Along

Rose Alexander has had more careers than she cares to mention and is currently a secondary school English teacher. She writes in the holidays, weekends and evenings, whenever she has a chance, although with three children, a husband, a lodger and a cat, this isn't always as often as she'd like. She's a keen sewist and is on a mission to make all her own clothes.

Rose Alexander

ALONG
the
ENDLESS
River

CANELO
US

San Diego, California

Canelo US
An imprint of Printers Row Publishing Group
9717 Pacific Heights Blvd, San Diego, CA 92121
www.canelobooksus.com

Printers Row Publishing Group is a division of Readerlink Distribution
Services, LLC. Canelo US is a registered trademark of Readerlink
Distribution Services, LLC.

This edition originally published in the United Kingdom in 2021 by
Canelo.

Published in partnership with Canelo.

Correspondence regarding the content of this book should be sent to Canelo
US, Editorial Department, at the above address. Author inquiries should be
sent to Canelo, Unit 9, 5th Floor, Cargo Works, 1–2 Hatfields, London SE1
9PG, United Kingdom, www.canelo.co.

Publisher: Peter Norton • Associate Publisher: Ana Parker
Art Director: Charles McStravick
Senior Developmental Editor: April Graham
Editor: Traci Douglas
Production Team: Beno Chan, Julie Greene

Design: Brianna Lewis

Library of Congress Control Number: 2022940660

ISBN: 978-1-6672-0383-6

Printed in India

27 26 25 24 23   1 2 3 4 5

Going up that river was like travelling back to the earliest beginnings of the world, when vegetation rioted on the earth and the big trees were kings.

An empty stream, a great silence, an impenetrable forest.

Joseph Conrad, *Heart of Darkness*

Prologue

Brazil, 1876

The rainforest is never silent.

Even in the dead of night, it is alive. The spine-tingling cries of howler monkeys, the guttural call of an owl and the cacophonous croaking of a million frogs fill the damp-laden air.

But tonight, the activity is not just of the animal kind. A quickening swash of water disturbs the shallows, giving rise to the tell-tale groan of wood rubbing on wood as the launches, canoes and rafts moored along the river's edge rise and fall against each other. Usually, the darkness is left to the lurking caimans, the prowling jaguars and the softly swooping vampire bats but tonight, humans are around.

For this is no ordinary night.

A silent column of men leads down to the water's edge, forming a line along which they stealthily pass hand-woven baskets interlaced with banana leaves. Basket after basket passes down the file, swinging from hand to hand, one after another. The man looking on, the overseer of this bizarre nocturnal ritual, appears nervous. He strokes his beard and smooths his impressive whiskers, shifting his weight from one foot to the other, gazing first at the swaying receptacles and then into the navy sky, where clouds shroud the stars and the moon is a sliver of silver.

'Watch out!' he hisses under his breath, as one of the baskets lurches precariously almost out of the receiver's grasp.

Inwardly, he curses the carelessness of the man. Does he not realise how precious the contents of each and every one of these meticulously packed panniers is? But no, of course he doesn't. The workers are ignorant as to what they are handling. The only person who knows is him, the mastermind, the architect of what will be — if he brings it off — the greatest feat of international smuggling the world has ever seen.

In a series of small boats, the baskets are painstakingly paddled out against the current to the waiting ocean-going steamer. Eventually, all the cargo is loaded. The hold is full, baskets swinging from ceiling hooks to allow for adequate ventilation. The clink of the anchor chain as it begins to wind makes the man catch his breath in fear. When the splash as it exits the water is partially masked by the haunting cry of a night bird, he breathes a sigh of relief. He manages to flash a nervous smile of reassurance to his wife and the small bronze-skinned boy, both his adopted son and his servant, who is sitting next to her. They have waited silently on deck throughout.

The *Amazonas* shudders as the engine starts, and almost immediately she's under way. The water before the bow swirls and seethes as the steamer glides purposefully downriver. The man stands against the gunwale, transfixed by the moiling eddies as if within them he sees all the trials and tribulations of the preceding years, the years of hardship and loss and disease and disaster that have seen the deaths of almost his entire family — but which have ultimately led to this heroic achievement.

As the vessel picks up speed, he descends to the hold and surveys the cargo, the most precious ever shipped from the Amazon to Europe. He fingers the shiny green banana leaves that protect the seeds, 70,000 of them, encased within their silken folds. Seeds of the rubber tree. They must be kept secret and intact at all costs. On them, reputations rest and, more than that, the future of the British Empire depends. But although the man is full of hubristic pride, neither he, nor his wife, nor his son, nor the captain of the ship knows the full enormity of what he has achieved.

2

Under the noses of officials, a Brazilian gunboat patrolling nearby, Henry Wickham, who first came to the Amazon to collect colourful feathers for the millinery trade, has committed the crime of the century. The contraband he is shipping will change the world forever.

And it will take little more than thirty years to do it.

Part I

1890 – 1899

Chapter One

An expanse of water surrounded them, so vast that it was impossible to tell where the sea became the river or the river the sea. The sky above hung heavy with lowering clouds and the air and the water seemed to fill the whole world so that there was nothing else at all. Along the widest horizon Katharine had ever seen, sheet lightning played in a frenetic, never-ending ballet without rhythm or choreography, competing in its performance with the last valiant glimmers of light from the day's end.

So, this was the Amazon, Katharine thought, as the steamer's engines changed tune to cope with the strong current in the estuary. The greatest river on earth. She could hardly believe she was here. Sweeping her unruly red hair into her hand to stop the vigorous breeze blowing it across her face, she looked back towards the Atlantic, from where they had come. Her grey eyes narrowed against the ocean wind, she uttered a silent goodbye to Europe, to London and to home.

She had no idea when, or if, she would ever return.

Everything had happened so quickly. At first, her husband Anselmo's grand plan had been no more than a crazy idea, a pipedream, a fantasy. As it had taken shape, it had still seemed unlikely, fun to talk about but nevertheless distant and implausible.

And then, suddenly and somehow inexplicably, it had become a firm decision, an actual arrangement, tickets booked, final farewells exchanged.

Of course, now she thought about it, Katharine realised it had not begun with the late-night discussions, their wild imaginings of another life conjured up in the cosy safety of their marital bed. Really, it had all started with their marriage itself, undertaken with an almost unseemly haste, though it was not a wedding of necessity. There had hardly even been time for the little embarrassment of a pre-nuptial pregnancy. No, it had been the lure of the Amazon that had compelled Anselmo to wed his bride in the shortest time possible, so soon after that first fateful meeting in a back corridor of Fortnum & Mason's department store in London.

It had been a long day.

Katharine's back was aching, her feet were killing her in shoes that pinched, and her head throbbed. As she passed through the doors that led off the shop floor, she ran her hand across her forehead and paused to lean against a stack of shelving. She longed for the warmth and comfort of her mother's snug kitchen and the hugs and kisses of her many siblings that always greeted her on her return. Particularly those of Mabel, the only other girl and so her only sister who, with her caramel brown eyes and silky blonde locks, was so pretty and cute and undisputedly Katharine's favourite, even though she knew she shouldn't really have such a thing and should love all her kith and kin equally. And she did love them all. It was just that Mabel melted her heart in a way that none of the others quite equalled.

Their mother Mary had been very ill after Mabel was born and so Katharine had more or less raised her for the first few months, stopping attending school for a while, only handing the baby to Mary to feed. It was as if those early days of closeness, inseparability in fact, had forged a bond between them that was even greater than that which normally exists between siblings, even in a tight-knit family.

She would be home soon, Katharine reassured herself, choosing to ignore the long omnibus journey to Clerkenwell that she would have to endure to get there. Closing her eyes, she imagined snapping her fingers and summoning a magic carpet that would fly her, in a matter of minutes, high above the grey and sooty city streets all the way to Hawthorn Road, to their front door with its proudly polished step. She would make her vision into a story for Mabel and the other little ones, she thought, smiling as she pictured their eager faces begging her for more. They always loved the tales she told.

Since her elder brother Mayhew had left the country to make his fame and fortune in America, Katharine had shouldered the bulk of the burden of helping her parents cope with their large brood. Though her mother was no longer unwell, she was tired out from relentless work and childbearing, and her hardworking father, enervated by a lifetime of toil on the docks, frequently came home too exhausted to do anything other than eat, then sleep.

Katharine bore no resentment about what was required of her. She was young – only eighteen – and healthy, and she had energy and stamina to spare. But the monotony of it all got to her sometimes. The feeling that nothing could, or would, ever change.

'Slacking again?'

At the sound of the voice behind her, Katharine jumped up from her unseemly position slouching against the shelves, a flush of red-hot embarrassment running through her. She wasn't doing anything wrong – she had clocked off now, her contracted hours of service completed. But still – she shouldn't be lolling around like a girl who had not had a proper upbringing. She was about to apologise but, as she opened her mouth to speak, realised that she didn't recognise the voice and had no idea who had spoken to her.

Slowly, she turned around.

A handsome, olive-skinned face greeted her, a smile slowly spreading across it.

8

Inexplicably, Katharine felt herself blush. Hurriedly, she attempted to compose herself. She knew the man by sight; he did some business in the food hall, something to do with cured meats from Spain. But she'd never spoken to him and did not know his name.

'Miss Bird, isn't it? Or Senorita Pájaro, as we would say in my language.'

The infuriating blush, the enemy of the fair-skinned who cannot possibly hide it, threatened anew. Katharine swallowed hard, lifted her chin and returned the man's steady, unsettling gaze.

'Pleased to meet you, I'm sure.' She held out her hand. 'And with whom do I have the pleasure of conversing?'

'Anselmo. Anselmo Ferrandis,' he replied, taking her hand in his and holding it for an infinitesimal second before shaking it. 'And, may I say – the pleasure is all mine.'

There was a silence, not awkward, more expectant, as if something new was occurring, something fresh and exciting and wondrous. Katharine was not beautiful. In some lights, on some days, she could be striking, with her high forehead, pale skin and Titian red hair. But most of the time she believed herself too raw-boned, too tall, too unfeminine to be pretty. She was plain Katharine Jane, nothing special, nothing to write home about. So, Mr Ferrandis' attention was unexpected and also delightful. A frisson of excitement curled in her belly as he spoke again.

'You look thirsty – and tired, if I may be so bold as to say so.' The man hesitated, as if testing out the words he wanted to say in his head before uttering them. 'Would you care to join me for a cup of tea and a sandwich, or perhaps a slice of cake? I've not had lunch myself and I'm parched.'

She should be getting home. She should be heading for the bus stop and waiting for the bus. She should be back in time to help her mother with the numerous infants, to rub her father's back with the linctus that aided his troublesome lungs.

9

Katharine looked at Anselmo Ferrandis, for a brief second meeting his eye. He was smiling, a smile that contained encouragement and cheekiness in equal measure. A beguiling, enticing smile. Perhaps what she 'should' do could be put to one side for a while.

'That sounds lovely,' she answered, keeping her voice light and casual. She was a modern, independent, working woman and entitled to some time to herself, she reassured herself. And, after all, no harm could come of tea and cake.

They stayed at the cafe for far longer than Katharine intended and she found out more about Spanish cured meats than she had ever wished to know. And when she finally left and was making her way to the bus stop, she walked on air, a dizzy, lightheaded sensation thrilling in her veins and a strange warmth suffusing her usually cold and aching limbs.

A week later, Anselmo Ferrandis, thirty, formerly of Madrid, Spain, now of Kentish Town, London, proposed to Katharine Bird, eighteen, of Clerkenwell, and three weeks after that, they were wed.

Chapter Two

On deck as the steamer approached Manaus, just three months married but with her entire life changed already, Katharine stood beside her husband and watched the fabled Meeting of the Waters. The black Rio Negro and the café-au-lait Solimões ran beside each other for a considerable distance, two stupendous bodies of water flowing concurrently but separately towards the sea. The sight, like so much she had seen since they'd reached Brazil and the mighty Amazon, was as fascinating and improbable as she had been led to believe.

As they'd ploughed their way inland on the long haul up from the Atlantic port city of Pará, the river had been constantly changing. Sometimes it was wide, a sea rather than a river, a vastness of water too big to comprehend. At other times it would narrow, lush vegetation sweeping the ship's sides, depositing leaves, branches and insects that littered the upper deck like misplaced, oversized confetti at a giant's wedding party.

One thing that never changed was the scenery. Land covered with trees as far as the eye could see, stretching thousands of miles to the foothills of the Andes: a living wall of one-hundred-foot trunks whose crowns, in their endless quest to reach the heavens, blocked out the light beneath. Katharine watched Anselmo's face, upon which was etched if not greed, then something very like it. His lips fluttered up and down as if involved in some silent calculation, counting. Counting the trees themselves, perhaps, though they were innumerable. Counting the cash that was to be made from them more likely, sizing up their potential. Because that was what they were there for, what had compelled them to travel so far.

Money.

'We've done it.'

Katharine started as Anselmo's voice roused her from her daydream. 'We're on our way – to our future and our fortunes.'

All around them, on all three of the steamer's decks, Katharine could hear the voices of others, so many others, speaking in all the languages of Babel, all with the same thought in mind. She nodded in mute agreement with her husband. She was too overwhelmed to speak, her brain too feverish with a befuddling mixture of newness and apprehension and trepidation to form a cogent opinion on anything. All she was certain of was that excitement and fear were fighting a battle to the death inside her. And at that moment, she couldn't tell which would win.

'There's white gold in that forest,' breathed Anselmo. 'Just think of it, Katy!'

He always shortened her name, a habit peculiar to him. Katharine wouldn't have liked it if anyone else had done it, but from him it was a form of intimacy that she cherished. Briefly, she rested her cheek against his shoulder. She needed his strength and courage, his unwavering self-belief, to shore her up. If anyone could convince her, it would be him.

'We'll be millionaires! Rich as Croesus. Just imagine…'

Katharine hardly could imagine, that was the problem. She tried her best. But where Anselmo was all vision and hope and confidence, Katharine often felt herself a poor companion, a vacillating, unreliable foot soldier to his assured, focused general. They just didn't *know* anything about this new world they were headed for. Or at least *she* didn't, which was perhaps more to the point.

'We'll be in Manaus any minute now.' Anselmo pointed ahead where the buildings of the jungle city were just coming into view, rising like beacons from the cleared plain. 'And then – onwards.' Anselmo was irrepressible, and, as if to prove it, he flung his hat into the air where it completed three perfect revolutions before he recaptured it, laughing.

He made it sound so simple. And he wasn't the only one. Everyone on this ship was the same, the Amazon itself full of hopefuls, of dreamers and believers, all putting their last pound or penny on the guarantee that, in this unpredictable, crazy world, in a century when prices rose and fell faster than a loose woman's girdle, there was one commodity, one crop that was failsafe. An elixir that was fuelling the world's development. Whose value would keep on rising, going inexorably up and up and up. Whose future was assured.

Rubber.

Everyone else was getting rich from it and Anselmo saw no reason why he and his new wife shouldn't reap some of the spoils, too. In the border lands between Brazil, Peru and Bolivia, far from the civilised world, rich expanses of forest full to bursting with *Hevea brasiliensis*, the rubber tree, were waiting to be tapped, to give of their bounty to the modern world that craved it so badly. But to get to these Elysian Fields, they would have to journey deep into the dark heart of the forest, braving whirlpools and waterfalls, snakes and savages, poisoned arrows and piranhas.

Katharine shuddered, shivering despite the intense, oppressive heat.

'What's wrong?' asked Anselmo, tenderly. He stroked her chin and looked into her eyes. 'Not having second thoughts?'

Katharine gave a short laugh. 'Of course not. Anyway – too late now. Here we are.'

As the steamer butted up against the floating dock, there was no disputing that. Here they undoubtedly were, on another continent, in a different hemisphere, a host of unknown challenges – and opportunities – ahead of them.

Looking out over the harbour, the control that rubber had over everything was immediately apparent. All along the

13

quayside whirred the cogs that oiled the trade: the offices of the *aviadors*, the merchants who controlled the movement of each precious *bolacha*, as the balls of rubber were called; the warehouses and the shipping firms. Squeezed into tiny spaces amongst them, the sleazy entrances to brothels and bordellos swallowed up a never-ending stream of customers, disappearing like night beetles into their dark interiors.

Milling around on the crowded waterfront were men of looks and stature that Katharine had never seen before: copper-skinned Indians; Black men; *mulattos*; *mamelucos*; *cafuzos* and *caboclos*. And then the dark-skinned Spaniards and Portuguese and the *flagelados da seca* from the drought-ridden Brazilian interior. The sheer number and array of humanity gathered here was dizzying, and they were all shouting and yelling in their impossible languages, calling up to the boat with offers of God knew what, scrambling to be the closest to the gangplank for when the passengers descended.

Even from the deck, high above the crowds, Katharine could smell the place, and the people, too: the sharp pungency of sweat; the ripe odour of rotten fruit; the earthiness of the brown, muddied water. A wizened beggar stretched stick-thin arms towards the disembarking passengers, then turned and spat onto the packed mud of the dockside. The spittle lay, foaming, glowing viscously in the light of a street lamp. Katharine looked away. It was too much, too soon.

A sudden, aching surge of homesickness lurched through her. She thought of the tall, thin terraced house in Clerkenwell, her mother's tired but kindly eyes, her father pulling on his boots as he made his way out of the door to work in the early morning. She heard the prattle of her brothers and sister, their small hands grabbing for their breakfast bread, their squabbling and laughing, and felt an aching, twisting stab of longing for them all, for home, for what she knew and what was familiar.

'Be strong,' she whispered to herself under her breath, the way she had when she was being teased at school about her height, her thinness, the colour of her hair or the pallor of her skin. Which had been ridiculous because everyone was skinny and pale; it was just that she was even skinnier and paler than the rest, as well as being tall and ginger, and so seemingly deserved to be tormented for it. She looked out again at the city, willing herself to fall in love with her new life. This was their chance, wasn't it? Hers and Anselmo's, their opportunity to make something of their lives.

If only it didn't feel quite so daunting right now.

Perspiration pooled between her breasts and trickled down her back, trapped by the tight constriction of her corset, and she shifted her shoulders, wiggling them to and fro in search of relief from the tightness, the pressure. Down on the dock, three majestic Black women were making serene and steady progress through the melee, huge water jars balanced on their heads, tiny infants on their hips. Katharine watched them, admiring their stately gait, the freedom of their movement, unencumbered by tight cords and bones around their ribs, gliding by as if the world belonged to them.

Perhaps it does, in this strange, foreign land, thought Katharine. *Certainly, more to them than to me.*

One of the women looked up at her, standing transfixed by the ship's railings. She smiled and waved, shouting something that Katharine couldn't catch as the words dispersed on the breeze and wouldn't have understood anyway. Katharine smiled and waved back, hope surging through her. If people were friendly, if they were at least that, then maybe everything would be all right.

Then her attention was drawn elsewhere, to another place in the crowd where a commotion had broken out. In the ensuing scuffle, Katharine heard the thwack of fist upon flesh, followed by animalistic cries of anguish. The fight brought forth the National Guard, dispersing the crowd with random blows of their night sticks, allowing the beggar man to come back into Katharine's sight, revealed as the throng took flight. Catching her eye, he lifted his reed-thin arm, stuck out his twig of a forefinger and drew it slowly and deliberately across his throat.

Horror curdled through Katharine's whole being, instantly obliterating the positive emotions of only a few minutes before. The beggar, recognising the look, opened his mouth to emit a beastly cackle that, though Katharine could not hear it amidst the din, rang in her head like the sounding of a death knell.

So, this was the Amazon. Life and death on all sides, slipping from one to the other in a heartbeat, safety and danger constantly vying for the upper hand. It was no place for the fainthearted, the weak or the weary. Katharine wanted so much to be as eager and ready for this adventure as Anselmo was. But as she followed her husband down the unsteady gangplank to the floating quay, her exhilaration mingled with her fear and the fingers of an indefinable dread pawed at her heart.

Chapter Three

Standing on the wide first floor veranda of an expansive villa in the smartest residential district of Manaus, Katharine looked around her doubtfully.

'Are you sure we were invited?' she whispered to Anselmo. A horse and carriage had conveyed them and their luggage speedily there; they were guests of Mr and Mrs Patrick McNamara, though he was currently absent, upriver on his extensive rubber estates. Anselmo had made his acquaintance in London before they had left, while doing his research about how to set up in business.

All Katharine knew was the little Anselmo had told her: that McNamara was one of the most powerful, and richest, rubber barons in the Amazon; his wealth legendary; his five children educated at the best schools and universities in England and Paris. He owned the leases on thousands of *estradas* of rubber trees and was said to employ over 10,000 workers. His house in Manaus, built from stone on two storeys, was surrounded by lush gardens and ringed by a high fence. The room they were in had tall windows and a plethora of decorative features: scrolls, carvings and elaborate flutings. Everything shouted money – and plenty of it. An introduction to McNamara was a golden ticket, Anselmo believed – he knew people in all the right places. And it had saved them from the expense of a hotel in a city where everything, Katharine had been told, was double the price of London.

But taking in the disarray that surrounded them, Katharine wasn't sure they'd made the right decision. Was Mrs McNamara in her right mind to be taking in house guests? She seemed to be in the middle of a major removal operation. Two huge trunks stood open-mouthed against the veranda railings, spilling forth a variety of beautiful fabrics – organdie, lace, tulle and velvet – while cascades of silk, cotton, gauze and Swiss dot billowed from the hands of an army of servant girls as they folded and tucked and rolled. Yet another trunk seemed to be full of sheets and pillowcases, all of the finest linen, the McNamara initials embroidered onto their corners. Perhaps, thought Katharine, Mrs McNamara was going home to Highgate before the rainy season came, when the river swelled to forty feet above its normal height and torrential downpours left the city prone to flooding.

The arrival of their hostess, accompanied by a flurry of greetings, heralded the possibility of Katharine getting answers to her questions.

'Please, call me Bernadette,' Mrs McNamara implored. 'We are really terribly informal here.'

She smiled brightly but without warmth as she spoke.

'We have come at a bad time,' apologised Katharine, 'just when you are leaving. Are you travelling to Europe earlier than planned?'

Bernadette, distracted by some inexpert packing, spewed forth a stream of reprimands at one of the Indian girls, then a further outburst of impatient instructions at others still arriving with armfuls of rippling cloth. There was something about her manner that was already putting Katharine's back up. Her voice was harsh and coarse and the way she spoke to her servants was unpleasant. Having been one herself, or close to it when she had been a shop girl, Katharine was always sensitive to the mistreatment of others in lowly positions.

Unfortunately, though, she presumed the servants were used to being shouted at as they appeared impervious to it. On the boat, at the ports where they had docked en route, and even on the way from the boat to this house, Katharine had seen how the indigenous people were treated – herded like cattle onto the lower decks on board, spoken to as if less than human, though ironically given superhuman tasks to accomplish, the men routinely carrying enormous loads on their backs, supported by thick webbing straps around their foreheads.

Composing herself after her tirade, Bernadette turned back to Katharine. 'No, of course we're not leaving,' she exclaimed. 'Whatever gave you that idea?'

Katharine, bemused and feeling more and more out of place by the minute, flashed Anselmo a nervous glance. She thought that the answer to Mrs McNamara's question was obvious but refrained from saying so. Anselmo grimaced back at her in silent complicity; he didn't know what was going on either.

'Shut it firmly,' ordered Bernadette, as three waif-like women struggled to pull down the lid of one of the trunks and to fasten the buckles that secured it.

'But where is all this – these things – going then?' Katharine asked, tentatively.

'It's the laundry,' replied Bernadette tersely, standing watching over the servants with hands on hips. 'Off to Portugal, to Lisbon, of course.'

'Of course,' agreed Katharine, weakly. 'It's just that I didn't realise—'

'Oh, you'll get used to it,' interrupted Bernadette. 'Everyone sends their linens and dresses back to Europe,' she continued, speaking as if Katharine really were the dimmest person she had ever met. 'The river water here is so dirty and muddy; it really doesn't do a good job at all. Everything gets spoilt.'

'Oh.'

Katharine couldn't think of anything more to say in response. This was a different world to the one she inhabited in Clerkenwell, where laundry day was a Monday and her mother boiled pans, scrubbed and mangled all day in the back courtyard of their terrace and hung up the clothes on a haphazard zigzag of washing lines where it swayed and blew in the wind until it was

19

dry. In a wet winter or spring, this could take several days. The extravagance of sending your dirty clothes and bed linen across an ocean to another continent was barely comprehensible.

Over the weeks they spent in Manaus, while Anselmo was busy setting up in business, Katharine had time to find out that extravagance was a way of life here. The city spewed wealth and luxury, conspicuous consumption was not only encouraged but expected. Brazilian banknotes took second place to gold and diamonds in terms of currency, and everyone seemed to be in a race to spend money, whether on ever bigger and better houses and offices, or on clothes, foodstuffs and luxuries from all over Europe. The shops were full of French champagne, Danish butter, Swiss watches, British firearms. Rubber barons clothed in white linen had themselves transported in sedan chairs so that they never need dirty their shoes in the tropical mud and rain.

The levels of debauchery, hinted at by the many houses of ill repute she had seen when they docked, shocked Katharine even more than the profligacy. Indian women were openly advertised as bodies for sale and brothel madams boasted river cruises with champagne and music for whoever had the cash and the desire.

The most eye-catching extravagance was the enormous, elaborate opera house that was under construction in the city centre. Designed in the Renaissance style, all the materials had been imported from Europe, including monumental blocks of Carrara marble that stood amidst the red Amazonian mud like white vestal virgins.

Rubber was fuelling the greatest consumer boom the New World had ever seen and no one was in any hurry to slow down.

Early every morning, when Anselmo had disappeared off to meetings with banks and *aviadors* and all the other movers and shakers it was necessary to grease the palms of in order to succeed in the Amazon, Katharine was left at a loose end. Though she and Anselmo were in this together, women were no more expected to play a part in business dealings in Manaus than they were in London. As she couldn't bear to stay in the house and listen to Bernadette McNamara berate the servants, she took to wandering the streets each day, getting to know the city, staying out for as long as she could bear the oppressive heat. The fear she had experienced at first had largely dissipated, to be replaced by a gentle melancholy, a loneliness characterised by a pervasive homesickness for her mother and father, her brothers and Mabel — always little Mabel at the forefront of her mind.

Telling her parents immediately after their marriage that she and her new husband would be leaving for another hemisphere had been so hard, though in the end Anselmo's absolute conviction that they could not fail had won them over.

'It's natural for young people to want to make their own way in the world, to plough their own furrow,' her mother had concluded, with a sad but benevolent smile.

'You have so many opportunities these days,' her father had added between the coughs brought on by an attack of pleurisy. 'So many chances that we didn't have. Everything's different now. It's right that you should take a few risks, go for gold.'

'Or rubber,' Katharine had interjected, and they had all laughed, lightening the mood.

She wrote to her family almost every day and longed for news of them in return, but the post, as everyone told her, was unreliable, mail taking an age to arrive if it ever got there at all.

One day, Katharine stayed out later than usual and found herself dizzy and lightheaded in the glare of the equatorial sun at its full height. The air was so thick with heat she could hardly breathe, and the river water that spewed prolifically from gold cherub fountains in the public gardens only served to intensify the thirst that had come upon her. Exhausted, she sank onto a bench beneath a silk cotton tree as tears of self-pity pricked behind her eyelids. Anselmo was too busy, and too fired up with excitement, to trouble with her doubts and worries; her family were far away and she had no idea when she would next hear from them, let alone see them. Mrs McNamara was a shrew of a woman whom she longed to get away from. Katharine was covered in heat rash and sweating unbearably in her tight corset and long dress. Out of sorts with everything, she let the tears fall. Why not? Who was there to see, or to care?

After a couple of minutes of doleful sobbing, a sound attracted Katharine's attention. She glanced around to be greeted by the sight of a delicate, exquisitely patterned little bird padding gracefully out from the undergrowth, lifting each matchstick-thin leg proudly at every stride. It strolled serenely towards Katharine, its small head darting from side to side, its eyes bright and enquiring. Calmly, it looked up at her as if asking permission, before bending its neck and plucking a spider daintily off the hem of her dress.

Katharine, tears stemmed, laughed out loud.

'Hello, little creature,' she said to the bird. 'What are you after?'

The bird dipped its beak in silent reply and then proceeded to trace a circle around her, keeping a watchful eye out for any other tasty titbits that her gown might be harbouring. Katharine observed it in rapt delight; she had seen birds like this before, in the yards and front rooms of several houses. They were a type of miniature heron, nicknamed *pavão* or peacock, and were a particular favourite amongst the Brazilians, who often adopted them as avian friends.

'Hey, tiny thing,' she murmured as the bird completed its circumnavigation, 'I'm going to call you Po-Po. You can be my very own special pet – while I'm here, anyway. I'll be leaving soon… but until then… would you like that?'

Po-Po flapped his wings and ruffled his feathers as if in hearty agreement.

Cheered, Katharine summoned the energy to walk back home, rummaging in her purse for the biscuit she had stored there in case of hunger pangs. Tempted by the treat, the little bird followed her all the way, for all the world like a faithful puppy. Katharine had always wanted an animal, a dog or a cat or a rabbit. But there had never been money, nor space, nor time in London. This little bird would be the first tangible bonus of having come to the Amazon.

That evening, Po-Po sat on the veranda as if he'd been there all his life, while Bernadette hosted a grand dinner party in honour of Katharine and Anselmo. Katharine wasn't entirely sure that they were worthy of such entertainment – it made her feel self-conscious; she was just a shop girl, after all – but Bernadette seemed certain. Anselmo, on the other hand, relished the chance to talk about rubber to anyone and everyone, especially such dignitaries as the Spanish consul, who had been invited, and Mr Phee, the corpulent, red-nosed owner of a chain of stores catering to those heading into rubber terri-tory, selling all the paraphernalia necessary for a journey into the forest. Mr Phee, Katharine was given to understand, had already done rather well from Anselmo setting up for their expedition.

As the courses were delivered one after the other, polished silver cutlery sparkled under the light from the enormous crystal chandelier that hung in the centre of the huge salon. In the corner, a pianist tinkled at a baby grand imported from England. Apart from the intense, unremitting tropical heat, they could have been in any grand salon in Europe.

Katharine had been placed on one side of Mr Phee and Anselmo on the other. The wine was flowing freely and tongues were loosened.

'So, I hear you've done the deal, young man,' chortled Mr Phee. Katharine pricked up her ears.

'More or less,' agreed Anselmo, in between mouthfuls of foie gras specially shipped in from Aquitaine.

'You didn't tell me,' interjected Katharine mildly, disguising her irritation. 'Is this something I should know about?'

Anselmo's eyes widened in surprise. 'Of course, my darling love.'

He must have had a lot of the claret, thought Katharine. He never usually spoke to her like that in public.

'I was going to tell you everything tomorrow, after I've shaken on the final details.'

23

'So, what is there to tell?' Katharine's voice was quiet but insistent.

'Well, we are now the proud owners of five hundred *estradas* of prime rubber trees on the Rio Poderoso! It couldn't be better.'

Katharine rapidly did the numbers in her head. An *estrada* was a looping path through the forest along which might be found one to two hundred rubber trees. That made a potential total of 100,000 trees. Katharine gulped, partly in astonishment at the sheer number, partly in consternation at how they would manage such an enterprise – and partly in admiration for Anselmo's achievement.

Meanwhile, Anselmo was still explaining the rest of his acquisition.

'There is a small settlement called Norwood already established there,' he elaborated, 'left by the previous proprietor, with a largish house for us and outbuildings for the servants. I've hired two Indians who can navigate us all the way there, splendid chaps by the names of Jonathan and Santiago, and employed a European clerk and a cook, both coming with their wives. So, you'll have some company!'

His gaze on Katharine's was willing her to agree that what he had achieved was magnificent, perfect. After a moment's hesitation, she pushed doubt aside and rewarded him with her widest smile. Anselmo had come good, as she had known he would, he had sorted everything out and the uncertainty was gone. They had a home and an address which gave them permanence and a future. She pictured a clearing in the forest, in its centre a wooden log cabin like an American prairie house, surrounded by a white picket fence. Sheltering the settlement were the trees of mahogany, kapok and Brazil nut, and beside them a small grove of banana plants, and açai palms dripping with nutritious berries. Orchids, passion flowers and heliconias bloomed in profusion, studding the green with their brilliant, eye-catching colours.

Mr Phee, who was busy stuffing a buttered asparagus stalk into his thick-lipped mouth, noisily interjected before Katharine had a chance to congratulate Anselmo, immediately shattering the charming mental picture that she had created.

'You'll be negotiating terms with McNamara, then, if it's the Poderoso,' he stated rather than questioned, grease making his lips glisten. 'Good luck with that.'

Anselmo barely seemed to acknowledge the implied warning. 'Nothing two gentlemen can't come to an amicable agreement on,' he responded, unabashed.

Mr Phee raised his glass and drank his wine with an air that doubted it would be quite that simple. Katharine's emotions, on a constant rollercoaster, plummeted anew, and the house with the picket fence evaporated completely.

'He's not going to be happy that you've snatched prime, virgin rubber territory from under his nose,' continued Mr Phee, in an ominous tone. 'He's been after that land himself for a long time. Can't say as I understand myself how you've managed it.'

Anselmo smiled with barely disguised glee. 'I am a master businessman,' he replied, as irrepressible as ever. 'It's easy when you know how.'

He turned to Katharine and whispered under his breath, 'Becoming English was definitely a good move. Opens all sorts of doors.'

Anselmo had taken the time to become a British citizen before coming to the Amazon, where anything British carried extra cachet. Half of the region was backed by the City of London, many of its businesses floated on the Stock Exchange and powered by British banks. Katharine felt a warm glow of pride in her husband for his forethought and good planning. He had sorted all this out himself, taken the initiative, worked tirelessly for what he had set his heart on. She was glad that Mr Phee was surprised at and, she was sure, secretly impressed with what Anselmo had achieved.

But she still didn't quite understand.

'What terms are you referring to?' she asked Mr Phee, innocently.

'Over the isthmus, my dear,' he responded, his double chins wobbling as he spoke. Little bits of spittle formed in the corner of his mouth and a quick, pointed tongue whisked them away. Katharine shivered in repulsion. She really did not like this man. 'McNamara discovered, and now owns, the land passage that links the Largo with the Poderoso. It takes weeks off your journey, as well as being the safest way to go.'

'But surely it can make no difference to him to allow others to use the route?' questioned Katharine, keeping her gaze wide-eyed. 'And if he doesn't allow it – well, we just take the longer way.'

Mr Phee choked with laughter, spluttering wine onto the pristine white tablecloth. Washed in Lisbon, I'll be bound, thought Katharine. Those poor Portuguese laundry women will have a devil of a job getting these stains out.

'The other options are a long detour through the forest, full of wretched savages who'll kill a white man soon as look at him, scalp him and put his head upon a totem pole,' chuckled Mr Phee, seeming to rather enjoy the thought. 'Or you portage all your worldly goods over fourteen deadly waterfalls. You can more or less guarantee to lose a significant portion of your equipment and luggage and at least one Indian per fall.'

The sinking feeling came back with a vengeance, and Katharine was momentarily silenced. So too, unusually, was Anselmo. *Perhaps he didn't know this*, thought Katharine. Perhaps all this is news to him. Perhaps he's put money down on property that we can't even get to. A searing flush of panic flooded through her. Anselmo's savings had been fairly sparse and Katharine was surprised that they had stretched far enough to get them such promising rubber land. But however good it was, it was no use to them if it was impossible to reach.

Anselmo must have seen her stricken look.

26

'It will all be fine, my sweet one,' he soothed, and then picked up his glass and drained it.

At the other end of the table, Bernadette's attention was on one of the servants, issuing long-winded and strident instructions about the bringing of the cheese course. Mr Phee glanced towards her and then motioned Katharine and Anselmo to come closer. Both leant in towards him, and Katharine got a whiff of bad breath and stale sweat. Forcing herself not to recoil in disgust, she strained her ears to hear his whispered warning.

'Take a bit of advice from me, who has seen so many would-be's disappear up this damn river, never to be seen nor heard of again. You would be wise to be careful of McNamara.'

Out of the corner of her eye, Katharine saw Bernadette dismissing the servant and, as she did so, resting her eyes on the three of them, huddled conspiratorially together. She had the sense that Bernadette was listening in, keen to hear what they were discussing.

'Find favour with him,' continued Mr Phee, bestowing a sickly smile upon Katharine. 'Which I'm sure, Mrs Ferrandis, won't be too difficult for a woman of your, er, finesse – and he will be the most powerful ally you could possibly have on the Amazon.'

Mrs McNamara tore her gaze away and fired a volley of further commands and reprimands at the hapless servant girl who had just appeared by her side.

Mr Phee looked slowly at Katharine, and then Anselmo.

'If you play your cards right, all will be well,' he concluded. 'But if you don't – who can say?'

Chapter Four

The Amazon, 1890

The odious Mr Phee's words rang in Katharine's ears as, two days later, she followed Anselmo down to the quay, picking her way between the litter of cans and bottles, piles of excrement, both animal and human, and the flotsam and jetsam of logs and branches and foliage thrown up by the volatile motions of a capricious river. She was glad to be leaving this opulent, degraded city where sleaze and corruption were a way of life, and decadence prevailed. However frightening the forest, however daunting to be waving goodbye to the last vestiges of civilisation, at least, she thought, the air there would be pure, fresh and free from the stench of obscene wealth.

At the top of the gangplank their progress was impeded by a commotion caused by a man who seemed unhappy with his class of ticket. As they waited, Katharine felt something sharp pressing against her calf. Anxiously, she glanced behind her, expecting to find a hideous bloodsucking insect enjoying a feast of her blood.

Instead, a bright eye gazed adoringly up at her, the head that it belonged to cocked invitingly to one side.

'Po-Po! What on earth are you doing here?'

Katharine burst out laughing as she bent forward to pet the little bird's crown. He probed his beak up towards her hand.

'I don't have anything for you,' she told him regretfully. 'And you shouldn't be on this boat – you haven't got a ticket.'

Po-Po darted his head back and forth in ardent disagreement.

Katharine looked around to seek Anselmo's advice. He had moved up the gangplank and seemed to be getting involved in the fracas occurring there. She looked back down to Po-Po and shrugged.

'Well, now you're here – I suppose there's nothing for it but for you to come too.' The bird could always fly away if he changed his mind, she reasoned to herself, and perhaps Po-Po was exactly the good luck charm they needed for the challenges of the future.

The first of which the captain was soon explaining.

'The facilities for Madam and the other ladies in first class,' he proudly pronounced, pulling a hessian curtain across a roughly assembled rail, 'are here.'

Katharine stared in dismay at the chamber pot and bucket of water that stood on the deck. They expected to be on this boat for four to six weeks, travelling to Lagona, McNamara's settlement on the isthmus, where they would stay while negotiating their onward journey. Was this to be her apology for a WC for the entire duration?

'Where... what are the, um, arrangements, for the rest of the passengers?' she asked, suppressing her innate reluctance to discuss such matters. It simply wasn't a topic that women ever broached in public, to a complete stranger. Her mother would be horrified.

'Oh, for most it is fine that they sit on the railings,' replied the captain, breezily. 'We rarely have females on board, though the more people set off up the Amazon, the more are taking their wives with them.' He paused, seemingly lost in contemplation of a future filled with troublesome demands for toilet facilities. 'So, I suppose we will have to come up with something more – er, more permanent before too long.'

Katharine, baulking at the very idea of what he had suggested, thought that he probably would have to rethink the arrangements – and soon. But she didn't say anything. There was no point in making a fuss about something that clearly

29

couldn't be changed. And equally, there was no way Anselmo would agree to put off their voyage and wait for a more suitable vessel, even supposing such a thing existed; he was champing at the bit, desperate to get underway.

'Thank you,' she said, 'on behalf of myself, Laure and Clara. I'm sure we are most grateful to you for taking so much care to make us comfortable.'

Laure was the wife of Charles, the experienced Belgian clerk whom Anselmo was delighted to have secured to take charge of administration, and Clara the wife of Philippe, the French chef. Katharine had briefly met them both the day before; in appearance, they were complete opposites. Laure was older, comely and buxom, petite but well rounded, exuding a quiet competence. Clara was also small, but wiry with it and bearing an air of being pent-up like a coiled spring waiting to unwind. She was much younger than Laure, only a bit older than herself, Katharine reckoned, and despite her diminutive size, or perhaps because of it, it was clear to see that she was pregnant. Katharine guessed, having often seen her mother in the same condition, that she was quite far along. She hoped they would get to Lagona before the baby arrived.

Beneath, crammed like sardines on the lower decks alongside other second and third class passengers, were the labourers that Anselmo had employed – one hundred migrants from Spain, Portugal and Brazil's arid interior where periodic droughts sent entire families flocking to the Amazon in the hope of a better life, or at the very least survival. It wasn't nearly enough of a workforce, but it was all he had been able to recruit. Labour was in short supply and fiercely contested and Anselmo, as a novice, had to make do with the slim pickings left behind by greater masters. His coup had been to nab the two Indians, Jonathan and Santiago, who knew the river and all its many tributaries all the way to the mountains, and Katharine took as much comfort from their presence as she did from that of Laure and Clara.

As they pushed on upriver, towering red sandstone cliffs rose up beside them, topped by colossal trees that reached ever upwards towards the cloud-ridden sky. Branches over the water were hung with scores of the long, elaborate nests of the oropendola bird, a local species of blackbird. The forest grew thicker and more impenetrable with every mile covered, a tangle of lianas, creepers and vines, leafy green palms sprouting in every possible spare space between the mighty trunks, while in the river islands of aquatic grasses floated freely around them.

Every now and again they passed an Indian village, some poor and wretched with slovenly, broken-down huts and listless men and women swinging idly in hammocks, some much more lively, prosperous and thriving, with houses on stilts, livestock and sawmills and busy, energetic inhabitants. All along the way they were passed by canoes going up and down, loaded with anything and everything: turtle oil and Brazil nuts, pineapples and vanilla, great bunches of green bananas and bizarre collections of stuffed birds. It was as if the Amazon was the biggest, busiest, most prolific High Street on earth. Katharine thought of her mother Mary, who went out every day to buy such ordinary items as a penny loaf and a pound of carrots, and wondered what she would make of it all.

At least once a day, the steamer would pull into a trading post to unload supplies and deliver the mail, and there was always a small queue of people eagerly awaiting its arrival. Katharine watched as, at one such stop, a white man appeared, trailed by an Indian woman heavy with child, naked apart from a small skirt around her waist.

'Bush wife,' commented Charles, who had joined Katharine on deck. Charles' twenty years in the region made him an Amazonian veteran, and Katharine was profoundly glad of his calm common sense, his level-headed approach to everything.

'Some whites have twenty or thirty of them. Concubines, I suppose they should more accurately be called.'

Katharine blushed while Charles shook his head in silent disapproval but said no more. His discretion was absolute; Katharine had already noticed that he avoided saying anything overtly negative.

'Never speak ill of anyone on the Amazon,' he had counselled her at dinner the night before. 'This is not a place to make enemies – no more than already exist in the savage tribes deep in the forest, or in the lethal wildlife the jungle is full of. It's as well to remember that the law means very little here. And those you meet while you're on the way up – well, who's to say you won't come across them again on your way down?'

This was sound advice which Katharine took immediately to heart.

They continued up river, travelling through territory which was a battleground for numerous barons vying for supremacy. It was only now that Katharine had a chance to view the commodity they had come to harvest up close. Ranged along the riverbanks were countless *seringueiro*, or rubber tapper, encampments. In front of them teetered piles of fine, dry Pará, the best quality rubber in the world, waiting for whatever means of transportation had been arranged to ship them to the markets downriver.

Katharine was fascinated by the sight of so much rubber, and somewhat repelled by the *seringueiros* who gathered it. They were rough, tough looking men, thin from a poor diet, excessive drinking and the hours spent traversing the *estradas*. In the mornings, they would make the slashes in the bark, returning in the afternoons to collect the sap, and in the evenings sit over smoking palm nut fires to solidify the latex into *bolachas*. Most worked alone or in small groups, but some had families with them, women with rotten teeth and hunched backs, undernourished children clutching at their legs.

Despite the money to be made from rubber, it was immediately obvious that not a single one of these people was rich.

'They are generally indebted to their employer for their food and other supplies,' explained Charles. 'The manager sells to them at an inflated price – five times the real cost – and they have no choice but to buy. There are no shops deep in the jungle. And the amount they receive for each *bolacha* is one-fifth of its true value. They can never hope to pay off what they owe – so they work until the jungle or the drink kills them.'

Katharine thought for a while before replying.

'So they are little more than slaves, though slavery has been abolished?'

Charles shrugged and made a moue of resignation. 'Not really. They are free to leave – although, if they do, they are unlikely to get far.'

Katharine ran her hands down the skirt of her dress while considering her response. It felt damp, and the hem was dirty and mouldy. The climate got at everything, creeping over it, into it, tainting and disfiguring. She fingered her arms, the lumps where the reaction from bites she had got on the first boat still lingered. Sweat dripped from every pore and the accumulation of moisture had given her rashes in her elbows, behind her knees and beneath her breasts.

The Amazon could be a cruel and hard environment. But many of the people in it were, it seemed, even crueller and harder.

'You haven't answered my question.'

'The answer is in the question,' Charles replied somewhat enigmatically. Then, reluctantly, he continued. 'It is a duty, be it legal or moral, to repay a debt, so the rubber barons will ensure that this is fulfilled. However, the methods by which they can extract payment are less well-defined and perhaps here is where the powers of law and order have little jurisdiction to ensure that things are done by the book.'

'But why should they be held to a debt they had no choice but to incur and cannot hope to repay?' Katharine continued insistently, watching a group of *seringueiros* on the nearest bank sharing a bottle of *cachaça*, strong alcohol made from sugar cane.

A brief smile of cynicism mixed with humour flashed across Charles' face. 'I see that you do not give up easily,' he said and then, with a narrowing of the eyes, 'a trait which could serve you well – or not.'

Katharine leant on the railings and stared down at the water, black and turgid. She could hear the voices of the workers squeezed onto the lower decks, the ones who had been hired to labour for them. She was suffocating with the heat even here on the spacious top deck. She couldn't imagine how unbearable conditions were for those down below.

'Mrs Ferrandis,' Charles continued quietly, 'do not worry yourself about a situation you did not create and cannot hope to change. This is how the system works here.'

And with that, the conversation was over. Charles went to discuss some matter of planning with Anselmo, and Katharine was left alone with her thoughts.

—

In Iquitos, a grubby little town huddled on the bank of the river, Anselmo, Katharine, Charles and Laure went to dine on another steamer, the *Bolivar*, which had come all the way from Liverpool. When they got back to their own boat, which was due to set sail again before first light, they found a huge commotion afoot.

Anselmo and Charles went ahead of Katharine and Laure to find out what was going on. Half an hour later, Anselmo came back alone to accompany the two women on board. From the expression on his face, Katharine could see that something serious had happened.

'What's the matter?' she asked anxiously. She couldn't understand what could have gone wrong in the short time they had been absent.

Anselmo remained tight lipped until they had negotiated the wobbly gangplank. Then he flung his hat down on a table and ran his fingers through his already thinning hair.

'Labour, that's what's wrong.' He gestured resignedly to the stairs that led to the lower decks, on which had been housed the migrant workers. 'They've jumped ship, every last one of them. Frightened of the forest, so word has it. Frightened of hard work, more like.'

'So, what are we to do?' Katharine realised how utterly ignorant she was of the number of men needed to run five hundred *estradas* of rubber trees. Was it ten? Twenty? Two hundred? Two thousand? She really had no idea and hated herself for her ignorance. The heat and the humidity had enfeebled her, taking her energy away and allowing her to sit back and leave Anselmo to it, not questioning him enough, not learning enough about this new life, their new enterprise. Regardless of her sense of discomfort at the *seringueiros*' working conditions, there was no doubt that they needed such workers. And now disaster had struck and she didn't know how to help him.

'We recruit when we get there.' Charles' firm, steady voice intervened. 'This is not an unexpected event – it's often this way. Few immigrants want to go so far as the Rio Poderoso; it's so isolated, so far from anywhere. We will use local labour, the Indians, instead.' He paused, his forehead creased in thought, before adding, 'It will just take a little longer to, er, round up the number we need.'

Katharine saw bewilderment then doubt then relief sweep over Anselmo's face.

'Charles,' he cried, his voice over-loud with sudden happiness. 'I knew I'd picked the right chap in you.'

Katharine joined in with weak congratulations. Somehow, she was not convinced it could be that simple. And the hesitation she had spotted in Charles' reply only served to reinforce her uncertainty.

They went to their hammocks. Katharine had learnt how to lie diagonally and keep one foot on the floor to gently rock oneself back and forth. Now she was used to it, she found it as comfortable as a bed – almost. But that night she rocked for longer than usual, sleep eluding her. Charles's words 'round them up' reverberated through her mind until she fell into a fitful slumber.

He made it sound so easy – but what, exactly, did he mean?

Chapter Five

Lagona, 1890

It took six long weeks aboard the steamer, toiling against the strong downstream current, to reach Lagona, McNamara's forest home. Anselmo had had to pay a considerable amount extra to persuade the captain to add so many additional miles to his journey. The river continued to astound; sometimes so wide that the shore on either side was a narrow line far in the distance, other times no bigger than the Thames. Katharine thought often of her father, hard at work on the docks, loading and unloading cargo from all over the world, with never a thought of ever visiting the exotic locations from which the produce originated. She was still incredulous that she herself was here, a lowly working girl from London, now a rubber baron's wife.

When it didn't terrify her, it made her smile to herself in disbelief.

As they progressed, the water level became lower in advance of the rainy season and the river strewn with hazards that could not be seen: hidden rocks, submerged tree trunks and whirlpools that could seize a small steamer such as theirs and spin it as if it were light as a cork. It took all of the captain's skill and experience to pilot the boat safely. And it wasn't just the river that caused fear. Trepidation built in Katharine day by day at the thought of finally encountering Patrick McNamara. She imagined an ogre, a man with a tongue as strident as his wife's and a bloodlust to match.

But when they at last clambered off the boat, legs wobbly after weeks away from dry land, the infamous gentleman's appearance took Katharine by surprise. He was short and compact, with sandy hair and a handsome, freckled face from which shone out a pair of startlingly blue eyes. He was smiling broadly in greeting.

'Welcome to my humble abode,' he said, waving his hand expansively around him at the two-storey villa surrounded by well-tended gardens and a small vegetable patch. Katharine was impressed; it all looked enchanting and she was already planning in her mind's eye how she would make her home as welcoming and pretty as this place. For a moment she forgot how sweaty she was, the raw and chafing skin of her armpits and inner thighs, the unpleasantness of the onboard makeshift toilet and lack of washing facilities. The discomforts melted away and she imagined a sunny future, her and Anselmo, building their business, earning enough money to go home rich, showering their largesse on each and every member of their families, and never having to work again.

A large and handsome dog came bounding eagerly up, completing this idyllic picture. Katharine bent down towards it, ready to pat its back and fondle its ears.

Without warning, it leapt towards her, emitting a blood-curdling snarl, yellow teeth bared and ready to bite. Katharine recoiled in terror, finding Anselmo and clinging desperately onto him as the dog continued to threaten, making small, aggressive jumps in her direction, accompanied by low, rumbling growls.

'Down, Hamlet, down,' ordered McNamara fiercely, grabbing at its collar. 'So sorry,' he continued, turning to his guests once the dog had been restrained and the bloodthirsty growling reduced to intermittent, angry yelps. 'He is a guard dog, after all. We have to be vigilant.' He snapped his fingers and an Indian servant appeared instantly and led the dog away.

As it passed Katharine, it took its chance to lurch towards her anew, lips curled back in vicious contempt, jaws chomping and slathering. Katharine froze. Her heart, which had been pumping at ten times its normal rate, now seemed to stop completely.

It only restarted when the dog was finally out of sight.

Trembling, she glanced fearfully over her shoulder. The trees had been cleared for some way around but that only seemed to make the forest, when it began, darker, denser and more forbidding. She and Anselmo had to brave that forest, to set off into its deepest depths, to places few, if any, white men had ever trod – and they didn't have a Hamlet to guard them.

And once the three to four week journey had been accomplished, she and Anselmo, Charles and Laure, and Philippe and Clara would be quite alone; six Europeans stranded amidst a galaxy of untold numbers of trees, all around them savage tribes of head-hunters and poison arrow bowmen, not to mention the fierce Aráras of the river Madeira, the Majerónas cannibals of the Jauarí. Stories were told of travellers killed, roasted like pigs on a spit and feasted upon. And on top of that there were deadly jaguars and anacondas, spiders and centipedes.

Danger lurked everywhere.

Katharine knew that to be a true Victorian was to be an adventurer, to travel bravely and intrepidly to the furthest reaches of the earth for the sake of Queen and empire.

She just kept having the awful feeling that she wasn't up to it.

–

They didn't see much of Patrick McNamara for the first few days at Lagona, but towards the end of the week a few visitors arrived from a different branch of the river, and so, on Friday night, they were quite a party for dinner. Their host was genial and personable, as affably welcoming as the Irish were always said to be. Despite Mr Phee's ominous warnings, Katharine found she liked him. She had been placed next to him at the table and took advantage of that to ask numerous questions about life on the Amazon, what jungle plants and berries could be eaten, how to keep supplies away from insects and whether it was really true that, in the forest, the Indians wore no clothes at all. He answered in detail; in fact, he talked so much that Katharine began to suspect that he didn't get much chance at conversation most of the time, so was making up for it now he had company.

'And how often do you travel to Manaus, Mr McNamara?' she asked. 'You have such a beautiful home there – although Lagona is lovely, too, of course,' she added hastily, in case he should think her rude, 'but your wife is in the city, and your friends. You must miss them all.'

'Please, Mrs Ferrandis, everyone calls me Mac and I insist that you do, too.' He took a long draw on a huge Cuban cigar and exhaled the smoke in a choking cloud of wispy tendrils that floated in front of her face, making her nostrils flare in distaste. 'You are right that it can be hard to be away from home comforts. But my wife does not like the primitive way of life here, nor the isolation. And, given that I have control over all the routes to the interior, and have been charged by the government with opening them up to the flow of rubber, then it's important that I am on hand to police who gets to use them. And who does not.'

He smiled at her. Katharine smiled back, the warmest, friendliest smile she could manage. It was crucial that she and Anselmo were in the 'use' category.

'And on what basis is such a decision made?' She kept her voice light, trying to keep out of it the urgency she felt.

'A strong woman with – how shall I put it? – personality, is always an advantage, so it is.' Mac's eyes twinkled and his Irish burr became more pronounced. Katharine almost spat out her mouthful of wine in surprise; was he *flirting* with her? Immediately, she dismissed the thought. The very notion! She'd been travelling for too long, and he'd been isolated up river for too long, leaving them both prone to misjudging social situations.

Mac took another lengthy draw on his cigar. 'Seriously now' – and Katharine immediately relaxed; he had just been teasing – 'I feel sure that we can come to a suitable arrangement. As sure as ever I could be.'

Katharine took a deep breath as relief flooded through her. If Mac was on their side that was at least one hurdle cleared.

The meal ended and the dinner guests drifted off to various pursuits: card playing, stargazing, more drinking. Mac and Anselmo huddled in a corner, talking business Katharine supposed. She excused herself to visit the bathroom, which was some way from the house, and the tiny Indian servant girl who had been assigned to her for the duration of their stay scuttled after her. It was such a strange thing, and one Katharine found hard to get used to, but in the Amazon she'd discovered that your servant accompanied you everywhere, even to the lavatory, and slept by your bed at night, at least one or two of them, their gaze always upon you.

This one, whose name was Esperanza, beguiled and horrified in equal measure – she was sweet and pretty but painfully thin. And very, very young – not more than eight, Katharine reckoned. She reminded her of Mabel, and that made her love her instantly. Immediately on first seeing her, Katharine had wanted to take care of her, to find out more about her, to dote on her as she did her sister. But Esperanza never spoke a word, whether she couldn't or didn't want to, Katharine had no idea.

That night, in bed, she turned to Anselmo. 'He seems nice,' she whispered, conscious of how thin were the partitions that divided rooms in this house, and of Esperanza's listening ears.

Anselmo took her in his arms and then quickly released her. It was too hot for any prolonged close contact.

'You sound surprised,' he replied, too loudly for Katharine's liking. 'What did you expect to find?' Without giving her a chance to answer this question, he rolled over onto his back, looking straight above him as if addressing the lofty ceiling, with its wooden struts and zinc roofing. 'He's a fine fellow and, what's more, not only has he signed on the dotted line regarding moving our rubber down river, he's given us rights to use the passage over the isthmus. All for a charge, of course, but he's been very generous, all things considered. And – I've leased a small steamer from him on very favourable terms!'

Katharine paused; her brow furrowed in concentration. Mac and Anselmo had clearly been even harder at work after dinner than she'd thought. 'That's great news.' She considered some more before adding, 'I mean, really great. Your achievements are very impressive – I'm sure lots of people back home didn't think we could do it. I wasn't as confident as you were from the beginning – but now I, well, now I see that the two of us together – we can do anything!'

Anselmo grinned happily. 'Well, my darling, you are prone to pessimism, are you not?' he replied. 'But I never had any doubts. I just know it's all going to be marvellous. And with Mac on our side – we cannot fail.' He sat up, leant in close to Katharine and whispered in her ear, 'I've heard he's mortgaged to the hilt, though. That's why he couldn't buy the land I've secured for us – didn't have any more cash to leverage.'

'Right,' Katharine said. And then, feeling that this was the first time since they'd arrived in Brazil that she and Anselmo had really talked about everything that was going on, added, 'So how are you – we – affording all of this?'

Anselmo dropped a kiss delicately upon her nose. 'It's very complicated, a matter of borrowing from one bank to put down money in another and then borrow even more from another, and so on. It's how the whole rubber shenanigans are funded, a kind of pyramid system. We were lucky to have your father's generous gift to give us exactly the deposit we needed to get the process started.'

Anselmo fell back onto the bed and stared up at the rafters again. In the moonlight, Katharine could just make out the satisfaction etched upon his face.

41

She opened her mouth to speak, shut it again, then began once more. 'My father's gift.' It was a statement rather than a question. 'What do you mean?'

Anselmo rolled over onto his side and took one of her hands in his. 'Before we left,' he said, 'I was explaining to him how difficult it was all going to be on the little cash that I had. One needs capital, Katharine, to set up in rubber. There's a lot of competition, as you've seen for yourself. And your father offered – I didn't ask – his life savings. To help us with our dream. A small loan that would make us all rich in just a few years. He'll get a return of 1000 per cent – more! – on rubber, instead of the paltry 5 per cent from the bank he's got it stashed away in.'

In the darkness, rendered speechless, Katharine's eyes widened and her mouth fell open. Her father's life savings. All his money, which wasn't just for him and her mother but had presumably been put away for all the children, too. In fact, she knew that her parents wanted the younger children to stay on longer at school if they showed the aptitude for it, so that they could get better jobs in the future. The boys could be clerks! Bookkeepers! Engineers! Mabel already knew she wanted to be a teacher. And both her parents needed to give up work at some time in the future and enjoy a peaceful retirement, even if for only a few years. Without what they had so diligently put away over their entire working lives, that would be impossible.

Anselmo seemed to take her silence as approval. 'I told him, that money will have quadrupled in just a few years and he was properly chuffed about it. What could possibly go wrong, I said to him, and he volunteered it, all of it, no further questions asked.'

Katharine pictured her mother and father and her little brothers and sister, sitting around a table bare of food, shoeless feet pitifully red and swollen in the cold of winter. She saw her father, slaving on at the docks for years, until the end of this century and into the next, despite his bad lungs, his constant coughs and chest infections, and her mother, worn ragged and half blind from taking in ever greater amounts of sewing to make ends meet. Neither of them was in the best of health, especially her father. One of her doubts about leaving had been whether they would survive until her return.

How could Anselmo have let her father give him all his money? Why had her father offered it? How come she hadn't known? She tried to convince herself that it would all be fine, more than fine, exactly as Anselmo said. Rubber was a dead cert, a sure-fire way of earning hard cash beyond anyone's wildest dreams. But with a further journey of many days through the most hazardous part of the rainforest before they even got to their land, let alone recruited any labour to work on it, let alone made a single rubber *bolacha*, it was hard, impossible in fact, to have Anselmo's sense of certainty. And then there were all the things she was finding out, the 'rounding up' of Indians that had such a ring of coercion about it, in addition to the fact that, however charming he was, they were effectively hostages to Mac when it came to his control of the isthmus.

Her feelings had oscillated backwards and forwards so wildly during their trip so far, between admitting defeat, giving it all up and going back to the comfort and safety of home, to plunging on ahead into the forest and making their fortune while also having the greatest adventure of their lives. But now, everything was different. Now, there was no choice.

She had something important she had wanted to tell Anselmo, but the shocking revelation he just shared had prevented her from going ahead. It wasn't the right moment and would have to wait. Anselmo was snoring already anyway, tired out by hatching plans and working on strategies – not to mention the great deal of strong alcohol that had been quaffed.

Katharine lay, struggling to nod off. Her last thought, before finally falling into a fitful sleep, was of whether they would ever be able to pay her father back.

43

Chapter Six

When she woke in the morning, Katharine was overwhelmed by a different agony to that caused by Anselmo's late-night revelation. This pain was a physical rather than a mental one, an intolerable need to itch her head. Not one particular part of it, but all of it, her cheeks, chin, nose and forehead, her eyes and scalp and crown.

She tried to sit up but found herself hopelessly entangled in the mosquito net which seemed to have become detached from its ceiling hook and to be swathing her in yards of gossamer-thin, grubby white fabric that became more knotted and invasive the more she attempted to rid herself of it.

Battling frantically with the net, desperate to get a hand free so she could assuage the maddening itching, her contortions roused Anselmo, who blearily opened his eyes. After all the alcohol drunk the night before, it took a few moments for his vision to clear. When he did, his shriek of horror made Katharine jump out of her skin.

'What? What is it? What's the matter?'

But Anselmo seemed to have been rendered mute and could only point a wavering finger towards her.

Finally free of the enveloping net, Katharine leapt out of bed and towards the dressing table, upon which was a looking glass. Picking it up, she held it in front of her. The sight that greeted her was nothing short of horrific. Her entire face was covered in mosquito bites, some swollen and red, some weeping a clear liquid and some bleeding freely. They were absolutely everywhere, from her eyelids to her ear lobes. She looked like an illustration from a penny dreadful, or an exhibit in a freak show.

'Oh, my lord,' she breathed. 'Oh, good grief. What on earth...?' Weakly, she replaced the mirror as tears welled in her eyes. 'What's happened to me?' she pleaded to Anselmo.

Each salty tear brought new agony as it coursed over the open wounds of the insect bites.

'Your head must not have been covered by the net during the night,' he said, 'and the mosquitoes have had a feast. My poor, poor love. That looks...'

'Say it,' moaned Katharine, her fists clenched by her sides to try to quell the desperate urge to scratch. 'I look horrendous.' She slumped down onto the bed beside him. 'I suppose my appearance doesn't matter much,' she wept, 'there's so few people here to see me. But still... it hurts, Anselmo. It really hurts.'

It must have been her extreme anxiety about Anselmo's confession that had caused her to toss and turn with such vigour that she brought the net down. What kind of a place was this that they had come to, she thought but did not say, that they now could not leave until they had made enough money? But how were they going to survive here, when everything around them seemed to want to kill them, from the savages to the wildlife?

Lost in self-pity, she became dimly aware of a scuffling around her feet and snapped her gaze towards it, ready to stamp on any species of invertebrate life that might be looking to have another go. But it was just Esperanza, come to investigate the fuss. She must have been asleep, thought Katharine, or she would have covered my head with the net. The child took in Katharine's hideous bites, shook her head in dismay and scuttled hurriedly away.

'I'm even bad enough to frighten the Indians,' she moaned, 'and look at them with their war paint and tattoos and practice of head mutilation of their infants!'

45

Anselmo was holding her hands, partly in sympathy, and partly to stop her from tearing at her skin with them.

'It'll get better,' he urged. 'In no time at all.'

But they both knew that most Europeans reacted extremely badly to the bites of the Amazon's voracious insects, that numerous hideous illnesses were carried by them and also that wounds of any kind took a long while to heal in this wet climate.

Esperanza came hurtling back into the room. In her hand was a plate on which stood green hillocks of halved limes.

Katharine grimaced. 'I don't want gin now, Esperanza. Thank you – but not now.'

The little girl shook her head. Climbing onto the bed, she knelt beside Katharine, picked up a lime half, and tenderly dabbed at her skin with it.

'Ow!' Katharine winced and shrunk back from her as the acidic juice bit at her flesh.

'Shhh,' soothed the girl, the first sound Katharine had ever heard her utter.

And it was true that, after the initial spike of intense pain, the lime did provide some relief from the incessant, tormenting itching.

Katharine sent down her apologies with Anselmo at breakfast time, telling him to let Mac know that she was indisposed. She lay on her bed, the limes by her side, continually dabbing at her poor swollen face, feeling utterly wretched. When Anselmo came back up to the room to tell her his plans for the day, she found it hard to summon the energy to even listen to him.

'We're going to take the steamer I've leased out for a spin,' he said, clearly making a great effort to staunch his glee out of respect for Katharine's misery. 'Me, Charles and a few of Mac's Indians who know the river well. Mac isn't joining; he says it's best if I establish myself as the one in command from the off. I'm sorry you can't come, my love. But I'm sure by this evening you'll be feeling a bit better.'

Katharine nodded feebly, making her best effort to smile. She didn't want her woes to dampen Anselmo's obvious eagerness to keep their expedition upriver on track, to press on as soon as possible to their rubber land. And, given that turning back was no longer an option, she herself was gripped with an overpowering urge to get underway in order to begin repaying her father without delay. Just that today, with her poor face so mutilated and painful, and with an enormous headache, she couldn't face going anywhere.

She managed to haul herself from her bed to watch from the veranda as the little party boarded the boat. Mac's soft voice with its lilting accent rose up to her in the clear air.

'Take as much time as you need to check out the goods you're paying for,' he chuckled, genially. 'The weather's set fair for now. With the rainy season approaching, that isn't guaranteed.'

Anselmo grinned and then, looking up at the villa and seeing Katharine there, waved brightly to her. A sudden desire to share the news she had kept to herself the night before and to say a proper goodbye surged through her, giving her an energy boost. Forgetting about her grotesque appearance for a moment, Katharine picked up her skirts, ran down the stairs and along the boarded walkway to the dock, Esperanza following in hot, uncomprehending pursuit.

Katharine ran to Anselmo and flung her arms around him. 'It's all right about the money,' she said, her words muffled from being buried in his shirt. 'You're right, we'll pay it back in spades.'

Anselmo smiled and kissed her forehead.

'And Anselmo – I have something to tell you.'

He looked at her enquiringly.

'I was going to last night but the news about my father's – um, my father's gift – took me by surprise and the moment passed.' She paused to catch her breath before resuming. 'The thing is that I think, I mean, I'm pretty certain – sure, in fact – that I'm pregnant. We're going to have a baby!'

The last words came out in such a rush that she had to stop, breathless again.

Anselmo seemed as dumbstruck about Katharine's announcement as she had been by his. But after a few moments of silence, he suddenly grasped her tightly to him, almost lifting off her feet, crying, 'That is wonderful news. The best I could ever have. Well done, my sweet one, well done.'

Katharine laughed out loud. Anselmo made it sound as if she had won a race or carried away a top prize, when all that she had really achieved was conceiving a child, and it hadn't been that difficult! As they stood looking at each other, Anselmo beaming with pride and pleasure and Katharine with delight in his delight, the steamer let off its horn.

'Time to get on board,' Anselmo said, and turned to go. And then turned straight back and grabbed her by the shoulder, pulling her towards him and kissing the top of her head. 'I'm so happy,' he whispered. 'So, so happy.'

But then Mac was calling, 'You should be on your way,' and, reluctantly, Anselmo followed the others up the gangplank and onto the boat.

'Remember the days are short in the tropics,' Mac added, 'you want to make the most of the light, so you do.'

He did not appear to have noticed Katharine and Anselmo's exchange, and when his eyes fell upon her disfigured face, he merely looked politely away as if wishing to spare her embarrassment. Katharine presumed he had seen it all before, that all his years in the Amazon had exposed him to every one of its many afflictions and ailments. There was nothing he could do to help and he was probably thinking it would teach Katharine to be more careful with her net in future. *An amateur mistake, a schoolboy error*, he was probably thinking, *so it is*.

'Goodbye, my darling love, my precious Katy,' Anselmo called down from the steamer's deck, looking wistfully back towards Katharine as if she already held their baby in her arms rather than it still forming inside her. 'I love you – even if you do look like the Elephant Man.'

48

Katharine had to laugh despite herself. He always had this power to lift her spirits. Thank goodness they had each other and were undertaking this epic journey together. It would be unthinkable to do it alone.

Po-Po came to join her in seeing the expedition party off, lured out by all the activity from wherever he'd been hiding.

'And I've got you, too, haven't I?' whispered Katharine to the little bird.

The ship's engines started up with a low, grumbling rumble, the water gurgled and churned beneath its bows and it was off, purposeful, like a pug dog running with its head down.

'It will all be fine,' called Anselmo to Katharine, clearly referencing the money and understanding that she still had doubts about it. 'Trust me, Katy. Trust me.'

'I do,' she shouted back. 'I always will.'

Po-Po brushed against her legs and gave a long, slow whistle as if in farewell to Anselmo.

'It will, won't it Po-Po?' Katharine said, bending down to her pet. 'It will all be fine.' Po-Po put his head on one side in that endearing way he had, his darting, intelligent eyes seeming to see into her soul. And then he was off, attention taken by a beetle in the mud, no longer concerned by human affairs.

Katharine looked back up, towards the boat, straining her eyes to see it, waving.

'I love you!' she mouthed, knowing that Anselmo could no longer hear as the boat receded into the distance. And then, as she watched, it disappeared from sight around a bend in the river and was swallowed up by the dark heart of the jungle.

Chapter Seven

The steamer did not return at the expected time that day. Katharine waited, on the veranda, on the dock, by the water's edge. But its solid bulk never hove into view.

In the afternoon, the sky darkened and a ferocious storm blew up, black clouds racing over the trees and catching in the branches. The tempest raged all through the evening and into the night, the wild wind whipping up towering waves and clouds unleashing torrential rain that fell like bullets on the saturated land. Squalls pulled young saplings out by their roots and flung them violently down to the ground where they broke like matchsticks.

'They must have gone further than expected – but they'll turn up soon, never fear. Time has no meaning in the Amazon, you'll soon discover that,' Mac assured Katharine and Laure, before lighting one of his noxious cigars and taking a puff. 'Apart from anything else, no one has a watch that works! The mechanisms rust in the damp and you're left using the sun like the damn natives.'

His chuckles ricocheted through Katharine's aching head, causing her to shrink back from him, from everyone.

By the following morning, calm had been restored, a rosy dawn revealing a newly benign river under a clear blue sky, scattered piles of debris the only signs of the night's savagery. The very air seemed freshly laundered, washed clean and full of hope.

Then the Indians returned.

Cries accompanied their arrival – of alarm and fear and consternation. Katharine, who had barely slept, rushed to the dock to be confronted by three prone corpses, lying in a row on the rain-dark wooden boards. Their faces were swollen and distorted from their time in the water, and their clothes torn to rags, but they were still identifiable. Two were Mac's servants who had gone on the excursion.

The third was Anselmo.

At first, Katharine could not comprehend it. She stood in stunned and silent disbelief, before sinking to her knees and throwing herself over the cold, wet figure of her husband. When she vomited, she just managed to miss the embroidered cloth that had been placed over him.

They left her for a while, Mac and Laure, Philippe and Clara, kneeling over the corpse. Only silent Esperanza kept her company, appearing by her side and slipping her hand into Katharine's in mute commiseration.

Despair gnawed holes in Katharine's stomach and grabbed at her heart, which felt heavy as a dead weight in her chest. Her bites itched and she scratched them, violently and vigorously, wanting them to bleed, wanting that physical pain to assuage the grief that was raging inside herself. It was too great for tears or sobbing or weeping or wailing. It was just a quiet, monumental agony that Katharine knew no way to express.

Eventually, after how long Katharine did not know, Laure reappeared and pulled her gently by the arm. Dazed, Katharine stood up. Her head spun and her legs wobbled and she slumped against Laure's petite frame, but somehow the two of them managed to stumble to a bench beneath the house's overhanging roof. Katharine sank heavily down onto the rough-hewn wooden planks, and Laure sat down beside her.

'Laure,' Katharine murmured, 'I'm so sorry. I haven't asked about Charles. Is there no word?'

Laure shook her head. Katharine could see blood on her lip where her anxiety had caused her to bite into it.

'Oh, my lord,' breathed Katharine. 'I'm so sorry. But...' the thought dawned on her as she was speaking, 'perhaps that's a good thing. If they haven't found his... him – perhaps it means he's all right.'

Laure nodded, fighting back tears. 'Maybe.'

Her voice was almost inaudible. Katharine took her hand. It was limp. Her whole body was bent forward as if she wanted to fold herself in half and disappear.

'We must hang on to hope,' she encouraged. 'We must believe Charles is... Charles will come back. I will believe it for you if,' her voice faltered, wavering, 'if you cannot.'

Laure nodded feebly then dropped her head, and Katharine saw fat, heavy tears fall to the sodden ground. She understood the woman's pain, the awfulness of uncertainty, the feeling of inevitability. If all the others were dead, why would Charles have been spared? But despite all this, Laure still had the possibility of seeing her husband again, and Katharine envied her that.

Anselmo, in contrast, was gone and although her numbness meant she couldn't really take it in, Katharine knew it was true. The awful, terrible reality of that made her feel hollow inside. Without him she had nothing, was nothing, had neither heart nor soul nor hope for the future.

Mac brought her and Laure whisky for the shock and, in a daze, Katharine drank the whole glass in one, even though she hated the taste. The lightheadedness that followed was a relief from the heavy, leaden feeling that loss had induced, but was quickly followed by overpowering nausea.

She had been feeling queasy since realising she was pregnant. Running her hand over her belly, she thought of the baby in there, Anselmo's baby, that he had only known about for a few brief hours before his death.

Now a dilemma raged within her – between cursing her mosquito-ravaged face for being the thing that had stopped her accompanying Anselmo and dying alongside him, and relief that she had kept herself safe so that her unborn baby had a chance at life. She wanted to cry because that might relieve her sorrow but she couldn't get the tears to come.

She went to bed and lay in rigid contemplation of the future. Because how could she possibly carry on with this madcap venture that had only just made sense when Anselmo was alive and now made no sense at all? How could she do it, on her own?

But then, when her father's money was at stake, how could she not?

Chapter Eight

During the night following the retrieval of the bodies, as if in supernatural response to Katharine's acknowledgement of her own condition, Clara went into labour. An Indian woman came to help, and Katharine and Laure joined her, at Clara's request. Katharine was sure there was nothing she could usefully do. Aside from being dazed with grief and exhaustion, the five brothers and one sister born after her in her family had all arrived when she was out at school, or at work, or had come like this one in the dead of night, and Katharine had no idea of the process by which babies were born.

The reality was horrifying.

The Indian woman judged it an easy birth, but to Katharine it looked like torture itself. Clara roared and screamed and panted and thrashed around as if possessed by the devil. The baby's entry into the world was accompanied by blood and excrement, causing Katharine to recoil in disgust. The Indian woman, completely unfazed by any of it, simply wrapped the newborn baby boy in a shawl and handed him to Clara.

After the turmoil Katharine watched, wonderstruck, as a quietude deeper and more intense than any she had ever known fell upon the scene, like the calm after the storm, like the river that very morning once the tempest had ended. Clara's face was adorned by a beatific smile such as Katharine imagined might have greeted the Wise Men at the nativity, when they found the baby Christ child sleeping in the arms of his loving mother.

This was the Amazon. Life and death on all sides, slipping from one to the other in a heartbeat.

The joy of the baby's safe arrival was short-lived, quickly replaced by mourning as next day they buried the bodies of the drowned men. There was no time to wait for a priest; the heat meant the burials must be quick and it would take weeks for a minister to be summoned and to arrive. If, in fact, one could be persuaded to come at all.

'We're lucky the piranhas didn't get them,' stated Mac, as he presided over the burial. He sounded unbothered but Katharine knew she must be wrong. It must be that he had become inured to loss. During his time on this beautiful, majestic but lethal river he would have seen scores of deaths. It was nothing new to him.

'When a boat ships water – it's never going to stay afloat,' he added, before solemnly reading a passage from the Bible.

He had had his Indian carpenter fashion simple wooden crosses from an Amazonian hardwood that, he said, would last for centuries. Katharine had the fleeting thought that this man, not her, would preside over Anselmo's eternal soul for all time. Then she dismissed the notion; she was not particularly religious and struggled with the idea of an afterlife – she was sure that, once you were gone, you were gone. Nevertheless, she still lingered by the grave long after the others had left so that she could tell Anselmo in private her hopes and dreams for the child he would never know.

Later that day, a stream of curses and insults woke her from an exhaustion-induced doze; she had not slept since Anselmo's death and had been starting to hallucinate with tiredness. She got out of the hammock that was strung between two lemon trees, her eyes picking out some distance away a couple of Indians, hunched and pitiful, being dragged by Mac's Spanish office manager and his clerk to a series of posts set into the hardened ground well above the water level. She watched in increasing horror as the Indians were tied up and a flogging began, both the manager and the clerk wielding a flailing whip similar to a cat o' nine tails.

The Indians' cries of pain and anguish seared through Katharine's heart. What had these men done to deserve this? Where was Mac? Why was he allowing this?

Rushing towards the scene, Esperanza hot on her heels, she suddenly pulled up short. Mac was there, leaning against an ironwood tree, smoking a cigar and watching what was going on. His eyes were expressionless but there was the faintest smile of satisfaction flickering on his lips. Katharine wanted to scream and shout at him to get the men to cease the flogging. But she stopped herself. Perhaps the men had committed some heinous crime. Perhaps, though it seemed unlikely, they deserved what was being meted out to them.

Swallowing her disgust and fixing her face into a neutral expression, she proceeded towards Mac.

'What did they do?' she asked, as inoffensively as she could while her insides were churning, sickened by the sight of blood pouring from the men's backs. She turned away, unable to stomach it.

Mac did not look at her as he replied. 'Left their *estradas*. Took rubber they harvested for me with the intent to exchange it for some tawdry tat that these ignoramuses value above money. Stole food.'

He dropped his cigar to the floor even though it was far from finished and ground it to shreds with his heel.

'One punishment for three crimes. I call that more than fair.' He patted his pockets as if seeking another cigar. 'The whip is the only thing these savages understand, the only thing that keeps them under control. You'll find that out, soon enough.'

Katharine grimaced. 'But surely they cannot endure more,' she said, struggling to keep her voice from trembling with suppressed anger. 'Surely it's enough now.'

Mac shook his head. 'I should tell you not to interfere,' he murmured, and then sighed deeply. 'But perhaps you have a point.' He held her with his gaze, considering. 'Perhaps it's good to have a fresh pair of eyes scrutinising how things are done here,' he added at last.

56

He turned towards the men.

'Stop now,' he ordered. 'Take them away.'

Katharine watched as Mac disappeared off to his office and the manager led the Indians to a row of buildings on the far side of the compound. Mr Phee had said that no one got as rich as Mac without the capacity to be ruthless, and this was no doubt true. Plus, Mac was only treating the Indians as everyone did – harshly, often brutally, believing that the only thing they feared was the whip. The prevailing attitude was that they not only needed it, but thrived on it, that they could not be made to work any other way. People who in every other aspect seemed good completely ascribed to this way of thinking.

But despite the body of opinion against her, Katharine could not convince herself that outright and deliberate cruelty could ever be right, that corporal punishment should ever be meted out to anyone, whatever the misdemeanour. She plodded back to the house, arms folded across her body, drenched in a cold sweat.

Already, before they'd even begun, her father had handed over his life savings, Anselmo had lost his life and Katharine was quickly learning that the moral and ethical codes that existed elsewhere did not prevail on the Amazon. Right there and then she determined that she would never follow the crowd on this, that she would not, under any circumstances, compromise her own standards of right and wrong. She would more than likely be as alone in taking this stance as she was now in her life, but that could not be helped. It was non-negotiable.

Nevertheless, despite the strength of her convictions, deep inside Katharine had a feeling of utter hopelessness, of everything being insurmountable. She and Anselmo had come to the Amazon to make their fortunes from rubber – but no one had told them of the costs.

Chapter Nine

Teams of Indians were still searching for the rest of the party who had gone on the steamer. Like a miracle, at four o'clock on the second day, they emerged from their canoes accompanied by a limping figure.

It was Charles.

Against all the odds he had survived and was able to reveal to them what had happened. Katharine could tell that he was sparing her the full truth of the accident, comforting her by saying that the end came quickly, that Anselmo had been hit by the stern of the boat and had not had a long-drawn-out, agonising death by drowning. She didn't – couldn't – fully believe him, but even in her dazed state, she appreciated his tact and concern. Laure was beside herself with joy and relief, weeping and laughing simultaneously; Katharine was glad that this tragedy had had a happy ending for her, at least.

But however big-hearted she was, watching Laure rejoicing in Charles' presence only made Katharine feel her own loss more keenly. Needing to clear her head from the sensory overload of all the problems assailing it – death, debt, joy, fear, brutality, trepidation, necessity – she went outside. Lagona boasted verdant grounds but they did not have quite the placid benevolence of an English garden, where green thoughts could be had in the green shade offered by drifts of rain-dusted roses and clematis, and where hedgerows buzzed with benign British insects that did not have as their central purpose in life the destruction, by bites or stings or scratches, of somebody else's.

Nevertheless, space to wander and to think was what Katharine needed and so, sternly instructing Esperanza not to accompany her, she set off. As she walked, she heard the sweet notes of a boy singing in perfect pitch, his song rising above the jungle's endless uproarious noise. Wondering who it was, she followed the sound; the melody rose and fell, leading her ever deeper into the forest where eventually it faded away.

At which point, Katharine looked around and found that she had no idea where she was. She was sure she had been on a path but now she could not make it out. The dense vegetation seemed to close in on her, the foliage and creepers and vines too tangled to penetrate, the palms and ferns and ramblers too thick to pass through. There was nothing like this forest in England, in London. The greatest number of trees Katharine had ever seen in one place before was in Highgate Wood, but there the oak, ash and sycamore left clear space between them and a soft, gentle light always dappled through the branches.

Here, beneath the canopy, darkness reigned, an obscurity which only accentuated the noise, the deafening humming and thrumming, hooting and howling, chattering and buzzing of the cicadas and frogs and birds and monkeys. You were never alone in the forest: life abounded, though much of it stayed always invisible, and much you didn't want to lay eyes on – bird-eating spiders, giant centipedes, pit vipers. Katharine was aware of the overpowering smell of decaying vegetation, damp earth and moisture that assailed her nostrils. But the boy she had been seeking was gone. Not a trace of either him or his lilting song remained.

And it was stiflingly hot – furnace hot, boiling fires of hell hot.

In the grip of panic, Katharine tried to force her way out through the tangle of undergrowth, desperate for the open, for fresh air and the sight of the sky. As she grappled with thick, tough branches and clinging vines, her foot became stuck, grabbed by a thick liana. Try as she might she could not release it and a judder of pure fear seared through her body, a terror that she might never escape, spending the rest of her life a captive, withering away and dying amongst these trees, no one able to find her. Or that she might be eaten alive by the army ants, battalions of them stripping her flesh to the bare bone, her skeleton the only thing remaining.

Dread gave her hidden strength and Katharine struck out with one last gargantuan effort, pulling with such might that suddenly her foot came free and she flew forwards, landing with a thump on the soft leaf mould of the forest floor. She sat for a moment, catching her breath and feeling her stomach as if she could tell from the outside whether anything had happened to the baby on the inside. She thought of the letter she needed to write, telling her family of Anselmo's death – but also of the new life she was harbouring.

Half walking, half limping, she dragged herself towards the relatively tame and familiar environs of the compound. Her nerves frayed and her heart pounding, she emerged into the sunlight and headed towards the house, feeling like a solider returning from a long and vicious war, but nevertheless triumphant, able to rise again.

Esperanza greeted her with her habitual blank-eyed expression. The only time the little girl had ever shown emotion was when she'd seen Katharine's bites. Like most of the Indians, she was generally impassive, unmoved by anything. Katharine had at first assumed that it was just the way they were. But more and more she reflected on whether it was the way the white man, over centuries of subjugation, had made them.

'Been for a walk?' Mac appeared beside her, smiling, his blue eyes as grateful a sight to Katharine as the cloud-studded sky had been.

'Just a little stroll,' she replied casually, surreptitiously brushing a few remaining leaves from her dress. She didn't want to confess to the blind panic she had so easily succumbed to. It hardly augured well for coping without a husband. 'I-I heard a little boy singing. He sounded so young – I haven't seen any boys that age at Lagona so I wondered if he were lost.'

Mac's eyes scrunched up, half laughing, half commiserating.

'That wasn't a child you heard, Mrs Ferrandis. It was a bird.'

'A bird?' Katharine couldn't believe it. The song had been so pure, the pitch so perfect, the sound so human and, at the same time, divine. Surely a bird could not produce such a sound?

'The organ bird,' continued Mac, waving his arm at the trees that stretched unimaginable miles in every direction. 'It is a favourite amongst us forest dwellers, heard but rarely seen.' He turned to Katharine with his twinkling smile. 'These woods are full of wonders.'

Katharine smiled back. 'Of course, I don't know them as well as you,' she replied, 'but it certainly seems that way.'

'When you are back in London, I hope you will take with you some fond memories of our Amazonian wilderness.'

Katharine opened her mouth to reply and then realised she had no idea what she wanted to say. Mac obviously assumed she would go straight home. But Mac didn't know the full story. By the time she had come to her senses he had gone, off to his office to deal with the affairs of the greatest rubber baron of them all.

Katharine went to her room and spent the remainder of the day in restless rumination.

That evening, Charles came to see her. Bandages covered the wounds he'd sustained in the water from bashing against rocks or submerged trees, but he'd had a bath and a shave and looked fairly chipper, all things considered.

'We're still with you,' he said to her, without preamble or explanation, his voice a bland monotone. 'Laure and I. If you decide to carry on – so will we.'

Katharine scratched at her face, which remained an unsightly mass of scabs and weeping sores and continued to itch intolerably. This affliction had saved her life. She still had no idea if she were glad about that or not.

'Thank you,' she said. She rubbed her hand across her eyes as if that would help her to see more clearly and took a deep breath. 'And yes – I will carry on.'

Right up to that moment she had not been sure which option she was going to take. But as soon as the words were out, she knew it was the only one. Charles looked at her uncertainly as if, when offering his support, he hadn't actually expected her to take up the offer.

'Right,' he uttered, tentatively. 'Absolutely. Well, tomorrow we must resume with our planning and preparing. I shall go and tell Laure.' He clapped his hands together and turned on his heel, leaving Katharine somewhat stunned about what she had committed to.

Mac also sought her out, later that evening.

'Of course, you'll be heading back to England,' he predicted.

It wasn't a question, rather a statement of fact, said with the same certainty of earlier.

'I'll be happy to take your *estradas* off you,' he continued, breezily, without giving her a chance to respond. 'Of course – well, the truth is that I wouldn't be able to pay you what Anselmo gave for them. He was, um, a little out of his depth, I fear.'

Katharine, watching him with a steady gaze, saw his face blanche as he realised his faux pas, referencing deep water that had caused Anselmo's death.

'You know what I mean, Mrs Ferrandis.' He coughed, cleared his throat, then carried on. 'As things stand, you'll be wanting to get out of here, to take your good self back to London where – well, where things are safer for everyone. So, I'm offering to buy you out. And I'll throw in your return passage, too. Least, I can do, in the circumstances.' He paused, gauging Katharine's reaction. When she didn't give one, he continued, as if compelled to fill the silence. 'He was a good man, your husband, and a brave one. I'm sorry for what happened.'

Mac propelled a piece of paper and a pen towards her. 'I can give you a couple of hundred, straightaway. We can sign on it now.'

Katharine regarded the document. When she had told Charles she would continue, she had felt so sure. Now she was filled with new doubt. And then a picture of her mother and father, waving them off at Southampton, leapt into her mind. Their faces had been full of hope, their smiles heaped with encouragement – but in her father's eyes she'd detected a tinge of anxiety. She had assumed it was just for her and Anselmo, for their safety, had not even imagined what she knew now. That Bill had lent – given, whatever – all his money to Anselmo. There was nothing left. Nothing for a rainy day. Everything he had, all he had spent a lifetime working for, was here, in the Amazon, gambled on rubber and the promise of a fortune. The money Mac was offering was a pittance, nothing like the value of the land. Nowhere near the amount Anselmo had borrowed, using her father's money as collateral.

Mac was watching her, waiting.

'You can't possibly run a rubber estate on your own.' His tone was gentle, kind and encouraging, as if reminding a young child that they were far too small to climb to the top branch of the tree. 'You know that, don't you? Women don't, a woman never has.' He shrugged, almost resignedly, as if he regretted this simple fact but knew it to be incontrovertibly true. 'A woman couldn't.'

The vision faded but Katharine's mind was made up anew. The bites had happened for a reason – to save her from the same watery fate that Anselmo had met and to enable her to make sure her father was repaid.

She picked up the document and read it, slowly and carefully, as if making sure to take in every word. With an expression of great relief, Mac proffered her the pen again.

She put the paper down.

'Thank you very much for the offer, Mac,' she said, politely and genuinely. She knew he was doing it to enable her to leave

63

before she got in any deeper, and to do so without humiliation. Despite what she had already avowed to Charles, and to herself, quitting would be the sensible thing to do.

But it wasn't the right thing.

'I can't give up now,' she said, softly but firmly. 'I came to the Amazon to harvest rubber and that's what I'm going to do.'

Mac held up his hands in protest.

'But my dear, that's simply not how things work here. A woman, on her own…' His words petered out at the impracticability, the sheer impossibility, of what she was suggesting.

Katharine took a deep breath before meeting his gaze. She needed to phrase things right. Mac was the most powerful man between Manaus and La Paz or Lima. At the moment he was her friend and ally and she needed to keep things that way. 'I appreciate your concern – I really do. And I understand that it's not going to be easy. But Charles and Laure are sticking by me and I'm going to continue to the Rio Poderoso and set up the business, just as Anselmo intended.'

Mac sat back in his chair, eyes wide with astonishment, too stunned to say more.

'Thank you for your help,' Katharine continued earnestly, as doubt flickered anew. Mac's dismay indicated to what great degree she was doing something unheard of. 'And all the hospitality you have shown us. Me. But my husband and I came with a mission and, in his name and for his sake, if for nothing else, I need to fulfil it.'

No need to mention the borrowed money, her family's life savings.

Mac rolled his eyes in a long-suffering way and grimaced regretfully. 'Your indomitability is beyond reproach.' He sighed.

He picked up the document he had wanted her to sign and held the edge towards the candle. It crinkled and browned before flaring up into a wave of red and orange flame. They both watched as the white ash it created drifted down onto the table.

'One last thing,' Katharine said, channelling a brazenness she didn't know she possessed. 'I'm sure a gentleman such as yourself will honour the agreement you made with Anselmo about passage over the isthmus – for us and for the rubber, once we are producing it. Won't you?'

Mac inclined his head in tacit agreement. Katharine nodded and got up to leave. She felt suddenly exhausted, needing desperately to sleep.

'A small matter remains.' Mac leant back in his chair and brushed invisible ash from his trouser legs before resuming, laconically. 'Unfortunately, I must still ask for payment for the steamer. Anselmo had already signed on it so I'm afraid he was the legal owner when it went down. I'm happy to take repayment in monthly instalments, as arranged.' He named a sum so enormous that Katharine had to forcibly stifle a gasp of dismay.

Before she had a chance to say anything in response, Mac added, 'This includes interest, obviously.'

Katharine bit her lip and took a deep breath. Another debt.

Anselmo had taken it on in good faith, to keep their rubber flowing downriver, to Iquitos and Manaus and Pará, to America and to Europe. That was the only goal of anyone in the Amazon, to harvest rubber and to sell it for the highest price. Now it was Katharine's only goal.

Because she had to pay her father back.

'I wish you the very best of luck,' called Mac in a low, soft voice as Katharine walked out of the room. 'You're going to need it.'

Chapter Ten

Twenty pounds.

Fifty-five pounds.

Three hundred and thirty pounds.

Five hundred and sixty-three pounds.

Over the next few days, Katharine found out the extent of Anselmo's borrowing.

His paperwork was well ordered and filed in true Anselmo-style so there was no escaping the scale of the problem. The number of promissory notes seemed endless; they owed thousands of pounds for the purchase of the *estradas* themselves and the compound of Norwood that went with them, plus all the equipment, for which Anselmo had been charged through the nose by the repellent Mr Phee, and of course wages paid to secure Charles who, as the most senior employee and an experienced clerk, could command a high salary. In addition, there was the fee negotiated between Anselmo and Mac to use his shipping route for the rubber, plus the cost of the sunken steamer, and commission paid in advance to the *aviador* in Manaus.

The total debt was colossal.

And as if that weren't bad enough, Katharine could not find the wallet that contained their cash, the £100 they had taken with them to tide them over until the rubber flowed. It must have been washed away when Anselmo drowned, was all she could think. Dropping her head into her hands, she felt despair sweep over her. The idea of ever repaying these vast sums seemed impossible, a Herculean task she simply wasn't capable of. Just thinking of it was gruelling.

She didn't know how long she sat like that. Only that the violent squawking of a pandemonium of red and yellow macaws roused her from her catatonic state. Glancing up at them, she wondered how their sight and sound had already become as familiar as the murmuration of starlings that used to gather in the smoke-smudged evening skies above her home in London. How things had changed. She had the sudden feeling that she could not keep up, that she needed the world to slow down to enable her to find her feet, as a widow, mother-to-be, business owner and employer. It was all too much, too soon.

Two days later, Katharine's dilemma intensified when Jonathan and Santiago rematerialised from the jungle where they had been dispatched before Anselmo's death to find men and canoes to take the newcomers upriver. They had no idea of the tragedy that had occurred and Katharine had no idea how to tell them. She did not know how they would respond to discovering a woman was now in charge.

Contrary to her concerns, the two men took it in their stride. They and the two-dozen forest Indians they had returned with would take Katharine, her employees and her cargo upriver, portaging them over the *cachuelas* and steering them through the rapids, just as previously planned.

I suppose white people are all the same to them, Katharine reasoned to herself – the ones who wield the power and tell them what to do. Why should they care if that person is a man or a woman? But she vowed to herself to stick to her determination that she would not stoop to the whip as the means of control, no matter the example that had been set by others.

Painstakingly, all the equipment that Anselmo had so carefully gathered for the expedition was packed on board the canoes. Katharine had gone through everything to make sure she knew what they had and to ascertain that it was all entirely necessary, and now they were ready to go.

'I'll honour our agreements,' Mac promised, observing her preparations, his desire to buy her out seemingly consigned to history. 'I'll keep your supplies moving upriver to Norwood and I'll keep your rubber moving downriver to – well, to whoever will pay the most for it!'

'Thank you,' Katharine said, and meant it. She knew she was lucky to have the friendship and support of someone so powerful and knowledgeable. And someone so rich; he'd lent her cash to replace what had been in the lost wallet. Yet more to be repaid, but utterly necessary. She had to keep them all fed, whatever else they went without.

'We Europeans have to stick together, so we do,' Mac insisted, and Katharine gratefully acknowledged this truth.

On her last night at Lagona, she ate heartily, filling her belly with imported delicacies of *confit de canard* and champagne. This would be the last good meal she would have until such time as they were established at Norwood, and she wanted to make the most of it. She and her unborn child needed all the nourishment they could get for the gargantuan task that lay before them.

Mac didn't see them off the next day. He'd set off before dawn on a visit to his *estradas*, leaving Katharine a note assuring her that he was there to help, that she could call on him any time if she needed anything. As they all climbed aboard the canoes, Philippe and Clara lingered on the bank, the baby wrapped in a shawl and cradled in Clara's arms.

'You need to get in now,' called Katharine from the first canoe. 'We should be off.'

Clara and Philippe exchanged a glance.

'We're not coming,' answered Clara, bluntly.

Philippe nodded and gave a Gallic shrug to accompany her words.

'We've decided it's too risky – with the baby and everything. There's yellow fever upriver, and malaria, as well as all the savages. And who knows what state the house will be in by the time we get there,' continued Clara.

68

'But what about your job?' Katharine asked Philippe. 'What will you do for work?'

Even as she spoke, she knew she was not going to persuade the couple to make a different decision. There was plenty of work in Iquitos, Manaus, Pará. Philippe and Clara had no need to follow her to the depths of a dangerous and disease-ridden jungle in order to earn a living.

'We will be fine,' answered Clara, and Katharine knew they would. They had each other, and that was always a greater guarantee of success than being alone as she now was.

'Goodbye then,' she called. 'And good luck.'

As the Indians stowed the last few items, she folded her hands around her belly. She needed to keep her own child safe just as Phillippe and Clara were protecting theirs. But its embryonic life made doing the sensible thing and going back to England even less possible than it ever had been. To turn up in Clerkenwell not only having denuded the family's savings account but also as a widow with an extra mouth to feed couldn't be contemplated.

Suddenly overwhelmed, tears pricked behind her eyes and a sense of utter despondency descended like the tropical rain clouds overhead. She had no one with whom to share this adventure, the future, now Anselmo was gone. Most likely she never would again. She would have to go through it all alone, make all the decisions, earn all the money to pay back Anselmo's numerous borrowings, all by herself.

Katharine wanted to buckle and collapse, to sink to the floor and hammer her fists into the ground, berating Anselmo for taking such risks with her father's money. She hated him for his profligacy, was furious at him for dying and leaving her alone, and she missed him so desperately she thought her heart might break with the pain. There was no one to call her Katy any more, no one to stand by her side – not now, and not when her baby was born.

She looked back at Philippe and Clara standing on the quay, holding tight to their precious infant, and allowed herself a moment of jealousy, a moment to long that she still had what they had.

But she didn't.

With an immense effort of will, Katharine banished her self-pity, which could do her no good. She gave a last wave to those who had gathered to see them off, including the little servant who had been like a shadow for the duration of her stay. Most of the onlookers were waving dutifully and mechanically, but suddenly Esperanza rushed forward, right to the water's edge and stood teetering there, tears welling in her eyes. Katharine looked at her helplessly. If only she could take her with her, this silent child. But she belonged to Mac and in any case, Katharine didn't want such a young servant of her own, no matter how often she saw others in the Amazon adopt this custom. It made her feel uncomfortable in a way she hadn't had time to digest or interpret yet.

Just as Jonathan was casting off, a scuttle in the undergrowth and a streak of colour, followed by a soft, long-drawn-out whistle, caught Katharine's attention. A familiar figure with dainty, poised gait emerged from the bushes.

'Po-Po,' she cried out, as the little bird advanced towards the river. 'Are you coming too?'

The bird halted, turning its delicate head one way and another as if considering what to do. And then it sauntered at a leisurely pace up to Katharine's canoe and stepped aboard, taking up a perch on the stern and gazing imperiously back at Lagona as it faded into the distance behind them.

Katharine was ridiculously glad to see her friend, who had disappeared the day of the storm and not been seen since. She'd assumed he had tired of human company and gone back to the jungle; his return aroused the faintest scintilla of hope. With or without Anselmo, Philippe and Clara, she had to carry on.

There was simply no other option.

Chapter Eleven

The Amazon, 1890

Just before they left Lagona, the mail arrived. There were five letters addressed to Katharine, as well as a few for Anselmo. Those with Spanish postmarks Katharine judged to be from his parents, siblings or other relatives. They were weeks or months old, written with no thought that Anselmo might not be alive to receive them. She fingered them gingerly before putting them away to deal with later. She needed to be strong to look at these, and even stronger to write the replies in which she explained what had happened to her husband.

As the convoy of canoes made their stately progress upriver, Katharine devoured her own letters greedily, two from her mother, one from Mabel, another from a friend called Elsie whom she'd met when working at Fortnums, and amazingly the last one from her errant brother Mayhew. Katharine read Mabel's first, savouring the words as if they were manna from heaven, eating them up voraciously. Mabel's handwriting was surprisingly well formed, despite her young age, and her childish voice sounded in Katharine's head just as if she were sitting right beside her. She wrote of the weather, and dad's cough, and school that she had only just started and loved every minute of. She described the travelling band that had played at the end of the street last Sunday, the organ grinder accompanied by a monkey in a little red woollen jacket.

Do you see monkeys in the jungle? Mabel wrote. *Can you send one home for me?*

Katharine smiled to herself and raised her eyes to the river-bank, where a family of capuchins frolicked in the boughs of a barrigona palm.

Elsie's letter had been penned in March, soon after Katharine and Anselmo had left, and it was now August. In Green Park, where she and Elsie used to walk in their lunch breaks, the mown grass would be parched by the summer sun, and in Hyde Park the flowers in the beds would droop and wither in the sere heat. Here in the Amazon, nothing was ever dry. Sudden deluges occurred almost every day and night all year round, and in the rainy season even more frequently.

Elsie talked of the usual things – the annoying manager who always tried to cut short their lunch breaks, the demanding customers who had more money than sense, the cold in the old building's basement where the staff changing rooms were located, a music hall concert she had attended. Katharine had a lurching surge of nostalgia for that old, familiar life, for its monotony and mundanity which also meant safety and surety, for the cool smell of long summer evenings, the taste of a cup of tea with fresh cow's milk, the sound of cartwheels on cobbled streets. She longed for crowds and noise and voices and composed music, instead of the constant, haunting, unchained melody of the rainforest.

Her mother's letters were short but loving, and though she never complained, Katharine was acutely aware of the responsibility that lay on her shoulders. Mary and Bill were getting older and they were tired, but with their retirement fund in the hands of the banks and businesses of the Amazon, they would have to continue working for some time yet.

Mayhew's letter, on the other hand, infuriated Katharine in equal measure to Mary's pulling on her heart strings. He was full of himself as always, living the high life in New York, waxing lyrical over the virtues of the Elevated Railway, apartments with steam heating and that marvellous invention the telephone that was already revolutionising communication in the most civilised parts of the world.

It was clear that he found her emigration to Brazil unfathomable, though he wrote that the jungle would probably keep her amused for a while, as she had such limited sophistication. New York would no doubt be too intimidating for an ex-shop girl such as her.

After Katharine had stopped fuming, and a sudden rainstorm had dampened the steam coming from her ears, she managed to smile to herself. At least Mayhew's arrogance had taken her mind off Anselmo's death, even if only for a few minutes. But her spirits soon fell again as they spent hours travelling through the dark gloom of the melancholy forest and she could not reach out her hand and feel her husband's reassuring presence beside her.

Only the friendliness of the Indian villages they passed through lifted Katharine's spirits and helped to dispel her despondency. At every one, if they did not stop, a woman would paddle out to deliver gifts of eggs or fruit, corn cobs or brilliant feathers, handing them to her and Laure with shy giggles and wide-eyed curiosity.

In the evenings, at some time that the canoeists seemed to understand without any obvious sign or signal, each would head for the bank and, when the bottom of the boat hit the sand, all the occupants would jump out and there they would camp for the night. Usually, the Indians chose a spot near a village for companionship and the possibility of supplies. If no food was available, they would go hunting, shooting with their bows and arrows wild pigs, monkeys or birds, and once even a small gazelle, their aim so true that Katharine never saw them miss. They only ever killed what was immediately necessary for everyone's sustenance and if bushmeat was scarce, the Indians would fish, either with their bows and arrows if the water were clear enough, or by gathering the sap of the barbasco vine and using it to poison the fish as they swam.

Katharine became more and more impressed by the strength and skill of the Indians, how they could carry the canoes over rocks and waterfalls as if they were no heavier than driftwood, how they could read the river like a book, could use the currents to propel them forward and avoid the rapids that might capsize them. In the settlements they passed, she saw *matirí* bags fashioned from plant fibres, and sewing thread made from the inner bark of the *uaissíma* tree. She could not understand why, when the lamentable traits of Indians were discussed by Europeans, their sloth and idleness disparaged, that no one ever mentioned their skills, their encyclopaedic knowledge of the rainforest, passed down through generations, nor their resourcefulness, nor their complete oneness with their ancestral jungle home.

At one far flung village, larger than the usual collection of half a dozen huts, Katharine was astonished to encounter a Catholic priest in full black robes and dog collar emerging from the undergrowth.

'We are working hard to bring civilisation and Godliness to the heathen,' he explained, in answer to Katharine's incredulous enquiry as to what he was doing there.

'Do you think we really need to?' she questioned mildly. 'Did they request it? I doubt it, for they seem perfectly content.'

The priest raised his hands in a gesture of exasperation and mystification. 'It's true that they often have little regard for the benefits we bring them, such as the word of the Lord. But we are doing what we can.'

Katharine didn't know whether to laugh or cry. She had an ingrained respect for the Church but felt no particular need for regular worship – and certainly didn't see why the Indians should be expected to respect a God they neither believed in nor needed.

'Perhaps their lack of gratitude is because they never asked for those benefits and do not value them,' she suggested, in a tone of innocuous enquiry.

The priest's mouth fell open in stunned disbelief. 'But, my child, it is our duty to bring all peoples into God's fold. As the superior race, it is imperative that we do this.'

Katharine did not reply, instead shaking his hand and excusing herself, hurrying back to the rest of her group. Though she disagreed with his proselytising, she understood that this was considered necessary, that the Indians and other native peoples the world over were judged as requiring Christian intervention from Europeans to save their souls. She had never thought about it much before, just known that this was the way, and it had never occurred to her to question it. But now she was here, amongst these people, she was beginning to see everything differently, to believe that the Indians should be left alone to worship, or not, exactly as they pleased.

They continued upriver, further and further into the untrodden Amazon. At times, the land sloped gently upwards from the water, at others, they were surrounded by lofty red cliffs gashed by waterfalls and topped by trees whose branches arched across the river, interlocking with those on the opposite side as if engaged in an eternal tug of war. The forest was old, so old that the tree trunks were cloaked by mosses and ferns, their exposed roots gnarled and discoloured like aged teeth, but still strong, clinging to the soil and to life with all their might.

The tribes they encountered were continually changing, along with the patterns and diagrams tattooed across their bodies and the piercings of their ears and noses. Jonathan and Santiago explained that each spoke their own language and that though some were mutually understandable, many were utterly unique. The deeper they penetrated into the forest, the more Indians they met who had rarely seen a white person, and never a white woman, before.

One evening, the convoy stopped at a sylvan paradise where a series of rocks formed a natural pool by the riverbank, fed by springs bursting forth from numerous dark crevices and cascading downwards like liquid silver. Overhead, the leafy fronds of the murumuru palm provided a protective canopy, while beside the pond the feathery plumes of arrow grass rustled gently in the hint of a breeze. As they made camp in a small clearing, the local women trooped down to the water to bathe and, seeing the travellers and being reassured by Jonathan that they came in peace, they gestured to Laure and Katharine to join them. Laure declined but Katharine leapt at the chance. She was hot and sweaty and longed to wash.

Stripping naked felt awkward for a moment – after all, she had not undressed in front of anyone except Anselmo since she was a small child being bathed in the iron tub in front of the fire in Hawthorn Road. But that awkwardness was forgotten the moment she unlaced her corset. It had pained her since their arrival in Manaus and releasing herself from its constraint was the most marvellous thing she had ever done. Once she felt the evening air against her skin and the cool, silky water lapping at her toes she experienced a sense of liberation she had never felt before.

The Indian women gathered around, picking up and examining the mysterious garment that was the corset, poring over its construction, holding it up around themselves and roaring with laughter, then scrutinising it again, clearly mystified as to how a body could fit within it. Once they had satisfied their curiousity, though still shaking their heads in disbelief, they handed it back to Katharine and she placed it by the rest of her clothes on a mound of sand.

Wading deeper into the water, Katharine realised that the women were now inspecting her naked body as closely as they had her underwear. Cautiously, they moved closer to her, then tentatively reached out hands towards her and began to fondle her hair, not just on her head but her armpit and pubic hair too, marvelling at it, signalling to each other their wonder at its abundance and fiery orange hue. They themselves were hairless apart from on their heads, so Katharine supposed it was bizarre to them to see such a different species of human being in their midst. They were also completely comfortable with nudity, wearing little if any clothing themselves. As their inspection continued she felt as if she were somehow being welcomed into a different state of being female, where a body was a useful tool and its incredible capacities – of strength and childbearing and milk-providing and nurturing – were lauded and acclaimed rather than hidden furtively away as her culture required.

Their inquisitiveness about her hair satiated, the women moved on to her belly. No one knew that Katharine was pregnant; she had not told anyone and her natural slimness, combined with the corset, meant that to most observers she did not show yet. But now, standing naked in the pool, she could see the slight swell of her belly, the increased fullness of her breasts, the pinkness of her nipples. The women recognised her state instantly, stroking and patting her while consulting with each other, exchanging knowledgeable looks and confirmatory glances of what they were discussing. Katharine stood in the middle of it, silent and content, letting these women analyse and conclude. She felt no discomfort at their gentle, caressing touches; instead, a sense of profound calm swept over her as if, here in this beautiful place, she had come into contact with the sublime. Suddenly, she felt a certainty that all would be well, that all difficulties would be overcome.

That she and her baby would survive.

The washing over, she and the women emerged from the water and sat on the rocks to dry off. Katharine went to collect her clothes. She picked up the corset and, taking hold of the torturous garment for the last time, she kissed it goodbye. With a huge intake of freely taken breath, she flung it into the air where it sailed like an ungainly bird for a few moments before settling in the branches of a monguba tree.

'No more corsets,' she said to the uncomprehending women watching her in bewilderment. Truly, foreigners had strange habits. 'Corsets are for the city, not the Amazon.'

She laughed and the women exchanged cautious smiles, then tentative chuckles. The ways of the white people were incomprehensible to them, inexplicable and unfathomable – so they didn't bother to try to understand. Instead, they went back

77

to their huts and their babies and their unfettered lives where no one told them to encase their ribs in the bones of other animals or to cover their ankles for fear they might offend someone.

The next morning Katharine rose early and wandered down to the river's edge, keeping a wary eye out for any jaguars that might still be prowling. There had been prints around their tents at their last camp and an attack could never be ruled out. But the only wildlife on view was a sombre gathering of pig-birds, seated in a tidy row beneath the silvery leaves of the trumpet trees, and a family of capybara. These rodents, that looked so sweet and charming, a bit like small, short-haired pigs, were ubiquitous all through the Amazon and had become as familiar to Katharine as cats and dogs on the streets of London.

Though the dawn light had come, the sun was still low behind the trees, the forest shrouded in cloud as if wrapped like a precious object. Katharine smelt the freshness of the air, the faint wisps of wood smoke rising from the nearby huts and the earthy, humus smell of the soil after rain. Raising her face to the rising sun, she breathed in the pure essence of her surroundings and sighed, long and low. Promise filled the air, the promise of a future that was hers to mould. She had never had such a feeling before.

In an azure sky now streaked with pink-tinged clouds, the sun rose further still. Its rays fell on Katharine's belly and something stirred inside her, a faint fluttering, an imploring scratch that said, 'I'm here.'

Casting her gaze downwards, Katharine felt her heart swell in delight as the motion, faint and hesitant as a butterfly's wings, continued. As the heat intensified upon her skin so did the movement within. It was her baby, calling to her, letting her know it was there, that it was alive and revelling in the new day, just as she was.

A slow, surreptitious smile spread unstoppably across her face.

'Hello, baby,' she whispered, and patted her stretched skin in a gesture of greeting. 'Nice to meet you.'

That day, freshwater dolphins tailed their canoe for hours, the type that Jonathan told her always travelled in pairs. The Indians feared the *bôto*, believing that they enticed young men to a watery death, but Katharine was fascinated by them. They performed their distinctive tumble-turns repeatedly throughout the day and only left as night began to fall.

Over the following days, the canoe convoy was forced by low water levels into a stretch of river known to be inhabited by hostile tribes, and the atmosphere changed from serene and joyful to one of nervous trepidation. The boatmen kept to the middle of the channel, as far from the reach of poisoned arrows as possible. The dangers were not just on land; one day, looking into the water, Katharine saw a dormant log transmorph before her eyes into a huge caiman, ten foot long, beady eyes piercing straight into hers. Snakes slid past them, on sea and on land, including the type with two heads that, if cut in half by a machete blow, simply wriggled away in opposite directions. Intermittent torrential rainshowers combined with gusty winds ripped trees from the banks and swept them downstream as if light as corks.

Katharine had the constant sense of eyes in the jungle, watching. At night, the habitual cacophony of animals, birds and insects, underridden always by the screeches of the howler monkeys, was occasionally disturbed by a sudden crash as a branch or tree fell to the ground, or the strange cries of unseen, unknown beings. The Indians put these down to Curupira, the wild man of the forest, who had cloven hooves and a bright red face and was covered in tresses of unkempt orange hair. The fiend even possessed backwards facing feet to throw trackers off his trail, so the legend went. Katharine wanted to dismiss such stories as superstitious nonsense, but in reality there was something about the density of the jungle, the silence amidst the noise, the melancholy that often hung about it, that gave her the feeling that it could be true, and made her look over her shoulder, half expecting to catch a glimpse of Curupira emerging, leering, from beneath the canopy.

For all the fears of monsters, in truth, it was the jungle's smallest inhabitants that caused the most harm. After the hideous experience of the face bites, Katharine had thought she had undergone the worst the Amazon could throw at her. But she hadn't bargained for the myriad insects the region specialised in, some active by day, some by night, making sure there was never a time when humans could let down their guard. Mosquitoes, ticks, centipedes and scorpions could all bite and sting and torture in their own, unique way. Swarms of pium flies surrounded the canoes and chomped at the passengers with a ferocity belying their minute size; blessed relief came only at nightfall as they were active only in sunlight.

Day passed monotonous day and Katharine yearned to arrive, to be able to sit in a chair rather than on a rock and sleep with four solid walls around her rather than in her canvas mosquito tent, which though it gave some protection against insects, was always soaking wet by morning. She longed to wash and dry her clothes which were permanently damp, green with mildew, and revoltingly smelly – a fact that was only tolerable because everyone else's were, too. As the journey wore on, she frequently felt alternately cold and shivery, hot and feverish.

Finally, after four long weeks on the river, Jonathan changed course, steering the canoe to the left bank.

'We are here,' he stated, blankly, as the boat's bottom hit the sandy shore. 'Norwood.'

He pointed to an area that had been cleared of primary forest but was now beginning to be engulfed by secondary growth. They were some way ahead of the other canoes so Katharine got her first glimpse of her new home before Laure and Charles were anywhere near. Rising up from the tangle of small trees and creepers was a low hill, and on top of that a house, smaller but not dissimilar in style to Mac's villa, the offices and storerooms on the ground floor, the living quarters above with the same wide veranda running all around.

There any resemblance to Lagona ended.

Half of the zinc roof had fallen off and the veranda sloped and sagged where the supporting posts had rotted or been eaten by beetles. And even from this distance, Katharine could see through the open sides that the rooms were bare, the furniture destroyed by the combined forces of rain, heat, humidity and voracious termites. It was so far from her vision of the log house with white picket fence that she could hardly believe her eyes. How could she have been so deceived? But then she remembered that no one had promised her anything – all Anselmo had said was that a house existed – not what state it was in.

One thing was certain. Her hope of a chair was not going to be realised.

Katharine got out of the canoe. Dizziness overcame her, together with an overwhelming feeling of nausea. She only got a few paces up the beach before vomiting profusely and sinking to her knees. Almost crawling, aware of the horrified glances of Jonathan and the other Indians, she made it to the house, pulling herself upright on the door and reaching out to open it. The handle came off in her hand and chunks of worm-eaten wood crumbled dustily to the ground. Before she could attempt to enter, a terrible curling pain in her belly forced Katharine to run for the shelter of the nearest bushes and squat down behind them. As she crouched, her guts twisting themselves inside out, a pair of sinister eyes nestled between the tree roots met hers.

'Ugh!' The scream was involuntary. Katharine flinched but couln't move far due to her state of half-undress. Wanting to look away but not daring to in case the spider attacked, she kept a wary eye on it, shaking with fear and fever in equal parts. It looked innocuous enough, but Katharine recognised it as one of those that Jonathan had taken particular care to tell her to look out for. It was a wandering spider, possessor of venom that was amongst the deadliest in the world.

Noisily, Katharine began to sob. The acute stabbing pain in her stomach and the terror of her new jungle neighbours assailed her, nailing her to the spot, incapable of movement.

An attack of dysentery, a ruined house, killer insects. It was for this that she had travelled thousands of miles up the Amazon. Any confidence she had garnerned deserted her anew. Tears rolled down her cheeks and despair overwhelmed her. She was filthy, smelly and ill, her head ached, her back ached, her legs ached and her belly was pure agony. She did not know how to cope with the conditions here in the tropics, was not equipped, either mentally or physically, to do so. Momentarily, she was jealous of Anselmo for having got out of this hell by dying.

Perhaps the truth was that he had had a lucky escape.

Chapter Twelve

Norwood, 1890

For three days, Katharine rolled around on a raffia mat, writhing in agony as the dysentery ate into her guts. She drank only boiled water brought to her by Jonathan, Santiago or Laure. The only way to combat the illness was to starve and stay warm. Throughout her rampant sweats, she kept her blankets wrapped around her. When they were soaked by perspiration or the general dampness in the air, someone – she was often too delirious to know who – replaced them.

On the day the fever lifted, she sat up and looked around in bewilderment. She had been placed on a roughly assembled platform on the ground floor of the house, and a fire kept burning to ward off insects and predators. Gingerly, she swung her feet to the floor and tried to stand. The noise as she stumbled and fell brought the seated Indian, left to guard her, rushing to her side. He called out in a language she didn't understand and within minutes Santiago and Jonathan were there, closely followed by Laure and Charles.

'Thank goodness you're on the mend,' said Charles, with characterstic understatement, at exactly the same time as Laure said, 'You look absolutely terrible.'

Katharine emitted a short, effortful laugh. It was all too ridiculous. How could anyone survive this purgatory? What were any of them doing here?

Laure sent the men away. Gently, she lowered Katharine to a sitting position on the makeshift plank bed. Katharine felt her bones creak with the unaccustomed movement. She ran her hands down her sides; she could feel her ribs and her hip bones.

'Katharine,' murmured Laure, quietly. 'You're pregnant, aren't you?'

The swell of her belly had been accentuated by the drastic weight loss brought about by the illness.

Miserably, Katharine nodded. 'I was,' she whispered. She gazed imploringly at Laure. 'But the baby won't have survived this, will it?'

Laure's face blanched momentarily and then was immediately restored to its habitual equanimity.

'It looks all right to me,' she replied, her eyes on Katharine's stomach. She reached out her hand and patted the bump. 'We could get the *feiticeiro* to come,' she said, 'some of them make effective potions from the forest plants. Others are nothing more than witch doctors. However,' she continued, after a pause, 'I think that all will be well. We just need to feed you up and get plenty of fluids into you.'

Katharine said nothing. She could hardly believe the baby could have made it through the wrenching nausea and diarrhoea. But on the other hand, she herself had, so maybe it was possible.

Laure, meanwhile, was now staring intently at her feet. Katharine had the urge to laugh again. Maybe her toes had fallen off. Nothing would surprise her any more. She wiggled them to try them out and they seemed to still be there, but then again amputees thought they still had their limbs, didn't they? She had read that in a magazine article about the American Civil War.

Laure leant forward, carefully lifted Katharine's skirts and picked up her right ankle.

'Excuse me,' she said. She raised it a little higher towards her eyes. 'I need to check something.'

'What?' Katharine was half alarmed and half resigned. She wasn't sure she could be bothered to get worked up about any more ailments. 'What are you looking for?'

'Chigger mites,' responded Laure, drily. 'They are rampant – and ravenous. But it looks like you've escaped their attentions – for now at any rate. The only way to be sure to prevent them is to cover yourself up. It's why I wear these.'

With a flourish of her hands, she lifted her skirts to show Katharine the ankle-length bloomers she sported underneath, with tightly tied bows to secure the bottoms. 'This way the mites cannot get a hold on me. You might want to make something similar. And remember to regularly check under your toe nails, as that is where they lay their eggs. If you find any, you have to dig the sac out with scissors and tweezers.'

Katharine shuddered in disgust.

'Or get someone else to do it. It's fairly painful,' added Laure.

Of course it was, thought Katharine, wryly. Why wouldn't it be? This was the Amazon.

Laure bent forward for one last look at Katharine's feet. 'You're fine,' she pronounced.

Katharine sighed with relief. She had been spared one torment at least.

'Now drink this,' Laure said, proffering a gourd of fresh water, 'and then sleep. You need all the rest you can get, you and the baby.'

When next Katharine woke she felt almost human. It was daylight and she could hear the bustle of people and footsteps and voices drifting towards her. She sat up, and this time didn't fall straight back down again. She stood, and was not overcome with dizziness.

Slowly, she moved towards the daylight, not entirely sure where she was or what to expect. She stepped out from under the shelter of the rickety house and looked around her, and the recollection of that first view of Norwood came back to her, as if from some long ago past, some almost forgotten history.

It dawned on her anew how much work there was going to be in making it a home fit for herself, a European woman used to a house built of brick with solid walls and floors and windows and doors – and for an infant. Her heart slowed in her chest. She couldn't face it. Rebuilding the everything, establishing the rubber business, caring for a newborn, simply finding enough for them all to eat when the arrival of supplies would inevitably be erratic – it was overwhelming.

Discombobulated, she wandered round to the front of the house and towards the river. Jonathan and Santiago were there, deep in conversation about something. They stopped as soon as they saw her, came rushing over, implored her to tell them how she was, to accept their suggestions of herbal teas and nourishing soups and other healing potions and potages. Katharine thanked them over and again.

When they left her side, anxious to set Rosabel, an Indian woman they had assigned as cook, to the task of preparing lunch for her, she sat down on a tree stump to think. Jonathan and Santiago and all the Indians had toiled so loyally and bravely, using all their practical skills and cunning to get them here safely. They were relying on her for employment, to pay them, to provide for them and supply them with things only money could buy. She couldn't crumble on them now. She just couldn't. Here she was, at Norwood, and the only way forward was to keep going. Though the constant effort required to battle against the jungle was utterly wearying, it had to be done.

Hauling herself upright, trying to shake off the weakness and lethargy, she went to survey their meagre supplies, the canned food and *farinha*, flour made from cassava root, that they'd brought with them from Manaus. Someone had piled it up in an open-sided hut where it was protected from the rain. It wasn't much.

'We will go hunting, Mother,' Santiago assured her, appearing beside her again. 'We will bring parrot, tapir, monkey, wild pig. I have already found turtle eggs and we have

86

peach palm fruits, berries and bananas, jungle pears and plums. We will plant yuca. It will be fine.'

Katharine smiled gratefully at him. He and Jonathan were always so positive. Nothing dismayed them, nothing dampened their spirits. They were like the trees in the forest, always there, always ready to give of themselves for human need. Most Europeans seemed to think that the Indians should make themselves more like them. But Katharine increasingly thought she should try to be more like the Indians. Indomitable. Unfazed by triumph or disaster. Stable and strong through anything and everything, resilient to whatever life or nature threw at her.

Later that evening, feeling somewhat revived after Rosabel's delicious offerings, Katharine took a walk around the compound. She needed to build up her energy again. As she strolled, she felt a little scratch inside her belly, and then a tiny punch, like a fist or foot reaching out to explore its cramped environment. She paused and waited, unwilling to allow herself to believe it was true. It came again, unmistakably. And again. Almost sobbing with joy, she went back to the fire and the remains of the dinner, where Charles and Laure were still sitting. Calling Laure to her, she whispered in her ear. 'The baby. My baby. It's alive.'

Laure laughed and smiled and told Katharine it was all the more reason to take good care of herself.

Dazed with unexpected happiness, Katharine went back to her bedroom where she took three of her dresses from her trunk, leaving the best in case of visitors. She had work to do, which began with some adjustments to her attire, and a renewed sense of purpose with which to do it. The dress she had been wearing on the journey and while she was ill could not be salvaged and was good for nothing but burning; it stank and was full of holes and irredeemable stains. Not even Bernadette McNamara's redoubtable Portuguese washerwomen would have been able to fix it, Katharine thought to herself with a wry smile. But the others were in fine condition.

Katharine had invested in the best needlework kit she could afford before leaving London and fortunately the needles rolled in asbestos and the high quality scissors had just about survived the rust and remained usable.

By the flickering light of a smoky candle, she ripped and tore and seamed and sewed, roughly and with much admonishment of her own clumsiness (sadly, she lacked her mother's skill at needlework) until she had constructed three sets of long trousers, with ribbons at the cuffs to tighten against any marauding insect.

'That'll show you, chigger mites and all the rest,' she said out loud, and then laughed at herself; wasn't it the first sign of madness to talk to yourself? But there was Po-Po, peeping his elegant head around the threshold, his darting eyes seeking her out as if eager to respond to her.

'I was speaking to you, wasn't I?' she said to the bird, and then, 'thank goodness you're here, Po-Po. We need to stick together. With enemies like the jungle holds, a girl needs all the friends she can get.'

Throwing the idiosyncratic garments over the rickety veranda rail, she gave a last satisfied glance of approval before getting into her hammock which, now she was well, she preferred to the hard, mattressless wooden bed.

Katharine Ferrandis fights back, she murmured to herself, and heard Po-Po's soft whistle of approval before she fell asleep and slept soundly until morning.

Chapter Thirteen

There was no time to settle in, no time to explore the area or to make the dilapidated house more homely. Katharine had to get to work. Jonathan constructed a makeshift desk for Charles, fashioned from the lid of a packing case and two giant upended ironwood logs that the Indians had felled with their machetes. The first thing that Katharine had to brave was revealing to Charles the extent of Anselmo's debts, just how much it had cost him to set up as a rubber baron – even before he'd paid the ultimate price of his life.

'The most important thing is to recruit workers,' Charles advised, 'only then can we begin to make the money to repay all these debts. And we need to do it now, so that we're ready for the main tapping season after the worst of the rains are over. You cannot collect the latex during the rainy season as it is all washed away by the downpours, so you have to allow for months of non-production as well as the times when it flows freely.'

Katharine sat down on a tree stump chair. 'Some time ago, you spoke of rounding the Indians up. What exactly did you mean?'

'Exactly that.' Charles laid down his fountain pen as if he expected to have to give a long explanation. 'We go out in recruitment parties and gather forest Indians. A kind of human harvest, I suppose you could say.' He paused, as if expecting Katharine to laugh at his joke.

She didn't.

'The fit and strong ones we take and the others we flog so that, when we let them go, they run as far and as fast as they can into the forest and don't bother us again,' he continued, his voice as passionless as usual.

Katharine stared at him open-mouthed. 'Are you serious?'

'Of course. How did you think it was done?' Now Charles' voice had a hint of sharpness to it, as if he was already preparing to defend the iniquitous practice he had described.

Katharine opened her mouth to speak and then quickly shut it again. She didn't have an adequate reply. From the very first time Charles had said the words 'round up' she'd had recurring moments of worry and anxiety – when she had had time to think at all in between all of the other worries and anxieties. It seemed she had been right to be fearful.

'But,' she remonstrated feebly, 'there are so few of us – just you, Jonathan and Santiago and the other dozen or so who came with us. How could we hope to recruit all the workers we need this way?'

It wasn't what she had intended to say, didn't even come close to asking the questions she wanted to ask – but these were the words that came out. Perhaps she was looking for an excuse not to follow Charles' method, hoping he would say, 'oh yes, I hadn't thought of that, you're absolutely right, we'll have to come up with another idea.'

He didn't.

'We have guns,' he stated simply. 'We have whips. We use them.'

And suddenly Katharine saw it. The reason Charles was a clerk and had never become anything else was because he had no imagination. He could not conceive of doing anything differently to how it had been done before, how it had always been done. And while the white Europeans of the Amazon were so quick to criticise the Indians of being without emotion, in fact Charles was the most dispassionate person she had ever met. And Laure, too – Katharine liked her but found her to be self-contained to the utmost degree, never opening up to Katharine. After all these days travelling with her, living in such close and intimate quarters, Katharine felt that she knew her no better than when they had started.

At that moment she felt the want of a companion even more than she had done at any point on this journey. She yearned for one so badly it hurt, the longing tearing at her heart. She pined for Elsie, to whom she could say anything, or Mabel who, though so young, understood without words. She ached for Anselmo who had been so cruelly wrested from her before their life together had really begun. She had no one to compare her own moral compass to, no one who shared her values to discuss things with. It was all down to her, and though the burden felt insupportable, she had to bear it.

Through the fug of her isolation, she made up her mind.

'No. We will not do that here.'

Katharine stood and walked to the battered and pock-marked door, which hung lopsidedly on rusty hinges. 'There will be no forced labour. And absolutely no corporal punishment of any kind.' This was what she had committed herself to when she'd decided to continue and she would not bend from that commitment. Slavery was a word she could hardly bear to utter; she had always believed it to be an abhorrent practice and was not about to be part of it. She wanted to work with the Indians, not against them, and had noticed how highly they valued items they lacked the materials to make for themselves – dyed cloth, steel tools, iron pots.

'In addition to their wages, we will put the word about that there's fabric, metal items of their choosing and tinned food for every man who signs up,' she said. 'Plus a year's supply of *farinha* for every tribe that sends us more than twenty men.'

'You won't make any money that way.' Charles' response was lightning fast.

Katharine paused for a moment to gather her thoughts.

'I don't think that's true,' she replied, speaking in as measured a tone as she could muster when her heart was beating wildly in her chest. 'I think it must be possible to be a good employer at the same time as being an astute businesswoman.'

In truth, Katharine wasn't sure about this at all. How could she be? She had no experience of being either. And she did need the money for her father so very badly.

Charles raised his eyebrows before speaking, very slowly, a strained edge to his voice. 'All right. I'll rephrase myself. You won't make as much money as you could.'

'Money isn't everything.' This was true; there were limits, boundaries she was not prepared to cross. But in the Amazon, the only thing that mattered was money, it was the holy grail that everyone was there to seek, what enabled rubber barons in Manaus not only to bathe in champagne but also to wash their horses and their carriages with it.

Charles shut his eyes and opened them again very slowly, as if expecting Katharine to have disappeared, her bizarre ideas with her.

Only when he realised she hadn't did he reply.

'They won't believe you. About the *farinha* and all the other – gifts.'

Katharine felt her habitual – and unhelpful – impatience well up within her.

'Then bring them here so that I can show them,' she snapped. And then, immediately contrite about her bad manners, continued in a more moderate tone, 'I'd like the opportunity to explain to them in person.'

With that, she went upstairs to her apology for a bedroom. She had no idea whether her gamble would pay off, or whether she would be forced to eat humble pie. But over the next days and weeks, Indians began to arrive, in pairs and groups, some with their wives and children. They accepted the conditions of employment, understood that they would get their goods as soon as the supply boats arrived, and melted away into the jungle, to the *estradas* that Charles assigned to them.

Katharine could hardly believe it. Her plan had worked. She had stuck to her guns and it had paid off. Briefly, she allowed herself to indulge in some self-congratulation. Maybe she would be able to pull this whole thing off, after all.

Weeks turned to months. Time lost all meaning, here where there were no clocks. Almost unbelievably, despite the sweltering heat that was only occasionally moderated by a cool breeze blowing down from the mountains, Katharine suddenly remembered that Christmas was on its way. It was hard to fathom that such a festival could exist without chill winter winds, without the hoar frost lying thickly on iron railings, without the smog produced by a thousand coal fires all battling to keep out the cold. But, she supposed, the 25th December was the 25th December, wherever in the world you were.

In a rare idle moment, lying in her hammock, Katharine rubbed her belly, now grown huge, the skin stretched taut across it, and fantasised about Christmas dinner. Roast turkey, potatoes – delicious, fluffy and crispy, not green, hard and tasteless as they were here – parsnips, carrots, bread sauce, and to follow a pudding, rich with fruit and brandy, set alight to the delight of all the little children in the family. She was permanently hungry, sickened by the lack of variety in the diet, the pungent, gamey bush meat, the *farinha* that had grown sludgy and unappetising in the damp.

Katharine hankered after chicken, a smooth white breast of luscious, juicy flesh, not the stringy, ancient birds they ate here when their useful egg-laying life was over. She hungered for sweet things: chocolate or jelly or a cake made by her mother and sliced into thick helpings oozing with sugar and lemon. She could feel her baby craving it, too, and she wanted to feed it and give it everything it needed for its health and vitality.

With that thought she looked down at the mound beneath her eyes. She could scarcely see her feet any more. She smiled to herself; though she was starving, her baby seemed to be doing absolutely fine.

A few days later, as if in answer to her prayers and longings, a canoe pulled up at the beach below the house. A couple of

Indians jumped out whom Katharine recognised from her stay at Mac's house. They were part of the informal delivery system that existed on the Amazon. People were always travelling up and down and they took the mail and sometimes other supplies if regular deliveries were not possible, using covered canoes called *cubertas*. These specially designed vessels had raised sides that arched over towards each other, allowing cargo to be piled high above the water line.

As well as letters from home, the Indians unloaded case after case of supplies. Katharine had sent orders for what she needed to pay her rubber tappers and also larder staples for the whole extended household at Norwood – tins of butter, meat, fish, beans and tomatoes, plus wine, beer and lemonade. But she had so little money to spare and, of necessity, had had to calculate quantities exactly so as to have enough to keep them going but nothing extra.

Mac, however, had taken it upon himself to include a plethora of treats: tea, coffee, condensed milk, Gilbey's gin from London, jerk beef from Argentina, and *bacalhau*, Portuguese dried salt cod. Unbelievably, there was also a tinned plum pudding; the label promised extra strong liqueur and 'at least 50 per cent' fruit filling. The final item that Katharine unloaded was a bottle of French perfume, Violette à Deux Sous by Guerlain, the bottle and the packaging both exquisite, and accompanied by a handwritten note from Mac wishing her a happy Christmas.

I hope you enjoy the gifts, the message ended, *and that they bring you happy memories when you are so far from home*.

Katharine laid aside the card and looked at the scent. She could not imagine when she would ever wear it. Her life had little use for such luxuries these days. As for the happy memories – well, there were plenty of those, but all tinged with the sorrow of Anselmo's death, leaving her no one with whom she could share them, or create new ones. She rubbed her hand over her belly. The baby. This new life, when it came, would be her companion, her friend and soulmate.

An Indian arriving with a message from one of the tappers on a far flung *estrada* distracted her. She put the perfume bottle carefully away in her trunk and forgot about it. She didn't, however, forget about the glorious abundance of food now in the store hut. Her stomach gurgled in anticipation as she finished the rest of the day's tasks, one half of her brain planning the evening meal even as she calculated latex yields and transportation costs.

That night they feasted: Katharine, Charles and Laure, together with Jonathan and Santiago and their wives, who were accompanied by numerous children. They could not possibly all originate from these two couples, Katharine reckoned, but must have been attracted by the strong smells from the open air cooking fire.

It was no matter. Every Christmas that Katharine could remember had been a riotous gathering of siblings, uncles, aunts and cousins, together with random neighbours who were invited into number 33 Hawthorn Road because they would otherwise be spending the day alone. She loved that here in the Amazon, so many thousands of miles away, she could enjoy a little of the bonhomie and conviviality she so closely associated with home.

In bed, a stomach ache brought on by eating too much rich food after so long on near-starvation rations made Katharine toss and turn and groan as sleep evaded her. But by the time morning came and the pains were worsening by the hour, she stopped cursing her gluttony and began to suspect that perhaps this was more than indigestion.

She was in labour.

A flash of panicked horror accompanied this realisation, soon wiped away by a searing cramp that tore at her insides. She had avoided thinking about the inevitable necessity of actually giving birth to her baby, especially since that dreadful, beautiful night accompanying Clara's infant as it made its way into the world. Even after witnessing that event, nothing had prepared

Katharine for the pain, the length of time it took, the excruciating agony of each and every contraction. She felt as if her body were splitting in two, could not believe that her skin and flesh could survive intact after being wrenched apart in this way.

The overwhelming emotion she had throughout her confinement was fear.

At times the pain, or possibly the tea the Indian women fed to her in spoonfuls urged between her gritted teeth, caused her to hallucinate. She had visions that she would die and her broken body be eaten by the ants that devoured everything. That the ants would get her baby too, and it would die, if not in the act of being born then soon after, eaten alive, its plaintive cries unheard by its dead mother.

She knew that Laure was there throughout but it was just a vague awareness. There was nothing Laure could do to help other than wipe her sweating brow and hold her hand, and Katharine's vice-like grip soon made Laure give her a stick to grasp instead.

After hours and hours of labour – fifteen or sixteen in total, Katharine found out later – in the dull light of a cloudy December day, a baby boy burst into the world. One of the Indian women laid him naked upon her chest and Katharine waited. Waited to experience that pure calm that had descended upon Clara that day, to feel that profound love that mothers must feel.

But all she felt at first was relief. That it was over, that they were both alive, and that now she could rest and, soon, sleep. She was so very, very tired.

'What are you going to call him?' asked Laure.

Katharine's eyelids, that had already begun to droop, flickered briefly open. 'Antonio,' she said, drowsily. 'I will name him Antonio.'

It was Anselmo's second name and one she knew he liked. As she drifted off, it fleetingly crossed her mind how much she had grown up during this journey. She had been eighteen when they set sail and was now nearly twenty. Over all these months, she had learnt so much about the ways of the world – and the importance of always acting in the way she knew to be right.

She had become a widow, and a mother.

Somehow, from somewhere, she had gained the strength to dig deep into the depths of her soul and to get this far. Now all she had to do was keep going.

Chapter Fourteen

Norwood, 1893

The months after Antonio's birth passed slowly but surely, imperceptibly turning to years. Each day was characterised by hard work and long hours, up with the sun, to bed with the sun, and barely a break during those twelve hours. Katharine was unstinting in her efforts, at first strapping her baby to her back in a shawl and then, once he learnt to walk at ten months old, using a liana rope to tie his wrist to hers so that he could tag along beside her and not run into the forest and get lost. When he got bored, she would hand him over to Rosabel or one of the other Indian women and they would feed him snacks of pineapple and banana and sing him lullabies in their own language.

Throughout each day, the compound bustled with activity. Several of the Indians showed great skill at carpentry so Katharine set up a workshop that could provide them first of all with repairs to the buildings and then with furniture. Gradually, they renovated or rebuilt the main house, offices and storerooms, though maintenance was an ongoing process. The palm thatching did not last long in the onslaught it received from sun and rain; Laure and Charles' house was being reroofed for the second time already. But there was progress, too – a new guesthouse for visitors was nearly completed and Katharine's efforts at an orchard were showing signs of success, with what had started as spindly saplings now growing into promising fruit trees.

The few miserable Indian huts that had still existed when Katharine arrived had been torn down and replaced by a dozen or so new ones, neat and generously sized to accommodate growing families. There was a central cookhouse with a covered fire over which Rosabel presided with fercious efficiency and iron discipline. She always knew exactly how many days' food they had and could calculate quantities in the blink of an eye.

None of it was luxurious, not like Lagona. There were no fine furnishings, no rocking chairs or writing tables imported from England and France, no silver cutlery or porcelain table-ware, no damask curtains or bedcovers. Their plates were banana leaves and their furniture, even as the Indian carpenters strove to make it comfortable, was hewn from tree trunks. Katharine joked in her letters to her family that the uneven surfaces of her desk made her handwriting even worse than ever. They did not have much, but what they had was service-able, and it was enough.

Likewise, though there was never a day without difficulty – a problem on an *estrada* with unreliable tappers, a snake bite, a fall – somehow they managed to weather them, and survive to see the next day and the next challenge.

–

One October afternoon three years after their arrival, Katharine and Charles were in the office as usual, working on rubber tapping plans. Antonio was running around outside with a big stick, shouting and looking for snakes. Po-Po, Katharine's faithful bird who had stayed with them through everything, was strutting after him, snatching – in his usual dignified way – any insects Antonio's flailing weapon unearthed.

A contented feeling surged in Katharine's veins. All was well. Antonio, approaching his third birthday, was healthy if a bit of a handful, the business was building and, though she hadn't acutally made any money yet, she would – very soon. It just took time to get up and running, to get the rubber rolling.

On her desk lay a pile of letters, all to do with business, or so she thought. She picked up the top one, recognising it as from Mac.

'We have an invitation,' she remarked, as her eyes scanned across the words.

Charles raised his eyebrows in his usual polite but non-committal way. 'Oh yes?' he questioned, clearly only half-concentrating.

'To spend Christmas at Lagona.'

Katharine folded the letter and rested her chin on her bent arm. It might be good to get away for a while.

'That's a surprise,' remarked Charles. 'But a pleasant one, nonetheless.'

Katharine nodded. 'Yes, Charles,' she replied. 'It is. And it would be a change of scene.'

Not that the scenery was substantially different at Lagona – it was still the forest, gloomy, dark and forbidding at times, green, verdant and welcoming at others. But there would be other visitors there, and conversation, as well as news of the wider world that wasn't six months out of date, unlike the newspapers and magazines she received in the post. Katharine gorged herself on any reading material that happened her way, and when she had finished with it the ants and termites did the same. Nothing lasted long in the Amazon: nature was always lurking, waiting to reclaim everything.

She went back to reading the remainder of the letter and was intrigued to find that Mac's eldest daughter would be staying at Lagona; she was spending some time with her father before being presented in London and doing the season the following year. Katharine was interested to meet one of Mac's children, especially one so clearly urbane and cosmopolitan, and it made her more intent on making the trip.

'I think we should go,' she stated, definitively.

Charles frowned. 'I suppose we could leave Jonathan and Santiago in charge for a few weeks. They've become very competent in office matters as well as supervising the tappers.'

Katharine's plan to encourage workers to her *estradas* had not lost its efficacy and she was nearly fully staffed now, with all but a few *estradas* manned.

'They have,' she mused. 'And it might be good for them to have the experience of coping alone. It will show them that they are trusted.'

And so it was decided. The journey would take a little less time than it had when they had first travelled to Norwood as the water lever was higher and tributaries that had been impassable at low water were now navigable. They would be able to bring supplies back with them; she would write out her order and a letter accepting Mac's invitation straightaway, and give it to the Indians who had brought the news.

Making her list, of fabric and clothing they desperately needed, foodstuffs, tools, alcohol and everything else she could think of, Katharine swallowed down the queasy feeling in her stomach that tended to arise whenever she had to spend yet more money. Despite the fact that things were going well, her debt had done nothing but increase. Their expenses, though minimal, all added up and though they were nearly in full production of rubber, it had taken three years to get this far, during which time nothing had been paid off. She'd even had to borrow again from Mac to tide them over, a fact she hated as she did not want to rely on him, or to impose on his goodwill and generosity. Nor did she want him to think she wasn't up to the job. But there had been no other option.

Taking a deep breath, she forced herself not to dwell on her finances. She was so deeply in hock to just about everyone, what difference did a little more make? And soon, very, very soon in fact, when they got back from Lagona and the river was ripe all the way to Pará for shipping the rubber, they'd be sending a huge consignment of *bolachas* to the *aviador* Anselmo had chosen. When Katharine had been paid for her goods, and despite the *aviador*'s cut and the hefty taxes levied by the Brazilian government – then they'd be well on the way to profit.

Antonio ran in, bellowing loudly, as he was wont to do, confirming to Katharine that her decision to go to Lagona was the right one. He might benefit from spending some time in rather more refined company than he was used to. He was frequently stubborn and obstinant, with a will of his own and a refusal to bend to his mother's. She worried that he lacked a father figure, and was growing up wild, learning not polite manners and fine habits but jungle ways: how to track a monkey, shoot an arrow, gut a fish. Useful in Norwood, no doubt – but Katharine hoped for a future for him back in Europe, where perhaps the money she would make (because she would make money, eventually, wouldn't she?) would equip him to set up in business for himself, to buy a comfortable house in a nice suburb and marry a lovely woman so that Katharine would have lots of grandchildren to dote on.

Pushing her tree stump chair backwards, she stood up abruptly. Daydreaming again! She should not map out Antonio's future like this, it wasn't fair on the poor boy. She was acutely aware that all of her maternal attention was focused on him because she had no other children and never would have. It was so different from her own family, when the siblings had come along every two or three years with remakable regularity. But that door had firmly closed with Anselmo's death and it would never open again. She contented herself with Antonio's admittedly sometimes truculent company, and busied herself with the mountain of daily tasks that faced her, so that matters of the heart need never surface. If she were honest, food preoccupied her mind to a far greater extent than romance – and she would have had a fruitless search if she tried to find a lover in Norwood. Under a banana leaf, perhaps? Behind a jauarí palm? Up in the branches of the towering Brazil nut tree? She smiled to herself at such thoughts and then dismissed them, as fanciful nonsense should be dismissed.

What couldn't be so easily pushed aside, though, was Antonio's more immediate future – and the small matter of his education. Katharine could teach him to a certain extent when the time was right and he was a bit older – but Latin? Greek? These were – quite literally – closed books to her. The prospect of sending Antonio all the way back to England for his schooling filled Katharine with horror; he was all she had, she couldn't bear to let him go.

Calling to the little boy, she took hold of his hand and walked with him beside her to give her letter of reply for Mac to the waiting canoe. She wouldn't think that far into the future right now. They would go to Lagona for Christmas.

They would have some fun.

Chapter Fifteen

Lagona, 1893–4

As the boat departed, Katharine took a long lingering look at her home. Her house, being two storeys tall, was still visible nestling in its forest clearing, but many of the low Indian huts had vanished behind the piles of *bolachas* lined up along the riverbank. Teams of her workers had been bringing them in for months now and there were hundreds of pounds worth of rubber awaiting collection in the new year.

In the canoe with her, Katharine had one small but perfectly formed ball of dry, fine Pará, the best quality rubber in the world, to show Mac. Usually, each *bolacha* weighed seventy to ninety pounds but Katharine had had a petite one made for easy transport to Lagona. Taking it was part of some subliminal need to prove to Mac what she had told him that evening when she refused his offer to sell her *estradas* to him – that she could cope, that she could run a successful rubber business when so many others failed, and that she could do so even though she was a woman.

She patted the *bolacha* proudly with one hand, while the other kept a protective grip on Antonio. But, unlike inert balls of rubber, lively little boys do not generally like to be restrained. Antonio soon pulled himself free of his mother's grasp and, reluctantly, she let him go. In all truth, she didn't know why she went through the motions of holding him back.

He'd been born by this river and knew it like the back of his hand. Knew how to swim like a dolphin, knew where piranhas lurked, knew the places where it was safe to frolic and splash and bathe. Already he was well versed in jungle lore; for example, never urinate in the river as the miniature catfish, the candiru, will swim up the stream of nitrogen and lodge in the urethra, causing intense pain. He was much more attuned to his surroundings than she was; it was all he'd ever known, and he was so independent already. Sometimes the fleeting thought crossed Katharine's mind that he seemed to have no need for her at all.

The journey to Lagona was uneventful, with none of Katharine's worst fears of capsizing or other disasters realised. The rapids they had portaged over on the way up were actually fun on the way down, everyone paddling like mad, flying over the water as it foamed and frothed and effervesced all around them. Just the nights were hard, with frequent soaking downfalls that were impossible to shelter from completely. *I must be getting soft*, Katharine thought as she awoke one morning, wet through and stiff from sleeping on an uncomfortable patch of lumpy ground. *Or old.*

When she said this to Laure, the Belgian woman just laughed. 'Oh Katharine,' she teased, 'you are not even twenty-five! Just wait until you're forty-five like me before you start talking about feeling old.'

Katharine grinned. 'Sorry,' she replied. 'You're right, I have nothing to complain about.'

'And you have your son to keep you young,' continued Laure, her gaze focused on the little boy who was busily helping, though in all truth getting in the way of, the Indians who were packing up their camp.

Katharine looked up sharply and scrutinised Laure's expression. It was the first time Laure had ever referred to her own childlessness, and Katharine could tell, even though her remark had been oblique, that she regretted her lack of a family. Etched on Laure's face was a wistfulness that Katharine had never seen before, a mist of longing for something that Laure must have accepted by now would never be.

'You would have liked children?' Katharine volunteered tentatively.

Laure shrugged, but the slightest hint of a wavering lip told Katharine that shrugging it off was an act.

They boarded the boats and set off again.

'I always wanted a large family.' Laure trailed her fingers in the water and then passed her cooled hand across her forehead. It was steamy hot today. 'Like your Queen Victoria,' she joked, but there was no laughter in her voice.

There was a long pause before she spoke again. Katharine waited, not wanting to break the invisible bond that had sprung up between them.

'I had a child,' Laure continued eventually. 'But he died during the birth and something had gone wrong that meant I never could have another one. I had lots of pregnancies but I lost all of them. All the babies I lost.'

She repeated this information with such utter sadness in her voice that Katharine felt tears springing to her eyes. Unconsciously, she shifted further towards Antonio, crouched on the floor of the boat, thumping his hands rythmically on its side in a call and response tune played with an Indian boy who was using a stick and a coconut shell as his instrument.

Life and death. Slipping from one to the other in a heartbeat. She was so lucky to have her son.

'I'm sorry,' she said, simply, to Laure. She recalled the fleeting look of anguish on Laure's face when she had realised Katharine was pregnant. Now she understood it. This was the first time the woman had ever opened up to her and she wished it had been with a happier story. 'So very sorry.'

'It's all right,' responded Laure, her normal equanimity restored already. 'I've come to terms with it now. I enjoy the fact that I have no responsibility to anyone. Just me and Charles, living life how we please, going where we wish, doing what we want. We fell in love with the rainforest and so we've stayed here. It would be a lot harder if we'd had children to worry about, to educate.'

Katharine nodded, though the topic of education wasn't one she particularly wanted to think about, having so recently resolved to postpone making decisions on that for a while. A long while.

They arrived in Lagona on the 21st December. Katharine's first priority was to show Mac the rubber so she immediately sought him out. She valued his judgement and recognised that, as a rookie in the rubber business, she needed all the help, advice and guidance that she could get. Mac scrutinised and appraised the *bolacha* carefully, finally pronouncing it of extremely high quality.

'It's as good as my own – nearly,' he teased. 'And I'll work out a price you should expect from the *aviador* – remember that everyone in that damned city of Manaus is out to swindle you.'

He looked from the rubber to Katharine and she was struck anew by the intensity of his gaze and the blueness of his eyes. They were the colour of the blue seas of home and the sky, of cornflowers – and of emptiness. She had no idea what could lie behind such a void. Mac, so it seemed, had it all – family, fortune, intelligence and good health. What more could anyone want? And yet it seemed that something was missing.

'But we should not hide ourselves away here in the office talking business,' he said, and the void vanished, to be instantly replaced by his characteristic twinkling kindness. 'I have guests to entertain. And my daughter is desperate to meet you. Alexandra has never come all the way to Lagona before,' continued Mac, 'so while she is here we must make the most of it. She's independent too, like yourself. Travelled on her own. It's more than her mother will do.'

In that moment, Katharine understood. The look was loneliness. She had suspected Mac of suffering from that affliction when they had first passed through Lagona. That was one thing they had in common, anyway. For Katharine, despite Antonio, was lonely too.

A servant showed Katharine to her room. She had hoped to see little Esperanza but there was no sign of her. That first visit had only been three years ago but already seemed like aeons in the past. Despite this, she had expected the girl to still be around. She would have asked Mac but something held her back. Not wanting to find out that something terrible had happened to her, perhaps? Servants were usually guarded like rare and precious possessions – chiefly because they were rare and precious possessions, not easily come by, and expensive. The girl's absence could well have an explanation that Katharine didn't want to hear. So many people died young in the Amazon. There were a lot of things to die from.

Lagona was exceptionally busy that Christmas time. There were visitors from all over the world: English scientists travelling through looking for specimens, a world-renowned botanical illustrator working on a book on jungle plants and flowers, plus some Irish musicians who'd been performing in the Theatro da Paz in Pará and had come upriver for an adventure, and finally a German man who seemed to be there for no particular purpose. And then, of course, there was Alexandra, who proved to be a charming and interesting young lady.

The days passed enjoyably, with convivial meals and plenty of free time for resting, or walking by the river. It took Katharine a few days to regain the art of relaxation – she'd been working so hard for so long – and of conversation. They had so little of either at Norwood, and had grown so used to each other, her and Charles and Laure, that they often spent whole days barely exchanging a word. Antonio, too, found it hard to settle down amidst so much unaccustomed jollity and unsolicited adult attention, not to mention the abundance of sugary foods. Everyone wanted to cuddle him and pet him and play with him, when all he wanted to do was run free in the garden surrounding the luxurious house.

In the evenings, after dining, they danced to the tunes of the Irish fiddlers or the German man's accordion: reels and jigs, waltzes and quadrilles. Katharine had moments of feeling almost carefree, something she hadn't experienced since Anselmo's death – or even before that. When they had first set sail for Brazil, she had been so filled with dread and excitement and apprehension and exhilaration she hadn't known how to cope with it at all.

'You don't come often to the Amazon, I believe,' Katharine said to Alexandra one evening as they took a rest from the dancing. 'And it's your first time at Lagona. So how are you finding it?'

'I find it – different,' the young woman replied, her eyes surveying the room bordered by the wide veranda, open to the vastness of the night sky. 'Father keeps himself well supplied with home comforts, of course – but it's the thought that out there is a panoply of insects and snakes and scourges that could kill you at any moment! I can't get used to it.'

At this, they both laughed, in a slightly desperate way.

'Mother completely refused to allow us to set foot out of Manaus when we were younger,' continued Alexandra. 'She was so terrified that something would happen to us. She didn't want me to come now, but I just told her I was going anyway, whatever she said.'

No one could accuse Bernadette McNamara of having an overactive imagination, Katharine thought. She glanced towards Antonio on the other side of the room, jigging about in the most uncoordinated way to the accordion music. All these fears she had for him, too.

'And even Manaus we only visited a few times,' Alexandra went on. 'Most of the time we stayed at home in Highgate with nannies. I regret that I saw so little of my father growing up. I feel that I hardly know him. That's why I was so determined to get here for this visit.'

They both looked over at where Mac was standing with a group of others, his usual huge cigar pinioned between finger and thumb. He was an unusual rubber baron. Most preferred to leave the running of their estates to clerks and managers and to spend their time in the city, enjoying the benefits of city life: soirées and dinner parties, visits to the theatre, shops with every European luxury. When Katharine had first passed through Lagona, he'd been preoccupied with establishing the rules of engagement for anyone using the isthmus. But now that was well in hand, there was no reason for him to be here so much. Fleetingly, Katharine wondered why he stayed.

At that moment, a servant approached her with a tray of drinks. Katharine recognised her as one of the girls who had waited at table on their first visit; she had looked around ten or eleven then and so must now be thirteen or fourteen. Though the girl was slight and thin like most of the Indians, she was obviously pregnant. Katharine wondered if she were married and then asked herself why it mattered. She tried hard not to judge the local people by European standards. They had their own way of life and, in her opinion, should be left to follow it untrammelled by white people's interference. But nevertheless, the girl was young to be a mother and Katharine hoped she would be well cared for when her confinement came.

On Christmas Eve, more passing travellers arrived and they were twenty-five people at dinner. Mac had received a huge wine delivery direct from France just a few days earlier, plus brandy, whisky and gin, and all of it flowed freely at the dinner table.

Katharine became aware, as the evening wore on, that everyone was a touch the worse for wear. It was hard not to overindulge when treats were so rare. Feeling a little nauseous herself from the rich food to which she was no longer accustomed, and far too much to drink, Katharine ventured out onto the veranda. It was hardly cooler out there but at least the air was fresher than in the smoke-filled salon and there was the tiniest hint of a breeze that fluttered welcomingly against Katharine's cheeks. She leant against the railings and let her head drop forward as she took deep breaths to clear the dizziness that threatened to overwhelm her. *Why* had she had that third glass of wine?

She didn't hear the approaching footsteps. Her mind was miles away, imagining her family in Hawthorn Road, the presents in their tantalising wrapping piled beneath the tree, the cards on the mantelpiece.

The touch on her shoulder made her jump out of her skin. Whipping around, she was confronted with Mac standing silently beside her. Stifling a small scream, she quickly tried to compose herself. She wanted him to regard her as a competent, sophisticated business woman, not a nervy girl.

'Beautiful, isn't it?' He hardly seemed to notice how he had startled her. 'I never stop thinking that.'

His voice was low, the words spoken so quietly that she could hardly hear them, as if he were imparting some secret.

Katharine looked up at the night sky, at the myriad stars that were unobscured by cloud, and at the pearlescent moon, nearly full, just a small bitesize portion yet to form.

'It is.'

'I had another look at that *bolacha*.' Mac shuffled his shoulders as if his jacket were too tight. 'Very fine, very fine indeed. Well, they don't call the rubber from the Amazon fine, dry Pará for nothing!' He laughed, somewhat drunkenly.

'Thank you.'

'You got much of it? How many pounds, do you reckon?'

Katharine pictured the piles of *bolachas*, growing by the day, waiting to bring in the money she so desperately needed. She did some rapid mental maths and gave an estimate.

'Very good. Exceptionally good, for a woman.' Mac leant over the veranda rail as if straining to see the latex pouring from multiple slashes in multiple tree trunks on his own *estradas*. 'It takes time though, doesn't it?' mused Mac. 'It took me ten years, fifteen, to get myself on a firm footing. Now the bright young things come in and expect to be millionaires in a year.'

Katharine lifted her hands in a gesture of resignation; Anselmo had been amongst this number.

'I suppose so,' she concurred. 'It's hard to know, exactly. But I'm determined to see it through.'

Down on the river's edge, a *jacaré* silhouetted against the black night sky opened wide its tooth-filled mouth and snapped it shut.

'You haven't reconsidered then?'

Katharine looked at him questioningly, even though she understood precisely what he meant.

Mac smiled knowingly, as if he knew her game. 'My offer for your land still stands if you care to change your mind.'

'No.' Her reply was instant, requiring no time for thought.

Mac's forehead creased in frustration – he clearly wasn't used to being thwarted twice – but then suddenly he laughed, a rollling laugh like water streaming down a gutter, and there was something so infectious about it that Katharine momentarily joined in.

'Katharine Ferrandis, you are a marvel, so you are,' he said, once recovered from his mirth. 'All those male empire builders should watch out. You'll beat them all at their own game.' He paused, pulled out one of his enormous cigars, struck a match against the wooden veranda rail and watched the sulphur flame fizz into a tiny flare of light. 'The last time I saw you I wished you luck. Now I see you have no need of it. I have to say it, Mrs Ferrandis, I admire you.'

He lit the cigar. 'And that's not a word of a lie. I admire you. And I can't even imagine what it would take to break you.'

Katharine regarded him closely, frowning, unsure whether he was teasing her. When she was sure that he was genuine, she began to smile and gradually the smile grew to a broad, delighted grin and her heart pulsed with something like pride. Patrick McNamara, the greatest rubber baron of them all, admired her, humble Katharine Ferrandis.

Now *that* was something to tell the grandchildren.

Chapter Sixteen

Norwood, 1894

The river swept around in a wide bend just before the little settlement of Norwood, whose houses, palm huts, fruit trees and carefully tended vegetable patch nestled in the crook of the turn and were therefore more or less invisible until you were right upon them. So there was nothing to warn Katharine of what awaited her until the sandy beach, the Indian huts and the house came into view before her.

The Indian huts. Visible before her.

That should not be possible.

When they had left, the heaps of rubber had obscured the low buildings from sight and more, much more, should have been piled up since then. The blood ran cold in Katharine's veins as the reality of what she was seeing slowly dawned on her.

The rubber had gone. All of it. It was all gone.

Any notion that Jonathan and Santiago might have shipped it early disappeared before it had properly formed. Because not only was the rubber gone, but so were the people. There was absolutely nobody around: no women cooking by their huts, no children toddling around outside, no men sorting and piling the rubber. The compound was deserted. And more than that, the Indian huts had been burnt and were blackened and half destroyed, gaping holes in roofs and walls letting in the rain which had begun to fall. The smell of charred straw and wet ash hung like a pall over everything. Where had everyone gone?

Had they been stolen, rounded up, forced to work for another baron? Or had they run away into the jungle and stayed there, too scared to come out again?

Antonio heard Katharine's stifled scream of alarm and, seeing the stricken look of dismay upon her face, began to cry, repeating, 'What's wrong, Mummy, what's wrong?' over and over again. The Indians were scared too, she could tell. They exchanged fearful glances, looking all around them, pointing and shouting.

Shushing her son distractedly, Katharine climbed out of the *igarité* – the two masted canoe Mac had given her to make her return journey more comfortable – and began to walk up the sloping beach to the settlement. The air was thick and heavy, the heat like a hellish blanket, and she moved slowly and with difficulty, feeling as if she were trapped in a dream, unable to connect with reality. Charles and Laure's boat was some way behind, just as it had been on their very first journey here, so she had no choice but to confront the scene of utter devastation that lay before her alone.

Up close, it was even worse than she had at first perceived. As well as the Indian huts, there'd been an attempt to burn her house down and licks of black soot darkened the slatted wooden sides like sinister tears. Chicken feathers had settled on the mud created by the churning of many feet, resembling some kind of macabre decoration. Undergrowth and trees bore the marks of machete blows indicating a violent and vicious attack. Her orchard, her pride and joy, had been obliterated, tiny oranges and lemons trodden into the ground, stamped upon and smashed open. Katharine pictured rampaging men, tearing through her home, her property, her life.

But why? Who would want to bring such terror to a peaceful place? Was it personal, a vendetta? Who hated her this much?

As she stood surveying the damage, an icicle of fear stabbed like foreboding inside her. She had the sudden feeling of being watched. Perhaps the marauders were still here, hidden in the forest.

Forcing down her fear, Katharine advanced a few more steps, round to the side of her house where the front door was. And then she stopped again, so abruptly she almost fell over her own feet. Bile rose in her mouth and she vomited, the contents of her stomach splattering onto the ground.

In front of the door, deliberately placed to obstruct the entrance, two dead bodies lay face down in the dirt. Already, they had been attacked by ants and beetles, and one was missing an arm and leg, so a jaguar must have got to them, too. Fat, pallid maggots crawled clumsily over their open wounds.

The men were rubber tappers, two of Katharine's longest serving employees, left to putrefy in the sun and decay like so much rotten, discarded vegetation. But they were not the only dead. On top of their bodies, carefully positioned across their backs, lay a skeleton, neck broken and turned grotesquely back on itself in a bizarre and macabre contortion, a few feathers still loosely attached.

Po-Po.

The faithful bird, her special pet, who had been by Katharine's side since that day in Manaus when his arrival had seemed like a promise, an answer to her prayer for a friend, was dead.

Murdered.

The whole ghastly scene bore all the hallmarks of a sacrificial offering.

Or a warning.

Katharine stumbled backwards, falling upon the scorched house wall, her legs unable to support her own weight. Her fingers scrabbled against the wood to try to get a hold upon it, upon something solid, upon what was happening. When she took her hands away, she saw that her fingertips were blackened with soot and, half crazed with despair, she ran them down her face, imagining the long dark streaks they would leave, the marks of her madness, her anguish. But then, after perhaps another five minutes wandering around, dazed, surveying the devastation, Katharine suddenly felt angry.

A furious, incandescent rage filled her being from her crown to her toes.

How dare someone come here and slaughter her people and her pet? Did they think that, because she was a woman, she was weak, enfeebled, unable to stand up for herself? Did they think their annihilation of what she had built, of all she held dear, would destroy her, make her give up? Because if they did, then they were wrong.

So very, very wrong.

She ran back towards the river to check on Antonio. He was sitting bleakly by the water's edge. The Indians were cowering in the boat and she shouted to them to pull themselves together, to get out and come and help her.

Then, still crazy with anger, Katharine stormed back up the beach, noticing for the first time that it was dotted with *bolachas*. Whoever had come here must have rolled all the rubber into the river and let it be washed away in the gushing currents. They had not even stolen it, had not wanted it for themselves, just wanted her not to have it. They had simply disposed of it so that she would lose all her money, her livelihood.

She strode to the store huts and found their doors hanging off, their floors damaged and all Rosabel's carefully curated supplies either gone or ruined, *farinha* sacks, tins and bottles slashed open or broken, the contents spilt and spoilt.

Whoever had done all of this didn't just want to cause her financial loss and frighten her – they wanted to make it impossible for her to live here by starving her, and all who lived and worked with her, to death. In a heartbeat, the fire left her belly and her resolve failed her.

Demoralised and despondent, she sank to her knees. Just then, it felt like her attackers had succeeded.

Chapter Seventeen

It was two days before the Indians started to emerge from the forest. First to return were Jonathan and Santiago. Katharine, having got to know them so well over the years, could see that underneath their usual inscrutable expressions lay a veneer of fear – and also apology.

'What happened?' she asked.

There was a pause and then Jonathan spoke.

'A hostile tribe came,' he said, 'with many men, and guns, poisoned arrows, knives, fire. We were not ready – they had surrounded us before we could even get to our own weapons.'

'I'm so sorry.' Katharine lowered her eyes and blinked back tears. She didn't want them to see her cry. She needed to be strong, to show them that she was invincible. If they didn't believe that, they'd melt away again, shrinking back into the enveloping vegetation. She couldn't exist here without them.

'But,' she added, looking Jonathan in the eye, 'no tribe has ever attacked before. Do you know who they were? Did you recognise them? Did something happen to provoke them?'

As she looked from one to the other she saw the two men exchange a quick glance.

'What?' she questioned sharply. 'What is it?'

Jonathan shook his head and Santiago shrugged.

'Nothing, Mother,' they said in unison. 'We know nothing.'

Gradually, the other Indians who lived on the compound also returned, slinking out from the canopy, going to their huts and quietly getting on with the repair work. Many decided to tear down the damaged, burnt structures and start again, and the newly built buildings looked so pretty, with their green palm fronds and intricate weaving patterns.

But nothing could take away the stench of death and fear that hung over them all. They buried the bodies and tided everything up but the fact remained that the intention had been to finish Norwood, to scare Katharine and all those who lived with her away and ensure they never came back.

As someone who had never threatened the tribes living around her, had not indulged in the Amazonian scourge of forced labour but had sought to work with the local people and to help them where she could, Katharine couldn't understand why they had targeted her. For being white? For being a woman? Just for being here? All were good reaons, she supposed. But none seemed enough – especially when there were so many others who had avoided such retribution, even though they may well have deserved it more.

Recognising that dwelling on it would only embed her bitterness further, she tried to move on from what seemed unfathomable, setting to work clearing and cleaning the house. Laure helped her, though Katharine couldn't help but notice that her efforts were half-hearted, even with her and Charles' living quarters. It was as if she couldn't be bothered any more.

One day, needing a few moments alone, Katharine retreated to the room on the upper floor of the house that she used for quiet reading and writing of letters. Before she'd had a chance to light a lamp, a scuffling noise from the corner caught her attention. She looked around, expecting to see a rat or a cockroach, both common housemates.

As her eyes focused in the semi-darkness, a flash of green and gold caused her to jump out of her skin and let out a blood-curdling scream. With a whip of shiny scales and an uncoiling of a body as thick as a tree trunk, a head was suddenly raised to almost the same height as her own, two beady eyes maniacally fixed upon her.

Sobbing with fear, hardly able to breathe, Katharine saw her life ebb away as the anaconda, the most powerful snake in the

Amazon, gathered itself for attack, slipping effortlessly across the room like liquid mercury. Terror paralysed her as she imagined the snake's coils around her, slowly crushing her ribs, draining her strength away, squeezing her out of existence.

And then she thought of Antonio, orphaned.

From some deep crevice of her heart, she summoned up her courage and her fighting spirit and began screaming for help. She could not hope to outrun the snake, or to overpower it – but perhaps she could scare it off for at least as long as it would take for someone to come to her aid.

Racing for the doorway, and then the rickety staircase, she was aware of the anaconda ravelling and unravelling around her feet, its shimmering body twisting and unfurling with such rapidity it was almost impossible for Katharine to jump and dodge the coils.

Somehow, she reached the top of the stairs and, grabbing the rail, tried to leap over the snake. But she'd forgotten the damage done to the building and the rail, burnt and smashed at the bottom, was no longer securely attached. It wobbled, pitching her forward, and then broke entirely, the banister rent apart from its supporting post.

Katharine fell, face down on the charred wooden floor, her fingers clawing in vain for something with which to pull herself upright. She felt the snake as it slithered over her; the weight of it, a fully grown adult, was astonishing, appalling. It could overpower her in an instant. It was worming its way above and beneath her, weaving between her legs and under her body like a grotesque piece of knitting.

She fought and struggled and kicked and continued to scream, even while she knew how futile her efforts were, how all they were doing were aiding her own demise, taking all her energy even before the snake had a chance to. Fear forced her eyes closed; she couldn't bear to see the dreadful beauty of the serpent, its glossy, shiny, irridescent scales, its inhuman gaze.

Then a hair-raising yell sounded in her ears. It took a moment for her to realise that it was not her own voice. Forcing her eyes open, she saw who it was; Antonio, open-mouthed in horror, running up the stairs towards her, shouting and bashing the stick he always carried against the wooden floor in anger.

'Stay away,' shouted Katharine, as the serpent fastened around her legs. 'Don't come near. Get help!'

Ignoring her, Antonio crashed on up the stairs, flailing his stick, hollering at the top of his voice. The coils tightened and she felt the blood flow to her limbs curtailed. Antonio was by her side, landing blow upon blow on the snake with a force that belied his young age. Some missed and fell on Katharine; she was glad of it, for the fact that she could feel them meant she was still alive.

And then suddenly the pressure on her legs released and she could move again. She pulled herself upright just as the snake lunged for Antonio, jaws wide apart, rows of teeth glinting in the muted light. With some superhuman effort of will and strength, Katharine flung herself forward, pushing the little boy out of the serpent's way, falling heavily against the wall and smashing her head. For a few seconds, the world went black and stars danced before her eyes. And then she came to, and she waited. Waited for the sensation of teeth searing into flesh, for the constricting hug of the killer snake, capturing her in a fatal embrace.

Instead, what she felt was a hand on her wrist. Not Antonio's, but Santiago's. Katharine exhaled in a ululation of relief as he seized her up and carried her downstairs and into the fresh air where he checked her carefully for wounds.

'That was the biggest *sucuruju* I've ever seen,' he said, whistling in awestruck horror. 'Twenty feet long and two around, I reckon.'

The numbers went right over Katharine's head. All she could think, when she could think at all, was of Antonio.

'Don't worry about me,' she insisted, gesticulating wildly. 'Where's Antonio? Is he all right?'

But the little boy had already disappeared off to regale his story of the enormous snake to Jonathan, who had missed all the action. He didn't seem bothered by the episode at all. Perhaps he was just too young to have realised the danger, or perhaps it was because he was used to snakes and liked to beat them with his stick. This had been no different – just a bigger, fatter, stronger snake than usual. Still – if it had come across him first and not her – Katharine shuddered to the core of her being at the thought.

Rosabel the cook, unaware of the drama that had just unfolded, padded over to ask about supplies. Discussing tinned beef, Katharine felt suddenly weak and lightheaded, as if the shock of it all had only just hit her. Or maybe it was the realisation that all they had to eat was what little she had brought back from Lagona – some rice, potatoes and a few cans of meat and butter. The yuca plants had been slashed down but the roots beneath might still be recoverable. Even if so, what they had would not last long with so many mouths to feed – herself and Antonio, Charles and Laure, Jonathan and Santiago plus all the rest of the compound dwellers. The Indians would have to organise a hunt – and soon. Sending Rosabel away with brief instructions about what to make for now, she turned her attention to Jonathan and Santiago.

'The snake must have got in when we were away and all the damage was done,' she said. 'We don't know how many days the doors were open for.'

'It was very big snake, Mother,' intoned Santiago, gravely. 'You are lucky.'

Katharine smiled. 'Yes, I am. I must say that I never expected to have an anaconda as a house guest. I assumed they would stay away from humans if possible. Its attack was entirely unprovoked.'

She looked around the compound, at the ruined huts and at her house, charred and smoke-damaged. 'As was that of whoever did this.'

There was a pause, filled only by the shrill shrieking of the forest.

'There are many types of snakes in the jungle,' said Jonathan.

This was true. The forest was home to venemous pit vipers, coral snakes and jararacas, the much loathed snake with two heads, as well as boa constrictors and anacondas. All abounded in Amazonia.

'But,' continued Santiago, 'not all are in serpent form.'

Katharine looked at him questioningly, trying to work out what he meant by such a cryptic remark, but the two men were already walking away, getting back to their work of gathering up the remaining *bolachas*, seeing what could be salvaged. It was probably another Curupira-type myth, she thought, trying to dismiss it from her mind. She really didn't have time for such superstition right now.

As she tried to focus on her paperwork, however, the Indians' words rang in her ears. *There are many types of snakes in the jungle, but not all are in serpent form.* She could not shake the profound sense of something going on that she didn't understand.

That night, once Antonio was in bed and fast asleep, she went out and surveyed the decimated compound. Though much rain had fallen, she could still smell the acrid stench of burnt rubber and torched wood. She wandered up and down the paths that ran in intricate patterns between the house and the huts, the storerooms and the cookhouse, doing mathematical calculations in her head. Her rubber trees, virgin and untapped before she had come, could go on producing latex for another twenty-five or thirty years. As soon as the rains had eased off, the *seringueiros* could restart collecting and smoking, and by next September or October, she could have another crop to send downriver. In the meanwhile, the debts would have got bigger and the time when she could begin repaying her father vanished even further into a murky future.

She knelt down by the dead *seringueiros*' graves, and that of loyal Po-Po, and uttered a prayer for the three of them. Such sentimentality about an animal was wrong, she knew – and yet

Po-Po had been a true friend, and she missed him, however stupid it was to miss a bird. A desolate sadness overtook her as she prayed for herself and her son, for her parents, for Charles and Laure, Jonathan and Santiago and all those who she relied on so greatly.

What was to become of them all?

Chapter Eighteen

Next day, the myriad pressing matters weighing on her mind woke Katharine early, just as dawn was breaking. Picking her way over the debris that still had not been gathered up, she made her way to the cookhouse. She was desperate for a cup of coffee and even Rosabel was not about yet so she would make it herself. Stooping low over the fire, a flash of colour disappearing over the rise of the land before it sloped down to the beach caught her eye. She straightened up and stared after it, puzzlement creasing her forehead. The figure was familiar, small and somewhat stout, walking with a striding gait.

It was Laure.

Katharine stood, consternation and bewilderment flooding her mind in equal measure. Why was Laure heading for the river at dawn? Where could she possibly be going? A dreadful truth began fomenting in her brain but she refused to contemplate it. Perhaps Laure fancied a bathe, or some silent contemplation on the water when only the sea birds and fish would be stirring.

Stumbling over some fallen roof parts, Katharine headed off on Laure's tail. She was sweating profusely; the violent thunderstorm of the night before had been followed, as was often the case, by suffocating humidity. At the top of the beach, she stopped dead in her tracks, her jaw dropped open in appalled understanding that her worse fears had been realised. A canoe, in which sat Charles and Laure, was already in mid-channel and heading fast downriver. Four Indians were propelling them through the water, strong, even strokes rapidly gaining them distance from the dock. It was clear that her clerk and his wife were intent on making a quick getaway.

Katharine, too stunned to move, watched as the craft became smaller and smaller. Only when it had disappeared around the bend in the river did she turn back, staggering up the beach, picking her way between the splintered ends of off-cuts of wood discarded during the rebuilding. She went to Charles and Laure's house, feeling no compunction about opening the door and marching right on in. It was clear that they had gone and were not coming back. That was the only explanation for a pre-dawn departure without a word said to anyone.

Lying on the table in the main upstairs living room was a letter. Katharine picked it up, turning it round and round in her hands before she opened it.

> *Dear Katharine,*
>
> *We have decided to leave Norwood, and indeed the Amazon. It is too dangerous these days and neither of us has the stomach for the adventure any more. We wish to return home for our twilight years, so we are heading to Belgium. We're sorry to leave you so suddenly but it seemed better this way, without long-drawn-out farewells or tearful partings.*
>
> *We wish you, Antonio and everyone at Norwood all the best for a happy, healthy and prosperous future.*
>
> *With much love,*
> *Charles and Laure*

It was the final straw.

The jungle was nothing more than a malevolent graveyard, that swallowed people up and spat them out when it was done with them. She couldn't cope any more, had no coping strategies left. Though losing her clerk was a blow, she knew as much about the business now as he did. And Laure, albeit an ally and a companion, had never truly become a friend. So the worst of it wasn't that she would never see them again, but what their departure represented. The fact that, without a ton of debts around their necks, they had the freedom to choose what to do, which she did not. And they never had to make that choice alone, as she did, because they had each other, and she had lost Anselmo for good.

In a state of nervous collapse, Katharine retired to her room. Heavily, as if her limbs weighed a ton, she stood on the veranda. On the balustrade, a silk moth casually unfolded its wings, revealing a pair of forbidding hyacinth blue eyes flecked with silver, immense and unfathomable. Katharine shuddered. It was as if those blank eyes could see into her soul and, looking, found nothing left.

She glanced away, towards the endless expanse of trees, craving silence, time to think, to plan what to do next – but the deafening noise of the forest surrounded her and precluded thought, the cacophonous screeching and chirping and calling and tweeting and the endless, endless din.

'Shut up!' she shouted. 'Just shut up and let me think.'

They'd think she was mad, screaming at the jungle. Jonathan, Santiago, the other Indians, Antonio. They'd all think she'd gone stark, staring mad. And perhaps she had. Sometimes it felt that way. Right now it definitely did.

Her rubber. Her money. Her clerk and his wife. Antonio's future. Her father's loan. It was gone. All gone. She was defeated. The Amazon had beaten her.

It had got what it had always wanted.

–

Katharine stayed in bed for three days, Rosabel sending meals she hardly touched and Antonio, unable to comprehend her mood, seeking more congenial company elsewhere. On the third night, she lay watching a firefly circumnavigate her bedroom again and again, winging its delicate way round and round as if locked in its own never-ending dance. Eventually, Katharine fell asleep, the bright pinprick of light still burning behind her retinas. Maybe it was hunger that caused her to hallucinate, but in her dreams, her little sister Mabel appeared before her, riding a huge anaconda that was bridled and saddled like a horse. Mabel was smiling beatifically and laughing her gurgling, water-down-a-drainpipe laugh, impervious to the bucking and rearing of the serpent horse beneath her.

'Don't give up, Katharine,' urged the vision of Mabel. 'You know you always told me to never give up.'

Then the anaconda neighed and slithered away into the distance as fast as any galloping steed.

When Katharine woke the next morning, she felt miraculously clear-headed and refreshed, renewed. Climbing purposefully out of bed, she ran down the stairs and out into the compound. The sky was clear and freshly laundered linen hung cheerfully from the washing line. Already, new greenery sprouted from the charred branches of those fruit trees that still stood. This was the wonder of the Amazon. Destruction could be quick, but regrowth was even quicker. In the sunshine, everything looked fresher, brighter, more hopeful.

It was clear that the Amazon demanded blood if you wanted to be successful; the blood of hands blistered by sawing and chopping wood for building and cooking, the blood of a thousand insect bites, the blood of sacrifices of chickens and goats made by the *feiticeiro* to bring them good fortune. The only way to combat it was to play it at its own game. Katharine would redouble her efforts, working harder and longer than ever before.

She gathered all the Indians around her to tell them what she had decided.

'Jonathan and Santiago,' she said, her clear voice carrying right to the furthest waiting ears, 'you will be my new clerks, replacing Charles. There is work enough for two these days and you have earned your right to promotion.'

She paused, and looked around at the expectant faces. 'Everyone else, we have two weeks to get this place cleared and rebuilt. During this period, wages are doubled – you will be paid the extra money at the end of the fortnight. Providing,' she added, 'the work is all done.'

Nods and grins and smiles of desultory appreciation greeted her words; applause and wild displays of emotion were not the Indian way. Even so, Katharine expected some action. Smoothing down her dress, she surveyed the crowd. No one was moving, no one was going anywhere.

'So,' she called, raising her voice very slightly, 'what are you waiting for? Off you go! Let's get Norwood back into business!'

And with that, her audience moved off as one, all setting purposefully to their tasks. Soon the compound rang with the sound of axe and machete blows, hammering and chiselling, shouting and whistling.

Jonathan came to her. 'Well done, Mother,' he said, admiringly. 'You are changed! Like a new person now. Perhaps you took a potion from the witch doctor?'

Katharine smiled wryly and shook her head. 'No.' She looked around at Norwood, her home, her livelihood. 'No, Jonathan, nothing magic, no spells or incantations.' She breathed in deeply, smelling the earth fresh from the overnight rain, the breeze that came all the way from the high Andes. 'Just my love of this place and all of you – and my promise that I won't let you down.'

Chapter Nineteen

Norwood, 1899

Over the next few years, everyone at Norwood worked without cease. In the office, Katharine, Jonathan and Santiago huddled over plans and maps, working out how to rotate the tappers across the *estradas* to maximise production, the best routes to bring the rubber to the compound, the most advantageous time to send it to Manaus and Pará.

Out in the forest, the *seringueiros*, alone or in groups of two, three or four, slashed the bark, climbed the trees, collected the latex and sat for days over palm nut fires, smoking the growing balls of rubber. They had to be constantly monitored to ensure that they tapped responsibly. In the quest for greater production, the temptation was always to cut too often and too deep, which led to rapid deterioration of a tree's health. Too many estates had suffered from the urge to make a quick buck.

They had their fair share of difficulties, with yellow fever epidemics, which always took some victims to their graves, as well as insect, snake and vampire bat bites, and only slightly less infrequent accidents with knives or machetes. Together, they endured rains of biblical strength, hunger when their food ran out and the supply canoes could not reach them, plagues of mosquitoes and the dreaded 'manta blanca' – dense blankets of microscopic midges that covered every square inch of flesh and inflicted bites that itched tortuously for days after.

All of this they went through.

Until, eventually, a couple of years after the raid, success rather than disaster once more looked them in the face. They were shipping rubber two, three, six times a year and finally Katharine was paying off her debts. She'd even managed to send a small amount of money home, enough to fix the roof and windows of the draughty house in Clerkenwell and install a tap in the kitchen, which would save her mother the time and energy involved in fetching water from the pump in the street.

But she was still some way from being able to make a sizeable dent in repaying her father's life savings. Every now and again, she allowed herself to feel a scintilla of resentment towards Mayhew, who several years ago had made an advantageous marriage, or so she understood, and was running a successful financial business in New York. His letters continued to extol the merits of America and everything about it, though Katharine had noticed a slight change in tone recently. A certain circumspection had replaced the previously overriding tone of triumphalism. She wondered if everything were quite as marvellous as he made out. But in any case, he persisted in absolving himself of any involvement in the family back home in London. Why couldn't he help out a bit, she sometimes asked herself. But then she would shake her head in self-recrimination. It was not her brother who had borrowed from their parents, it was her husband and, by default, herself.

It was her task, and hers alone, to put things right.

Mac, on the other hand, carried on being both friend and supporter. On a sunny morning in May, a letter arrived announcing that he was travelling to Anzo province to view some *estradas* and would like to stay a few days at Norwood on his way. Anzo, a vast area between its eponymous river and the Pura, was known to be the rubber El Dorado, an as yet untapped region where virgin trees in their thousands were ripe for exploitation. But it was also a dangerous place, desperate *flagelados* from the destitute Brazilian north-east region were flooding in on a daily basis and coming into conflict with those already there. Fighting broke out frequently, and every now and again bodies floating down river bore testament to it. Katharine considered Mac brave to be venturing there – but, as she already knew, Mac hadn't made his millions by shrinking from risk.

True to form, Mac arrived with an entourage of canoes and canoeists, and, immediately on arrival at Norwood's dock, had the Indians unloading delicious treats from Europe to alleviate the fish, *farinha* and bush meat diet of the rainforest.

They ate well that night and, to celebrate the occasion, Katharine even opened the bottle of perfume he'd sent her all those years ago and applied it delicately to her wrists and neck in defiance of the mosquitoes. Over a sumptuous dinner of paté, *confit de canard* and petit pois, followed by crème brûlée, all from imported tins, Katharine asked Mac about his plans.

'You are really considering buying land in Anzo?' she asked. 'You've been here so long and done so well. Are you not tempted to ease off a bit rather than taking on yet more work, tackling another challenge?'

Mac, intent on scooping up the last of his dessert, did not reply for a moment. When he did, his answer was brusque, as if brushing Katharine's enquiry off. 'Oh no, not at all. Not ready to be put out to grass quite yet.'

Katharine smiled inwardly at the thought of Mac placidly and contentedly grazing the green fields of Highgate and offered him some more wine. He could have it so easy but chose not to, which did seem strange. But lots of people in the Amazon were peculiar to various degrees. She had almost certainly become odd herself, after all this time.

The next day, she had a lot of office work to deal with so she didn't see Mac in the morning. In the early afternoon, needing to clear her head from all the figures and calculations that were tying themselves in knots, she strolled down to the river to be confronted with a sight that made her double over in laughter.

Jonathan had built a rope swing for Antonio; it hung on a liana from a high branch of a mighty Brazil nut tree and the seat was, of course, made from rubber. But rather than Antonio sitting on the seat and sailing back and forth over the river, it was Mac. His pale limbs and sandy hair glowed in the equatorial sun as he performed graceful oscillations back and forth. Every time he reached the exact right spot over the water, Antonio shouted, 'now!' and every time, Mac failed to loosen his grasp and swung straight back to the bank again.

In between his ever more frantic exhortations for Mac to let go, Antonio was also laughing, a carefree, joyous laugh that Katharine had rarely heard before. It gladdened her heart to see her son so happy, for he was prone to sulks and tantrums.

Eventually, after four or five more failed attempts, Mac finally detached himself from the swing, plunging down to the turbid water beneath him. But he had misjudged the jump, preempting Antonio's command by a second or so, so that rather than being on the turn of the swing, heading for dry land, he was beyond the safe point, pitching directly into the place where the current was strong beneath the surface.

Any object in the water there was dragged ever further out and eventually underneath the surface, never to reappear. For one dreadful moment, Katharine was frozen to the spot, unable to think, unable to move.

And then she was racing down the beach and along the dock, untying a canoe, jumping into it and paddling for all she was worth. As she strove to go faster, she saw Antonio grab the liana rope, hoist himself upon the seat and fly through the air. Instead of waiting until he was at the safe spot for letting go, he did what Mac had done, throwing himself down at the exact same place. He landed in the water with a tumultous splash.

Immediately, Mac was reaching out his arms to him, clutching him as if he were a buoy. Katharine, barely able to breathe for the exertion of paddling, watched in appalled horror as the full-grown man clung to her small son and their heads disappeared under the deceptively smooth surface of the capricious river.

She paddled harder, so hard that her arms screamed in protest and her heart all but burst in pain. The two heads reappeared, gasping for breath. Mac was panicking and Antonio was trying to calm him so that he could keep him afloat. But Mac was so much bigger, so much heavier, that Antonio, for all his superhuman effort, could stop neither Mac nor himself from sinking. And all the while they were being swept out, into the current, and held under the water for ever longer amounts of time.

Katharine, in a haze of dread and terror, unable to fully register what was happening, paddled on.

After what seemed like hours but was in fact only seconds, she got to the spot where she thought she'd last seen them. She'd lined it up with a palm tree on the bank and tried not to take her eyes off the place but even so, the water just looked like water; it had no distinguishing features. For a moment, she ceased paddling, falling forward as her breath came in ragged, painful gasps. Whatever was happening here she refused to believe. She could not lose her son, nor her friend. This river had taken her husband; it was not taking any others.

The canoe was turning on the current, the river wanting to snatch it up and send it oceanward. As it began to spin, a disturbance rippled the surface just a few feet away. Bubbles rose, and then a head emerged, just enough to take a breath before it was submerged once more. Mac. He was still alive. But Antonio?

Katharine plunged the paddle downwards, sweeping it backwards with such force she arrived at the spot with one stroke. The head rose up again, but this time there were two of them. Katharine cried out in relief, 'Antonio! Mac! Here, I'm here.'

Antonio flung out an arm and caught hold of the paddle. With the other hand, he dragged Mac towards him until he, too, had managed to fold his fingers around the wood. With all her strength, Katharine pulled the paddle towards the canoe, the two gasping swimmers attached to it. She heaved Mac into the boat where he fell on the bottom, retching and crying. Antonio, nimbly and without help, pulled himself up and over the side and sank into his mother's waiting arms.

'Oh, Antonio, my Antonio,' Katharine sobbed. 'You're alive, I can't believe you're alive.'

Antonio spat a mouthful of water into the river. 'Just about,' he agreed. His eyes were sunken with exhaustion and shock.

'You're a hero,' said Katharine, 'my hero. You saved a man's life.'

Antonio shrugged, no breath left to speak.

Mac sat up, revived, rubbing his knuckles into his eyes, still coughing. 'What the bloody hell kind of game is that?' he demanded. 'I've never felt such a bleeding fool in my whole life, so I haven't.'

'Don't worry,' said Antonio, sternly. 'You're never going on my swing again, at least not if I've got anything to do with it.'

And his tone was so reprimanding and, despite his young age and unbroken voice, so serious, that all three of them burst out laughing, a laughter that started slowly but, by the time they got back to the dock, had become hysterical.

That night Katharine wept for Anselmo in a way she hadn't for many years. If only she had been able to save him as she had managed to save Mac and Antonio. How different this past decade would have been, if that had been so.

If only.

Part II

1900 – 1909

Chapter Twenty

New York, 1900

The advert on the front page of the *New York Times* caught Mayhew Bird's eye as he ate his habitual breakfast kipper and drank his morning cup of coffee.

Amazonian Rubber Company Inc.
Millions of rubber trees ready for tapping NOW.
75% return for life on all investments; this is one
that cannot fail.

Not being overly troubled by close attachments or familial bonds, Mayhew didn't often think about his sister Katharine and the life she was trying to build in that god-forsaken country she had disappeared off to with that foreign husband of hers. But Katharine had gone in pursuit of rubber and rubber meant money and money… well, money was what made Mayhew's world go round.

Avarice had driven him throughout his life and, combined with his shame over his hardworking parents and their humble home in Hawthorn Road, avarice had propelled him to set sail for America to make his fortune the moment he'd turned eighteen. He wanted to be rich and he also wanted to be a gentleman, to be what he considered 'better' than the place he'd come from. To achieve his aims, he'd set as a goal finding a society heiress to marry, and, being extremely goodlooking, much taller than the average Englishman and in possession of charm in abundance, he had succeeded.

He had wooed the richest, plainest girl he had found in New York City, beguiling her with his perfect British accent and perfect British manners, taking her to the opera, the theatre, to literary soirées and art exhibitions, talking knowledgeably about the hottest new writers and most groundbreaking artists. When he wanted to, Mayhew Bird could enchant and seduce with ease.

His marriage to heiress Amy-Joanne Burnett had been a triumph of those enchantment and seduction skills. The ceremony had taken place in Grace Church on Broadway five years ago, preceded by a long engagement, necessary, his mother-in-law Emily had insisted, not just for propriety, but also to allow time for the preparation of the required number of dozens – the monogrammed and embroidered linens, handkerchiefs and underwear that all the best brides must have.

It had cost a huge sum of money, the wedding and the dozens, plus the Park Avenue town house and the country estate, but money was no object. The death of Mrs Burnett's husband had left her a millionaire and, as the only child, Amy-Joanne was set to inherit it all. She also had a substantial trust fund to keep the wolf from the door until such time as Mrs Burnett should pass on to a better world. Though there was no sign of that happening any time soon. As was often the way with widows, Emily Burnett boasted the rudest health, never suffering anything worse than a head cold. Her daughter, Mayhew's wife, was similarly robust, aided, Mayhew always supposed, by the ample layers of fat that encompassed her pudgy form.

He averted his eyes from Amy-Joanne on the other side of the breakfast table now. She had grown stouter and plainer during their union and it pained him to see her eating so heartily. He pictured, in contrast, his sister Katharine, the complete opposite in shape and size to Amy-Joanne, tall and thin and lanky though similarly unattractive, poor girl. He had always considered Katharine competent but undynamic; she had gone to work in a shop at age seventeen, and that is where he had expected her to remain, at least until she got married and started producing legions of children of her own.

He truly had never imagined that she had it in her to up sticks and move to another hemisphere. But there she was, busily plucking rubber from the bounteous forests of the Amazon and the material's rising fortunes might just turn out to be fortuitous, the spotting of this advertisement to be a case of right time, right place. Because Mayhew was unhappily aware that he was in a bit of tight spot just now, the life savings business, of which he was founder, chairman and chief executive, in a fair amount of trouble.

'Guaranteed returns,' the newspaper ad for the rubber enterprise affirmed, and further down, in the small print, 'this cannot go wrong. Invest $5 a month and accrue an annual income of $500. Invest $150 a month and receive $5,000 per annum.'

Reading these astonishing figures – even better than the ones he had promised to investors in the Ladies Deposit Association! – Mayhew pondered quite how it was that Katharine had not managed to get rich yet. Obviously, it can't have helped that her husband had upped and died almost as soon as they'd got to Brazil, but it seemed like this rubber malarkey was such a dead cert a chimpanzee could run it and make a fortune. Mayhew sighed, and watched as Amy-Joanne took another piece of toast. This was the problem with a woman trying to do a man's job. It was bound to end in failure, or at the very least, a great deal less success than should ensue. What a good thing he might be in a position to give his sister some assistance.

Amy-Joanne, arrested in the process of spreading butter on her toast by the sight of his eyes upon her, gesticulated towards the newspaper.

'Something interesting, my dear?' she asked, somewhat nervously. She was often cautious in her approaches to her husband, especially in the morning, when he was not at his best, and especially at the moment, for he had been in a particularly bad humour for some weeks.

'No.' Mayhew's answer was short and curt.

The maid stepped forward to offer more coffee and the trickle of liquid pouring from a pot was the only sound to disturb the silence for the next few minutes. Amy-Joanne turned her attention back to her toast and Mayhew became acutely aware of her attempts to eat and drink noiselessly. He'd told her once, mildly and for her own good, that she sounded like a pig at its trough at meal times and she'd been self-conscious about eating in front of him ever since, much preferring it when he had his luncheon at the club and his dinner out with friends.

'Do you have any plans today?' he asked her. He had no real interest in her reply, save for the fact that he wanted to know where she'd be. Over the last few weeks and months he'd been fomenting a plan for how he could deal with the awkward matter of his failing business, his sterile marriage and his uncertain future in one fell swoop. Amy-Joanne's whereabouts today was crucial information if the plan was to succeed.

'I'm meeting mother at Macy's,' Amy-Joanne replied. 'To do some shopping,' she added, unnecessarily.

'That's generally what people go to Macy's for,' commented Mayhew, drily.

Amy-Joanne blushed, embarrassed at her own stupidty. Mayhew felt a pang of guilt. The last seven years since their engagement hadn't been so bad, really. They lived in absolute comfort, holidayed wherever and whenever they liked and wanted for nothing. Or, at least, he wanted for nothing. For Amy-Joanne and her mother, things were rather different. Mayhew knew that there was something lacking from their union that most people were expected to produce within the first few years. For himself, he was glad that there were no children. But for Amy-Joanne, he knew it was a lack she felt sorely. Divorce, though, was something she would never have contemplated, however bad things got. Puritanism ran thick through the Burnetts' veins; godliness was the highest virtue.

'What are you looking for at Macy's?' he asked, deciding to be kind. Amy-Joanne's look of gratitude at his taking an interest in her potential purchases would have been touching if it hadn't been so pathetic. Irritation arose in Mayhew anew. It reminded him of when Emily Burnett had agreed to his proposal of marriage. The plain ones were always the most grateful. Their mothers, even more so.

He drained his cup of coffee and rustled around on the table for his glasses and the newspaper. He got up and made for the door, and was at the threshold before he realised he hadn't given Amy-Joanne a chance to answer. He turned back and looked at her expectantly.

'Mother thinks we need some new linen for Turbury,' she answered, obediently.

Mayhew raised his eyebrows. There was linen aplenty in every one of the houses, so this mission seemed unnecessary. But if it kept Amy-Joanne occupied, he didn't much care. He had far too much on his mind.

At the office, he gathered up the day's pile of mail. The amount of letters arriving was doubling by the day. It had started as a gentle flow, become a torrent and was now a veritable tsunami. A knock at the door drew his attention away from the tidal wave of post that lay in front of him.

'How are you doing, old man?'

It was Robinson, a stockbroker acquaintance with an office down the corridor.

'Good. And yourself?' Mayhew hastily shoved the letters inside his roll top desk so that they would not be visible to his visitor and sat back in his chair, looking every bit the successful life savings investor.

Robinson pulled a disgruntled face. 'So so. It's always slow in the summer, isn't it? But I've had better seasons, nevertheless.'

Mayhew grimaced in sympathy. Whatever Robinson's troubles were, they couldn't be anything like as bad as his own. His chickens, as the saying went, were well and truly coming home to roost.

'You getting any time away from it all?' he asked. He knew Robinson's wife and children had gone to the coast and were not due back until September.

'Going next week,' replied Robinson, suddenly cheered. 'Yourself?'

'Amy-Joanne and her mother are planning to spend the summer at Turbury,' he shrugged, 'so I'll go at the weekends. When work allows.' He gestured towards his desk.

There was a short, awkward pause. Mayhew had a sudden premonition that Robinson was not just here to make idle chat and the stockbroker's next words confirmed this supposition.

'I heard a few investors were pulling their money out.' Robinson made it a statement, not a question, as if he had no doubt as to the correctness of the fact.

Mayhew shifted awkwardly in his chair. He didn't know how Robinson could have got hold of this information and was momentarily disconcerted.

'There is quite a bit of movement at the moment,' he responded, smoothly. Recovering his equanimity he raised his hands in a dismissive gesture. 'But nothing too serious. People are entitled to take their money out as well as put it in. Indeed, I'm glad if they do. Shows we are achieving our aim of a happy financial future for ladies everywhere.'

He gave a loud, hearty laugh but Robinson didn't join in.

'My aunt invested with you,' he continued. 'What she doesn't have in stocks and shares, she entrusted to the Ladies Deposit Association. She loved the proprietor Miss Jennifer Jones, her picture in the adverts, the information in the brochures, felt she was a woman just like herself.' He paused. 'I've never seen Miss Jones here.'

The words were conveyed in a tone of innocent observation but they fell on Mayhew like a ton weight.

'No, well.' He grimaced regretfully. He recalled the tense afternoon he'd spent in Greenwich Village with the aged German artist who had drawn the sketch of Jennifer Jones that adorned all Mayhew's advertising and marketing material. The old gentleman's charcoal pencil had flown across the stiff paper, skilfully capturing the likeness of someone who didn't exist, creating lines and curves, the slick of an eyebrow, the gentle curl of lips, gracefully sculptured cheekbones. As the bonnet began to take shape, Mayhew remembered wondering fleetingly if he had been right to go for that type of hat. But then he had focused on Jennifer's Mona Lisa smile, the demure, almond eyes and the becoming bow beneath the chin and had been more than satisfied with his decision.

'She's not in the best of health,' Mayhew said, pursing his lips regretfully. 'A lady of a certain age can have, how shall I put it, difficulties in getting out and about. But fortunately, because of sensible investments made in her very own company, she can live in great comfort while also being housebound.'

Upon finishing this statement, Mayhew struggled to keep the triumphant note out of his voice. *I'm good at this*, he thought, caught up in his own solipsistic bubble, *really very impressive. What a shame it's all got to come to an end.*

But Robinson wasn't giving in. 'My aunt told me she wrote to ask for a full withdrawal six weeks ago but has heard nothing. Do you know why that is?'

Mayhew's pulse quickened as his heart slowly sank within his chest. He placed his hands together, fingertips to fingertips.

'I have found some, how shall I put it, irregularities in several requests for the withdrawal of funds,' he said, slowly and sonorously, as if there was a danger that Robinson would not understand. 'Quite a few older, unmarried ladies saying they want their money out because their nephew or godson or whoever has told her she should give the cash to him instead, that he'll take better care of it.'

Mayhew tapped his fingertips against each other. 'Now, I'm sure you can understand that, as a responsible businessman, I need to be certain that this money, when I release it, is not going to fall into the wrong hands.'

Robinson stared at him. Gradually, it dawned on him what Mayhew was suggesting and his face turned an uncomfortable shade of puce. 'You mean you think I'm trying to steal my aunt's money?'

Mayhew made a moue of disappointment tinged with the sadness of experience.

'Not you, no of course not. But you understand that I have to examine all requests to ensure that no one is being exploited. It takes time. But it's in my clients' best interests.'

Fortunately for Mayhew, Robinson seemed to fall for this, even expressing his contrition. 'Very good,' he said, and then added, 'well I'm glad you're taking such good care of her. It's a pity not all financial advisers are so honest.'

Mayhew accepted the compliment with a modest inclination of his head. And then, with an air of finality, he concluded the conversation.

'And now if you don't mind, I must get on with my work.'

Robinson left, shutting the door behind him. Mayhew folded his arms upon the desk and let his head fall onto them. That had been a close shave; he had no idea that Robinson's damned aunt was an investor in his fund. But though he'd put Robinson off the scent for a while, he wouldn't stay away for long, Mayhew was sure. He needed to act – and fast.

Opening his desk, he swept the letters, unopened, into the wastepaper basket. He cleared a few items from the table top; his fountain pen and a photo of Amy-Joanne. It always showed that a man was a good sort if he proudly displayed a picture of his nearest and dearest – and of course such a man would take it with him when he left. Exiting his office, he locked the door securely and pocketed the key.

At the bottom of the stairs he said a friendly goodbye to the security guard in his navy uniform.

'Off early today, sir?' said the guard, always pleased to be noticed.

'Summer, isn't it?' answered Mayhew. 'All work and no play makes Jack a dull boy.'

'Oh yes, indeed.' The guard nodded in hearty agreement even though, as far as Mayhew knew, he hadn't had a day off work in all the years Mayhew had had his office here.

He doffed his hat at the charwoman forever cleaning the marble floor with her grey, fetid cloth.

'A good evening to you,' he said and she blushed and grinned toothlessly back at him.

'And to you, Mr Mayhew, sir,' she burbled, like the guard always gratified with being singled out for his attention.

A couple of police officers were coming up the gleaming stone steps as Mayhew approached the revolving door. He pulled his hat as far down over his forehead as it would go, then took a copy of the *New York Times* from his briefcase and bent low over it, pretending to be absolutely absorbed in its contents. As he stepped into one glass segment of the door and followed it round to the exit, the police officers entered another to arrive in the foyer, intent on cornering their prey inside, oblivious to the person going around with them but in the opposite direction. Emerging unnoticed, Mayhew tucked the newspaper under his arm and, whistling as he went, took the monumental marble steps two at a time, the perfect image of a successful businessman without a care in the world.

–

At Kitty Little's house, he found her lying idly on a couch eating grapes, which she was sharing with the lapdog that sat at her feet. Her maid, who had let him in, swiftly made herself scarce.

'It's been too long,' Kitty murmured, nestling her face in his chest as he knelt beside her.

'You know I've been busy,' he said, soothingly. 'I have responsibilities, don't I?'

'But they should only be to me,' she said with mock-childish petulance, and then laughed.

Mayhew smiled indulgently. Her looks were coarser now, lacking the fresh-faced sheen of youth and untouched beauty.

But his mistress was still the most attactive woman he'd ever laid eyes on. After Mayhew's marriage, she had disappeared, apparently to Italy to try to repair things with her husband, from whom she had long been separated. Then the story had changed to Kitty being there to sign divorce papers, and to try to extract an appropriate sum of money from the man as a settlement. Either way, she had been gone for a number of years.

But then she had returned, and so had the feelings that existed between her and Mayhew. Mayhew, who had the glorious attribute of being unaffected by moral scruples of any kind, had had no hesitation in rekindling a relationship. With the benefit of his own burgeoning business, and Amy-Joanne's overflowing bank account, he had helped to set Kitty up in this house and bought her a sky-blue coupe to get about town in style and comfort.

Pulling Kitty up from her sofa, he led her to the bedroom where he buried himself in her, suddenly desperate for this escape from real life, for this stalling of time for half an hour or so. She was getting plumper, but her voluptuousness only made her more attractive, more alluring. And there was still no comparison between her luscious softness and Amy-Joanne's rolls of fat. At the thought of his wife, Mayhew groaned and thrust himself harder into Kitty.

'Oh yes,' responded Kitty, automatically.

This was the problem, his little difficulty in the bedroom. What happened so wonderfully, so magically, with Kitty or any other lady of the night he sought the company of, was not possible with his wife. Mayhew simply couldn't perform with Amy-Joanne. This was why there were no children, and as of today, it was assured there never would be.

Afterwards, he and Kitty drank champagne and Mayhew felt something unfamiliar stirring within him. He hardly recognised the emotion. Was it sorrow? Love? He drank more champagne and dismissed it, whatever it was.

At the door, Kitty lingered, not letting him go. Trying not to show his impatience, Mayhew gently detached her limpet arms from him.

'I need to be off. I'm expected… somewhere.'

Kitty nuzzled her lips against his neck. 'Can't you stay a bit longer?' she murmured. 'There's something I want to talk to you about.'

'It'll have to wait,' he whispered gently, kissing her forehead. 'I really do have to go.'

She was trying to arouse him again, to beguile him into staying the night with her. He did that sometimes. But not tonight. Not ever again.

'We'll talk tomorrow, sweet one,' he said, 'once Amy-Joanne and her mother are ensconced at Turbury, we'll have all the time in the world for sharing our secrets.'

'Take this then,' Kitty said, thrusting a pale pink envelope into his hand. 'And let me know as soon as you've read it.'

Mayhew eyed the missive suspiciously, as if it not sure what it was about to do. What could be so important that Kitty had taken the trouble to write it down in anticipation of a hurried visit – or no visit at all?

A siren in the distance made him jump, and his heart lurched. He gave himself a little shake. He was letting his nerves get to him and that would never do. Hurriedly, he backed out of Kitty's door. 'I'll see you again soon, little one,' he whispered softly, layering his voice with the impression of sincere love. There was no time to lose. If he was going to get out unscathed, and with the money, this was his only chance.

Waving, he set off purposefully down the narrow, cobbled street, briefly pausing to blow Kitty a kiss before he turned the corner and disappeared out of sight.

–

He could already smell the sea air, taste the salt blowing from the ocean in the brisk breeze. He'd picked Brooklyn Bridge as the place to do the deed. It was the wrong time of year, only just getting dusky at seven p.m., but he had no choice. It was now or never. Putting a hand in his pocket, he felt for the passport. It was still there, safely nestled against his hip.

Beneath the bridge, the footpath was deserted. It smelt of urine and garbage and rats, and Mayhew's nose wrinkled as he undressed. He piled his clothes up neatly, casting quick glances to the left and the right to ensure he was still alone. He placed his watch, his pen and the photo of Amy-Joanne on the heap and, last of all, his carefully handwritten note which he weighted down with a stone. The murky river water sloshed incoherently against the banks and he thought, briefly, of his sister's drowned husband. It was a shame Anselmo had had his life taken from him so early, and it would be a similar shame when Mayhew himself was gone.

But Amy-Joanne would get over it, just as Katharine had. As would Kitty.

Thanking his lucky stars that he was still undisturbed, Mayhew hurriedly dressed in the workman's clothes he'd purchased a few weeks previously. Blue denim dungarees, a loose jacket and a cap. He had a false beard for now, which he could ditch as soon as he'd grown his own; even he could see that it wouldn't stand up to close scrutiny. But it had been enough to get him the fake passport and he was sure it would be enough to get him on the boat.

Mayhew shivered as he pulled the jacket around him and shoved Kitty's as yet unopened letter into the pocket. Turning on his heel, he left his few worldly possessions sitting forlornly by the water's edge, and scarpered.

The forces of law and order were closing in on him. Those police officers at his workplace had been after one thing, Mayhew was absolutely certain. That one thing was him. Investors wanted their money out but there was no money. It hadn't been invested in stocks and shares that would generate capital growth and interest, as promised. It had been spent, or ferreted away in secret accounts. The dividends he had paid out had come from the money invested by new clients, but over the last few months there had been more requests for withdrawals than deposits. So it would be only a matter of time before the whole façade collapsed like a house of cards. The demolition had begun, and the wrecking ball was a big one.

It was time for Mayhew to get out.

Boarding the boat at the harbour, doing his best to lose himself amidst the crowds, he felt a brief pang of regret. For the most part, he'd enjoyed his time in New York. He watched as the city's familiar skyline faded into the distance, and only when he could no longer see the tallest buildings silhouetted against the night sky did he turn to face the direction of travel. The boat was headed for the Caribbean; he'd get there, wait a while for the hullabaloo of his demise to die down and then move on to Brazil, pay his little sister a visit. The Amazon was the perfect place to hide out: miles from anywhere, virtually lawless and outside American jurisdiction. He reached into his pocket, extracted his office key, the last remaining remnant of his old life, and flung it into the sea.

And then, almost against his will, his hand went to the pocket again and pulled out Kitty's letter. Mayhew stared down at it, tempted to jettison it without reading it. Everything to do with Kitty was yesterday's news already. There could be nothing in it to concern or interest him.

But curiosity got the better of him. As the boat rocked on the open sea, he tore the letter open, his eyes scanning rapidly over the words. He read to the end and then slowly and carefully folded the paper into a tiny square which he encased within his curled fist, its corners and edges hard against his palm. He could sense that the colour had drained from his cheeks, feel his irregular heart beat.

It couldn't be true. And yet he knew that it was.

Kitty was pregnant. She was expecting a child and it was definitely his. She wanted money for maintenance but more than that, she wanted him. He should leave Amy-Joanne and set up home with her.

For a brief, fleeting moment, on the swaying deck of a boat bound for the southern hemisphere, Mayhew imagined it. He pictured himself and Kitty walking along the waterfront in Greenwich Village, taking in the exotic smells and sights of men from foreign climes, swinging a giggling little tousle-haired boy between them. He had never thought he wanted children, but for those few short seconds, he felt the joy in it.

And then he immediately dismissed such useless and unwanted emotions. It was a shame Kitty had left it until the last minute to tell him (although, to be fair to her, it was only he himself who had known that that visit was the last one). But nothing could be done to change things now. He had no doubt that Kitty would cope; she was a survivor. She'd bring the child up perfectly well by herself. He had other plans.

Dropping the tiny pink square into the water, he set his gaze to the ocean and the future.

A new life beckoned. A new beginning. Mayhew Bird would rise, phoenix-like from the ashes of his old life, and remodel himself anew.

Chapter Twenty-One

Norwood, 1900

Silently, Katharine surveyed *bolachas* of rubber worth thousands of pounds and allowed herself to feel a scintilla of pride in what she and her team had achieved. At precisely the right time, every *estrada* was in full production; the price had tripled over the past year. Jonathan and Santiago were about to set off downriver to sell it all, and would undertake all the negotiations themselves as Katharine had long since disposed of the services of the *aviador* Anselmo had contracted to; he had cheated and underpaid from the word go and she'd got rid of him the moment the agreement had expired. There were still extortionate taxes to pay, of course, plus Mac's fee for crossing the isthmus but nevertheless, her profit would be considerable.

To add to such positive thoughts, it was a beautiful day, the sun lancing through a thin layer of cumulus clouds, the tiniest hint of a cooling breeze blowing down the river.

It was a day when it felt good to be alive.

Katharine walked down to the water, where the cargo canoes would be pulling in over the next few days. At the moment, there was no one on the shore but Antonio, idly throwing stones into the shallows.

'Antonio,' she called, annoyed, her relaxed mood disappearing, 'you're supposed to be doing the maths problems I set you. What are you doing here?'

Antonio shrugged, a response that infuriated Katharine and he knew it. He had become ever more reluctant to engage in his school work and these days was often openly defiant when it came to instructions to study.

'What does that mean?' demanded Katharine, coldly. She found it hard, when he was sullen and obstinate. Was it her fault? Had she been too indulgent with his upbringing? Left him too much to run wild and not overseen his manners, not disciplined him sufficiently?

'It doesn't mean anything.' Antonio's reply was sulky and surly.

'Well it should,' she snapped. 'Go back to the school room and do your work! Do you think that you'll get anywhere in life without putting in the hard graft?'

Antonio lingered, digging at the sand with his bare foot.

I better check for chigger mites, Katharine thought distractedly. And then – 'NOW!' in her strongest voice as Antonio showed no signs of obeying.

Abruptly, the boy turned on his heels and walked back up the beach towards the compound.

Katharine sighed. At ten years old, her son was strong and fearless, but too apt to be resentful and wilful. It was an everyday, ongoing battle to get him to do any school work at all. She ordered books which sat on shelves and curled in the damp, nibbled by insects and soon growing a fine layer of hairy fungus, and the time she put aside each day to tutor him was frequently cut short by arguments and temper tantrums. Maths, her own favourite subject, was his most hated one, and history, geography and science fared little better. Katharine had started worrying about his education when he was only three and was still doing so all these years later. She despaired of getting him to pay attention and put pen to paper.

She shook her head as she followed him over the sand. Something must be done, but what? She could hire a tutor, send to England or France for a suitable young man to come and teach him. But who would want to bury themselves so deep in the jungle, far from any kind of social life, from friends and family, in a place that often felt like the end of the world? That to all intents and purposes *was* the end of the world. She thought more and more of moving to Manaus and enrolling him in one of the many new schools there. But she hadn't liked the city when she'd stayed there a decade ago and was sure it could only have got worse, and in any case Norwood wasn't on a firm enough footing yet for her to be an absentee boss.

At the brow of the hill above the beach, she took a moment to survey the river, the wide bend that opened up and quickly narrowed again so that it was fast flowing past the house. Floating islands of aquatic grasses bowled downriver and, to the west, a bird flew low, searching for fish. For all Antonio's lack of book learning, he was an expert scholar in the ways of the jungle. Which was more important? Katharine was torn; to know the forest was a special art, something the Indians had in their blood but that Europeans gained by special invitation only. But society did not value such knowledge. This society that she so wanted Antonio to be able to participate in required Greek and Latin, maths and science.

She looked back in the other direction, towards Manaus and Pará and the Atlantic, as if the answer to her dilemma lay there, in the vastness of this land, in the miles and miles of jungle that separated her from the country of her birth.

As she gazed, a canoe slowly hove into view, the oarsman working hard against the current. The mail boat!

No matter how long she lived here, the shudder of elation, the thrill of anticipation, on catching sight of the post never diminished. She could go without news from home for months at a time so whenever the boat did arrive, all she could think about was how many letters she'd get, how long she could spin out reading each one, teasing every ounce of love and meaning and companionship from each word.

Eagerly, she ran back down to the water's edge and stood, fidgeting on tiptoes, almost jumping with excitement. She was longing for news from everyone – most of all, Mabel. She had sat school exams and hoped for good results that would enable her to stay on, improve her French and, in due course, become a teacher.

The canoeist handed over the budget, the leather purse used to safely store mail on its journey up and down river. Eagerly, Katharine pulled it open and delved inside. But it contained just one letter and Katharine felt a frisson of disappointment on recognising the handwriting.

Mayhew's.

Katharine had always made sure to write to him every few months but his replies were rare as hen's teeth. When they did come, they were generally short and boastful; a new property bought with his wife's money, a new carriage purchased to show off around town in. He'd always been embarrassed by the humbleness of their childhood home, the many children, their tired and overworked mother and father. The last thing Katharine remembered him telling her was that he was going to get rich and become a gentleman, like Pip in *Great Expectations*. And look how *that* story had ended, she thought ironically.

Going into her office to read what he had to say today, she picked up her paper knife and slit the letter open. At each word, her heart sank further and further into the soles of her feet. Mayhew was coming to the Amazon. He wanted to visit her, to stay with her and assist her in making the most of her 'embryonic business'. He felt sure he had skills that she lacked and that he could ensure that she profited from the rubber price which, he helpfully informed her, had risen exponentially and looked set to continue in the same way far into the future. He worried that she would be too 'soft' and her femininity would preclude the making of sound business decisions.

Katharine flung the letter down onto the table in frustration. How she detested Mayhew's patronising attitude towards her. It had always been like this. He was the eldest, and a boy, and he'd always taken both as imbuing him with a natural and inviolable superiority. He was the one who had to have the first bath, to get the best piece of pork crackling, to be the first to walk on newly fallen snow, making her follow in his footsteps so as to avoid messing up the pristine surface. It had driven her mad then and it drove her mad now. There was no doubt that when he wanted to, he could put on winning ways. Their mother Mary had always said that he could charm the birds out of the trees. But he was also devious and bullying, always out for the main chance, and not above lying and deceiving if it suited his purposes.

Katharine groaned out loud to herself at the prospect of Mayhew's arrival. She'd thought travelling thousands of miles up the Amazon was far enough to get away from her brother. But obviously not.

With a heartfelt sigh, she picked up the letter, noticing as she did so a postscript on the back. It would be helpful, the note said, if she didn't tell anyone else that he was coming, or of his presence once arrived.

Katharine's eyes narrowed in puzzlement. Why the big secret? She had no idea. But, given he'd made no mention of bringing a wife with him, perhaps he was getting divorced and didn't want the shame to follow him. That was all she could think. She looked outside to the forest, where scarlet, green and black tanager birds fluttered amongst the vegetation and brightly coloured butterflies flitted between the searing red of passion flowers. There was no one here who could care less about her brother's marital situation and she herself most certainly didn't want to get involved. Mayhew was a law unto himself and always would be and Katharine was not going to interfere.

Tucking the letter back into its envelope, she comforted herself with the fact that he wouldn't be here for ages yet – if he made it at all. A slow, wry smile played on her lips as she contemplated Mayhew's love of indulgence, his craving for action and an audience. With a bit of luck, he'd get distracted by the bright lights of Manaus and never make it as far as Norwood;

most people had no idea of the rigours of the journey, how long it took, how isolated they were. She hoped that would happen, anyway. But if it didn't — well, Mayhew was family — and, as their parents Mary and Bill had always insisted upon their brood, blood was thicker than water. And by and large, Katharine agreed.

Even if they did drive you mad.

Jonathan called her with an issue that needed resolving urgently and, gratefully, Katharine diverted her attention away from her brother and onto her business. When Mayhew's impending visit crept into her consciousness every now and again, she tried to look on the positive side. One benefit might be, it dawned on her gradually, the possibility that he would build a good relationship with Antonio, and might be able to help her modulate his moods and mediate in their constant arguments about how much school work he should be doing. Such thoughts helped mitigate her concerns about Mayhew's arrival.

Later, preparing the budget to send back downriver, she noticed that she'd missed something earlier. Tucked at the bottom was another letter, squashed and crumpled. Taking it out and smoothing it down, she saw instantly that it was from Mac. A sudden sense of foreboding gripped her. Why was he writing to her? The arrangements for the imminent rubber shipment had been finalised some time ago. Picking up the missive, she dispensed with the paper knife and tore it open with shaking hands.

Dear Mrs Ferrandis, the letter began.

> *It is with regret that I must inform you of a change in the terms and conditions accorded to the passage of goods over the isthmus. Our previous ten-year agreement of 1890 has now expired and, on the orders of the government, I enclose here a new contract for you to sign. Please note an increase in charges to take account of the additional*

> *traffic on the river, the commission I am entitled to claim*
> *and associated costs, plus inflation.*

The price quoted was four times what Katharine had been paying for the last decade. It seemed grotesque, unfair to the highest degree. But then again, inflation in the Amazon was running out of control, prices of ordinary consumer goods doubling overnight, and Katharine knew that all the national and local governments were trying to make as much money as they could from taxes and fines and levies. If Mac was being pressurised to increase the revenue that passage over the isthmus gleaned for the powers that be, he would have little option but to obey.

It was called the rubber business, not rubber friends. She would just have to pay up and work even harder.

Chapter Twenty-Two

London, 1900

Mabel Bird chewed nervously at the inside of her lip. She had done it so often there was now a lump there that her tongue constantly sought out when her teeth weren't making it worse. Her stomach fizzed and churned as she waited for her mother to get ready. She hadn't been able to eat any breakfast; she knew that it would have come straight back up again even if she had managed to swallow it down. She buttoned her coat tightly around her, not just because of the cold but as a kind of armour against the harsh world that she must go out and face.

If only Katharine were there, she would know what to say to make Mabel feel better, to shore up her confidence. But Katharine, thousands of miles away, did not even know that Mabel had had to leave school to go out to work. She had no idea about the terrible accident their father had had, falling from a scaffold on the docks, leaving him unable to work any more. Mabel's mother Mary had insisted that Katharine not be told, reasoning that her eldest daughter had her work cut out for her as a widow bringing up a child alone and at the same time running a business single-handedly.

Mabel was not convinced, feeling sure that Katharine would want to know and to send money, if she had any to spare, but Mary was adamant. And in any case, whether Katharine knew or not, Mabel could not possibly continue with her education. There was no option but for her to take a job so that she could not only pay her own way but also contribute to the family economy.

Though she had had a couple of weeks to get used to the idea while she had been job hunting, Mabel felt entirely unprepared. Today was her first day of employment as a housemaid, a maid-of-all-work to be precise, and she was terrified.

'Ready?' Mary was suddenly beside her, grey hair neatly pinned, hat and gloves donned.

Despite her mother's matter-of-factness, Mabel could tell she was nervous and that only served to heighten her own fear. Her stomach somersaulted. She tightened her grip on the handle of the cloth bag that contained her purse, her toothbrush and soap. Her mother carried her box with her uniform, underwear and the few personal items she possessed. Mary had made the required garments – a print dress for the morning, black for the afternoon, and the aprons – though Mabel had helped. She would have done it all, but Mary was insistent that the work must be faultless, every stitch perfect. She didn't want anyone thinking that her daughter was not properly equipped for her first situation. They'd had to buy the collars and cuffs, but even so they'd made a considerable saving on the normal £4 cost of purchasing everything ready made from a shop. Mary's skill with a needle had seen to that.

'Well, are you?' Mary questioned, waiting for Mabel's answer. 'Ready?'

'Of course.' Mabel hadn't intended it to but it came out as a whisper.

Mary's face broke into a sad smile of sympathy. 'I'm sorry it's come to this, love,' she said. And then she bolstered herself, throwing her shoulders back and marching out of the house, waiting for Mabel to follow and then banging the door purposefully shut. 'But seeing as it has, we just have to make the best of it. It won't be as bad as you think – you'll soon settle in and learn the ropes and you'll probably find you enjoy it once you've got used to it.'

There was silence, broken only by their brisk footsteps on the cobbles. They both knew that this was unlikely to be the case – it was common knowledge that a housemaid's lot was unremitting toil and drudgery.

They took the omnibus all the way through the West End, down Oxford Street to Marble Arch, hardly speaking. Neither could trust themselves not to break down. The remainder of the way to Brampton Square they walked. The house was tall; Mabel counted six levels of windows plus the basement. In the middle of the square lay a garden, filled with dark and forbidding trees which cast a gloom over everything. Or perhaps that was Mabel's mood, which was sinking along with her heart, as she realised that there was no going back. She had to go into that austere building and begin a new life, working for others, doing exactly as she was told and never, God forbid, getting above her station. She chewed the lump in her cheek and clenched her fists, feeling the welts made by her nervous, clenching grip on the cloth bag's handles.

'Here we are then,' said Mary, making a feeble attempt at sounding cheery. She put Mabel's box down on the pavement. It stood there, a symbol of Mabel's future.

They stood staring at each other. Then Mabel flung her arms around her mother and buried her face in her neck, it smelt of home and safety and familiarity. It would be two weeks before she got an afternoon off and would be able to visit her family. She didn't know if she could last that long. It was unimaginable, unbearable. She had never been away from home for more than the hours of the school day before. How on earth was she going to survive a whole fortnight?

Mary let the hug continue for a few moments and then gently pushed Mabel away. She reached out her hand and wiped the tears from her daughter's eyes. Mabel was her youngest child, the only girl other than Katharine.

Mabel caught her hand and kissed it. 'Sorry, Mother,' she murmured. 'Sorry for being weak and pathetic.'

'Silly girl,' admonished Mary, kindly. 'You're nothing of the sort. Just nervous, and what fifteen-year-old wouldn't be?'

Mabel sniffed and fumbled for her handkerchief to blow her nose.

'Can you see that I've been crying?' she asked anxiously. 'Do you think they'll notice?'

'No,' answered Mary, definitively. 'Now, on you go. Let's be off with you. No point in delaying.'

Neither of them moved.

'Come now, Mabel, you must go.' Mary's voice was quiet but insistent, then suddenly urgent. 'One last thing. Be careful. Of – of men and… well, remember that great harm can come to a girl who fraternises. And one as beautiful as you might – you might attract attention. Unwelcome attention.'

It was the closest her mother had ever got to talking about relationships. Mabel, hazily understanding what she meant, mustered a nod and turned away, towards the tradesmen's steps leading down to the basement. Ignorant though she was of the world, she knew that servants never used the front door. Faltering at the gate, fumbling with the latch, her heart was beating twice as fast as normal, her stomach flipping back and forth. She was glad again that she hadn't eaten breakfast.

Hoping for a last glance of Mary she turned back, holding on tight to the black ironwork to steady herself, to anchor herself to this job and this future, to prevent herself fleeing back to the security of Clerkenwell. If she'd spotted Mary then, she would have run. But her mother had disappeared, melting into the streets beyond the darkness, and Mabel could no longer see her.

The door of the neighbouring house opened and a smartly uniformed nanny emerged, pushing an enormous black Silver Cross pram. With her came two footmen, who lifted the pram as if it weighed nothing and carried it to the pavement. Regally, the nanny followed. Taking a firm hold on the handle, she strode off briskly in the direction of Hyde Park, giving neither word nor gesture of thanks to the footmen. None of the three of them took the slightest notice of Mabel. She was clearly the lowest of the low.

Taking a huge breath, steeling her nerves, reminding herself why she had to do this, she descended the area stairs, box and bag precariously clutched in her arms. A black door with a brass knocker greeted her, as uninviting as the lowering square itself. Reaching out her hand, she rapped three times and then waited.

This was the end of childhood, the end of freedom. The lump in her cheek grew bigger.

Chapter Twenty-Three

Norwood, 1900

With no one else to confide in, Katharine sometimes found herself turning to Antonio. So, she told him about the unexpected price rises. She could see the mist of incomprehension covering his eyes as she spoke; it made her feel selfish as well as lonely. It was wrong of her to burden the poor boy with problems he had no concept of.

Antonio, for his part, made no effort to hide his lack of interest.

'What are you going to do about it,' he asked, his eyes already on the river, planning a fishing trip or a swim.

'I'll just have to pay what Mac has asked for,' she replied, 'and keep working as hard as I can so that we still make some money.' Antonio was fidgeting, eager to be gone. 'It'll be all right in the end,' she concluded. She didn't want her son to worry. For once he had actually put in five hours of relatively concentrated studying that day. 'Run away and play now!'

Instantly, Antonio turned on his heels and fled to the riverbank, joining a bunch of his Indian friends by the water's edge.

'Get an *acari* for our supper,' called Katharine after him, smiling to herself as she saw the carefree way he moved, the swiftness of his gait, his relief at being free. No wonder he resented being tied to his school desk. Who wouldn't, with the whole vast jungle playground constantly beckoning?

Back at her desk, Katharine turned once more to her account books, which she had pored over all the previous evening. There were no magic formulae to make the sums add up. With Mac's new charges and the tax, it was more important than ever to keep all the *estradas* in production, the *seringueiros* tapping the latex and smoking it as fast as they could. The fact that she treated her tappers fairly, paying them well, not over-charging them for supplies, providing them with the benefits in kind that she had promised right at the beginning, meant that the money she made from one *bolacha* of dry, fine Pará was much less than that garnered by the unscrupulous rubber barons who ruled over most of the Amazon.

So many lives were lost in the pursuit of rubber. The forest workers often succumbed to accidents, to the multitude of local diseases, or to tribal rivalry. Many *seringueiros* became so lonely and depressed, living their lives in the melancholy, oppressive atmosphere of the deep forest, their huts on poles surrounded by flood water during the yearly inundations, that they committed suicide, killing themselves with the guns they were given for protection or, slower and more painful, drinking themselves to a lonely death. Only the favoured few lived long lives in the Amazon.

Thinking all of this rekindled Katharine's determination not to chase the quickest dollar, whatever the temptation. Her prin-ciples, as Charles had so often pointed out, had cost her dearly in financial terms. But while there was breath in her body, she would not give them up. Those in her employ could be sure of conditions that were as good as she could possibly provide – and never, ever would anyone be forced to labour on her land. Nothing would change that. She would not lower her standards for convenience's sake – not even to repay her father more quickly. Instinctively, she knew that he would not want that either.

Over the course of that afternoon and evening, as arranged, the *cubertas* arrived in ones, twos and threes at Norwood. Jonathan and Santiago oversaw the loading of the *bolachas*. Katharine was apprehensive at being without her key lieu-tenants for the two to three months that they would be away.

This was the first time the amount of rubber her *estradas* had produced had necessitated two supervisors to travel with it. They had been busy training up junior colleagues to cover their absence but it wouldn't be the same.

At first light, she bid the huge convoy farewell, waving them off until all had rounded the bend and disappeared out of sight. Even then, Katharine stood on the ridge above the beach, forlornly looking after them. Of course, it was good to be selling rubber, and so much of it – but she would miss them. Shaking herself off and giving herself a strict internal talking to, she was about to trudge back to her office and get to work when an *igarité* hove into view. Straining her eyes, she tried to see who was aboard but the sun-awning hid all the occupants except the Indian paddlers.

As she looked on, the boat bumped onto the beach and a man slowly unloaded himself, moving awkwardly as if his limbs were stiff from a long journey in cramped conditions. Katharine gazed down at him. There was something familiar in his stance, an unmistakeable arrogance about his posture. With a slow dawning of realisation, she understood who it was.

Mayhew.

Her long-lost brother who, having conquered North America, had arrived to take on the South.

He strolled up the beach towards her as if his arrival was nothing out of the ordinary and greeted her with a casual handshake.

'So, this is what you've been up to all these years?' he remarked. He was looking around with calculating eyes as he spoke, surveying the surroundings, as if adding up the sum worth of Norwood. 'Who would have thought my little sis had it in her?'

Bristling at his insinuation that she was incapable, Katharine swallowed down a sharp retort. He had got to Norwood far sooner than expected but now she wanted Mayhew's visit to be harmonious – and short! The best way to achieve that was to be welcoming and hospitable and for him to find out for himself precisely how dull life was here, and what hard work. Then, hopefully, he'd take himself off, back to America or Britain or anywhere where he couldn't bother her any longer. In the meantime, she was determined to bite her tongue, avoid altercations and encourage the good relationship between Mayhew and Antonio that she had envisaged. The boy needed a father figure and it would be beneficial for him to spend time with his uncle.

Katharine showed Mayhew around the various buildings that had been constructed over the years: the office, the storerooms and the guesthouse. Travellers were infrequent as far upriver as Norwood, but they did come, and when strangers arrived it was customary to welcome them in, providing them with accommodation and food. That was just how the Amazon worked. These days the scientists and plant-gatherers had been augmented by politicians, brought here by the constant vying for control of the region that was going on between Brazil and Bolivia. Fortunately, they had no one staying at the moment, so Mayhew could have the place to himself, which at least would keep him from being constantly under Katharine's feet.

'You don't have much luggage,' Katharine commented mildly, as she and Mayhew sat down for coffee at the end of their tour.

'There's another couple of canoes coming on behind mine,' Mayhew replied, waving a hand in the vague direction of the river. 'They've got my clobber, such as it is. And someone I've brought with me.' He tasted his coffee and almost spat it out. 'Don't you have any fresh milk instead of this damned condensed stuff?' he demanded, petulantly. 'I can't abide the taste.'

Katharine smiled. 'Look around you. Do you see any cows?'

Suitably silenced, Mayhew sipped at the coffee with a long-suffering air.

'So, who is this mystery companion?' Katharine asked. 'Someone from New York?' She assumed it must be a friend or acquaintance who wanted to take the opportunity to explore the Amazon, or maybe someone hoping to benefit from the rubber boom. There were always plenty of those.

'A manager,' stated Mayhew, baldly, his tone implying that this was all that needed to be said on the matter.

'A manager?' repeated Katharine, as if she didn't quite understand the word. 'Why are you bringing a manager?'

'For you,' Mayhew said. 'To help you out, bring some order to this operation.'

Katharine bowed her head over her steaming coffee cup and counted to ten slowly in her head. She felt as if she might explode. What right did Mayhew have to come here and instruct her on what she did or didn't need? He was acting as if he knew the first thing about her business, about the rubber business in general, which he most certainly did not.

'Mayhew, I appreciate your concern for my wellbeing,' she replied eventually, concentrating on modulating her tone of voice. 'But I don't need a manager. I'm *managing* perfectly well by myself with the help of my clerks and have done so for the last ten years.' She stressed the word *managing* to emphasise her capabilities. 'My Indian clerks,' she reiterated, to make sure that Mayhew understood that the native people were trustworthy, not the idle, thieving layabouts they were so often portrayed as.

'His name's Thomas Smart,' continued Mayhew, as if she hadn't spoken. 'Found him in Barbados looking for a job. Fine fellow, over six feet tall, strong as an ox, black as night. Family were slaves once upon a time, before abolition.'

Katharine greeted this information with a stunned silence. It was totally unexpected, and she had no idea how to react.

'Men like him are all the rage on the rubber estates, so I've heard,' said Mayhew, still taking no notice of Katharine's reaction – or lack of one. 'Skilled, literate and no strangers to hard work. Though I say it myself, I did rather well in recruiting him – and I think you're going to find that Mr Smart is the perfect solution for you, really get this little enterprise you've got here operating on another gear.'

Mayhew sat back with a satisfied smile and drained his mug of coffee, seeming to have forgotten his dislike of tinned milk.

–

It was late by the time the second and third canoe pulled up on the beach.

Katharine had walked down to the water to see the full moon reflected on the still surface of the river. It was absolutely flat tonight, a black mirror so smooth it seemed that she could walk across its surface right to the opposite bank. Ibis and sandpipers waded in the shallows and an egret, hanging on a thermal, suddenly swooped low and then, with a piercing call, disappeared into the night. The profuse white flowers of an orchid that garlanded the trunk of a Brazil nut tree glowed opalescent in the silvery moonlight.

The mosquitoes were out in force so Katharine had not taken a lamp, but the sky was cloudless, the moon and stars bright enough to see by. As she gazed upon the river that she knew so well, the canoes materialised out of the distant darkness, slowly developing into recognisable shapes.

Thomas Smart was the first person to step out. It could not be anyone else but him. He was exactly as Mayhew had described him, tall and well built, with an air of carefully conserved energy about him, as if at any moment he could out-sprint the wind. In the white light of the full moon his burnished skin glowed and his dark eyes pierced straight through her.

He stretched out his hand in greeting and Katharine responded. His grip was deft and assured, and as they shook, he smiled at her. Ex-slave or not, it was impossible to imagine this man being subservient to anyone.

'It's a pleasure to meet you,' he said.

'And you,' replied Katharine, working hard to present a demeanour of perfect composure. She had lived so long at

Norwood, barely meeting anyone new. This stranger's presence was unsettling, unnerving. She didn't know what to say to him.

'You are absolutely as your brother described you,' Thomas added, filling the silence.

A sudden, furious blush rose inexplicably on Katharine's cheeks. Turning abruptly to hide her face, Katharine gestured to Thomas to follow her.

'I'll show you to your accommodation,' she muttered, trying not to let him see how flustered she was. 'The men will bring your things. And tomorrow – well, tomorrow we'll discuss what you're doing here.'

As soon as the words were out, she realised how rude they must have sounded, but she was too confused and discombobulated to work out how to put the matter right, and annoyed with herself – and Mayhew for putting her in this awkward situation. Thomas seemed a fine fellow, exactly as Mayhew had said, and it was a pity she was going to have to send him away when he'd undertaken the long and arduous journey to get here in good faith. But she had neither asked for nor wanted a manager and so send him away she would.

'Here is your room.' She opened the door of the bedroom next to Mayhew's. 'Please make yourself comfortable.'

She was about to head straight back to her house when something made her falter. She turned around to find Thomas looking at her with his steady gaze and unfathomable eyes.

'Thank you, Mrs Ferrandis, for your hospitality,' he said, his voice deep and sonorous.

'Yes, well – you're very welcome, Mr Smart.' Katharine paused, fighting back another blush. '*Até amanhã* as they say in these parts. I'll see you in the morning.'

She managed a brief, uncertain smile in his direction before turning on her heels and walking as regally as she could over the rough, trampled ground to the house, conscious all the way of his eyes burning into her back.

168

Chapter Twenty-Four

A regular, rhythmic noise, the thud of the woodcutter's axe, woke Katharine the next day, filtering in and out of her dream as she surfaced from unconsciousness. The unsettled feeling of the night before still lingered, but was gradually soothed by the regular morning sounds of the cockerels crowing, the Indian women talking as they prepared food for their families' breakfasts, and the little children laughing and playing. Outside her window, hummingbirds thronged around profusions of orange blossom, and patches of dappled sunlight shone a morning welcome. She rolled out of bed, dressed quickly and went outside to greet the new day.

Rounding the corner of her house, she looked to see which of the Indians was chopping the logs; it was a least favourite task and one that rarely got done without specific orders. But it was not an Indian. The man wielding the axe, letting it fall with perfect, arcing motions, was Thomas. His chest was bare and a slick of sweat covered his back; it glistened in the sun and accentuated muscles hard as rock.

Katharine was almost too embarrassed to look. She hadn't a clue why he had taken it upon himself to do this chore, though was grateful that he had, as the woodpile was woefully low right now. The fires were kept constantly burning, not just for cooking, but also for drying laundry, for the heat of the flames was the only way to banish the pervasive dampness that seeped into everything. But Thomas was supposed to be a manager and above such menial labouring work. And anyway, she had been about to send him packing.

Pausing to wipe his brow, Thomas caught sight of her watching him.

'Good morning, Mrs Ferrandis,' he called, seeming perfectly at ease. 'I saw your firewood stash was somewhat depleted, so I decided to help out. I woke so early I needed to do something, and after so many weeks sitting in a canoe, some exercise was essential.'

Katharine moved slowly towards him, not wanting to shout across the compound. 'That was a very kind thought, Mr Smart,' she said, 'but you really didn't need to. And you can't even have had any breakfast yet; I'll get Rosabel to make you some.'

Thomas smiled and stretched out his arms. 'That would be marvellous,' he replied. 'I am rather hungry.' He leant the axe against the hut wall and gathered together the last few logs he had cut, stacking them carefully inside. 'And afterwards – perhaps you can take me through the essentials and give me a map of the *estradas*. I'd like to get straight out into the forest, check on whether they're all being tapped efficiently, how much of the latex is lost during transportation or washed away in the rains. I've brought a prototype of a new collecting cup I picked up in Manaus that looks very promising to reduce wastage…' Thomas tapered off, noticing Katharine's lack of response.

'Oh.' Katharine was at a loss for words. Thomas was so interested, and knowledgeable. He'd clearly done his homework on the rubber industry and knew far more than she had imagined.

'But of course,' Thomas said, 'you must tell me what you would most like me to do, what would be most useful. My enthusiasm gets the better of me – but it's your business. You must instruct.'

'Yes, umm, definitely,' muttered Katharine.

Thomas' candour, combined with his energy and obvious capability, had taken the wind out of her sails. Maybe she had been too hasty in thinking she must dismiss him immediately.

Perhaps it would be worth giving him a trial period – three or six months – and then reviewing the situation after that. Apart from anything else, he seemed to have taken it for granted that the job was his and had already set about settling into it, and Katharine didn't think she had the heart to disabuse him of that understanding.

And so, Thomas stayed and almost immediately proved himself indispensable, not just as an employee but also as a friend. For Katharine it was miraculous to at last have such a person in her midst. For all she trusted and relied upon Jonathan and Santiago, they were very different to her, their culture and traditions totally separate. Not only that, they had their own families, their own lives and though Katharine was never excluded from them, she could never truly be a part of them either.

Thomas was different. He had not had many years of formal education, but he had grown up reading anything he could get his hands on – books, papers, periodicals – and was there-fore conversant on world affairs, aware of people and places far removed from their Amazonian home, which often felt so remote as to be a hermitage. Though the place he had come from was as different from Clerkenwell as it possibly could be, he appeared to Katharine as her equal and her respect for him and his abilities grew by the day.

Over the next few weeks and months, Katharine taught Thomas every aspect of the business, going over maps of the estate, explaining about how transportation was arranged and shipping organised. She told him about Mac's cripplingly expensive terms for crossing the isthmus, as well as the payments she had had to make for the scuppered steamer, which were only just coming to an end. Thomas' attention and interest were unwavering, his suggestions unfailingly measured and valuable. In addition to Thomas' assiduity, for all the things about Mayhew that irritated Katharine, he had turned out to be something of a godsend, taking it upon himself to be exactly the father figure to Antonio that Katharine had envisaged. The boy doted on his uncle and didn't display to him any of the sulks or stubbornness that he so often dealt out to Katharine. Everything seemed to be happy and harmonious, for the time being at least.

So much so that Katharine decided to take a trip to market in a settlement about two hours by canoe upriver. It was a place that, when Katharine had first arrived at Norwood, had been nothing but a small *seringueiro* outpost. Over the years, as more and more people flooded into the area, it had developed into a sizeable town, even boasting a resident Spanish pharmacist who was the first to bring modern medicine to the region.

Katharine needed to go; she had completely run out of reading material and she knew that an English gentleman who lived even further upriver would be there and would bring books and periodicals for her. Even if the magazines were two years out of date, she didn't care. She needed words, stories, news, to keep herself from going mad. She asked Thomas if he would accompany her, telling him that as they journeyed along the river they would see much of her land and he would be able to get his bearings for when he ventured into the forest himself.

The town was bustling, the market already in full swing when they arrived, with canoes, launches and *igarités* jostling for mooring space all along the waterfront. As soon as they had disembarked, Katharine and Thomas were swallowed up by the crowd, frequently being forced apart as they tried to navigate through the hordes.

'What's going on over there?' asked Thomas, when they found themselves in slightly calmer spot for a moment. He pointed towards a pool of eager shoppers gathered around a podium. All around them was noise, people talking, children wailing, chickens clucking, goats bleating and, above it all, the auctioneer's patter ringing out.

Katharine had a sinking feeling in her stomach. 'I think it's a sl… an auction.' She couldn't bring herself to say the word 'slave' in front of Thomas. Who knew what effect that word would have on him, how much he and his family, in generations past and probably still today, had suffered from the whole awful business of slavery and its aftermath?

'An auction of what?' questioned Thomas, quietly insistent.

Katharine steeled herself. 'I think they're selling children. They – people, I don't know who – they raid the tribes' home-lands and take them from their mothers when they're really small, just babies. They bring them up until they are around eight, or ten, or twelve, and then they sell them as servants, or rubber workers.'

Katharine had heard the appalling stories, of infants torn screaming from their wailing mothers' arms, of the brutality they often faced during their upbringing and when sold to new masters. She abhorred everything about it. But, like many nefarious practices, it was rife throughout the Amazon.

'Servants.' Thomas said the word as both a statement and an accusation. 'People treated like animals.'

'I know,' replied Katharine, softly. 'I hate it, too.'

They moved closer to the podium. A small procession of boys and girls for sale moved across it. Some were frightened and crying but others looked utterly emotionless, as if they had given up caring what happened to them. Boys went for more than girls – the going rate seemed to be about £50 for a male, £40 for a girl – a lot of money in either case. Katharine shuddered at the thought of how much toil and servitude would be expected of these poor mites to make good on that level of investment.

A small girl was pulled up onto the podium. Her hair was matted into ragged knots and her face besmirched with mud and snot. It was impossible to tell her exact age through the dirt, and she was dreadfully thin. Yet Katharine could still see that she was on the cusp of puberty, small breast buds outlined by her thin, skimpy clothing. The girl trembled, half hiding her face behind her hands until her seller grabbed them away, revealing a sad pair of eyes that glistened with unshed tears. Her expression seemed to hold within it all the pain she had endured since being separated from her family.

Katharine's heart ached for the child, who reminded her of little Esperanza, Mac's servant who had not been at Lagona on her last visit but instead had vanished without trace, or of Mabel. Her heart lurched as she remembered her little sister's face when she had bid her farewell all those years ago, how sadness and uncertainty had been etched upon it as she waved solemnly to Katharine and Anselmo's departing train. Only Mary and Bill had gone all the way to the port at Southampton to see the couple off, so those glimpses of Mabel on the station platform had been Katharine's last.

It had been such a wrench to leave, and Katharine knew how Mabel had dreaded her sister's departure. How much worse for the tiny children of the Amazon, wrested from their families, enduring such unimaginable loss and heartbreak. Katharine felt that Mabel would not survive it – and this small girl seemed to be hanging to life only by the most brittle of threads. For their mothers, too, the agony was incomprehensible. Mary would never have got over one of her children being snatched away like this. But it happened to the forest women all the time.

The bidding for the girl was laconic, just a few hands raised to start things off. Katharine scrutinised the bidders. There was a Brazilian man she vaguely recognised as owning extensive lands about three days' journey from Norwood, but the other two she didn't know at all. Of these, one was staring eagerly at the child, a lascivious expression plastered onto his red and pock-marked face. Katharine felt a sudden flush of revulsion. She had seen that look before on a certain type of man and it repelled her. Her imagination saw him pawing lecherously at the girl, doing unspeakable things to her, disregarding completely her fear and cries of distress. She glanced from the man to the girl and back again and something about his leering mouth and beady eyes compelled her to action.

'Thirty!' Her hand had shot up and the bid been made before she had time to think about it.

Thomas looked at her in astonishment. And then, seeing the anger in her gaze and the firm set of her mouth he seemed to understand what she understood and to know, without any explanation, what she was doing and why.

As the auctioneer cast around for rival bids, Katharine also looked anxiously about her, sizing up the competition. She was reminded of why she so rarely ventured out and why she did not fraternise with the rubber community in her isolated, lawless neighbourhood. The more she saw of some of the other settlers in the area, the less she liked, so she stayed at home and left others to their sins. She had no desire to mix with men who used their money and power to buy children like they would an animal, and to use them however they pleased.

'Thirty-five pounds.' The sleazy man had made a counter bid.

Katharine saw the look of anguish on the little girl's face, the fear of the unknown fate that awaited her, the terror of what the future held. It was already a good price for so scrawny a girl and he seemed prepared to go higher. There could only be one reason why he was so keen to get his hands on her. Katharine would have to beat him at his own game.

'Thirty-eight,' she shouted out, making sure her voice was loud enough to be heard above the constant murmur of the crowd. She could feel Thomas beside her, silently approving.

Katharine's opponent faltered.

'Thirty-nine,' he called, but his tone was nowhere near as definite as it had been.

'Fifty.' Katharine injected her voice with an air of what she hoped was indisputable finality. Her bid broke all the rules of auctions, going up far too much in one jump, and the sum she had put forward was way more than anyone in their right mind would pay. But she wasn't buying a slave to add to her collection but instead to save the child from a fate worse than death.

The sleazy man dropped his hands to his sides, shrugged as if it was no matter, and slunk away. Katharine almost laughed. It was that easy. Cash was king. He who pays the piper calls the tune… She went to hand over the money and collect the child. Kneeling beside her in the mud, amidst all the people and the chickens and the pigs, she took the girls' gaunt hands in hers. Her fingers were skin and bone.

'What's your name?' she asked.

'Fortunata,' muttered the girl, almost inaudibly.

Fortunate. How horribly inappropriate, like a cruel joke, thought Katharine. She said as much to Thomas.

'But you have saved her now,' he pointed out.

'I suppose so,' responded Katharine. 'But I can't give her back to her parents, can I? I can't take her back to her tribe, to her people. I don't know who they are, or where. And it would be impossible to find out, in this vast wilderness where no one keeps records of anything. She will always have that loss in her life.'

Fortunata's skin was dry and mottled and her lips dreadfully chapped, and Katharine was sure she was dehydrated as well as malnourished. She offered her the water gourd but Fortunata wouldn't drink deeply, taking only small sips when urged, casting fearful glances at Katharine as she did so as if waiting to be punished.

Later, their business done, they ate at a small water-side restaurant. Here, Fortunata succumbed to her hunger, ravenously stuffing the food into her mouth and then promptly vomiting it all back up again. Thomas cleaned her up and soothed her crying, handling her so gently, with such tender confidence that Katharine felt her own efforts to comfort the girl clumsy and inept. He was huge and strong and could probably kill a man with his bare hands but far from being violent, or bitter about the past, he exuded kindness. Perhaps there was hope that Fortunata, too, could overcome her terrible start in life.

A group of elderly but rowdy white men, speaking English with American accents, came in and took the table next to them. Fortunata flinched away from them. Katharine wondered what associations the child made with such people. Thomas' demeanour had also changed, a look of utter hostility covering not only his face but also the set of his shoulders and the rigidity of his back. Katharine glanced back at the men and then at Thomas.

'What's wrong?' she asked, quietly.

Thomas indicated towards the group with a sneer and a flick of his head. 'Confederados,' he muttered, as if barely able to form the word.

Katharine's brow furrowed quizzically. 'How do you know?'

'I just know,' stated Thomas in a voice that brooked no argument. 'They came here to Brazil, many of them, after they lost in the civil war, unable to accept an America without slavery. I suppose they thought that here in this inhospitable terrain their evil habits and beliefs would go unnoticed.'

The bill paid, they headed back to the canoe. Thomas strode on ahead, his body full of animosity. Katharine wasn't sure if the hostility was directed at her, the Confederados or her impulse purchase. He had seemed to be on her side during the auction, but since then had barely said a word in her direction.

Fortunata fell asleep almost as soon as they were underway, and then Katharine knew she had to broach the subject with Thomas.

'What's wrong?' she asked, gently. 'You seem to be displeased with me and I'm not sure why.'

Thomas let out a long hiss of air from flared nostrils. 'Not you, Mrs Ferrandis. Not you at all.' He paused and then flung his arm wide as if embracing the entire Amazon. 'It's this. Slavery, alive and kicking, when it was supposedly abolished years ago. People who cannot recognise its evil. I have lived with the consequences of the slave trade, seen its trauma in the eyes of my parents and grandparents. I thought that they would be the last, that no other peoples of the world would have to suffer the way my forebears did.'

He looked at Fortunata, curled up in the bottom of the canoe.

'But it seems the subjugation of the weak by the strong will never end. While there are oppressors, there will be the oppressed.'

Katharine's heart broke for Thomas, so noble and proud, but still capable of being bowed by the legacy of slavery, and for Fortunata, so innocent and vulnerable. It broke for Esperanza and all the stolen children of the Amazon. She wanted to save all three of them, to save the whole world.

But of course, that was impossible.

Chapter Twenty-Five

London, 1900

At the end her first day's work, Mabel was so tired that she almost crawled up the many flights of stairs to her attic bedroom. It was cold, with bare floorboards and a tiny window with grubby, ill-fitting panes of glass that looked out on an endless array of grey slate rooftops. The iron bedstead's mattress was lumpy and damp, the sheet and blanket mended so often it was hard to find a square inch without darning stitches. But nevertheless, Mabel sank gratefully into bed and lay down, unable to muster the strength to undress. Huddling into the covers, pulling them tight around her, she shut her eyes and tried to squeeze back the tears.

She had to be strong, she had to get through this. She thought of her sister, deep in the Amazonian jungle, the trials and tribulations she had faced since setting sail all those years ago. If Katharine could survive and overcome all the dangers and difficulties she had encountered, then Mabel must also be able to. But just then, lonely and cold and exhausted to her very bones, it was hard to summon the courage to believe she would ever get used to this new life.

She clasped her hands together and glanced down. Even in the gloom, she could see dark spots staining the white sheet. Blood was oozing from her fingers, which had been virtually skinned by the caustic substance she had been given by Cook to scour the pots and pans. Her fingertips throbbed, her knuckles were red raw and the worst thing was that she was going to have to put her hands through the same torture again the next day. And the next. Her knees, too, were agony; when she was not washing dishes she was on all fours, scrubbing and polishing, the floors, the outside steps, the passageways, the hearths and fireplaces… There was nothing in this house that didn't seem to require her ministrations and all the elbow grease she could muster. Everything ached: her limbs, her bones, her soul.

At that moment, Mabel's life stretched out before her, an endless grey monotony interspersed with pain. Her mother had always taught her that self-pity was indulgent and unallowable. But Mabel couldn't help but feel sorry for herself as tears trickled down her cheeks and she wondered how she would get through another day, let alone a lifetime.

The next morning, she jumped awake, sure she had over-slept. She trembled, imagining Cook's wrath, being summoned before the mistress – whom she had only briefly met at an inter-view in the employment agency offices – and given her notice for slacking. Leaping out of bed, she looked frantically around for her clothes and then remembered that she was wearing them all. Shivering, she rubbed her arms with her sore hands and moved towards the door. As she put her hand upon the door handle, a church bell sounded four long, sonorous chimes.

Four a.m.! She'd got up an hour early. She stumbled back to her bed and half lay, half sat upon it, dozing fitfully until the five o'clock bells rang. Dragging herself up again, she hauled her weary legs and tired body down the stairs to work.

A few hours later, crawling on her hands and knees the length of the long, wide hallway, smoothing the fringe of the rug so that every strand was absolutely straight, Mabel found herself convinced that this was the most pointless, sadistic of all the tasks that anyone could be asked to perform. Every day it had to be done, after she'd whitened the front steps until they were gleaming.

Then she had to clean the drawing room, which was stuffed full of heavy, dark furniture and tables covered in ornaments.

First, she had to sweep the floor and clear the grate, then leave the room for fifteen minutes for the dust and soot to settle before going back to complete the task. The rule was to start on the right-hand side of the door and work all the way around until she got back to the left. The room was huge and this took ages, and though it had a large window and should therefore have been full of light, in front of the glass and almost totally obscuring it was a miniature forest of potted plants. A strange earthy smell always filled the air and Mabel hated dusting the thick, unwieldy foliage, imagining that, if she tripped, the leaves would swallow her up and consume her so that she would never be seen or heard of again.

Once this despised chore had been completed, and assuming she was not incarcerated in the deathly embrace of a Swiss cheese plant, she moved on to the rest of the fireplaces, the downstairs ones first and, when the mistress was having breakfast, those in the bedrooms. The handle of the ash pail had slipped out of its anchor on one side so she had to carry it clutched to her bosom. This meant her hands weren't free to hold anything else and so involved twice as many trips up and down stairs.

By mid-morning, it was into the kitchen to help Cook prepare the dinner, endlessly peeling and chopping vegetables. Tedious in the extreme but better than what came after – the washing-up. Then more cleaning, more meal preparation, more scrubbing dishes.

The first days of Mabel's employment all went like this. Already she thought that she could not bear it.

There was no one to talk to as she went about her work. Apart from Cook, there was only one other indoor servant, a lad called Joe, whose jobs included fetching the coal and carrying the scuttles up the many staircases, as well as cleaning the shoes, answering the door to tradespeople when Cook was too busy and various other odd jobs such as going to fetch a hansom cab when the mistress wanted to go out shopping or visiting. An old man named Mr Harrison worked mainly outside, cleaning the windows and tending to the extensive garden, but he didn't live in. Cook's room Mabel never saw but Joe's lay on the half-landing up to the attic and was even more barren and miserable than Mabel's. It had three external walls and a flat roof that must leak badly, for when Mabel glanced inside on her way upstairs, she saw big, mouldy damp patches on the wall, lurking like beasts ready to pounce.

It was breakfast on the sixth day before Mabel heard Joe speak.

'That ash pail,' he said, in a voice that sounded husky from lack of use, 'I've mended the handle.'

Tears sprang to Mabel's eyes. 'Thank you,' she muttered, overcome with a gratitude that far exceeded what was necessary. It was such a small kindness – but so completely unexpected. 'Thank you very much.'

The words were out before Mabel remembered the nanny next door and the footmen; presumably you weren't supposed to thank someone lower in the pecking order than yourself. She caught Cook's quick glance of disapproval. But it was too late to take it back, and it was polite to say 'please' and 'thank you'. That's what she'd been brought up to believe, anyway.

Joe was a workhouse boy who ate all his food at triple speed, as if he were expecting it to disappear before he'd had a chance to gobble it up. He eats as if he's never seen a proper meal before, Mabel thought, and then acknowledged that this was probably exactly the case, given where he'd come from. Servants from those institutions were cheap, badly paid and poorly treated, because employers knew they wouldn't leave. They had nowhere else to go.

'I'm lucky,' Mabel told herself sternly. 'I have a loving family, a home, a happy childhood to look back on. How dare I complain and moan? I'm a thousand times better off than Joe.'

Shoring herself up with these brisk words, she set to cleaning the silver cutlery, yet another of the repetitive, monotonous tasks that now took up her time. Day after day went by in a flurry of fetching and carrying, cleaning and laundering, sweeping and polishing. Mabel tried to keep smiling but it was hard to be always bright and sanguine when the mistress and Cook seemed to constantly find fault, not just with her work but with everything about her.

One Wednesday morning, having been asked to serve at the lunch table, Mabel traipsed up and down the stairs with dish after dish of meat, vegetables and sauces and reflected that at least when the servants ate, their food was hot. By the time she'd got everything into the dining room singlehanded, the first lot would probably be stone cold.

Waiting at table under the scrutiny of all the diners was a nerve-wracking experience, with so many rules of etiquette to follow – curtsey before leaving, go out backwards to avoid turning your back on your superiors, never utter so much as a word. Mabel chewed and chewed at the lump in her cheek with the effort of remembering it all.

'Oy,' Cook snapped on her fourth or fifth return to the kitchen for yet more dishes. 'Stop making that strange face. Mistress will think you're being rude or cheeky or something.'

Abruptly, Mabel stopped the chewing. Immediately, her tongue flicked towards the place and found the lump, examining it.

'I said, cut it out!' Cook was really cross now, or perhaps just anxious to ensure Mabel didn't attract the ire of the mistress, which would, inevitably, backfire onto her.

'Yes, yes, sorry, I'm sorry,' stuttered Mabel. She felt three years old, scolded for picking her nose or wiping it with the back of her hand or some other disgusting habit.

Steeling herself, she went back up the two flights of stairs to the dining room. She knew, and had already been told, that yet another rule decreed that you must never look your employers in the eye. Nevertheless, she couldn't help casting a quick glance towards her mistress: an elderly woman, around fifty-five Mabel reckoned, but she looked older. She was tiny, much shorter than Mabel, but she was swathed in so much fabric from her multi-layered elaborate clothing – velvet, brocade, taffeta – that she appeared to be as wide as she was high. She wore strings of jewellery that Mabel assumed were family heirlooms. There couldn't be any other reason for adorning oneself with items that were so ugly and heavy and old-fashioned. Extraordinary attire, Mabel thought, for the daytime, but who was she to judge? She was nothing but a lowly servant, who many of the higher classes ranked on a par with dumb animals.

Master was not there, presumably at work. Mabel rarely saw him, and when she did, the impression she got was of sinister massiveness. He was tall, fat and always clothed in a black suit, with a thick black overcoat and top hat for when he went out. When he was around, his dark shadow seemed to loom over every corner of the house. Mabel already knew that he and his wife didn't share a bedroom, let alone a bed. She didn't know if this was usual or not, just considered her employers lucky to have so much space just for them. In Clerkenwell, Mabel shared with two of her siblings and many families, poorer than the Birds, lived in only one or two rooms for everyone, up to twelve people crammed claustrophobically together. But on the other hand, she thought with an inward ironic laugh, if the mistress wore as many layers at night as she did in the day then that, combined with the master's bulk, would mean one bed wouldn't be big enough for the both of them.

Forcing herself to concentrate on her task, Mabel placed the last platters on the table as delicately as she could. Shame over her scabby, calloused hands, combined with the disdainful expression that always came over Cook's face when she caught sight of them, meant that Mabel wore cotton gloves when doing anything that brought her into the presence of company.

But they made gripping things harder, especially if they got wet, and on her final exit from the room, she not only collided with an occasional table, sending photo frames and knick-knacks flying, but also lost hold of the empty serving bowl she'd been taking away. The clatter of falling objects combined with the dull thud of the dish upon the floorboards were like the rattle of gunshot about her ears. Mabel's heart stopped momentarily as she fell to her sore knees and desperately scrabbled around for the scattered items.

'Hurry up!' commanded the mistress, in a voice so deep Mabel at first thought it was a man. 'You are completely ruining our meal with your clumsiness.'

'S-s-sorry,' stuttered Mabel. Terrified and gasping for breath, she staggered to her feet and this time got through the door in one piece.

Later, Cook called her down to the kitchen.

Now I'm for it, thought Mabel, bracing herself for a stern dressing down for being so ham-fisted. But instead, it was another infraction that she was found guilty of.

'The mistress wants you to act more modestly next time you wait on table.'

Bewilderment engulfed Mabel's mind. More modestly? In what way, exactly, had she been immodest?

'I'm not sure what you mean,' she said, doubtfully. 'What the mistress means.'

Cook tutted in irritation. 'There was an occasion when you did not curtsey. And you spoke in front of both your employer and her guests.'

Mabel lowered her eyes. Cardinal sins, both, it was clear.

'You were *noticed*, Mabel, when you should be invisible.' Cook's emphasis on the word 'noticed' made it sound like Mabel had performed some kind of vaudeville act in the staid and stuffy surrounds of the dining room. 'You realise how unacceptable this is?'

'Of course,' Mabel murmured. She had no idea how it was possible to be invisible but looking for logic or further explanations would get her nowhere.

Hateful, hateful job. Tears stinging her eyes, she marched back up to the third floor and stabbed her feather duster at picture frames and ornaments with an aggression she couldn't hide. She could not see how any of this was ever going to get any better. The gloves that had let her down so badly she'd discarded, shoved into the deep pockets of the dress that Mary had made. Mabel looked down at her hands. She hated the bloodied skin, the split knuckles, the badly-healing blisters. Though she was not vain, and rarely looked in a mirror, she was used to being loved, to being told she was lovely and loveable, and to being praised for what she did well. These things were part of her identity, what made her Mabel Bird – but she seemed to have left them all behind when she had come to live in Brampton Square. The sorry state of her poor hands symbolised everything she had lost and made her feel lonelier than ever.

She wanted to go home, to find her mother and hold her tight, or to write to Katharine, defying her mother's ban on her sister being told the truth, and hear her wise words of advice and encouragement.

But she couldn't tell anyone what she was feeling. It was nobody's fault that she'd had to take this job, just dad's rotten bad luck to have that terrible accident, and even if Katharine suddenly bestowed on them a fortune, she wouldn't resign. She'd never want to be a scrounger. It was right and proper to work for your living – everyone else at Hawthorn Road had to, and moaning about it would not only do no good but also make her seem lazy and begrudging or as if she somehow thought she was worthy of special treatment. Mabel was old enough to contribute to the family purse now – more than old enough; many girls started in service aged eleven or twelve. She just had to knuckle down and get on with it.

However hard it was.

Chapter Twenty-Six

Not long after the purchase of Fortunata at the auction, Jonathan and Santiago returned, triumphant, having sold all the rubber at an excellent price. They'd spent most of the proceeds on paying a mass of bills and debts, but on Katharine's instructions had also wired a small sum to London. On hearing this news, Katharine breathed a sigh of relief. She was plagued by a constant feeling of guilt at the length of time it was taking to repay her father and although her mother's letters revealed nothing untoward, she had a sixth sense that something was wrong. Nevertheless, the sending of the money meant she went to bed on the night of their return more contented than she had been for many years.

Meanwhile, as the days, weeks and months passed, Thomas was becoming more and more invaluable. Katharine could not imagine what she had done without him. He was full of interesting plans, considered opinions, new strategies, and they spent many enjoyable hours discussing business, batting ideas and suggestions around. Secretly pleasing, though, was that her command of maths was better than his. Katharine didn't want her manager to outclass her in absolutely everything.

The flies in the ointment – and there were no shortage of them in the Amazon at any rate – were Mayhew, Antonio and little Fortunata. Antonio would be ten at the end of the year, Fortunata two or three years older, Katharine reckoned. She had grown no taller and was barely any fatter than when Katharine

187

had rescued her, and still regularly ate dirt, an inexplicable habit that was common amongst the forest Indians, especially children and pregnant women. Katharine had tried to find out why they did this, but no one knew, not even the Spanish pharmacist who lived in the town where the slave auction had been held, nor any other passing doctor or scientist she had quizzed about it over the years.

Antonio, on the other hand, was a tall and stocky lad who looked older than he was and whose temper was not improving with the years. He was often obstreperous and difficult, and Katharine was beginning to despair of how to cope with him.

And added to that was Mayhew. While she valued the time he spent with Antonio, he was increasingly becoming an irritant to Katharine. He complained constantly about the food, the house, the Indians, the forest, the isolation. Katharine often looked at him, amazed at how little they had in common even though they were of the same flesh and blood. Having brought Thomas here and imposed him on Katharine and her business he seemed to be oddly jealous of the man, frequently admonishing him and trying to muscle in on plans she and Thomas were hatching. What made him even more annoying was that, when he did put forward ideas for the business, they were invariably rather good ones, revealing a level of business acumen that Katharine hadn't realised her brother possessed.

It made everything worse to have to concede that Mayhew, on occasion, was right.

One night after supper, Katharine and Mayhew were sitting in the sparsely furnished open-sided living area of the main house. Mayhew was being particularly aggravating, constantly shifting in his chair and muttering, exclaiming about what he was reading in the three-month-old Manaus newspaper, and obviously wanting to evince some kind of response from Katharine, which she was equally determined not to give him. She just wanted to read quietly with the familiar night sounds of the jungle to keep her company.

She became aware of Mayhew looking critically around him, as if sizing up the setting, the room and the dark river beyond, the forest surrounding everything like the sides of a stage set.

'I don't know how you can live here,' he blurted out.

Katharine smiled. She wanted to say something rude in retort but resisted the urge, instead trying to humour him. 'As I've told you before, I've grown used to it. I like it.'

'It's not suitable for the boy.' Mayhew made this fact sound incontrovertible.

Annoyance rose up and Katharine clenched her fists tightly. 'What do you mean?'

'He's not being educated. He's learning nothing. You're a woman of status now, you've climbed the social ladder. But he'll stay right at the bottom where we both started if you don't get him an education.'

Mayhew lit a cigar and a cloud of noxious smoke surged towards Katharine. She batted it away. It smelt artificial, a vile human invention in a place where the natural scents of the forest should reign unchallenged.

'Think about it. You know I'm right.'

Mayhew's pomposity knew no bounds.

Katharine sighed. 'All right, I'll think about it.' She paused. Mayhew didn't know how heavily worries about Antonio weighed on her mind. When she spoke again, she made it sound as if something had just occurred to her.

'I've an idea,' she cried, excitedly. 'Why don't you relocate to Manaus? You could be Norwood Enterprises' representative there. Since I got rid of the *aviador*, I've run things from here but now we are making serious money, I really could do with someone on the spot. And it would save Jonathan and Santiago from always having to make the journey downriver with the rubber.'

Mayhew's expression changed in an instant. Katharine could see him evaluating her words, considering them, working out if Katharine's suggestion was a trick. He always assigned the worst

189

of motives to anyone, presumably, Katharine thought, because that was how he himself operated.

'You are absolutely right, my dear sister.' Mayhew suddenly seemed quite overcome with the delightful nature of the plan. 'What a brilliant idea!'

Katharine had to hold back a cheer. Mayhew was supremely aggravating, but for their mother and father's sake, she would always stand by him. And his innate love of money and success would mean that he'd make sure that Norwood Enterprises thrived – he wanted the rewards as much as – if not more than – any of the rest of them. In Manaus he would, quite truthfully, be an asset to her.

She could see him thinking it all through, his eyes bright and calculating. 'I'll go right away.'

'So soon?' she replied, surprising herself with how genuine she managed to sound.

'Oh yes, no time like the present.'

Katharine could hear the cogs whirring in his mind, imagining the house he'd have, the life of decadence he'd lead.

'I need to have everything in place for your next shipment,' Mayhew continued. 'Not a moment to lose.'

'Well, if you really feel you must go straight away…' Katharine let the words trail away as if too sad to finish the sentence, somehow managing to keep a straight face.

'I really must,' affirmed Mayhew, with an air of finality. 'I know you'll miss me but it's for the best. I'll organise a canoe for the day after tomorrow and get the hell out of this god-forsaken place.'

He disappeared off to find Jonathan and arrange his transport and Katharine allowed herself a little giggle. Standing up to stretch her legs, she caught sight of a shadow beside the staircase. It was Thomas'.

She went towards him and he jumped guiltily backwards.

'I'm sorry, Mrs Ferrandis,' he apologised. 'I didn't mean to pry, I was at the top of the stairs when you started to talk and then I felt that things were of a sensitive nature so I shouldn't interrupt and then suddenly I'd heard everything.'

It was the first time Katharine had ever seen him flustered.

'Well, Mr Smart, what can I say?' Katharine tried to look and sound stern but couldn't suppress the smile that broke across her face. 'You are really very... very... imperti... impertinent,' and then, before she could say more, she started to laugh. Astonished at first, Thomas stared at her. Then, after catching her eye, he seemed to suddenly get the joke and began to laugh with her and soon they were both holding their sides and roaring with irrepressible mirth.

When they were finally able to speak again, Katharine leant towards Thomas and whispered, 'I know it's awful of me to feel so, but I'm so glad he's going. I can't be myself when he's around, putting me down and treating me like the incompetent little sister.'

Thomas nodded, conspiratorially. 'I agree that a representative in Manaus is exactly what you need, Mrs Ferrandis. It can't come a moment too soon.'

'Please call me Katharine,' she said, 'and I will call you Thomas. We know each other well enough to do away with the formalities of Mr and Mrs by now.'

Thomas smiled and inclined his head gracefully towards her in acceptance of her offer.

Once Mayhew's decision had been made, and even more so after his departure twenty-four hours later, Katharine felt liberated, as if she had been given a new lease of life. She walked with a spring in her step and approached all her daily tasks with an alacrity that had been lacking of late.

The worry that remained was that of her son's reaction to his uncle's sudden absence. To make sure he didn't have too much time on his hands for fretting, she decided that Antonio should go with Thomas on his next trip into the interior, to some *estradas* that were not proving as fruitful as they should. It was planned to take place after Christmas and his birthday, in the new year, and Katharine anticipated their absence with equal amounts of enthusiasm and dread. It would be so quiet at Norwood, just her and the Indians.

The night before they left, she and Thomas stayed up late putting together the route for the journey, finalising the *estradas* Thomas would survey and the list of *seringueiros* he should expect to see there. Several Indian porters would go with them, carrying supplies for the tappers and gifts for their families, strings of beads and squares of fabric, small toys for the children.

'That's it,' sighed Katharine eventually, passing the hand-drawn map to Thomas. 'You see that section there? That's your last port of call. All the Indians going with you know the area well. You won't get lost.'

A silence descended. The lantern glowed on the table between them, lighting Thomas' eyes so that the whites seemed whiter and the irises darker than ever. His skin gleamed, and his kind face was drawn into an expression of intense concentration as he stared from the map up to Katharine.

'On the contrary, Mrs Ferrandis,' he said, his voice even lower and more sonorous than usual. 'I think I will be very lost indeed.'

Katharine stared at him, forehead furrowed in puzzlement. Why had he gone back to the 'Mrs' moniker already? And what did he mean about being lost?

'I assure you that your companions are experienced, as well as being local,' she reiterated, 'so I'm not sure I know what you mean.'

But even as the words were spoken, she realised that she did know, that she understood perfectly. And that this under-standing had existed between them for some time, and had grown and grown until finally, now, Thomas had not been able to keep it in any longer.

Very slowly, and very carefully, Thomas moved the lantern from where it lay between them and placed it out of the way. He reached out and took her hands in his. All her life, Katharine had felt her hands too large, too angular, too clumsy, too masculine. But now, cradled in Thomas' deft and dexterous grasp, they felt fragile and delicate, and in turn she felt precious and desired in a way that even Anselmo had never made her feel.

There was complete silence in the wooden office. For a moment Katharine couldn't hear the forest, the frogs and bats and birds and insects. All she could hear was Thomas' breathing, and her own, quickened with desire.

'You're so beautiful,' he whispered.

She gave a small half-smile in response. 'No, I'm not. Really I'm not.'

Thomas shook his head, refusing to give in. 'Beauty comes as much from the inside, Mrs Ferrandis,' he said. 'Therefore you are beautiful beyond measure.'

The compliment was so unexpected and so lyrical that Katharine was still revelling in it as Thomas leant forward, finding her mouth with his and kissing her with hard, purposeful lips. The kiss brought stirrings to Katharine's belly that she had long forgotten.

They kissed for a long, long time, and it was only when they finally released each other, starry eyed with the novelty and the joy, that it suddenly struck Katharine what she had done. How wrong it was, how completely and unutterably not allowed, that a widow should hanker after an employee, that a white woman should kiss a Black man.

And yet...

She could not deny, at the same time could not put into words, even to herself, how much she felt for Thomas. How she had, quietly and unobtrusively, over all these weeks and months, been falling in love. And now she knew that he felt the same.

She looked at him and he at her, their gaze locked together in the half-darkness.

Then she leapt up, suddenly, knocking the lamp over and extinguishing it, plunging them into obscurity. Feeling her way, navigating by instinct and knowledge of her surroundings, she fumbled unsteadily to the door and fled.

This couldn't be. It absolutely couldn't be.

Chapter Twenty-Seven

London, 1900

Reading the latest letter from Katharine, Mabel sighed deeply. She felt terrible for keeping her sister in the dark about their father's accident. And yet she knew their mother was right and it was for the best, that knowing would only send Katharine into paroxysms of worry. Katharine always enquired over Mabel's education, the development of her French, her desire to be a teacher. If she knew that Mabel was scrubbing steps and scouring pans rather than studying, she would be devastated. So it was better that she didn't know.

Meanwhile, life had settled into a steady, if monotonous, routine of drudgery. Mabel had Thursday afternoons off and at first, if she had time, she went back to Clerkenwell to visit the family. But they were busy, her brothers doing apprenticeships or working on the docks and Mary always sitting with head bent low over her sewing table, intent on the intricacy of her work. Mabel felt duty bound to join in and help her, or to do the housework for her, so it wasn't much of a break.

And watching her father sitting dozing in his armchair for hours on end, no longer the vibrant head of the family he had always been, upset her deeply. She didn't know what to say to him, couldn't bear to see him so diminished. Katharine had sent enough money to alleviate the immediate concerns about paying the rent or buying food, but it wouldn't last for long. The happy, optimistic, rambunctious atmosphere that had always pervaded the family home was no more. Mabel began to find ways to avoid 33 Hawthorn Road.

In any case, she soon discovered that, on a Thursday, numerous extra tasks would mysteriously appear, urgently needing completion so that, because she couldn't leave until all her work was finished, she often had only a couple of hours left to herself. This wasn't enough time to get to Clerkenwell and back so she began to explore the local area, staring into the windows of Bayswater's smart shops – full of clothes and hats she could not afford in a million years – and the restaurants, with exotic menus of dishes she had never heard of.

She went to Hyde Park and Kensington Gardens, despite Cook's warning that girls who were 'no better than they should be' hung around in parks on their afternoons off. Mabel loved the mown lawns, majestic trees and rippling lakes there, and the light and fresh air were a blessed relief after the sombre, deadening environment of Brampton Square. Plus, dismissing Cook's instructions was a small, if rare, act of defiance that gave Mabel great satisfaction. She was unlikely to be seen by anyone who would report back to the mistress and if they did – so what? It was her free time and she could use it how she pleased.

One balmy summer afternoon Mabel was released on time for once and by two o'clock was sitting on a park bench enjoying the sunshine when a girl of a similar age came and sat down beside her. She was also in service, she told Mabel, after introducing herself as Kirsty, and was from Scotland, which to Mabel seemed impossibly far away. Her accent was so strong that sometimes Mabel struggled to understand her, but after her a while her ears attuned to her different pronunciation. Kirsty's mother had died some time ago. Her grief-stricken father had taken to drink and an aunt had agreed to care for Kirsty's younger siblings, but at age thirteen, Kirsty had been deemed old enough to work and to make her own way in the world.

On being chucked out of the house, she'd decided to get as far away as possible and hence had ended up in London. She worked as third housemaid in a big house in Hyde Park Gardens – a good job, she maintained, for a girl from nowhere.

'How long have you been there?' asked Mabel, curious about Kirsty's assured air and self-confidence.

Kirsty shrugged. 'Five years, more or less. I should be looking for somewhere new, really, but, on the other hand, it's not too bad. The family have a massive estate in Bedfordshire, with all its own staff. When they go there for the hunting and shooting season, we stay in London with less to do. As long as we keep the dust down, the housekeeper gives us a bit of leeway. So, I'm sticking it out for the moment.'

Mabel looked at her enviously. That she could talk so glibly about getting a new job, that she seemed so certain that such a job would materialise the moment it was sought. And that she didn't always have to work sixteen hours a day. She snuck a look at Kirsty's hands. They were in much better condition than her own, though the nails were ragged and torn, indicating that she bit them.

'You're lucky,' she said. 'I'm on the go all day, every day. The master goes out but the mistress almost never does. She's always there, an invisible presence criticising and judging the four of us.'

'Four!' shrieked Kirsty, so loud that Mabel shrank back into her coat. 'You've only got four servants at your place? That's a pathetic amount for the toffs. They must have money troubles. Do they?'

Mabel looked at her, eyes wide in puzzlement. 'Do they what?'

'Have money troubles,' repeated Kirsty, somewhat impatiently.

Mabel was bemused. 'I don't know. How would I know?' And then, 'how do you know if they've got plenty of money or not?'

Kirsty burst out into a loud chortle of gurgling laughter. 'You've answered your own question. If you don't know whether they've got it or they haven't, then they haven't. Why? Because if they're rolling in it, they make sure everyone knows it.' She drew out the word 'everyone' to add emphasis.

'And,' she went on, 'if they're really not that much posher than you are, those are the people who treat servants the worse. The real toffs, you know, dukes and lords and stuff, they don't need to make the point that they're better than you by treating you bad.'

A silence descended. Then Kirsty nudged Mabel's arm with her elbow.

'Come on, hen, don't look so down. It doesn't matter that yours aren't as well heeled or as high up the social ladder as most. It just means you've got more reason to get out of there.' She stood up and held her hand out to Mabel, pulling her onto her feet.

'You need to look out, though. Don't ever take a job that someone offers you in the street.'

Mabel couldn't imagine doing such a thing.

'There are always people out looking for girls to put in... well, to go with gentlemen.'

Kirsty's tone was infinitely worldly-wise. Mabel, chewing her cheek, was somewhat unclear about what she was referring to. But 'going with gentlemen' sounded like something her parents would definitely disapprove of, related in some way to fraternisation. She wondered, not for the first time, how Kirsty knew all this, where she got her information from. Before she had a chance to ask, Kirsty had moved on to the next subject.

'Right, let's go down to the Gardens,' she burbled happily. 'And if there's any young men there on their afternoon off, you know, valets or counter assistants or whatnot, we might get asked to walk with them. You feel ever so, I'm telling you, promenading with a handsome man on your arm.'

They set off, Mabel having absolutely no idea what she was doing or why. Presumably stalking shop workers in Kensington Gardens was different from going with gentlemen, fraternising, or being 'no better than you should be'. In any case, Kirsty was fun, her sense of humour infectious. Mabel trusted her and she had nothing better to do so why not go?

A fresh breeze had blown up, rippling the water on the Round Pond. Gulls bobbed on sparkling wavelets, and the gleaming leaves of the plane trees glistened in the sunshine. Mabel was gripped by sudden joie de vivre. She'd never done anything like this before, and since she'd left school, she didn't really have any friends. All her classmates were still studying or had perhaps taken a job in a factory or stayed at home to help their own mothers until they got married. Spending time in a London park with an entertaining companion watching the off-duty guardsmen parade past in their smart uniforms seemed infinitely preferable to any of those options.

'Hey,' said Kirsty, suddenly nudging Mabel again. 'There's a couple of lookers over there. We'll just tag along behind them, all right? We can chat with them if they want to, but remember, no funny business.' She seized Mabel's arm and dragged her towards them.

Funny business? Again, Mabel wasn't sure what she meant but was bedazzled anew by Kirsty's superior knowledge and information about absolutely everything. Maybe she was talking about kissing or something? At the thought, Mabel shuddered involuntarily. Obviously, she wouldn't ever do anything like that with someone she wasn't formally engaged to. Who would?

Her eyes slid sideward to Kirsty, whose walk had taken on a more purposeful gait now she'd spotted her prey. It struck her that possibly Kirsty would. A frisson of excitement slid through Mabel, tempered with trepidation. There was something beguiling and exciting about breaking the rules. But on the other hand, how to navigate all the regulations about what was, and what was not, acceptable?

Arm-in-arm, she and Kirsty promenaded down Lancaster Walk behind the two men in breeches and jackets, who feigned complete indifference. Kirsty imitated their upright stance and stern expressions so that Mabel had to stifle her giggles and look away until she had composed herself.

When they reached the park gates, the men turned around.

'Has anyone ever told you how beautiful you are?' said one to Mabel. He was extraordinarily handsome, with China blue eyes framed by long pale lashes.

Emboldened by the fresh air and sense of liberty Kirsty had bestowed on her, Mabel replied with a swift, 'Yes, they have.'

Her mother was always telling her this, and he hadn't asked if it was a man who'd said it.

The young man looked briefly taken aback, but what he did next, Mabel didn't know. She and Kirsty did not hang around to find out. Laughing and shrieking, they hared through the iron gates and along Bayswater Road, running until they were so out of breath they had to stop.

They went to a cafe and Kirsty made Mabel giggle even more with her stories of her households' eccentricities, including the visiting aunt who always left a coin somewhere in her bedroom – under the rug, on the bedside table, beside the water jug – to check both Kirsty's honesty and the thoroughness of her cleaning.

Laughing, Mabel ate her bun and drank her tea and, once they'd finished, had to run like the wind to get back before the curfew. She flew up the stairs and into bed as if she were on wings. Nothing extraordinary had happened – but she'd made a friend. It was so long since she'd spoken to anyone who wasn't either a work colleague or a member of her family that she had almost forgotten how good it could be.

As she closed her eyes and drifted off to sleep, she thought of Katharine. She knew her sister had been lonely over the years, especially after Laure and Charles had deserted her; she'd written to her of how much she missed Elsie and all the family, especially her only sister Mabel. And Mabel missed her too, desperately. Despite how young Mabel had been when Katharine left, she remembered her vividly, and if the mental image she had of her ever faded, she would study the one family photograph they had at Hawthorn Road, taken the day before Katharine and Anselmo's departure for Brazil, and imagine the conversations they'd have if Katharine were there, the secrets and confidences they'd share. She wished her sister were here to tell of her exciting day.

That night, Mabel dreamt of the dancing water in the Round Pond, the handsome, pale-lashed man, and Kirsty's laugh, and suddenly saw a future that was a whole lot brighter than she had envisioned for a long time. She would share what she could with Katharine, without giving away her father's accident or the fact that she was working in service.

It was good to have positive news to put in a letter.

Chapter Twenty-Eight

Norwood, 1901

Katharine was grateful for Thomas' absence over the next few weeks. It meant that she didn't have to make a decision on what she should do about him, how she should behave towards him. She kept thinking that she should ask him to leave, should send him away to find work on another estate. After all, she had always intended to take him on for a trial period only. But the very thought made her feel utterly miserable. The heat, always oppressive, was exceptionally suffocating and depressed her mood still further.

She coped by keeping busy and renewing her efforts to restore Fortunata to health, tempting her with tasty food, saving for her the best bits of the fish the Indians caught, or the wild pig and tapir they hunted. But the child ate almost nothing, periodically supplementing her meagre diet with more chunks of dirt.

Fortunata insisted on doing the laundry and Katharine hated seeing her struggle with bundles of cloth heavy with the weight of water, but she refused all offers of help or exhortations to have a rest. Once she started, she would not take a break until the job was done. Ironically, despite her lack of interest in eating, she loved to help Rosabel with the cooking and was developing a range of skills in preparing the different meals they all enjoyed.

In this way, the days ticked by under the equatorial sun, the rain fell, the puddles evaporated and the river rushed past as it always did.

One day, just as Katharine was starting to long for and to dread in equal measure the return of Thomas and Antonio, she heard a commotion coming from the jungle. Calling Jonathan to come with her, and to bring a gun in case the visitors were unwelcome, she headed towards the source of the noise. A man stumbled out from between the mighty tree trunks, his bow and arrows slung untidily over his shoulder, his body smeared with mud and a wild expression in his eyes.

It was Fabio, one the Indian trackers who had gone with the expedition.

'Mother,' he called, his voice faint and weak, 'come quick, very quick. Bring men.'

Katharine and Jonathan exchanged looks of alarm, and then she turned back to Fabio. 'What's the matter, Fabio? How many men and why do you need them?'

Fabio gesticulated wildly towards the forest, 'Mr Thomas and the boy – they sick. Very, very sick.'

Katharine's heart stopped beating for a moment and sweat broke out on her forehead.

'Fabio, come with me and show me where they are. Jonathan, gather some more of the men together to help. Follow our trail – as quickly as you can.'

Dreadful fears crowded Katharine's mind; an attack by a jaguar or snake, or fever – yellow, dengue, blackwater – all could kill and often did. And then there were bites, infected wounds, dysentery, or any number of other unnamed and unidentified jungle diseases that could take a life, even those as strong and vibrant as Thomas' or Antonio's.

Following Fabio through the dense undergrowth was exhausting and difficult. The day was drawing to a close but no cooler for it and though Fabio vociferously slashed away at creepers and lianas to clear a path, leaves and branches still flashed into her face and her arms became grazed and torn from pushing her way through. Eventually, her lungs heaving and her heart racing, sweat pouring down her back, they arrived at a small clearing on a low cliff, below which a waterfall thundered, sending spray flying high in the air where it caught the light of the morose, dying sun.

There, lying on makeshift mats of layered palm leaves, lay Thomas and Antonio. Both were semi-conscious, perspiration slick on their brows, their feverish eyes half closed, mouths murmuring with almost-silent pain or incantations.

'Oh my God,' gasped Katharine, 'oh God, oh God.' She rushed towards her son and flung herself down beside him, placing her hand on his forehead and covering his cheeks with kisses. His skin was burning up, his breathing laboured and slow and a trickle of dried vomit stained his chin.

'Bring him water, Fabio,' she called. 'He needs water.'

Tears were streaming down her face and she wished she could use them to staunch the boy's thirst.

'Water gone, Mother,' pleaded Fabio, showing her an empty gourd attached to the loin cloth around his waist.

'Well get some more,' she yelled. 'There's a whole bloody river down there, isn't there! There'll be a fresh spring some-where.'

Fabio jumped back in amazement and then, without a second glance, headed to the low cliff to make his way down to the river.

Katharine's head fell into her hands and rubbed her eyes in distress. She should not have shouted like that, she hated to let herself go. And to take her fear out on Fabio, who had done everything he could to help, was completely unfair. Plus, what she had sent him to do was dangerous; he could slip and fall, dashing his head on the rocks below, or be swept over the waterfall and drown. All she'd done with her idiocy and impatience was make a terrible situation worse. But he had disappeared already, and it was too late to call him back.

Trembling with self-loathing and terror, she crawled towards Thomas. In contrast to Antonio, his skin was clammy and cold and he was shivering, teeth chattering, intermittently letting out piteous moans.

Oh God, she thought again. Oh God, oh God, oh God. They can't die, she kept repeating to herself inside her head, they cannot die.

It seemed an age before Fabio returned safely with the water, at the same time that Jonathan appeared with a troupe of other men. Immediately assessing the situation, Jonathan set about cutting down long, thin stems of a stiff plant that grew in abundance, then slicing lianas to make a webbing base for his makeshift stretchers. Helpless and useless, she watched him work, admiring even in her atrophied state his skill and brilliance at improvisation.

'Mother,' he said, once the stretchers were complete, 'we can take them home now. I've sent two men to collect the bark of the fever tree to combat the shaking.'

'Right,' replied Katharine, still befuddled and uncertain. 'That's... that's good, Jonathan, thank you.'

The men lugged Antonio and Thomas back to the compound. Katharine, stumbling beside them, was besieged by memories of Anselmo's body lying beside the river at Lagona. She wept for her son and for Thomas, her... But what was Thomas? Her manager? Her best friend? Her lover? Or all three of those things? Katharine did not know exactly what Thomas was, and could hardly bear to contemplate that she never might.

Her last action had been to reject him; she had not told him how much she loved him.

The Indians brought the cinchona bark powder, a remedy for malaria that the people of South America had used for centuries. For that is what they were sure Thomas and Antonio were suffering from. Katharine sent for the Spanish pharmacist and, while she waited for him to arrive, tried to persuade herself that malaria was better than yellow fever, the disease that she had seen so many die of over her years in the Amazon. You could survive yellow fever – but most didn't.

Senhor Garcia, when he arrived a day later, confirmed both the diagnosis and the treatment, and had little more to offer.

'Plenty of fluids, rest, soup or a light diet when they are able, and they will probably do well,' he advised.

'Probably?' probed Katharine, wanting to know and not wanting to know what percentage likelihood 'probably' related to.

'More than likely,' said Senhor Garcia, with what Katharine felt was a misplaced cheerfulness. 'And your men are doing a great job, Mrs Ferrandis, so I really wouldn't worry too much.'

And with that he was off, back to his canoe, with a jaunty wave and a tipping of his hat. 'Let me know how they do,' he called, as he embarked.

'I will,' she answered faintly.

She kept vigil over them night and day, barely noticing anything else that was going on around the compound, leaving Jonathan and Santiago to run the business. Rosabel and Fortunata brought her water and tea and meals they'd tried to make extra tasty, but Katharine could hardly eat. She sat with her hand in Antonio's, flickering her eyes from him to Thomas and back again, checking for any signs of improvement – or worsening – of their condition. Time lost all meaning and, although she was aware of the passing of the days and nights, she lost count of how many.

In all those silent, mind-warping hours, she went over and over her and Anselmo's decision to come to the Amazon, the reasons why they had done it – for adventure, for riches, for excitement, to achieve something. All seemed selfish, futile and empty now. She had borne the death of her husband because she'd had to; there had been no other choice, no other possibility. Giving up, giving in, was even more impossible once she'd found out about the loan from her father – and that she was pregnant.

The need to pay her father back, to provide for her son, to honour Anselmo's memory, had driven her on through all the years of hardship. But for what? Yes, she had made some money, and would make more – much more, probably. But meanwhile her son might follow his father to an Amazonian death. And the life of the man she loved was also ebbing away in front of her eyes.

Nothing seemed worth it any more.

Chapter Twenty-Nine

London, 1901

The optimism engendered by meeting Kirsty didn't stay with Mabel for long. The days returned to their dull and mundane turning, and though her afternoons off were something to look forward to, they were also fraught with guilt. If Mabel went home to Clerkenwell she felt guilty about Kirsty; if she went out with Kirsty, she felt guilty about her mother. Christmas came and went, with her day off on the 26th, but with everything that had gone wrong that year, the celebrations at Hawthorn Road were a pale imitation of what they had been during Mabel's childhood.

Nothing is simple, she sighed to herself as she scrubbed the front steps on the first day of the new year. She understood, with more clarity than ever before, why Katharine and Anselmo had taken the leap of faith required to travel thousands of miles to make their fortunes. She wished she would be lucky enough to meet a handsome, exotic foreigner who would whisk her away to some tropical future. But there was no way her parents would let her marry until she was eighteen, she was certain about that, so she'd just have to wait a while for her dreams to come true. Not to mention how she would ever meet a prospective husband, when she worked her fingers to the bone sixteen hours a day. And, talking of fingers, her hands were still a mess, but she counted herself lucky. At least she could function. Kirsty had told her that lots of girls' hands got so bad that they had to give up work completely.

The best that could be said at that moment was that things were ticking over, and Mabel assumed this was what life was all about – a long process of getting used to your lot, with always at the back of your mind the hope that one day, you might end up with something better. At work, she obeyed all the rules and did exactly as she was told, in part for a quiet life and in part due to her fear of being dismissed. With Kirsty, she let her hair down a bit. But she never overstepped the mark – and she worked without cease on her 'modesty'. By this time she was well versed in the practice of giving room to her employers and their guests, stepping back and turning away if they passed her in a corridor, never getting in their way.

So when one miserable, rainy afternoon she stood aside for the master as he walked towards her along the corridor, she knew she must have imagined his hand brushing against her skirts. Inwardly, she reprimanded herself for not flattening herself against the wall adequately. He would undoubtedly complain to the mistress, who would in turn instruct Cook to give her a dressing down. She spent the rest of the week on tenterhooks, waiting to be hauled over the coals, glad only that it was unlikely to happen again as it was fairly rare to come across one of the family around the house. When nothing happened – no telling off, no reminders of her 'modesty' – she almost forgot about the incident.

But suddenly the master seemed to be around a lot more than usual, not just in the house rather than out, but in Mabel's vicinity. And on several occasions, their paths crossed in narrow passageways or on the back staircase. Whenever this happened, the same thing occurred: Mabel tried to shrink to nothing but however hard she breathed in, clamping her arms against her sides to take up the least space possible, she still couldn't make herself small enough to allow the master to pass without touching her, his hand glancing off her bottom, his fingers trailing across hers.

She had no idea what was going on – but it made her increasingly uneasy. Her nervous anxiety reached a height when Cook called her into the kitchen and told her she had something serious to discuss with her. Immediately, Mabel's heart began thumping wildly in her chest and her palms became damp with sweat. The moment she had been dreading had come. She tried to convince herself it was just about the plate she'd broken last week. That would mean money deducted from her pay packet to replace the item but this seemed infinitely preferable to being challenged about her inability to keep out of the master's way.

But when Cook spoke, the problem didn't seem to be the master at all, but Mabel's conduct on her afternoons off.

'There is a rule, Mabel, which I'm sure you are aware of,' Cook intoned, sounding as if she were giving a sermon.

Mabel stood meekly, trying to keep her face expressionless in case she was accused of being cheeky or pert. There were lots of rules, a plethora of them and she didn't need to ask what this particular rule was; for certain, Cook was going to tell her.

'You know that there is a rule which says there must be no followers.'

Mabel nodded mutely. She wasn't allowed a man friend; servants never were. Well, that was all right because she didn't have one.

'The mistress is worried that you… that you are not taking the care of your reputation that you should be.'

Mabel was stumped. She didn't know what Cook was referring to. All she and Kirsty had done was have a few cheeky exchanges with young men in the park. The conversations had never lasted longer than a few minutes and never led to anything else.

'I don't have a follower,' she answered, trying to sound as innocent as possible. It was only the truth so she didn't know why she was feeling so caught out, why her heart was pumping so hard.

'Hmm.' Cook pursed her lips. 'So, make sure it stays that way.'

Mabel wasn't sure whether she was more indignant or furious. There was clearly no evidence behind this discussion, no real problem. It was just to intimidate her, to put her in her place.

'I've done nothing wrong,' Mabel said, with more boldness than she felt.

Cook sighed elaborately. 'Don't answer back,' she retorted.

They stood staring at each other for a moment before Mabel conceded defeat and dropped her gaze. There was no point in standing up for herself. They'd think what they thought whatever she did.

'Listen,' continued Cook, her tone suddenly more conciliatory. 'Just be careful. You're a looker; you must know it. All the men will be after you. Don't think that posh people, the m—' she faltered, corrected herself, carried on. 'The mistress' friends are no more immune to female charms than anyone else, even those of someone so much beneath them in the social hierarchy.'

Mabel's confusion was written all over her face. What on earth was Cook referring to? Perhaps it did have something to do with the master's bizarre actions, after all. She wanted to ask Kirsty, but at the same time knew she wouldn't. This was too perplexing and embarrassing to mention to anyone. Cook, seeing her expression, clearly felt it necessary to elaborate.

'The mistress says that you caught the eye of one of her acquaintances in the dining room the other day.'

Mabel almost sighed with relief and then the words sank in. So not the master but another male visitor? She frowned. She had no recollection of such an event. There had been a guest – a portly, bald man with gold-rimmed spectacles – who had ogled her for the entire time she was in the room. But she had done nothing. So, she was getting into trouble, she was being blamed, for his actions. The injustice of it seared through Mabel's very being. But she was helpless.

'I was pretty once, when I was young.' Cook seemed to have forgotten that she was supposed to be admonishing Mabel. She was looking into the distance, seeing something Mabel couldn't.

Mabel tried to imagine her with a figure, instead of the oblong brick she was now, to picture her with cheekbones and a chin rather than her present shapeless, jowly face. She couldn't. But she sympathised. She understood that it would be terrible to look back with regret at what you once were.

'I had to work hard to stay on the right side of the rules, I can tell you. Just remember that pregnancy is always the girls' fault.' Cook twisted her mouth into a sad half-smile. 'Even though it's the man's.'

They stood for a moment in silence.

'I wish I could help you, Mabel,' she sighed, looking down at the tabletop, pitted and rutted from years of use. 'But I can't.'

Mabel's forehead creased in puzzlement. Cook was being so cryptic, but she knew better than to quiz a servant so much higher in the ranking than herself. Then Cook came to and shouted at Mabel, 'What are doing, lolling around there as if you've not got work to do? Get on with it.'

Suddenly angry, Mabel marched off, head held high. There was a lot she didn't understand. But Cook was right about one thing, which is that girls always got the blame. As for the mistress – she thought Mabel was a bad egg, did she? The unfairness of this seared through her veins and continued to do so over the next few days. She was in the housemaid's closet where the brushes, dusters, brooms and mops were kept, bad-temperedly wrestling with the clutter, not entirely sure what she was looking for, when things took a terrible turn for the worse.

Just as she'd bent over to reach for a cloth, she heard foot-steps. The room was situated next to the narrow back staircase that the servants had to use, and only another servant would come anywhere near it. What did Cook want now she inwardly groaned. Not another scolding already, surely?

But when the footsteps stopped; instead of Cook's strident tones, sending her off on a task or berating her dilatory habits, there was nothing. Mabel became acutely aware of the smell of damp that infiltrated the closet, and of ash from the pail, of the hum of the silence that reverberated in her ears. Slowly, her heart in her mouth, she made to stand up straight.

'Stay there.'

Mabel's heart almost jumped out of her chest. Her breath was coming in gasps and sweat prickled on her back and ran down the backs of her legs.

It was the master.

He crossed the threshold and shut the door, quietly, careful not to make a noise. She could not begin to imagine what he was doing there, what he wanted from her. But a servant never disobeyed her employer. Neither did a servant ever question their employer. So Mabel stayed where she was, her hands clenched tight, her palms dampening.

Threat filled the air but Mabel did not know what that threat was.

Until, all of a sudden, it was upon her.

A heavy weight pressed against her as the master grabbed her from behind and pushed himself into her. Mabel froze. What was he doing? She couldn't fight, couldn't scream, was paralysed with fear. He grappled her to the ground, onto her knees, in between the metal buckets and mops and brooms, the shoe scraper that had somehow found its way here, the box of carbolic soap provided for the servants' use. His fingers gripped her tighter, burning hot through her dress and bloomers and she felt something hard digging into her, insistent and unforgiving. The master's breathing was heavy, snorting through his nose and hissing out of his mouth. For a crazy moment Mabel thought she was going to laugh. They were in the maid's closet, both on their knees, as if playing some childish game, hide and seek or forfeits.

But it was not a joke, it was a nightmare. So many thoughts tumbled around Mabel's mind – what if the mistress came along? What had she done to cause this? Was this punishment for all the times she'd been an annoyance to him lately? What did the master want from her?

Then all thoughts deserted her as one of his hands released its grip on her hip and was thrusting between her legs, fumbling through the layers of cloth towards her private parts.

Mabel thought she was going to be sick. She should fight, shout, but she had no strength, no energy.

The hand met flesh, the soft, white flesh of her inner thigh. The fingertips were creeping upwards. The horror of it was unbearable. Then the fingers were poking her, forcing their way inside her. She felt faint, her head whirling, giddiness overtaking her. She started to scream but he stopped her, whipping his other hand over her mouth, leaning forward and hissing in her ear.

'Keep quiet.'

The words echoed around her head which was suddenly empty of everything except what was happening here and now. She had no past and no future, just this horrendous, terrifying present. She didn't know if she would survive. Was he trying to kill her?

His fingers continued their groping and she got her answer. No, she wouldn't die. But she would feel as if she had.

The master took his hand away from her mouth but she knew better than to make a sound, was too terrified to be able to, even if she'd wanted to. He was doing something to himself, to the thing in his trousers, and his breathing was coming faster and faster as his wrist moved quicker and quicker until he let out a moan and fell forward, crushing her into the floor. Her head hit the ground with a sickening thump, the crack of bone against hard wood. The cold solidity of the floorboards was the only thing that was real, that and the mop leaning against the wall. Its dirty grey fronds were comforting somehow, familiar and friendly, like a friend with messy hair smiling amusedly at her while wondering what she was doing down there.

A couple of seconds passed. It felt like half of Mabel's life. Then the master calmly stood up, rearranged his dark suit and lumbered heavily away without another word. Mabel stayed where she was until she was conscious that so much time had passed Cook would be wondering what she was up to.

In a daze, she stood up, staggering as did so, her head spinning. She leant her hands against the wall, using it to ground herself, to support her. Picking up her feather duster and her cloth, she left the closet, fear of being caught slacking almost as strong as the terror and disgust of what had just happened. There was a fearful irony in the fact that she had been told to stay away from men, but this man thought he could treat her how he liked. She knew what the master had done to her was wrong. But what she could do about it? Absolutely nothing. Complain, and she'd lose her job instantly. Protest, and he'd throw her straight out on the streets. No one would listen and no one would believe.

Cook was right. It was always the girls who got the blame.

Chapter Thirty

Norwood, 1901

It was a week before Antonio began to show signs of improvement.

'Why are you looking so sad, Mother?' he asked, as his eyes flickered fully open for the first time since he'd collapsed in the jungle outside the compound. 'What's the matter?'

Tears burst from Katharine's eyes, the pent-up, stifled weeping that she had staved off for so long. She didn't want to worry him by crying in front of him but once it had started, she couldn't stem the flow.

Alarmed, Antonio tried to sit up, but did not have the strength and sank back wearily into the bed. Gradually becoming aware of where he was, he looked around him in puzzlement.

'I've been ill,' he said, as a statement of fact rather than an enquiry. 'That's why I'm in bed. And why you're crying.'

Katharine wept some more and then finally, with a few hearty sniffs, managed to stop.

'Yes,' she said, and then added with a weak smile, 'right on both counts.'

'Huh,' grunted Antonio, as if he'd run out of energy for speech already.

Rosabel bustled in with chicken soup and pity. 'My boy is awake!' she cried. 'After so many days.' She patted Antonio's forehead and smoothed his hair. With a faint, fragile smile, Katharine watched as Antonio flinched away from the unwelcome attention and fuss.

'Your mother!' continued Rosabel. 'Your mother has not left your side. She love you so much, she do anything for you!'

Wary of offending her, but conscious that Antonio needed as much rest and peace and quiet as possible, Katharine managed to manoeuvre her in the direction of the kitchen on the pretext of cooking something delicious for his supper. When she'd gone, Antonio met her eyes.

'Thank you for looking after me,' he said. 'I knew you were there, even during the fever. Everything was muddled – but I knew it was you. I could feel you willing me to get better.'

Katharine gazed upon her only child with a look of raw, exposed adoration.

'Of course,' she murmured. 'I love you more than the world, more than any other living being. I could never love anyone more than I love you.'

'You shouldn't love anyone but me,' demanded Antonio, suddenly petulant, showing himself as the immature ten-year-old boy he was. 'Don't love anyone else but me.'

Katharine leant forward and kissed his forehead. 'No, of course not. No one but you.' She said the words, knowing that she was lying because she also loved Thomas, but told herself that didn't count, that filial love was different to romantic. Antonio didn't need to know about Thomas, not now, not for a long time, not until he was old enough to understand.

Over the next hours and days, Antonio became more alert, able to sit, and then stand, for longer periods every day, although the fever returned in twenty-four-hour cycles, knocking him flat again for a few hours. Katharine continued to treat him with the fever tree powder that the Indians collected for her and allowed herself the faintest glimmers of hope – that he would survive, that his strong young body could fight this infection and conquer it.

Thomas, meanwhile, suffered on, sometimes racked by shivering chills, at other times by overpowering sweats. He drifted in and out of consciousness, in his more lucid moments complaining of terrible headaches and nausea. Though Katharine administered the same treatment to him as to Antonio, it did not seem to be having the same effect. Panicking, she asked Santiago for his advice.

'Be patient,' he said, sympathetically. 'It can take time for the medicine to work. All will be well, believe me.'

Katharine wanted ardently to do just that. She forced herself to keep calm, to eat and drink to preserve her own strength. It would only make matters worse if she got ill or collapsed. She tried not to think about the future because she couldn't envisage one without Thomas in it.

Eventually, three weeks after she'd found them lying on the forest floor, Thomas finally took a turn for the better, sitting up in bed and asking for water, calling to Rosabel for a cup of hot coffee and pancakes.

Katharine laughed when she heard him, from relief tinged with hysteria. Ill for so long and now all he could think about were pancakes? She rushed to his side to help him to the table, but he gently shook her off.

'I'm fine,' he insisted, clearly hating any thought that he might be dependent on her or anyone. 'Absolutely fine.' He looked around anxiously, scouring the compound. 'But where is Antonio?' There was a hint of alarm in his voice, as if he were thinking the worst. 'He was ill, too – and now I can't see him anywhere.'

Katharine touched his hand. 'It's all right,' she reassured him, 'he's well. Much better. So much so that he's gone to mess around with the Indian boys, swimming and fishing.'

'Thank the Lord,' breathed Thomas, pausing on his way to the dining table, clearly finding the activity, however minimal, taxing to limbs that had lain prostrate for days. 'I had dreams… I saw him… I couldn't have borne it if something… if he…'

Unable to finish the sentence, he sank heavily to a chair. He looked up and met Katharine's eyes with his, which were still yellowed and blurry with sickness. 'You know what I mean.'

Katharine nodded silently. She poured him water and passed the tin mug of coffee that Rosabel brought.

'Pancakes are cooking, sir,' said Rosabel. 'Ready soon.' No one had told her to call Thomas 'sir', she just did.

'I know exactly what you mean,' said Katharine, softly, when the cook had returned to the frying pan. 'You don't need to explain.'

He smiled at her and she smiled back because they both knew this, that the understanding that lay between them was deeper than words, deeper than what needed to be articulated.

After this, the illness and the recovery, everything was changed.

Katharine no longer had doubts that she and Thomas should be together, no longer told herself that Thomas was an impossible dream, a forbidden fruit. Life was short – in the Amazon, more so than anywhere – and needed to be lived to the full, all opportunities for happiness grasped with both hands. She had spent precious time before Anselmo died worrying about their future, but if she had known how brief that future was to be, she would have tried to behave differently. She didn't want to be plagued by such regret ever again.

She and Thomas would have a relationship, even if it had to be kept a secret.

One evening, they found themselves alone together in her living room on the first floor of the house. An opalescent moon hung low in a navy blue sky dotted with smudged stars. All around them, the jungle hooted and shrieked but between the two of them a silence fell.

Katharine ran her hands over Thomas' face and shoulders, along his arms to his hands. He had lost weight, his collar bone protruding like a hollow, curved bow, but some of his vitality had returned, and she knew his body would soon be as powerful as ever. As their fingers touched, he grasped hers in his.

'Thank you for all you did for me,' he whispered.

Katharine glanced away, at the river down below them, calmly racing on its way to the ocean, its many-thousand-mile journey only just begun.

'It was nothing,' she replied. 'I would have done it for anyone. But for you – and my Antonio – I would lay down my own life for either of you.'

'I know.'

Thomas pulled her towards him and held her close, so close that they could feel each other's hearts beating.

'And I would do the same for you,' he murmured, brushing her red hair softly with his lips. The contact seemed to remind him of something and he moved her slightly away from him, raising his arms to remove the pins from her hair and let it fall. He picked up thick tresses in his hands and watched them ripple through his fingers. 'Such beautiful hair,' he said. 'I never saw such hair before.'

Katharine gave a short laugh. 'You wouldn't believe how it is ridiculed at home, how teased I used to be about it.'

Thomas shook his head in disbelief. 'I wouldn't, you are right.'

He stood up, leading her by the hand to her bedroom, where he shut the door and put a chair under the handle in case Antonio should stir in the night and come to find his mother. With that precaution taken, the atmosphere changed, becoming frenetic and frenzied as they tore off each other's clothes and then fell onto the bed where Thomas made love to Katharine in a way she had never experienced before, nor even imagined.

'We can't tell anyone,' she told him in the morning, when the dawn light woke them. 'No one can know.'

'Yes,' he agreed.

It was difficult, with so many people around, but in snatched minutes and furtive hours, they got to know each other and to forge bonds so tight that Katharine knew nothing but death could ever sever them. Giddy with joy, she went about her business with her head in the clouds. One day, she watched her lover and her son as they played on the liana rope swing, their strength and fitness restored. One after the other they swung out, then dropped to the water with bodies straight as dice, barely rippling the surface, before swimming strongly back to shore.

Katharine, feasting her eyes upon the joyous sight and laughing, thought she had never been this happy, had never imagined such happiness. And even though the illness had been terrible, both it and the journey that preceded it had served one useful purpose, which was to take Antonio's mind off the absence of his adored uncle. Mayhew was safe and sound in Manaus, getting up to goodness knew what extracurricular activities, but actually doing a good job of representing Norwood Enterprises' interests there. Katharine hoped, for her son's sake, that he would come back for a visit soon – but perhaps not *too* soon.

A huge splash took her attention off Mayhew and back to the here and now. For a second, her heart lurched as she recalled her frenzied rescue of Mac and Antonio all those years ago. But it was a false alarm; everything was fine, just Thomas doing a belly flop to amuse the child.

'Hurrah,' she shouted across to them, and they waved back in reply. Observing them now, so full of life, of vigour and vivacity, she could hardly believe that so very recently, she had thought she might lose them both.

It was a miracle.

Chapter Thirty-One

Mac and Mayhew relaxed down onto the soft cushions of the steamer's luxurious sofas. Mayhew smiled to himself as he thought of the rough wooden chairs of Norwood. Oh, my sweet little sister Katharine, if only you could see me now. The words flitted through his head as a beautiful, pale-skinned girl brought them champagne, ice-cold and effervescent. Mayhew narrowed his eyes to scrutinise her intently. Polish or Russian probably, and Jewish. Such fair, blonde women from Europe were the mistresses of choice for the wealthy in Manaus. He'd make sure he tracked her down later. In this city, everything and everyone could be bought – for a price.

His mind dwelt briefly on Kitty, and Amy-Joanne. They seemed to belong to another lifetime, to have been part of someone else's past, not his own. He rarely thought of either of them, these days. Though it was true that every now and again he recalled Kitty's last words to him, and her letter, and was smitten by the realisation that, somewhere out there in this big, wide world was a child who was part of him. His child. His and Kitty's. But then he would push this unwelcome notion from his mind and forget it. There was no point in dwelling on what was, after all, an unfortunate occurrence. He should have been more careful. *Kitty* should have been more careful.

In any case, he needn't worry. They were unlikely to ever be able to track him down and anyway there didn't seem to have been any attempts to find him. It had been impossible to discover how his death had been reported, as news of such limited significance outside his own small circle was never going to make it to these parts. So, he just had to assume that they all believed him drowned, exactly as he had planned. That, unable to bear the shame of his company's collapse, he had taken his own life.

'How's business?' asked Mac, jolting Mayhew back to the present. His tone was laconic, but Mayhew spotted the shrewd look in his eye. Nothing was ever idle conversation with Mac.

'Good,' he replied. 'Can't complain.' There was more he could add but wasn't sure that he would. Or should. He drank a slug of champagne and decided to, after all.

'Just a shame my poor sister did not know enough to dispute your fees before they were signed and sealed.'

It was a challenge and both men knew it. In the silence that followed the phonograph played out, scratchily, a Richard Strauss melody. The Brazilian girls were gathering on the stage, dripping tassels and raw sexuality, preparing for the dancing to begin. The opportunity for business talk was limited.

'She's a hard nut to crack, your sister,' responded Mac, which was not really an answer.

The fair European girl arrived with refills of champagne. Mayhew ran his finger along her thigh as she passed by. She smiled at him and he mouthed at her, 'Later.'

'When I... when those savages came out of the forest to attack Norwood, I – most people – thought that would be the end of her.' Mac drew on his cigar, forehead creased in thought. 'But she's clearly made of sterner stuff. I can't imagine many women sticking it out in the Amazon, alone.'

The record changed to something more stirring. Mayhew knew nothing about music but had to concede that this modern invention was marvellous.

'If, that is, she can be called alone any more.' Mac's voice was level and even, without emotion.

Mayhew snorted into his champagne glass. The bubbles went up his nose and he shook his head in annoyance.

'What do you mean? She's as alone as any widow could be. She's hardly going to settle down with one of the forest folk, is she? They're half her size, for one thing.' Mayhew chortled to himself at the mental image he'd created of his tall, milk-white sister with a diminutive bronzed Indian, preposterous as it was.

'She has a sentimental edge, under her veneer of calm respectability and reliability.'

Mayhew frowned. Mac was speaking in riddles this evening. It must be the drink.

'That ridiculous duck she befriended,' continued Mac, staring at his glass of champagne with glazed eyes. 'Gave it a quaint name, Po-Po, as I recall. She really loved it. It was very touching.' He seemed to be talking to himself or to the wine as much as to Mayhew, who had no idea what he was referring to.

'That poor boy of hers,' Mac burbled on, 'being brought up amongst the savages. It's not right, so it isn't.'

Mayhew's interest was suddenly piqued. He'd had to concede a reluctant admiration for Katharine during his time at Norwood, though he'd been only too happy to leave and return to somewhere more to his sybaritic tastes. And for Antonio he had developed a genuine fondness. He might even go so far as to say he missed the child – though of course what he also missed was someone who looked up to and idolised him so unquestioningly. Sometimes, it even crossed his mind that his baby might have been a boy, that Kitty might have given birth to his son… But no. Such ruminations were pointless and must be strongly discouraged.

The music paused and the silence filled with the noises of the river, the churning engines, the performers' high-heeled shoes clacking on the decking in readiness to tantalise.

'You know there are whispers about her on the river?' Mac seemed suddenly more focused, his blue eyes restored to their normal acuity. 'Katharine, that is. Your sister.'

Mayhew bridled. What the hell was Mac on about?

'What do you mean?' he demanded for the second time that evening, his voice coming out in a high-pitched, strangulated tone. He was infuriated, could sense the flush mounting in his cheeks, the blood pumping faster. If anyone was going to spread rumours about a member of his own family, it should be him.

'Not a savage, good lord no.' Mac seemed to be harking back to Mayhew's earlier comment. He was definitely the worse for wear, but then Mayhew was starting to feel a little tipsy himself. 'You're right, that would be nonsensical.' Mac stubbed out his cigar and waved for another one. Mayhew reflected that he couldn't match him in smoking, even if he could in drinking. 'No, it's that Black man you took to Norwood. I think he's ended up becoming more a part of the clan than you intended.'

Mayhew stared at Mac, open-mouthed. Was he suggesting what Mayhew thought he was suggesting?

'I don't know what you're talking about,' he expostulated, coldly, quick to protest his sister's innocence. Mac's accusation was outrageous. 'And I think it would behove you to hold your tongue. Idle gossip helps no one.'

But despite what he said, he remembered. Remembered the looks, the smiles, the eager conversations. The evenings the pair of them spent on the dock, talking. Could it always have been about the *estradas*? He felt anger rise within him, as well as bile at the thought of something so disgusting. Bloody hell, what had he done, delivering that man to his sister?

Mac leant back on the cushions, puffing intently. Shrouded in a pall of grey smoke, the outline of his face was hazy. But Mayhew could tell he was smiling. Smiling at his sister, his flesh and blood, his kith and kin. Such things had never mattered to him before. But, given that his fortunes these days were so closely bound up with Katharine's, they did now.

He looked towards the stage where the dance continued, the troupe of exotic girls like colourful caged birds, nimbly and erotically performing bodily feats of great agility. A Brazilian beauty came over to where he and Mac sat, all French perfume and nipple tassels and a feather boa that stirred up some quite exquisite emotions within Mayhew, not felt since Kitty Little's silken caresses. Distracted, he stuffed some notes inside her garter. He could spend what he liked. Norwood was making good money now, thanks to him.

Thanks also to Smart. He had turned out to be a good manager, Smart by name and Smart by nature and – smart enough to beguile his lustful sister with his dark arts.

Mayhew felt his face flush several stages redder as anger subsumed him while he contemplated Katharine – that pale white woman – bedding that coal-black man. What about her child, Antonio, to whom Mayhew had dedicated so much time and attention, trying to civilise him in the barbarian jungle? The boy must be saved from the ignominy of a mother who went with a Black man. She hadn't even gone native; it was far worse than that. But she seemed to value savages more than her own kind. What about the pathetic slave girl she'd bought? What was wrong with the woman? With women generally?

The dancing performance over, he hauled himself up from the sofa and stomped furiously down the stairs to the lower deck. Mac's revelations had thoroughly unnerved him, setting him on edge and ruining the mellifluous ambience. He thought he might explode with rage and mortification. Did Katharine want to be the laughing stock of all Brazil?

But then he saw the European girl, waiting by one of the cabin doors and his thunderous mood lifted. He followed her over the threshold and into the sumptuously appointed room. Almost immediately, wonderful things started happening and Mayhew dismissed all thoughts of anything but the here and now. It was a remarkable facility he had that made life so much easier than for those who had that pesky attribute called a conscience.

As for Katharine – he decided he could do no more, he could not save her from herself. As long as she stayed in the jungle, it was clear that the habits of the jungle would stay with her.

Chapter Thirty-Two

London, 1901

Mabel cried herself to sleep the night of the master's assault. She longed for her mother, her sister, even her noisy, rowdy, boisterous brothers. Disgust enveloped her, for what the master had done and because she hadn't stopped it. Surely she could have thrown him off, if she'd fought harder? But she hadn't had the strength, had been weakened by terror and shock, and by the total surprise of it all. And he was huge, his girth and weight far greater than hers. Plus it had been so unexpected, so completely out of the blue – though as she went over and over it in her mind, she realised that it had actually been anything but. Those had not been chance encounters with the master in corridors and passageways; all had been deliberate, leading to this. How stupid she had been not to understand. How pathetic her situation that she wouldn't have been able to prevent it, even if she had understood.

She ran her hands over her stomach and hips to see if anything was broken or damaged, and then snatched them away, as if they were straying into forbidden territory just like the master's had. She felt dirty and cheap, aware that she had failed in some gargantuan way.

She chewed at the lump in her cheek until it became a mountain.

Mabel did not go to the park the next Thursday, nor to Clerkenwell the week after. She wrote to her mother to say she was not well and wanted to rest. Kirsty, whom she had no way to contact, would just have to wait for her in vain. Even if she ever saw her again, Mabel knew she would never tell Kirsty what had happened. She would never tell anyone.

The only thing she could do to try to expiate the horror was chronicle it in her diary. But, having done so, she spent fearful hours worrying that the mistress would find her journal, read it, and thus discover what had happened. Employers could do that if they wanted to, could enter your private room and go through your private things. They would reason that it was their house and everything in it belonged to them so they could do what they liked.

Mabel considered tearing the pages out and burning them. Indeed, she nearly did so. But then, in a sudden act of rebellion, she decided not to. Instead, she hid the notebook under her mattress. It wasn't the safest hiding place in the world but if the mistress were so nosy as to look there and to read it, at least she would know what sort of a man she was married to. If she didn't already.

Cook noticed her mood, and her lack of appetite.

'What's wrong, girl?' she asked. She was brusque and could be harsh and punitive. But she had a kind heart underneath, Mabel thought. She was just like everyone else: terrified of losing her job, of falling out of favour with those of higher status who controlled the lives of everyone beneath them.

Mabel shrugged and shook her head. 'Just feeling a little under the weather, that's all.' She could barely get her voice above the volume of a whisper these days.

Cook looked at her sharply. She pursed her lips and scrutinised Mabel before speaking. 'You're not…? Tell me you've not got yourself in trouble? I warned you about followers, didn't I? Please tell me you've not gone and done something stupid.'

Mabel's face blanched. Her stomach churned and bile rose in her throat. Cook knew. Cook knew what Mabel and the master had done. And she knew it was Mabel's fault.

'N-no,' she stuttered, and then hurriedly stood up, grabbing her wooden cleaning box and fleeing the kitchen. She didn't even know what she was saying 'no' about.

Over the next days and weeks, Mabel lived on her nerves, constantly on edge, her body always tense and waiting for the unexpected, for someone to creep up behind her in the darkness. The master went away for a while, but even then, she couldn't relax. She dreaded going into the housemaid's closet where *it* had happened. Even just passing near to it made her head spin, and her guts wrench in anguish.

One day, Cook told her she had to clean the closet out, sort all the equipment and give the walls and floors a good scrubbing. Dragging her feet, clutching her cleaning box in sweat-dampened hands, she made it to the room. Her knees trembled; her legs shook as if they could no longer support her weight. She was suddenly incredibly thirsty, as if she'd die of thirst. Desperately, she gathered saliva in her mouth and swallowed it down, trying to quench the dryness.

Wedging the door open with a bucket of water, she made sure that she was always facing it as she worked. For some reason, there was a picture on the wall even here, of a dour-looking man behind whom a three-masted schooner rocked on a dark and stormy sea. The man's eyes followed Mabel as she worked, assessing her, judging her. It was as if the master was watching her, undressing her with his eyes.

Somehow, she got the job done, and immediately on finishing, rushed to the privy and threw up. She was sure Cook heard her. Now she'd be even more convinced that Mabel was pregnant. But could you get pregnant from what the master had done? Mabel didn't think so but there was no one to ask. Anyway, she thought, looking down at her bony hips and hollowed out stomach, she certainly didn't look pregnant. Her loss of appetite and constant state of stress meant she was skinnier than she'd ever been.

A few nights later, Mabel woke abruptly in the night. It was almost midnight and at first, she could not work out what had disturbed her. Then she heard the unfamiliar sound of footsteps on the rickety steps that led to her attic room. No one else slept up here. Joe had his room on the half-landing and Cook, as the senior servant, had much larger and nicer accommodation on the floor below.

Mabel's heart stopped. Who could be coming up here at this time of night? A burglar? A ghost? Oh, please God not the master. If she lay in bed, covers over her head, perhaps whoever it was would think there was no one there and go away. But she couldn't move, just sat there, upright, wide eyes staring at the door. Tiny sobs rose in her throat, whimpers that she tried to suppress for fear of whoever or whatever it was hearing her. She willed, with all the force of her mind, the door not to open.

Creaking on its ancient hinges, the door slowly opened.

In Mabel's heightened state of awareness, every nerve on edge, she was sure she would snap or crack or break apart if she moved. She should have put a chair under the door handle or pulled her chest of drawers across it. Why hadn't she done that? She couldn't think now, just that it had never occurred to her that anyone would venture up to her hovel under the eaves.

If it was the master, what was he planning to do to her? She quivered in the darkness, heart full of dread.

The door was open wide now. A shadowy figure hove into view. Involuntarily, Mabel shrank back, pressing herself painfully against the metal bed head, and emitted a strained, strangled mewl.

There was a desperate, pregnant pause that seemed to last a lifetime. And then a familiar voice sounded out into the emptiness.

'It's all right, miss,' said the voice. 'It's only me, Joe. I ain't going to hurt you.'

The fear turned to fury in an instant.

'Joe!' Mabel's cry was a whispered shriek. 'What are you doing? You're not supposed to come here.'

Joe slunk into the room and shut the door quietly behind him but did not come any closer. The room was so small that he was only the length of the bed away from Mabel.

'I need to tell you something. And I can't do it during the day because Cook's always there with her pricked ears and eyes in the back of her head.'

Mabel nodded, mutely. Now the terror had abated a wave of exhaustion swept over her, leaving her almost too weary to speak.

'It's the master. And the mistress. They've been arguing about you.'

'About me?' questioned Mabel, faintly. She couldn't believe she was important enough to either of them to cause an argument. She assumed employers never thought about their servants – out of sight, out of mind.

'Yes,' Joe continued. 'I don't know exactly what's gone on. But the mistress thinks – well, she thinks that you've been making eyes at the master. And that he's got a soft spot for you.'

'How... how do you know?'

'I heard them, didn't I? They talk in front of us as if we don't have ears or can't understand. She was right cross with him, telling him to leave you alone,' Joe explained, his voice getting louder as he warmed to his subject.

'Shush,' hissed Mabel. 'Someone will hear.' She couldn't imagine how much trouble she'd be in if anyone caught Joe in her room. The disgrace that would entail was unimaginable.

She was silent for a moment, her mind working overtime, her thoughts flitting all over the place, trying to figure out what were the consequences of what Joe was saying, what might happen next.

Joe provided the answer.

'I think she's going get rid of you,' he hissed, in a stage whisper. 'That's what I wanted to tell you. Coz you'll need another job and I don't reckon on her giving you a reference.'

Mabel's mouth fell open. Shock surged through her body. She was going to lose her job. Get the sack. Be let go. However, you put it, it was a disaster. Her reputation would be tainted, her ability to get more work greatly diminished. And she had no idea what she could say to account for her dismissal, or how she would get another job without references. Though Katharine, still ignorant as to their father's accident, was helping her parents financially, Mabel still needed to work. She could not afford to be idle and unemployed, nor did she want to be. She took pride in earning her own keep.

'Go now, Joe,' she demanded. 'Just go.'

He slid out of the door and pulled it shut. Mabel sank down into her bed and lay flat on her back. That was how she felt: flattened. Erased, eradicated.

When the bells rang five a.m., she had not slept a wink. Her whole world had fallen apart. And worst of all, she had been rude to Joe. She hadn't been able to find the grace in her heart to thank him for letting her know and she hated herself for that.

Chapter Thirty-Three

Norwood, 1901

A dreadful scream roused Katharine from her bed. It was only a few days after the Spanish pharmacist, on his promised return visit, had declared Thomas and Antonio fully recovered from the malaria that had threatened to kill them, but immediately she assumed that something terrible must have happened to one of them. Once it had infected you, malaria could return at any time.

She was up, dressed and down the stairs in seconds, sure that Antonio had had a relapse. Oh, please God, not Antonio. And not Thomas either. Nor Jonathan or Santiago, or any of the Indians who lived in the compound and surrounding jungle.

She reached the ground floor just as a frantic slamming began upon the door. Wrenching it open, she was greeted by the sight of Rosabel's tear-stained and anguished face.

'Oh, Mother,' she cried, barely able to get the words out. 'She dead, she dead.'

She? So it definitely wasn't Thomas or Antonio – but who could Rosabel be talking about?

'Who, Rosabel?' she demanded. 'Calm down and tell me who.'

'Fortunata,' sobbed Rosabel, 'Fortunata is dead.'

Katharine stared at the distraught woman as her words gradually sank in. A wave of nausea surged through her. She had hardly thought of the girl since the malaria episode had begun, just been aware of her bringing food and water, slipping word-lessly in and out of shadows, hiding herself away from any kind of scrutiny.

'But how?' she gasped. 'Why? What happened to her? Did someone hurt her?'

Rosabel shook her head. 'No, Mother. She die of thinness. She eat nothing but dirt.'

The cook took Katharine to the hut where Fortunata slept. She was still in her hammock, looking as if she were asleep. But when Katharine leant over her and felt her brow it was stone cold. In the stillness of death, she could see how emaciated the girl was, more than she had noticed before, all skin and bones and angles, her cheeks pinched so tight they looked as if they might meet in the middle of her mouth.

'Oh God,' she murmured. 'Poor, poor girl.'

Anger flared through her; she remembered the man who had been bidding for her at the auction, the things she'd imagined he wanted to do to her, to use her for. And who knew what the person selling had been doing before that? Fortunata had had a horrendous life before Katharine, so full of big ideas of saving her, of nurturing her, had bought her. And yet here she was, dead, and it was all Katharine's fault for taking her eye off the ball, for being so concerned with Thomas and Antonio that she had neglected the little girl, hadn't seen that she had lost an impossible amount of weight.

She took Fortunata's hand in hers, feeling her skeletal fingers, like Hansel's chicken bone that fooled the witch and thought that she, too, had been fooled. She had assumed that bringing Fortunata to a place of safety, away from abuse and neglect, would make her well. She had not understood the depth of the sickness that infected the girl's soul. Far from making her well, she had let her die.

This was the Amazon, slipping from life to death in a heart-beat. But this time, it was Katharine's fault.

The whole compound attended Fortunata's funeral, everyone drenched in sadness. Antonio lit a candle and the

Indian women sang a song of grieving that they said would send her on her way to the next world, where the catfish were plentiful, huge and juicy and the jaguars slept with the chickens. A peaceful world, with no slavery.

A world where rubber did not exist.

'I really loved her,' Katharine murmured to Thomas as they stood by the grave, next to the burial place of the rubber tappers who'd been killed by the hostile tribe, and Po-Po, another lost friend.

'I know you did,' replied Thomas.

He had made a cross for Fortunata's headstone, engraving her name upon it and decorating it with carvings of flowers and leaves.

'But I didn't do nearly enough for her.'

'You rescued her from that – that man,' he reminded her, gently comforting her. 'You made her last months the best since she was stolen from her family. She had nothing to fear here.'

'Yes, but she shouldn't have been stolen in the first place, should she?' Katharine was shouting now, enraged by the injustices she saw all around her, the heartbreak that rubber and greed and the thirst for more was inflicting on the Amazon. 'It's not fair!'

Thomas grimaced resignedly. Katharine bit her tongue. She was conscious of sounding like a child. And how insensitive of her to remark on what was fair and what was not to Thomas, whose own family history, culture and ancestry had long ago been lost, obliterated by the scourge of slavery.

'You did what you could,' said Thomas, his tone as measured and reassuring as ever. 'And that's all any of us can do.'

His words were a comfort, his solid, indomitable presence even more so. But with Fortunata's death, following so closely on from his and Antonio's near fatal illness, Katharine saw afresh the myriad dangers of the Amazon, and she became fearful in a way she had never been before.

A few days after Fortunata's funeral, the budget brought a letter from Mayhew. The rubber price had risen again. He was

235

on his way to Norwood from Manaus – what a city! What an establishment he had set up there! – to discuss the twin issues of their increasing rubber production and Antonio.

Katharine showed the letter to Thomas.

'He wants to talk about rubber and Antonio,' she said, her voice a dull monotone. 'And I don't know what either has got to do with him.'

Thomas laughed. He understood the antipathy that often flared up between the siblings and he was always good at calming Katharine down and helping her to laugh off some of Mayhew's most objectionable and annoying traits.

'Just humour him,' he advised. 'And don't let him get to you. When he sees you rise to him, it only makes him worse.'

Katharine put her head in her hands. The thing was that Mayhew might be right that talking about Antonio was necessary. There was fighting again not far away in Anzo province, and yet another yellow fever epidemic. The jungle seemed to be becoming ever more dangerous. Maybe it would be best to get Antonio well away from this place.

It was broad daylight and everyone was out and about – Katharine could hear the chattering of the women around the cooking fires, the men lolling in their hammocks having good-natured arguments, the children grubbing in the sandy earth – but they were all some way away from the office. She turned to Thomas, needing him, his warmth and strength and solidity, wanting it so much that, even though she knew she shouldn't, she went to him now and laid her cheek against his shoulder.

She had taken so many decisions alone over the years, coped with so much that had been thrown at her. She was weary. She needed help.

'Hold me,' she whispered, 'please hold me tight.'

Thomas did as she asked, fastening his arms around her.

'Love me,' she murmured, 'love me above all else. Love me like I love you.'

Her eyes flickered open and shut, and briefly the light through the window dimmed and then re-illuminated. For a fleeting second, she wasn't sure if it had been her closed lids that had caused the light to go, or a shadow from a passing figure. But then Thomas pulled her further into him, kissing her forehead, her nose and then her lips, softly at first and then with an increasing urgency, and Katharine dismissed as fanciful, the product of a guilty imagination, that there had been anyone prying from outside.

–

Taking them all by surprise, Mayhew arrived only a week later.

'I left early,' he told Katharine, breezily, as he instructed the Indian canoeists to carry his luggage up to the house.

Antonio ran to greet him. He'd been exceptionally surly over the last few days, hardly speaking to Katharine or Thomas. Katharine's heart usually sank at the thought of a prolonged period of time spent with Mayhew, and she'd not been happy at the prospect of this visit, but now she was actually genuinely glad to see him. He, at least, always seemed to be able to communicate with Antonio, and Katharine was grateful that her brother could bring her son out of himself and his solitary nature.

'He's a youngster,' Thomas reassured her. 'It's a phase. He'll get over it.'

Katharine appreciated his efforts to put her mind at rest but wasn't convinced. At the same time, there was much to catch up on with the business. Though she had offered Mayhew the position of her representative in Manaus as a last resort, and had not thought it through at all, it had turned out to be a fortuitous decision. Everyone in the city loved money, but none more so than her brother. Motivated by the deal he and Katharine had struck where he got a percentage of the profits Norwood Enterprises made, he had every incentive to work hard and had proved to be an astute businessman.

Going through the accounts, completing entries in the profit and loss book and making price graphs absorbed all of the siblings' time for a few days. For a while, everything went smoothly. No arguments, not too many disagreements. But Katharine knew it was too good to last and so it proved to be. What she hadn't bargained for, or rather had chosen to ignore, was Mayhew's unfailing ability to sniff out a secret. It was as if he could sense the illicit on the air, and then follow it like a bloodhound.

'Thomas is shaping up as a good manager, isn't he?' he questioned as they sat by the river one darkening evening, watching egrets, herons and storks pick morsels from the shallows. 'You were so quick to say you didn't need anyone – now I don't think you could do without him, could you?'

Katharine sighed in agreement. 'No, I couldn't. I concede that you were right.' She turned to face him and smiled. It couldn't hurt to humour him every now and again. 'Thank you for being so wise.'

'I brought him here to help you keep the Indians in their place, show them who's boss,' continued Mayhew, living up to Katharine's expectations that he would always be the brother who knew it all. He paused, threw a stone into the water and watched the ripples as it sank.

'I didn't think you'd end up fornicating with him.'

Katharine's mouth fell open, her eyes widening in horror.

'Hah!' gloated Mayhew. As he'd suspected, the gossip Mac had shared with him in Manaus was true, not just idle rumour. The bush telegraph was surprisingly efficient, despite everything else in the jungle being so primeval and rudimentary.

'I thought as much,' he continued. 'I had no proof – none at all – but I've noticed the way you look at him, and him at you, full of lust.' There was no need to mention to Katharine that it was Mac who'd let him in on the secret. Let her think it was his intuition. Then she'd be less ready to keep secrets from him. 'And the fact that you contrive to spend every possible minute with him.'

Katharine gulped. Fear had stilled the blood in her veins and she was cursing herself for giving herself away so easily.

238

'It's – it's not what you think,' she said, lamely, and imme-diately hated herself for being so weak, for pandering to his prejudices, for making it sound as if she were ashamed of her relationship with Thomas. The problem was that, exposed to the light of 'civilised' society, she did feel shame – but only because society told her she should.

As if reading her mind, Mayhew continued. 'You've been away from civilisation for too long – you've forgotten what it is. You're no better than those savages out in the woods, living in the dirt, engaging in all sorts of filthy practices.'

Katharine held back a sharp retort. From what she remem-bered of Manaus, it was the city dwellers who were engaged in filthy practices if anyone was but she refrained from saying so. There was no point in provoking an argument. She'd just sit tight, let Mayhew get it all off his chest. And then hopefully he'd get bored again and rush off back to the so-called civilised city and leave her alone.

But Mayhew showed no inclination to move on from this particular subject.

'A so-called respectable widow canoodling with…! I don't need to say more. But then, I suppose it's no surprise you've gone native. I mean, what else is there to do here?'

There was a short silence while Mayhew lit a cigarette. The packet bore the imprint of a French brand, imported and sold at a huge mark up in Manaus, Katharine supposed. Of course, Mayhew couldn't slum it by smoking a local variety. She thought about getting up and walking off, leaving him alone with his vile suppositions. But she didn't want to let bad feeling curdle. Perhaps smoking would calm him down and they'd be able to have a rational discussion.

When he spoke again, he had completely changed track.

'Antonio's asked me to take him to England to school.'

Katharine's mouth fell open again.

'To school?' she spluttered, as if she'd never heard of such a place. 'In England? Why? Where?'

The evening was taking on shades of a nightmare, Mayhew doling out one horrific shock after the other.

'What does he know of England? Or of school, for that matter?' she added, frantically, helplessly. Even though she'd thought about it often enough herself, it was something completely different coming from Mayhew.

'He wants to get away from – this.' Mayhew waved his arm vaguely around him. 'And in all honesty, Katharine, I think it would be good for him. He's becoming a lily-livered mummy's boy.'

Rage exploded in Katharine's chest. Lily-livered? Nothing could be further from the facts; Antonio was brave and courageous to a fault, scared of nothing and no one.

The only scintilla of doubt was about the 'mummy's boy'. Could it be true? Was she stifling him, holding onto him for her benefit but not for his? She had never considered this before. But perhaps Mayhew was right. Perhaps it was pure selfishness to keep him here. Maybe it was precisely her suffocating love that was making him so uncooperative and difficult.

'I've told him about the schools in England, the kind of place he could go to,' Mayhew continued.

'What kind of place would that be?' Katharine thought of the school in Clerkenwell that she and her brothers and sister – including Mayhew – had all attended. It was hardly anything to boast about.

'Winchester, I think would be best, or perhaps Eton or Harrow.'

Katharine gazed at him in bemusement and then burst out laughing. Mayhew was being ridiculous. People like them didn't go to the oldest, most elite, most expensive public schools in the country.

Mayhew shot her a look that managed to be angry and patronising at the same time. 'Of course. Why not?'

'Winchester? Eton? Are you out of your mind? Those schools are not for people like us. We can't send him somewhere like that! It's ridiculous.'

Mayhew dismissed Katharine's protestations with an irritated tsk. 'I have money. Plenty of money.' He still had cash squirrelled away from his long defunct pyramid scheme, not that Katharine knew anything about that. She would undoubtedly disapprove. He'd been cautious about unearthing the funds in case anyone was onto his fake disappearance and watching him. But he reckoned it was all long enough in the past now.

'But I'm not wasting it on my siblings before you suggest that,' he continued. 'It's the next generation I wish to invest in.'

'Right.' Katharine was stumped. She didn't know what to think. Or perhaps she did. School abroad was probably the best thing. She just hadn't had the courage to face up to that fact yet.

'It's a chance for him to rise up in life,' continued her brother, his tone gentler now, encouraging, cajoling. 'Against all odds, you've made something of yourself. So have I. Now he can make something even better. If only I'd had the opportunity for the best education money could buy – just think what I could have done.'

Katharine hardly dared to. Surely he couldn't be even more of a bully?

'All I want to do is help my nephew. I know we don't always see eye to eye and we have – well – a lot of differences. But we both know that our parents put family above all else. And this is something I can do for a child I really love. It can't be easy for him, not having a father and all.' Mayhew sighed and pursed his lips, shaking his head as if evaluating Antonio's parlous situation. 'Let me do what I can for the boy, I implore you.'

Katharine nodded sadly. Of course, she wanted the best for Antonio. Keeping him here was selfish, to do with her needs, not his. Sending him to England for a few years would be for the best – and after all, it was only what everyone did, all the 'traditional' colonialists who lived in India or Kenya or Ceylon.

Mayhew was offering a golden chance to Antonio. How could she possibly say no?

'I think we should change his name to Anthony,' Mayhew concluded, assuming Katharine's silence as acquiescence. 'Make him sound more English. It's always best that way.'

Katharine stared sightlessly ahead, unable to look at her brother. She rubbed her eyes as if she could erase the inevitability of what was going to happen. But when she glanced up again, it was all still there. Mayhew surrounded by his plume of blue smoke, and Norwood, soon to be missing her son.

Chapter Thirty-Four

London, 1901

In the end, the mistress of Brampton Square gave Mabel a month's notice and a reference. She said that she and her husband were going to the South of France for an extended holiday and therefore she would no longer be needed. Cook was going with them, and Joe would stay in London to look after the house. Prior to that, the master was going to be away for work.

She spoke in a monotone, her voice expressionless and she did not accuse Mabel of anything. Mabel was bewildered that she wasn't being put out on her ear right away, but profoundly grateful that the mistress had made sure to let her know that there was no chance of *it* happening again, as the master wouldn't be in residence.

Nevertheless, she puzzled over the enigma of what lay behind her dismissal for the rest of the day. Whose side was the mistress on?

'*She was right cross with him, telling him to leave you alone,*' Joe had said. Perhaps this had happened before. But then, wouldn't Cook have said something? Immediately, she realised that was never going to happen. Cook was loyal to her employers through thick and thin; she would never speak ill of them. Brainwashed. That's what Kirsty said about these older servants who'd forgotten what freedom was, who were so used to being subservient that they didn't even realise that they were.

But however sure Mabel was that the master was far away and she'd never have to lay eyes on him again, she couldn't get him out of her head. She saw him in every dark corner, behind every piece of dark, heavy furniture. She felt his weight upon her, his hands all over her.

Her flesh crawled.

She wanted to write to Katharine to tell her about losing her job, to complain – because where else could she do so? – of how unfair it was. But she couldn't. Katharine didn't even know she was working rather than attending school.

Mabel tried to imagine Katharine being there, telling her stories as she had when she was little, combing her blonde hair and plaiting it for her, covering her with love and kisses. She thought of Antonio, who was now the recipient of all that love, and felt a moment of jealousy, which immediately made her feel guilty. She had no right to resent a son for having a mother who loved him. And anyway, it wasn't as if she wasn't loved by her own mother. It was just that she was so ashamed of what had gone on, what she had let happen, of *it*, that she could never tell Mary, and that drove an invisible wedge between them that was proving immoveable. And anyway, her mother was so preoccupied with nursing her father, she had little time for anything else.

On her last Thursday in the house, Mabel went to Hyde Park. She wanted, and didn't want, to see Kirsty, vacillating between going and not going for the entire week beforehand. In the end, her sense of duty made her go. It was unfair just to walk out on Kirsty; she might be imagining that she'd upset Mabel in some way, would not understand why Mabel had dropped her. Or she might be worried that something had happened to Mabel. There had been a scarlet fever epidemic, and there was always measles. People died of those diseases – not often, but sometimes. Mabel felt awful to think of Kirsty conjuring up all sorts of terrible fates for her when none of them were true.

She sat on the bench by the Long Water and watched the wind make crystals dance on the gleaming surface. Gulls swooped and screeched and the immaculate nannies with their enormous prams bowled past, small wool-coated children skipping in their wake.

Kirsty arrived. She fell on top of her friend, clasping her into the tightest hug. 'Where have you been,' she cried. 'I've missed you so much.'

Mabel shrugged and chewed her cheek. 'Just busy. I had to...' she paused, quelling a sudden urge to tell Kirsty everything, to get this hideous secret off her chest. 'I had to go home and help Mother, you know how it is,' she concluded, brightly.

Kirsty shook her head. 'Well, I don't know, given that we buried my mam ten years ago, but...'

'Oh, Kirsty, I'm so sorry.' Anguish gripped Mabel and she wrung her hands in sorrow. She was so thoughtless. Nothing was worse than what Kirsty had gone through, losing both her parents and being all alone in the world.

Kirsty laughed. 'Don't be daft. Of course, I understand. I'm just glad you've reappeared, a phoenix from the ashes.'

Mabel smiled weakly. She hadn't realised how much she'd missed Kirsty, her energy and optimism. The world felt just a little more normal, now they were together again in the park and the fresh air, away from the torpid atmosphere of Brampton Square.

They stood up and Kirsty linked arms with Mabel and pulled her off towards the Italian Gardens. Amidst the flowers, fountains and ornate urns, the sun seemed to shine a little brighter.

'Do you think this is what Italy is really like?' mused Mabel. 'It must be pretty if it is.'

'I haven't got a clue,' responded Kirsty. 'But the statues are all nude so maybe the Eyctics go around with no clothes on.' She roared with laughter at the idea, but Mabel's stomach churned.

They walked into the grasslands of the park. Mabel had seen pictures of Scottish grouse moors and imagined them like this, but wider and wilder, bigger and more barren. 'What's Scotland like?' she asked.

'You're full of questions today, aren't you?' teased Kirsty. 'Is this like Italy? What's Scotland like?' She mimicked Mabel's

London accent, and then said something in her broadest Scots so that the only word Mabel could make out was 'wee'.

Mabel couldn't help but giggle. Kirsty always raised her spirits. She shouldn't have stayed away for so long.

'My sister lives in the Amazon,' announced Mabel, apropos of nothing, when Kirsty had fallen silent. She just suddenly thought about it, as they were talking about distant places.

'The Amazon!' Kirsty stopped short and turned to Mabel in amazement. 'Really? Why? What does she do there?'

Mabel smiled. 'Now who's curious?' she retorted, in mock retaliation. They both laughed.

'She's a rubber baron's wife,' continued Mabel. 'Or at least she was, until her husband died. But that was when they'd only just got there, so I suppose she's the rubber baron now.'

Kirsty shook her head emphatically. 'No. Us girls never get the top jobs and the way I look at it, we never will.'

'What about Queen Victoria?' objected Mabel.

Kirsty flicked her head in irritation. 'That fat old cow doesn't count. She's dead now and anyway, royalty's different, isn't it? They don't care if you're a boy or a girl as long as they can keep the power and money and status.'

She paused for thought. 'The rubber baron's widow, that's what your sister is,' she continued.

'I suppose so.'

'I wish I could go to the Amazon,' continued Kirsty, pensively. 'Hang on,' she went on, stopping short as she thought of something, 'why don't we go? Both of us, you and I?'

Mabel blinked in astonishment. 'I don't know. I don't think we could. It's an awfully long way – it took my sister ages to get there. And how would we afford the tickets?'

Neither had an answer to that and they walked in silence for a while. Mabel's thoughts drifted, to Katharine in the jungle, running her business, seeking her fortune. She was so brave! Mabel wished she were as brave as that. These days even coming to the park felt like an impossible challenge. To reach the Amazon, even if money were no object, was unthinkable.

They rounded the corner of the path and past a clump of bushes. From behind it, they could hear strange noises, grunts and groans and yelps. The girls looked at each other, Mabel alarmed, Kirsty amused.

'Shhhh,' she hissed, motioning with her finger against her lips for Mabel to be quiet. Together they crept forward until they could see where the sounds were coming from. There in the grass were a man and a woman. The woman was on all fours, her dress pulled up around her waist. The man was behind her, his trousers pushed down to his knees. He was moving backwards and forwards against her, rhythmically and forcefully, his white forearms gleaming in the sunlight.

Mabel felt faint. She clutched tight to Kirsty's arm as her head spun. Stars danced beneath her tightly shut eyelids.

Kirsty was giggling and pointing.

'Look at them,' she said, 'he's going for it!'

The couple were so involved in what they were doing that they took absolutely no notice at all of the two onlookers.

Mabel, sickened, turned around, pulling Kirsty with her.

'Aw,' shrieked Kirsty, far too loudly for Mabel's liking. 'What are you doing that for? I was enjoying the show.'

Mabel's could feel her face bright red with embarrassment. Kirsty spotted it.

'What's up with you?' she joked. 'Haven't you ever seen anyone at it before? There are always couples in the park – they've nowhere else to go, have they. You want a bit of hanky-panky, you head for the trees or the bushes – and God help you if it's raining or snowing.'

She roared with laughter. Mabel's stomach tightened. She couldn't be cross with Kirsty. Her friend was not to know why it was affecting her like this.

'*Haven't you ever seen anyone at it before?*' The words rang in Mabel's head. No, but she'd experienced it. It was just that she couldn't tell Kirsty, couldn't tell anyone.

'The men beg you and beg you for it,' Kirsty was saying, though she sounded far away, her voice echoey and distant.

'That's what I've been told. But it's not fun for women. Only men enjoy it.'

She said this last so definitively, as if she knew from experience. Mabel was feeling dizzier and dizzier. A vision of the woman's face, showing layers of expression from pain to ecstasy, hovered behind her eyes. She hadn't looked exactly happy. But on the other hand, she hadn't looked as if she wanted it to stop. And she certainly hadn't looked as Mabel had felt when the master… She didn't understand any of it.

They walked back to the park exit, Mabel with her eyes half closed, as if seeing only part of the world made it less frightening.

'I won't be able to meet you again,' she blurted out, as soon as they reached the black iron gates. 'I'm…' she paused, realising she hadn't thought about what to say, what excuse to give. 'I'm leaving my job and the next one is far away from here.'

It sounded lame and Mabel could tell Kirsty didn't believe her, that she knew there was more to this story. But she didn't pry.

'That's a pity,' she said, lightly. 'I enjoyed our afternoons in the park. Still, never mind. I hope it goes well for you.'

She patted Mabel on the arm, then turned and left, striding purposefully towards Hyde Park Gardens.

'Goodbye,' called out Mabel to her rapidly receding form. 'Goodbye, Kirsty.'

Sadly, she headed in the direction of Brampton Square. She knew she would never see Kirsty, who'd been a good friend to her, again.

Chapter Thirty-Five

In November, Antonio's journey to England and to school began. Katharine accompanied him and Mayhew as far as Lagona, from where she would see them off. Mac greeted them on their arrival and immediately gave Katharine a bundle of letters that he'd kept for her. As soon as they were settled into their rooms, she ripped the first one open. It was from Mabel.

But the missive's contents were disappointing. Her sister wrote almost nothing about her education, did not mention anything about how her French was coming along – and her words seemed stilted and forced, as if writing the letter had been a huge effort without reward.

'The house is quiet these days,' one paragraph read. 'Alf and Jim have started their apprenticeships and are working long hours. I am sure they will prosper in their new professions. A new omnibus service has begun which runs from Clerkenwell to the docks which is most convenient for their transportation to and from their premises of employment.'

Katharine frowned as she read these lines. Since when had Mabel used such terms as 'prosper', 'profession' and 'premises'? She sounded as if she were talking to someone who was not only fifty years older than her but also at least three tiers higher in the social hierarchy, rather than to her own sister who had more or less brought her up in her earliest days. More than anything else, she sounded impossibly faraway, unreachable, like a stranger.

With a heavy heart, Katharine stored the letter safely in her pocketbook. The passing years, so many of them, were distancing her from her family, gradually but inexorably. If she only knew, if she could just explain to Mabel, that she had to stay in Brazil until all the money was repaid to their father – then maybe they would be as close as Katharine wished.

But that moment, when the debt was no more, was still a long way off.

At dinner that night, Katharine tried to hide her sadness, laughing and joking merrily with Mac and his usual array of guests of varying degrees of eccentricity. Mac updated her about his daughter, Alexandra, who Katharine had met at Lagona, that Christmas of 1893 when all her rubber was destroyed.

'She's Lady Cardburn now, married with two children,' he told Katharine proudly, pulling a wrinkled and mildewy picture from his inside pocket to show to her. 'She's got a lovely house by Regent's Park. Bought it for 'em when I was back two years ago.'

Katharine studied the sepia tinted image.

'She's done well for herself,' she affirmed. 'And she's still so lovely.'

Alexandra was brunette and in her late twenties now, where Mabel was blonde and years younger. But something about Mac's daughter, her clear gaze and luscious locks, reminded Katharine of her sister. Mary had sent some photographs a year or so ago, and Katharine had carried them everywhere with her until they finally disintegrated, destroyed by the insidious damp.

'My sister is beautiful, too,' said Katharine, her voice almost a whisper as she tried to hide her homesickness. She had thought, after so much time, she would be immune to this ailment, but it seemed it could still creep up to broadside her at unexpected moments. Combined with her continued mystification about the stiffness of Mabel's latest letter, it did so now.

Mac looked at her in astonishment. 'You have a beautiful sister?' he questioned. 'Well, I never would have thought it, so I wouldn't.'

Despite her melancholy, Katharine had to laugh. Was Mac surprised she had a sister, or that she had a beautiful one? Was it really so hard to imagine that not all her siblings were as plain as she was?

As if realising his mistake, Mac hastily covered up. 'It's just that you hadn't mentioned anyone else in the family, apart from your brother of course.'

Katharine knew this was utter waffle. But she appreciated his efforts not to hurt her feelings. To move the subject to safer ground, she asked Mac about his plans.

'I'm off to London myself, actually,' he replied. 'Taking the steamer from Iquitos. I should be there in six weeks or so. Travel is so much quicker these days, and more convenient of course.'

Katharine sighed and smiled sadly. Everyone was leaving, going somewhere, headed someplace. Her friend, Mac; her son, Antonio. Thank God for Thomas, without whom she would be alone again, which she did not think she could bear.

Late into the night she wrote letters for Mac to take to England. He would get there first as Mayhew and Antonio were stopping for a short while in Manaus while Mayhew tied up some loose ends before his lengthy absence. Writing was the only contact she had – and suddenly it didn't seem enough any more.

The day of her son and her brother's departure dawned mistily and overcast. Katharine, after a sleepless night, woke early. She wandered out of the house, not sure where she was going or why, and found herself down at the landing stage, where soon she would be catching her last glimpses of her son as the steamer bore him away. She imagined him on deck, watching and waving until Lagona had disappeared into the distance. And then, with a deep, heavy sigh, she wiped that image from her mind. The way Antonio had been treating her lately, he wouldn't wave at all, he'd just board the boat and set off without a second thought about whom he was leaving behind.

Rain began to fall, the sudden, deadening rain of the forest, pattering heavily against the sand and red earth of the riverbank. Katharine stayed where she was, not caring how wet she got. The deluge fitted with her emotions and she almost welcomed it as some form of catharsis. Lost in thought, she jumped when a voice spoke to her.

'Mother.' It was Antonio, suddenly by her side.

'Ant... my boy.' Katharine halted, about to fling her arms around him and then stopping herself. Lately he had shrunk from her embrace and shouted at her if she protested, and she did not want their last hours together to be tainted by an argument or ill humour. 'What are you doing out here in the wet?'

'Nothing much,' he responded. 'I don't mind the rain.' He held his hand out to catch the drops as if to prove his statement. 'Why are you here, anyway?'

Katharine sighed and gave a small shrug. 'Just thinking.'

'What about?'

'Of how much I'll miss you.' She had not been going to say this as the last thing she wanted was for Antonio to feel guilty. He should be looking forward to his school days, to mixing with his contemporaries, to expanding his knowledge of the world in a proper classroom. She could not allow her own misgivings to hold him back.

Now it was Antonio's turn to shrug. 'I'll come back,' he replied. 'One day.'

One day. Why did he say that and not 'in the holidays' or 'next year'? It was so vague, as if seeing his mother again was unimportant, of no concern to him. Perhaps that's how he feels, thought Katharine miserably. Perhaps that's how I've made him feel, though I don't know how or why. They walked back up to the house for breakfast. Antonio ate heartily as always, as did Mayhew. Katharine could not swallow a crumb.

Later, seeing them off, Katharine felt that a part of her body was leaving with them, sailing away on an inexorable current of love and despair. She knew it was for the best. But an inner foreboding nagged at her heart then settled low in her belly. The fact that Antonio fulfilled her worst premonitions and barely said goodbye as he stepped aboard made it so much worse. Thomas told her it was natural for a boy to withdraw from his mother as he grew older and that it was nothing to worry about. But Katharine wasn't so sure. She could only hope that being with others his own age, exercising his mind as well as his body, would be good for him.

But nothing eased the gnawing ache of loss. Back at Norwood, she wandered in and out of rooms, down to the river, to the edge of the forest and beyond, longing to hear Antonio's youthful voice ringing through the still, heavy air.

Chapter Thirty-Six

The Atlantic, 1901

Two months later, Mayhew and Antonio's journey to Liverpool and to England began.

'I'm sorry it came to this,' Mayhew said to Antonio, the day they sailed out of the Amazon estuary and into the Atlantic.

'What do you mean?' Antonio, who'd been fine while on the river, was already starting to look a bit green around the gills. Mayhew recognised the signs and felt sorry for him. The sea was rough at any time of year, but especially in December and January, and it was miserable to be a poor sailor. Though he had never suffered himself, he had seen countless fellow passengers laid low on his passage to America all those years ago, and again when he'd made his escape from New York. It looked like Antonio wouldn't be much of a companion for the rest of the voyage.

'Your mother — well, she means well,' he replied, shaking a cigarette out of the packet.

'Does she?' Antonio asked, sounding defensive. 'In what way?'

Mayhew patted the boy's hand. He was so young, just at that age when a lad is at his most impressionable. Momentarily, he thought of Kitty. The baby she was having – his baby – would be around a year old now, though Mayhew hadn't done the maths to work it out precisely. Boy or girl, what nonsense would Kitty fill its head with? He had given up the right to provide a good influence when he faked his own death.

Observing how Antonio was sweating with nausea and the heat, Mayhew passed him a handkerchief to wipe his brow. It was a pity, he mused inwardly, that his nephew had to learn the harsh realities of human fallibility so young. Mayhew wished it didn't have to be this way, that he didn't have to be the one to spell it out. But sadly, in the absence of anyone else who would be honest, that task fell to him.

'Well you see, Anthony,' he began, adopting a sage and worldly tone. 'From her point of view it seemed best to get you as far away from the Amazon for your teenage years as possible. You being around – well, it was likely to prevent her from following her, er, how shall I put it, her natural inclinations in the way she wished to.'

'I don't understand.' Antonio's tone was plaintive. Confused. 'What are you talking about? She told me it was just about learning, education. And because I was so ill that time, and she wanted to protect me.'

Mayhew tapped ash into the ashtray. He sighed, deeply and regretfully, as if he really didn't want to say what he was going to. Antonio was staring at him, his eyes narrowed in puzzlement. Or possibly because Mayhew's smoke was all pervading in the confined quarters of their cabin.

'Your mother. She's not been honest with you. She and, er, she and Thomas, well, let's just say they're more than just colleagues.'

Antonio blinked. 'I know. I saw them. Holding hands and… and stuff. One evening when they were in the office and they didn't know I was outside.'

Mayhew's cigarette halted halfway to his mouth. This was news indeed. He'd had no idea the boy had any inkling of his mother's shenanigans.

'It made me sad,' Antonio continued, 'but I don't really know why, because I like Thomas.'

Mayhew's mind whirred. He'd thought that he was going to have to break the news of the relationship between Katharine and Thomas to Antonio, but as the boy already knew, he'd have to change tack.

'Well, it's perfectly fine to *like* Mr Smart,' he answered, cautiously. 'He's a splendid chap. It's just that… well, not to put too fine a point on it, he's Black. And I'm afraid – well, it's not just me, it's the way of thinking the world over – it's just not right for a Black man and a white woman to… you know, to be in a relationship. To sleep in the same bed. Not right at all. In the jungle – well, all sorts of unsavoury things go on. But you need to know that, in polite society – quite simply, it's regarded as, if not illegal, at the very least indecent.'

Antonio looked startled for a moment, and then anger spread across his face like a dark cloud during the rainy season. 'That's why she was hiding it from me. Kissing in secret, not telling me anything – because she knew it was disgusting.' His eleven-year-old face was screwed up in pain, red with fury. 'I was cross because she'd always said that no one could replace my father. And she promised she'd never love anyone but me, that she'd always love me best of all! But I didn't know that her being with Thomas was actually wrong.'

Mayhew nodded resignedly. It was a shame for the boy to learn the harsh truth, but better that than be kept in ignorance. Although seeing Antonio so agitated, Mayhew felt a momentary twinge of alarm, and something that was almost remorse.

'Look, my boy,' he said, in an attempt at mitigation. 'Out in the jungle different rules apply. People become isolated and that makes them develop strange habits and do things they wouldn't if they were somewhere more developed, like London, say.'

As he finished speaking, Antonio stood. Far from being mollified by Mayhew's words, instead he picked up the ashtray and flung it forcefully at the cabin wall. The thick glass did not shatter but threw off a few dispirited chips and then fell, with a dull thud, to the wooden floor. The extent of his nephew's rage both alarmed and confused Mayhew. Antonio was so truculent, so stubborn and at the same time so credulous. It was hard –

impossible, in fact – to read him. He had certainly taken it all rather more to heart than Mayhew had anticipated. Mayhew watched him nervously as he paced up and down the few square yards of the cabin floor, clenching and unclenching his fists. At least anger seemed to have banished his incipient seasickness, Mayhew thought grimly.

'Come on, young man,' he volunteered, using a hearty tone of voice to try to dispel the tension in the atmosphere, 'let's get some fresh air and then have dinner.'

Perhaps it was good it would be up to Kitty, and Kitty alone, to bring up their baby. It was harder than it looked, this child-rearing business; Mayhew had had a lucky escape from the responsibility. Locking the door hurriedly behind them as Antonio stormed along the corridor, Mayhew shook his head grimly. All he had wanted to do was to make the boy aware that his mother was far from perfect and ensure that he understood who really had his best interests at heart – namely, his Uncle Mayhew.

But it seemed that his words had set a fire burning that he had no idea how to put out.

Chapter Thirty-Seven

London, 1901

Mabel gazed apprehensively around her at the gleaming marble tiled floor and the gracious oak staircase, at the high, vaulted stucco ceiling decorated with elaborate carvings and at the plethora of gas lamps that meant the entire space, cavernous though it was, was brightly lit. Opulence screamed out from everything she could see. Patrick McNamara's Highgate mansion was a fitting abode for one of London's richest men.

Mabel could still hardly believe she was here.

Determined to pick herself up after the ignominy of being sacked, Mabel had summoned all her courage and taken herself off to Mrs Hunt's employment agency on Duke Street. She'd decided (perhaps spurred on by the thought of what Kirsty would have advised her) that the only way forward was to look for a job higher up the rankings than housemaid. She'd saved a bit of money while at Brampton Square and had put some of it towards cloth for a new uniform dress that Mary had made. She spoke properly and, thanks to her mother's expert craftsmanship, was well presented; she had experience and a reference and knew French.

All of these attributes meant that Mabel did not see why she should not apply for a position as a lady's maid. Though the master's assault had crushed her spirit in many ways, in others it had galvanised it into action. Her reasoning was that becoming a servant of higher status might afford her some protection from the same thing happening in the future, and this gave her the confidence and strength to enact her plan.

Once in the solemn, silent chamber of the agency, she'd begun to have second thoughts. To take her mind off her anxiety, she'd perused the numerous thick cream cards stuck into the custom-made wooden boards that adorned the walls. All had details of jobs on offer: third housemaid, cook, chamber maid, scullery maid.

And then the words 'lady's maid' had jumped out at her and she bent forward to read in closer detail.

Lady's maid required for
Lady Alexandra Cardburn.

Usual duties, £32 pa.
Must be young and presentable.

Apply to Mr Patrick McNamara,
Priests Avenue, Highgate.

Patrick McNamara. She recognised that name. Wasn't he Katharine's friend from the Amazon, the rubber baron on whose estate she'd been staying when Anselmo died? Mabel was sure he was. And she remembered Katharine writing about his daughter, Alexandra, whom she'd met when she'd visited one Christmas. Katharine had liked her and that was good enough for Mabel. So was the prospect of £32 a year – more than double what she'd been earning previously.

Purposefully pulling the card out of its holder, she went to sit down and await her turn to be interviewed. When her name was called, she had produced the card and insisted, politely, that this was the only position she was interested in.

The redoubtable woman sitting opposite her had read her credentials then invasively run her eyes up and down Mabel's person. After a pause to show who was in charge here, she had acquiesced to her request.

'Interview on Monday,' she had said. 'Twelve noon, don't be late.'

And now here Mabel was, overawed at her own boldness and wondering what on earth had possessed her to apply for the job. She had no experience as a lady's maid; the very thought terrified her. She chomped on the inside of her cheek until it was raw.

But Patrick McNamara, when she was eventually taken into his office to speak with him, was kind. He sat behind an enormous mahogany desk with a green leather top, a variety of expensive gold fountain pens arrayed on the blotting paper before him. The trappings of wealth pervaded every part of his home and himself, but his intense blue eyes twinkled encouragingly as he regarded her and he did not stop smiling throughout the brief interview – at the end of which he did what Mabel had least expected and offered her the job! Bluffing as she had been every inch of the way, she'd had no idea it would be that easy.

As she left, he looked her up and down. 'Your sister was right,' he said, still smiling.

Mabel hesitated. She'd told Mr McNamara as soon as they'd been introduced who she was. She'd hoped – and perhaps she'd been right, given the result – that it might make him look favourably upon her. She wondered when he and Katharine had been talking about her, and then whether Mac, as she knew Katharine called him, was going to explain. Should she ask? But Mr McNamara was bidding her farewell before she'd had a chance to. In the few moments before a servant arrived to see her out, Mabel knew she had to say the words that had been burning inside her since the interview began.

'Mr McNamara, sir,' she began, falteringly, 'would you mind very much, sir – I mean what I wish to say is…' She stopped, flustered, palms sweating. Mac lifted his eyes from the papers he had retrieved from a drawer. He waited, patiently.

Mabel tried again. 'Please, sir, I would be very grateful if you wouldn't mention the matter of my employment to my sister, should you see her again. I mean, you will see her again, obviously, when you go back to the Amazon...' Mabel tailed off. Had she said too much? But it had to be done. She began anew, firmly now, her voice unwavering. 'I would rather she didn't know that I'm working, you see. She thought... she thinks... that I'm still in school. And I'd rather it stayed that way. If you don't mind.'

Mac stared at her intently for a good few minutes after she'd finished. And then he leaned back in his chair, rocking it onto two legs, and began to guffaw with laughter. Surprised and shocked, Mabel looked on speechlessly.

'Oh, that's funny,' gasped Mac, as he recovered himself. His valet had arrived by now to escort Mabel away and was watching his employer, bemused. 'That's a rum request if ever I heard one.' It was as if he were talking to himself. And then he abruptly stopped laughing and looked straight at Mabel, into her brown eyes with his startling blue ones. 'But of course, my dear,' he said. 'I will, of course, follow your request to the letter.'

Thankfully, Mabel breathed a sigh of relief as she left the Highgate mansion. She would start her new job in two days' time. She still didn't know what Katharine had told Mac that he now knew was true but it didn't seem to matter any more. She had landed the job, plus a huge pay rise and she felt, justifiably, somewhat pleased with herself. It wasn't a feeling she indulged in often, but while it lasted it was a good one.

Chapter Thirty-Eight

London, 1901

By the time Mabel was ringing the bell at the tradesman's entrance of the elegant Nash house on Hanover Terrace, her nerves had returned and she was practically shaking.

'Lady Alexandra,' she kept repeating to herself in her head, 'Lady Alexandra.' She had to remember that was the way she must address the person who Katharine merely called Alexandra. She wondered if she'd be allowed to keep her own name. She'd been lucky so far. Employers often changed their servants' names to ones they thought more suitable such as Emma or Lucy, or to the one associated with the job, such as Mary for scullery maids.

Led into the house by a servant, Mabel was taken straight to see her new mistress. She was too nervous to notice much about her surroundings but Alexandra Cardburn, she saw immediately, was tall, slim and very beautiful, though Mabel thought her features had a sharpness about them that hinted at a quick temper. She was also exquisitely dressed and Mabel felt self-conscious in her plain dress, however carefully made by her mother. She had worn uniform, assuming that was what was expected. And in any case she would have felt uncomfortable in anything else, worried that it would make her look forward, as if she was trying to be noticed or to upstage her boss.

But as soon as Lady Cardburn spoke, Mabel realised she had made a mistake. 'How curious,' Alexandra said, forehead furrowed in puzzlement. 'Did you have to wear uniform in your old post? That's unusual, for a lady's maid. Usually, one would expect such a person to wear their own clothes.'

'Oh, I was...' Mabel, biting her tongue, checked herself just in time. Mac must have told his daughter that she was experienced in this particular area, not just that she'd done domestic work before. 'I-I wasn't sure what my lady would want,' she stuttered. She couldn't let on that she hadn't realised that her wardrobe was no longer restricted to print and plain dresses, with or without an apron.

'Well,' smiled Alexandra, sweetly, 'now you know. Mrs Bustle, the housekeeper, will show you your room and around the parts of the house that concern you.'

No one, apart from the butler and the housekeeper, had access to all areas of such a grand establishment as this.

Mabel nodded. 'Yes, my lady.'

Mrs Bustle, Mabel soon discovered, lived up to her name. She was less than five feet tall and round as a barrel, and she scurried about like an overgrown hedgehog, her numerous bundles of keys rattling like spines. Mabel's bedroom was right next to Alexandra's and was twice the size of her attic in Brampton Square. It had a bed with a much better mattress than she was used to, a chest of drawers, a kidney-shaped dressing table with a damask curtain and, best of all, a large window that looked onto the mews behind where the coaches and horses were kept.

She could hardly believe all this space was just for her. There was even a bathroom with running water for the servants and she was allowed two baths a week. The Bird family wasn't the poorest in society, not by any means, but the Clerkenwell house burst at the seams with two adults and six children still in residence, and bathing was done sporadically in a tin tub in front of the fire.

Mabel was grateful for this new-found luxury. In fact, she even started to think that she was going to like this new job, this new life, hobnobbing with the aristocracy, having, at last, a status within the household. She could begin seriously saving for the future with her new wage, to put money aside with which she might, one day, be able to achieve her dream of travelling to France and becoming a teacher of French.

Next, Mrs Bustle introduced Mabel to the butler, Mr Robson, and she curtsied gracefully, slightly overwhelmed at being in the presence of the most exalted servant. Brampton Square had not given her any opportunity to get used to the hierarchy of the servants' hall.

As they were heading through the front hallway, Mabel caught sight of a pair of footmen, resplendent in scarlet breeches, waiting by the door. They looked so alike that Mabel wondered if they were twins. Kirsty had told her that it was the last word in fashion to have matching footmen, and the taller the better; six footers held a premium in terms of status and wages. These two were both at least that height, towering over Mabel and the diminutive housekeeper. Mabel caught the eye of one and instantly looked away. But not before she'd seen the faintest hint of a smile cross his lips.

'His lordship is about to go out,' said Mrs Bustle proudly, as if this were a magnificent and princely achievement that only the highest echelons were capable of.

At that moment, a door was thrown open and a man who must be Lord Cardburn strode into the marbled hallway. Another man followed close behind; it was Patrick McNamara.

Roughly, Mrs Bustle almost manhandled Mabel against the wall. As the two men walked past, she curtsied, and Mabel followed her lead. But rather than walk straight past them as Mabel had hoped they would, they paused in front of the two women backed up against the blue-painted plaster like hostages. Mabel knew what Kirsty would be thinking in this situation: why should we cower and hide ourselves away, just because we're not posh? But Mabel had no thoughts of rebellion. All she wanted was a quiet life, not to get into trouble, to earn her wage and do a good job well.

And never, ever for *it* to happen again. Clearly Mac was not a concern in that regard. But Lord Cardburn? Who knew?

'Ah,' said Lord Cardburn.

He looked her up and down, appraising her. 'She looks promising.'

The comment was addressed to Patrick McNamara, not to Mrs Bustle or Mabel herself.

Mac gave a nod of acknowledgement and smiled at Mabel, a reassuring, comforting smile that creased his blue eyes charmingly.

'She's a lovely one, isn't she?' he remarked.

'She'll do,' responded Lord Cardburn. 'Quite nicely, I'd say!' He scrutinised her again. 'Bit too thin, but they eat well in my servants' hall. She'll put some flesh on and then be more than passable.'

Pleased with his quip, he laughed long and loud but Mac did not join in.

'I know from personal acquaintance that she's from the best of families,' he said, a trifle coldly. Mabel felt a warm rush of gratitude. He was sticking up for her. She had known this would be a good situation.

And then Lord Cardburn's laughter stopped and the men moved on, deep in conversation, the insignificant maid forgotten. Mabel breathed a sigh of relief: being ignored by the master of the house was far more preferable than being noticed.

The footmen snapped to attention as the men passed, then followed them out to the carriage that awaited them. Through the open doors, Mabel saw that the horses, like the footmen, were perfectly matched: black and glossy, hooves impatiently stamping against the paving slabs, manes tossing in the wind. The two men climbed aboard and the carriage rolled away, accompanied by the cacophonous clattering of wheels on stone.

Downstairs in the basement, Mrs Bustle showed her to the tradesmen's door. As Mabel went out, she passed her a package wrapped in brown paper.

'What's this?' asked Mabel. Was Lady Cardburn expecting her to start mending and darning, one of a lady's maid's key tasks, even before she'd actually begun working for her?

Mrs Bustle clicked her tongue against her teeth. 'A couple of my lady's old dresses for you. You'll need to shorten them considerably and take them in a bit, on account of you being nothing but skin and bone, but otherwise they should do you fine.'

Mabel fingered the package gingerly, as if it might explode at any minute.

Mrs Bustle smiled. 'That's one of the perks, my dear. My lady has all the latest fashions and she never wears anything two seasons running. That's a finely made black dress you're wearing there but I'm willing to guess it's your only one, and it's rather dull and plain. You need to look the part and this—' she tapped the parcel decisively, 'will help. Your wardrobe won't recognise itself.'

She didn't ask Mabel if she'd ever been a lady's maid before but Mabel could tell she knew she hadn't. She'd given herself away by not knowing the dress code – or that her employer would pass on cast-offs to her. That evening, she and her mother stitched and pressed and turned Lady Cardburn's dresses into beautiful outfits for Mabel. The fabrics were lovely, far lovelier than any Mabel had ever been able to afford: the best, softest wool and silk, the most luxurious organza and velvet. Mabel had never had garments like this before. Now she had a chance to enjoy fine apparel for the first time in her life.

That last evening in Clerkenwell though, she cried quietly to herself before she slept. Her mother thought she was just nervous at taking on more than she could chew. She didn't know that Mabel was full of self-loathing and confusion. That alongside her gratitude for getting the job was her terror, arisen anew after a period during which she had forced herself to be strong and confident. Lord Cardburn, the handsome footmen, Patrick McNamara – there were unfamiliar men everywhere and though the latter had shown her nothing but kindness and the two former nothing of harm, Mabel was frightened.

What was the secret of it all? Why did she garner unwanted male attention? At seventeen years old, she longed to know.

Chapter Thirty-Nine

London, 1902

The days in Lady Cardburn's employ were completely different to Brampton Square. No more washing dishes, scrubbing pans and polishing cutlery with varying substances of equal corrosiveness. Mabel, looking at her hands, could hardly believe that they appeared normal again, her fingers no longer swollen cabbages, her nails no longer ragged and split, her skin healed, smooth and flawless again.

1901 turned to 1902 and, despite her initial worries, Mabel picked up on the demands of the job quickly and easily, and her natural flair for fashion and style rapidly brought her Lady Cardburn's approval.

'You are always one step ahead,' her mistress said one late afternoon, as Mabel was helping her into her carefully chosen outfit for that evening's dinner. Caring for and choosing Alexandra's clothes was Mabel's main duty and took nearly all day, as her ladyship might change up to five times, depending on what her engagements were. 'I don't know what I did without you.'

Mabel never knew how to respond to statements like this.

'Thank you, my lady,' she said, thinking that you couldn't go wrong with such an answer.

The truth was that she loved dealing with all her ladyship's clothes, hanging and folding, mending and ironing. Now she was sewing on a daily basis she was becoming as competent and skilful with her needle as her mother, and she possessed a great eye for what would suit someone. She made sketches of the most striking outfits she and her ladyship saw each day, or found inspiration from the fashion plates in magazines, and then turned these prototypes into unique designs that either she or the dressmaker would make up.

Once Lady Cardburn was dressed, Mabel did her hair and make-up. She'd spent her first few afternoons off prowling the Harrods beauty hall, learning everything she could about face creams and powders, the latest anti-ageing remedies and trends in eye shadows and lipsticks. She soaked up all the information, fascinated by everything that was available to make a woman more attractive and beguiling – but never to use for herself of course, only ever for her ladyship.

Mabel loved that the house was always full, life and laughter spilling from every room. Many of the guests were famous or titled, or eminent in some sphere of government or industry, the legal profession or banking. Their shine rubbed off on the servants and made all of them seem more glamorous as a result.

Kirsty had been right that it was much better working in a larger household. Apart from anything else, there was much more fun to be had in the servants' hall. The Cardburns had provided a piano, and a couple of the servants could play the fiddle, so in the evenings they'd sometimes have music, singing and dancing, which Mabel adored. She became friends with Hannah the nursery maid, a girl about her own age who worked with the terrifying nanny, Nanny Hoskins, looking after the Cardburns' two sons, Michael, aged eight and William, aged six. Apart from Hannah, the other person she got to know well was one half of the handsome footmen pair, whose name was Archie. The other was called Arthur.

'That's funny,' she said, when Archie told her this. He was shy and courteous, with none of the arrogance of Arthur's haughty gaze. 'You look the same and your names sound similar. What a coincidence!'

'They're not our real names,' he explained. 'They gave us new ones, to make us a pair, like the horses are Belle and Beauty.

My real name is Terence – but it's not a servant's name, is it? I think my father had delusions of grandeur.' He laughed then, self-deprecatingly.

'Oh, very posh,' teased Mabel, warming to him further for his modesty and humility. 'But I like Terence.' She paused and then added hastily, 'I like Archie too, of course.'

In the evenings, the footmen worked together waiting at the dinner table and sometimes they both accompanied the family on an outing. But on a normal day, Archie went out with Lady Cardburn and Arthur with his lordship. Almost every afternoon, Lady Cardburn would call for her carriage and change into her second or third outfit of the day. Together, she and Mabel would proceed downstairs to where Archie would be waiting to open the carriage door and help them in, making sure they avoided any muddy puddles that might lie in the way. Then he would climb aboard himself and take his seat next to the driver. When they had done their shopping, he'd be there, faithfully waiting to carry the parcels and purchases.

There was something cosy and wonderful about bowling over the cobbles, skimming through the wind and rain, a handsome young man at their beck and call. Shoving the bad experiences of the past out of her mind as best she could, Mabel managed to reach a level of contentment that she'd thought would never be possible again.

Over the weeks and months, she also cast aside some of her doubts and inhibitions. Kirsty would say that life was for living and it was time for Mabel to abide by that mantra. So, when Archie invited her to walk with him on their afternoon off, and to have a cup of tea and a bun afterwards, she agreed.

'Where do your family live?' she asked him, on their second or third outing. He had a lilting, beguiling accent she couldn't place.

'Newcastle,' he replied.

'Oh,' Mabel said, not knowing quite how to respond. Newcastle was so far away and all she associated it with was coalmines about which, being a Londoner, she knew little.

'My family are miners.'

Mabel smiled. 'So why aren't you?' she teased. 'Why this job, why here?'

Archie shrugged. 'Me da didn't want me down the mines. We lost my brother in the pits, and my uncle. A footman's job seemed a safer choice and with my height, I could earn a fair bit, especially down south. I was lucky that I was a match with Arthur.'

He laughed. Mabel was curious. She wondered how the two of them got on, beneath the façade of oneness and teamwork they had to display to the household and the wider world.

'Though he's first footman and I'm second,' continued Archie, as if reading her mind.

'Does it make a difference?'

'About £10 a year!' Archie exploded into laughter again and it was so infectious that Mabel had to join in, though it seemed unfair that one should earn more than the other when they were both so handsome and good at their jobs.

'So, unless he leaves or I bump him off,' Archie continued, 'I'm destined to be second fiddle forever.'

Mabel chewed her lip. 'I'm sorry about that,' she said.

Archie shrugged. 'I'm teasing you. But we'll be gone soon anyway,' he said, suddenly pessimistic. 'They'll be getting one of these motor cars that are all the rage. The Bedfords have had one for a while and I'm sure his lordship won't be left behind for long. He always likes to keep up with new technology. I think the only reason he hasn't already bought one is because he loves the horses so and doesn't want to lose them.'

This was the longest speech Mabel had ever heard Archie make. She felt a pang of fear, or panic, at the thought of Archie being let go. If that happened, he might have to become a miner after all, risking his life.

'Maybe you could become a chauffeur,' she suggested, desperately trying to be positive.

'Maybe,' said Archie. He looked doleful for a moment, his long eyelashes drooping over his kind hazel eyes. Then he shook his shoulders out and sat up straighter. 'But there's no point in worrying, is there?' he said, with renewed cheeriness. 'Now, you be mother and pour us another cuppa, and then we'd better be getting back.'

Before they got too near the house, they parted company. It was an unspoken agreement between them that no one else needed to know how they spent their afternoons off. There was so much gossip in the servants' hall and Mabel did not want to be part of it.

In her room, she sat on her bed and thought about the rise of the motor car, the way it seemed to symbolise how much was changing. Electricity was coming, too; Lady Cardburn had told her that, in the next year or so, the whole house was to be fitted out with electric lighting to replace the gas. Nothing lasted forever and the same was true of the position of lady's maid – it was not for life. You needed to be young and fashionable and attractive for this job; unlike with other professions, lady's maids earned less and less as they got older. Mabel could probably count on only around ten years on her current salary; she must think about the future.

That evening, she asked Lady Cardburn if she would have any objection to her signing up for a French course at the Working Women's College.

'It would be useful when my lady is entertaining guests from France,' she suggested. She didn't mention her ambitions to be a teacher one day. Even though Lady Cardburn was kind and forward-looking, most employers were disdainful of servants' attempts to better themselves, much preferring the lower classes to know their place and keep to it. Mabel didn't want to put a spanner in the works by coming across as if she were above herself.

'Of course, Mabel,' answered Lady Cardburn, without hesitation. 'I think that's a splendid idea. And as his lordship doesn't speak a word of any language other than English, it will be a wonderful way for us to keep secrets from him, should we wish to do so.'

She laughed heartily at her little joke and Mabel, tentatively, joined in. She didn't know what she might need to discuss with her ladyship that couldn't be heard by her husband but it wasn't her business to ask. She was just glad she'd been given permission to study.

When she told Archie, he was most impressed.

'Well, who'll be the hoity-toity one,' he teased in his lovely accent.

Emboldened by her recent successes, she plucked up all her courage. 'Why don't you join me?' she suggested. 'We could learn together.'

Archie almost collapsed in gales of laughter. 'Me? Talking French? You're having a lark, aren't you? And anyway, I don't think the Working Women's College would take a six-foot man, would they?'

Mabel had to concede the accuracy of this fact.

But then, a few days later as they waited while Lady Card-burn chatted to a friend she'd met coming out of Fortnum's food hall, he whispered in her ear, '*Parlez-vous français?*'

Mabel turned to see a cheeky grin spread all across his face. 'What?' she murmured, not wanting to attract Lady Cardburn's attention. 'Where did you learn that?'

'Got a book out of the library,' pronounced Archie, proudly. 'I've done chapters one and two already.'

Before Mabel could respond, her ladyship was upon them, thrusting packages at Archie and then sweeping up her skirts as she climbed into the carriage.

Archie stood on the footplate rather than sitting beside the driver on the way back. Mabel was sure he was doing it so she could see him. She felt a sudden, devastating pang of despondence at the thought that the Cardburns might buy an automobile and no longer need their footmen. And the irony that it was her sister's rubber, and Mac's of course, that was making the huge expansion of the motor trade possible did not escape her.

At that moment a car, noisily backfiring, overtook them on the left, setting the horses Belle and Beauty stamping and tossing their heads. Mabel recognised the man inside as the Duke of Bedford.

'Do you think his lordship will acquire one of those?' she enquired of Alexandra, as casually as she could. 'It seems to be the fashion. My sister says they even have them in Manaus now, though there are only a couple of miles of paved roads.'

Lady Cardburn smoothed her coat over her knees. 'I think he probably will, Mabel. But,' she peered out of the window and gave a small, gracious wave to someone she knew, 'I don't think he'll let go of Archie and Arthur. After all, I'll still need someone to carry my parcels and we'll always require servers at dinner. I think their employment is safe for the foreseeable future.'

Somehow, this news sent a warm glow of relief coursing through Mabel's veins and she spent the rest of the journey in a reverie of contentment.

Chapter Forty

Norwood, 1906

Time and the river swept inexorably on.

Somehow, inexplicably, a year passed, and then another and another. To Katharine's huge relief, Mabel's letters were markedly more cheerful these days. Even though she had left school, she seemed to be content helping Mary around the house and in caring for their father, and the good news was that she was continuing to study French at evening class. It was right that she should stay at home while she was needed. Her time to work, to be a teacher, would come.

Her brothers, too, were all now gainfully occupied by apprenticeships or jobs, one an engineer, another a stonemason, a third a silversmith, while the other two had followed their father into the docks, though both had secured administrative positions as clerks and so did not have to risk their physical safety in manual work.

Antonio was a harder nut to crack. His brief, terse letters from school gave little away about what he was really feeling. And Katharine was unlikely to see him any time soon – he had been dreadfully seasick on the voyage and was reluctant to undergo the journey again just for the duration of the holidays, even the long summer break. And anyway, as he casually informed her, he preferred to spend his time visiting the country estates of numerous well-heeled friends. He'd become a good shot, he boasted, and learnt to ride a horse to hounds.

Katharine always had the impression that his letters were written as a duty, not a pleasure, because school Sunday afternoons were set aside for that purpose and missives to parents had to be produced. It saddened her. But, unlike her business, her relationship with her son did not seem to be within her control. Things had gone wrong and, other than always professing her unconditional love for her son, she simply didn't know how to put them right.

Meanwhile, the price of rubber rose and rose. In the summer of 1905, it had hit $1.50 a pound – and since then had continued upwards. Every time it was thought to have reached its limit; it went higher. The increasing production of tyres for the automobile industry, and the growing popularity of cycling, had led to an insatiable demand for the material, and that was only increased by ever-widening requirements for its use in industry.

The *bolachas* kept rolling out and the money kept rolling in, and everywhere on the Amazon, people were getting rich. Including Katharine. But still she missed her son like one of her own limbs.

By October 1906, two months before Antonio's sixteenth birthday, Katharine made a decision. She would travel to England herself. She didn't really want to – the journey was long and arduous, and, more than that, she loathed the thought of a prolonged absence from Thomas. But of course, she would do anything for her son, and she abhorred the distance that lay between them, both geographical and emotional. She knew a teenage boy would never be as doting to his mother as she would like, but still. She needed more than that offered by Antonio's stilted letters that focused on his activities and lessons, but never so much as mentioned emotions.

Sitting at her desk, she drifted into a daydream about what she and Antonio could do during the long summer months in England. One thing she was really looking forward to was bringing the family together. Antonio and Mabel still had not met, and Antonio never visited his grandparents at Hawthorn

Road. He had grown accustomed to much grander establishments over his years at Winchester. Katharine feared he was like Mayhew, ashamed of his mother's humble beginnings, shunning contact with his relatives.

She would try to heal that rift. And as well as spending time with Antonio, she desperately wanted to see Mabel, to rekindle their bond with face-to-face contact after so many years apart, and to help Mabel plan her future. With a sigh of pent-up anticipation about their reunion, she called to Rosabel to bring her coffee. She had a strange, metallic taste in her mouth that she couldn't get rid of. But when the coffee arrived, she didn't fancy it, pouring it away when Rosabel had gone to avoid hurting her feelings; she took it very personally if anyone didn't finish what she had made.

Over the next few weeks, Katharine's appetite completely deserted her and she experienced intense bouts of nausea, not actually vomiting, but constantly feeling as if at any moment she would. One fine, sunny Sunday, the failure of her monthly to arrive for the fourth time forced her to confront what was going on. She looked at herself in the mirror that she'd bought from a travelling salesman who had somehow found his way to the Rio Poderoso a few years ago. It was a prized possession but was already deteriorating, dotted with spots of rust, silver fish eating at its edges and blurring the outlines of the reflection. She turned sideways and then face on again. You couldn't tell yet. But soon, it would become obvious.

She called Thomas to the office. There was some talking to be done.

Thomas stood looking at her expectantly. Katharine had a sudden premonition that he knew what she was about to say.

Exactly at that moment, he spoke.

'You're expecting a child,' he said, matter-of-factly, as if this were an everyday occurrence.

Katharine bit her lip. 'Yes.'

Thomas' stern expression softened, and a broad smile of sheer delight broke over his handsome face. 'So, we should rejoice!'

Katharine shook her head and looked at the ground, not wanting him to see her incipient tears. A baby was always joyful, a new life, a new beginning, something to celebrate.

But not when the infant had been conceived out of wedlock and with a Black man.

'What will we tell everyone? What will we say?'

In reality, she wasn't thinking about those who lived at Norwood, in the compound, or in the nearby village, nor even those in Iquitos or Manaus – apart from Mayhew. The Indians would accept the baby as they accepted everything: with perfect equanimity. No, the people she was really worried about were her beloved parents, and their relatives, friends and neighbours, back in the safe, homogeneous environs of Hawthorn Road, where white women did not have Black men's babies. It had been bad enough telling them she was marrying a Spaniard. A Black man descended from slaves? It was simply inconceivable.

'We will tell the truth.' Thomas interrupted her fevered thoughts, calm and controlled as always.

'But Thomas, we're not even married!' The words burst out and then, immediately after them, the weeping.

In addition to the shame of it, she felt old to be having a baby. Though she knew her mother had had her last at age forty-one, and she herself was only thirty-five, soon to be thirty-six, the difference was that in her case there had been no pregnancies in between. She worried that her body would have forgotten how to do it, that she wouldn't be able to deliver this baby. Once or twice she imagined losing it, and felt momentarily relieved, and then disgusted with herself for having such treacherous thoughts.

Thomas came to her and took her in his arms. 'So, let's get married. We're both free people.' The word 'free' had particular significance said by him. 'There's nothing to stop us.'

No, thought Katharine, *nothing but a world full of prejudice and judgement and censoriousness.*

But as she pondered on it, she gradually accepted that, whatever anybody else thought, she wanted nothing more than to be Thomas' wife, and to call him husband. The terror she had felt when he had been stricken with malaria had made her realise that she could not bear to be without him. Why shouldn't they marry, and hold their heads up high? Not to mention that a recognised union would mitigate at least some of the stigma this baby would experience.

Her mind made up, Katharine wrote a letter to the newly appointed priest at the church in the town upriver where she had bought Fortunata. She had been so disparaging about the ever-encroaching Christian faith, always maintaining that the Indians were much better off being left alone to enjoy their own rituals and beliefs. But now she needed the Church, she had to eat her words.

A month later, she and Thomas set off on their wedding journey. They took the opportunity of the visit to see the Spanish pharmacist. He led Katharine into his consultation room and examined her. When they came back out again, his face was grave.

'I think you should go to Manaus to have the baby,' he said, 'where you can get better care. There's an excellent hospital there now, with a brand-new maternity department employing highly skilled obstetricians trained in London and Paris. It's expensive of course...' here he broke off to rub his fingers together in the universal gesture indicating money, 'but you would have the peace of mind of knowing you are in the best hands.'

'Why does she need a hospital?' asked Thomas, his tone as calm and measured as always. But Katharine could see his lips were trembling. He was worried. 'She had her son at Norwood.'

Katharine thought of that long and dreadful labour, the details of which she of course had never shared with Thomas, and suppressed a small shudder. It would be easier the second time. That's what the Indian women said, anyway.

But Senhor Garcia would not hear of it.

'Mrs Ferran—apologies, Mrs Smart's age mitigates against an easy delivery,' the pharmacist insisted, 'and the baby seems small for the dates you've given me. I would prefer her to be in the hands of those with proper experience of more difficult labours. Out here...' He flung his arm in the general direction of the forest and the rivers, the intricate network of waterways that made their part of the Amazon so inaccessible. 'You know what I mean,' he concluded, lamely. 'And − I would recommend going early, staying a few months.'

Thomas and Katharine exchanged glances.

Senhor Garcia, perhaps sensing their doubts, fired his parting shot. 'You know that even Queen Victoria took advantage of pain relief in two of her confinements,' he exhorted them. 'So, there's no reason not to. But you will have to go to hospital to get it.'

That decided it for Katharine. She didn't give a hoot about Queen Victoria but the thought of not having to experience the full agony of Antonio's birth was enough to dispel all hesitation. They would go. And that would mean, inevitably, Mayhew finding out sooner rather than later. Katharine dreaded his reaction. She would like to keep this baby a secret, hidden from the cruelty of the outside world, cocooned in the privacy of Norwood. But the word would out somehow, whatever measures she took to hide it, just as news of her relationship had filtered all the way downriver to Manaus, so she might as well get it over with. And now she had overcome her initial mixed feelings about being pregnant again, she was desperate for the baby's arrival, already head over heels in love with this new person she and Thomas had created.

In her bliss of pregnancy, she even believed that Antonio, too, would love unconditionally his little brother or sister.

Chapter Forty-One

London, 1906

Lady Cardburn, Mabel discovered over the years at Hanover Terrace, was a generous employer as long as she knew that her employees' loyalty was guaranteed. Every now and again, she treated the housemaids to afternoon tea and the theatre. When it came to Mabel's twentieth birthday, she organised a special lunch in the servants' hall for her, complete with a massive cake bursting with fruit and cream.

After the festivities, Alexandra called Mabel to her room. She passed her an oblong-shaped gift wrapped in shiny gold paper.

'Thank you so much,' gasped Mabel, opening the box and taking out a sterling silver chain from which dangled a delicate pendant in the shape of a feather. 'It's beautiful.'

Her heart was beating in double time and she felt crippled by embarrassment, not knowing quite what to say in the face of such unexpected munificence.

'You're very welcome,' replied Lady Cardburn. She coughed slightly, as if clearing her throat.

'Mabel,' she said, and then paused.

Mabel stared at her, her stomach churning. There was something in Alexandra's tone of voice that scared her.

'Don't look so terrified, you silly goose,' she continued, smiling amusedly at Mabel's stricken demeanour. 'I just wanted to say… I've noticed the – liaison – between you and the second footman, Archie.'

Mabel gulped, and her heart sank. Was she in trouble for spending time with him? In truth, their friendship had become deeper over the years and, though nothing specific had been said, by now it was generally known in the servants' hall that they were courting. When they were together, Mabel always felt a little fizz of excitement in her belly and, when he took her arm in his to walk around the Rose Garden in Regent's Park, she stood taller and prouder to have such a handsome, kind man as her escort. But perhaps all of this was wrong. Forbidden. She waited for Lady Cardburn's next words with dread in her heart.

'It's all right, Mabel. It's natural for young people to enjoy each other's company. It's just that—'

'There's nothing improper, your ladyship,' Mabel burst out, interrupting her employer but not being able to stop herself. She'd lost her job at Brampton Square after getting the blame for the master's behaviour, and though that had turned out to be a blessing in disguise, she didn't want the shame of being sacked to occur again. 'I swear on my life,' she insisted.

Lady Cardburn shot her a sharp look. 'I'm not accusing you of anything,' she said, sternly. 'You are a beauty, Mabel,' she continued, 'so it's hardly surprising that you catch the eyes of men. But you are so sweet and naïve and innocent that I don't think you realise the power you have.'

Mabel chomped on her cheek, utterly confused. Was she being told off or congratulated? 'No, your ladyship. Sorry, your ladyship,' she whispered, utterly unsure what her response should be.

Lady Cardburn burst out laughing. 'Oh, Mabel! It's nothing to worry about. You are not in any trouble.'

She waited until Mabel had plucked up the courage to meet her gaze before continuing.

'I just feel – and I know my father agrees, in fact it was he who asked me to speak to you – that a young woman of your calibre and intelligence and looks could do better than a footman. We don't want you to tie yourself down too soon.'

Lady Cardburn sighed and looked carefully at Mabel, a resigned expression on her face. 'But servants will be servants, I suppose.'

And with this cryptic comment, Mabel was dismissed. She scurried out of the room, Alexandra's words ringing in her ears. She felt as if the conversation had taken place in a foreign language, one she had no command of. Though Archie seemed to be the problem, it was Archie, with his calming presence and kindness, she desperately wanted to see.

Fortunately, she didn't have to wait too long. She had been given the afternoon off and it was also Archie's so she'd arranged to spend it with him. He took her to the lake in Regent's Park, hired a boat, and rowed her over to the island to see the families of cygnets and mallard ducklings. One matriarch had a brood of eight, just like the Birds themselves, and looked as harassed and worried about them all as her own mother Mary always did, Mabel laughingly told Archie. As they watched the family take to the water in a long line like the beads of a necklace, a sudden noise of flapping wings and rustling grasses disturbed the peace. A heron appeared, flying low. The mother mallard squawked and quacked fit to burst but to no avail. The heron swooped purposefully down, plucked up one of the baby ducks as if it were weightless and soared away. Mabel watched in horror as the duckling's fluffy body, its tiny feet and fledging wings, disappeared inside the heron's long beak.

'Horrible,' she breathed to Archie, mournfully. 'Poor mother duck. Poor baby.'

Archie shrugged. 'Nature,' he said, as if that explained it all. Which, Mabel supposed sadly, it did. But nevertheless, the snatching of the duckling left her with a feeling of foreboding that she couldn't shake.

Archie had an errand to run and could not accompany Mabel back to the house. On the Outer Circle, just before they parted, he handed her a present. It was wrapped in plain brown paper and string and was a hard, stiff rectangle.

'I'm serving at dinner tonight,' Archie said, 'so open it later and tell me what you think of it tomorrow.'

Mabel blushed. 'I will,' she whispered.

And as Archie turned towards the house, he called softly, 'Thank you.' He turned back, bent forward and kissed her cheek, quickly, just a peck – but one that burnt into Mabel's skin like a tattoo. And then he was gone. Mabel leant against the railings for support. That was the closest they'd ever got to intimacy. The horror of what had happened in Brampton Square had hindered her from letting the relationship proceed in a truly 'romantic' way. Suddenly Mabel knew that the incident had receded so far into the distant past that she could move on from it, that she was ready to put it fully behind her and not think about it again. It was time, she decided, for her and Archie to make their arrangement official.

Smiling blissfully to herself, she set off back to Hanover Terrace, clutching Archie's plain and simple gift in her black-gloved hands. Lost in thought, she almost walked straight into a man coming in the other direction.

'I'm so sorry,' she apologised, and then, after a couple of moments, realised that the man was Mac. She had hardly seen him at the Cardburns' house for the last few years, and assumed he'd been in the Amazon. The time disappeared in an instant. He didn't look a day older. If anything, his eyes were bluer than ever, his face more charming. 'Oh, Mr McNamara, I do beg your pardon. I wasn't looking where I was going.'

'The fault is mine entirely,' he responded, his voice as smooth as melted chocolate. Mabel had almost forgotten his Irish accent, how lovely it was. Almost as lovely as Archie's Geordie one. 'And it's been so long you've been working for us; you really must do as your sister does and call me Mac.'

'Oh,' gasped Mabel, 'but I couldn't do that. Her ladyship... I'm sure she wouldn't like it.'

Mac gave a dismissive flick of his head. 'Given that I pay for everything that goes on in that house, it is I who calls the tune. And I insist that you call me Mac.'

Mabel flushed a deep red. It felt uncomfortable to have financial information about her employer divulged to her so

283

freely and openly – though it was only what was whispered around the servants' hall, so it wasn't exactly news – but Mac didn't appear to think he'd said anything particularly noteworthy.

'As you please, sir,' she muttered. 'I mean, Mac.'

'My daughter is very pleased with your work.' Mac offered a small smile. His tone was avuncular, protective. 'She says you're a wonder. Indeed, in the short time I've been back in town I've heard you being talked about all over the place. Lady Cardburn's divine maid, people say. Have you seen her they ask? An utter beauty, they carol.' Mac paused, observing Mabel's reaction. Her blush deepened. 'And they're all correct,' he concluded. 'I see that I made the right decision, employing you on behalf of my daughter all those years ago.'

Mabel's heart was beating so loud against her chest she was sure Mac could hear it. All these compliments were so unexpected, so extraordinary. They were simultaneously uncomfortable and strangely pleasing; there was something nice about being singled out for praise by such a powerful and important man. And of course, he was right that she was indebted to him for all her current contentment.

'I saw you walking with the footman, Archie or Arthur or whichever it is,' Mac went on. Mabel's bashful pride at his words of praise vanished in an instant and she became wary. Should she own up?

'I would avoid the young servants,' he advised, his tone markedly cooler now. 'It's better that way.'

Mabel's mind filled with confusion for the second time that day. Why was he saying almost the same thing that Lady Cardburn had? She shot him a cautious glance from underneath her eyelids to see if he was angry. But he was smiling again, his usual warm smile.

'A beautiful girl like you could do so much better,' he concluded, definitively.

Mabel attempted a feeble smile. 'I don't know, sir. I just want to do my job properly.' Bring it back to work, that was the safest option. All the other stuff seemed unfathomable.

'Indeed,' he replied. 'I'm sure you do, and you are.' He stood looking at Mabel, fixing her with his piercing blue eyes that were simultaneously knowing, and enticing.

Mabel's skin prickled with sweat but along with the embarrassment was a frisson of something else, something indefinable, but not unpleasant.

'I must get back to my duties,' she muttered, hastily. 'Goodbye.'

She didn't breathe freely again until she was safely in the servants' quarters of the house, where Mac would never stray. He'd made her feel awkward, and excited, and strange all at the same time, and the encounter had left her discombobulated in a way she couldn't explain. Mac – and Lady Cardburn – had said she could do better than a servant and of course there were stories of those who worked below stairs catching the eye of a dashing gentlemen from above stairs – usually someone foreign, and not bound by English class distinctions. But they were rare. And Mabel wasn't looking for anyone other than Archie, anyway. He was so sweet. She was beginning to understand that she loved him.

On her way into the house, Mrs Bustle told her that her ladyship needed her for something, so Mabel only had time to take her coat and the present to her bedroom before attending to her duties. Later, her chores done for the day, she went back to her room, her candle throwing delicate shadows on the walls. The electricity supply hadn't been extended to servants' rooms.

As soon as she opened the door, she saw it. A parcel wrapped in glossy pink paper and tied with an enormous bow was lying on her bed. Mabel's mouth fell open in astonishment. Who on earth had given her such an elaborate looking present and not only that but had it delivered to her room?

Plumping down onto the mattress, curiosity drew her to pick up the surprise gift before Archie's. She handled it carefully, examining its pink beauty, turning it around and around in her hands. Undoing the meticulously knotted ribbon and unfolding the paper so as not to tear it, she extracted a long rectangular box. Inside was an impossibly elegant pair of cream kid-leather gloves in her exact size. There was a note tucked between them.

> To Mabel,
> A small gift to wish you a very happy twentieth birthday and to thank you for all you do for my daughter.
> I will be abroad for a while, but I hope to see you wearing and enjoying these on my return. They will be some improvement on those cotton ones you have now.
> With warm wishes,
> Mac

Mabel's heart skipped a beat. A birthday gift from Mac? But why? She fondled the gloves, feeling their softness, examining the exquisite workmanship. They must have cost a lot of money; everything about them exuded luxury and expense. And they were, as he had pointed out, a world away from her black cotton ones. She was not sure, though, that she'd ever be able to wear them – it was very important that a lady's maid never outdid her mistress, unthinkable that she should have nicer garments than her. But oh, they were lovely, things of indisputable beauty and quality.

Mabel put them on and took them off again. Thank goodness her hands were no longer blemished and swollen the way they had been in the Brampton Square days, but were now smooth and dainty once more; these were gloves for well-kept hands. No one in Hawthorn Road had ever had such gloves as this – not her mother, nor herself and most likely not Katharine, either, for all her success.

In a daze, Mabel painstakingly rewrapped the gloves in their tissue paper and replaced them in the box. She would take them out and look at them every day, even if she couldn't wear them.

Only then did she remember Archie's package. Inside the brown paper wrapping she found a book, in French: *Madame Bovary* by Gustave Flaubert. It was brand new, the pages uncut, the embossed cover faultlessly displaying an engraving of a beautiful woman holding up a looking glass to appraise her own reflection. Archie must have saved for ages to buy this; books were expensive, ones in foreign languages even more so, and hard to find, too.

Mabel sat for a long time considering the two gifts. Both were lovely, chosen with such care especially for her. Both were undeserved. And both aroused powerful and conflicting emotions that she could not make sense of.

Chapter Forty-Two

London, 1906

The next day, a new footman stood alongside Arthur in the marbled hallway. He was shorter by a few inches, and there was no similarity between the two men.

Mabel's eyes flitted between the mismatched pair as she walked with her ladyship to the front door, trying to hide the horror and astonishment on her face. She was sure she caught a smirk on Arthur's face.

Where on earth was Archie? Was he ill? He must be ill. How ill? Fevered thoughts hurled themselves around Mabel's mind so that she could hardly concentrate on putting one foot in front of the other.

The new footman escorted them to the carriage.

'Thank you, Algernon,' said Alexandra as he helped her in.

Algernon? Who was this man and where had he come from? Mabel felt sick. She was desperate to find out what had happened to Archie, but too full of dread to ask.

Lady Cardburn answered her unspoken question. 'You are wondering what has become of Archie,' she said, bluntly.

Mabel nodded, mutely. The capacity for speech eluded her.

'He has been sacked. I believe he's gone back to County Durham. Or is it Northumberland he's from? I forget.'

Mabel's mouth fell open in shock and disbelief. Sacked?

'It was found that he had stolen some money,' continued Lady Cardburn. 'I sent him to make some purchases and he forged an invoice in order to keep several pounds for himself.

Of course, he had to be dismissed immediately.' She pursed her lips in righteous disapproval.

Mabel gulped. She had forgotten how to breathe.

'He's lucky we didn't have him arrested,' Lady Cardburn added, 'but my father insisted that we just send him away with a warning. He's sure he'll never do such a thing again.' She folded her hands decisively upon her lap. 'I must say I was surprised. I had never seen an ounce of dishonesty in Archie, nor thought he was capable of it. He didn't seem the sort.' She looked expectantly at Mabel as if waiting for a contribution on this topic.

Tears pricked behind Mabel's eyes and she forced them back. Lady Cardburn must not see her cry.

'No, my lady,' she muttered. 'He didn't.'

Lady Cardburn smiled sympathetically and reached across to Mabel, patting her hand gently. 'You will be upset,' she said, kindly. 'We had only just discussed that you and Archie – that you were fond of each other. That you had an – arrangement.'

Mabel nodded, not trusting herself to speak. How could she have been so taken in by Archie? He must have stolen the money to buy the book for her birthday. She'd wondered how he could afford it but never thought he'd stoop to theft. She had totally misjudged him. And even worse – had he thought of her as the sort of girl who would only be impressed by an expensive gift? When nothing could be further from the truth. He hadn't needed to give her anything to win her affection. He had already had it.

'Well, least said, soonest mended,' intoned Alexandra, decisively, interrupting the whirling tornado of Mabel's thoughts. 'It's a good thing you and he didn't get even more deeply involved.'

'Yes, my lady.'

The desolation that engulfed Mabel only intensified over the next couple of days. A heavy band settled around her chest and pulled tighter and tighter with every hour. She would find herself looking out for Archie, resplendent in his scarlet livery, and then suddenly remember that he was gone, and why.

In her bedroom, she looked at the gloves and the book, her birthday presents, as she sewed a loose button onto a blouse. She was convinced that it was all her fault, that something about herself had made Archie commit the crime. The tension and stress transferred to her hands and the sewing thread, stretched too taut, snapped. It felt like the violent breaking of Mabel's heart. Archie must have been so ashamed he had not even tried to contact her, to explain himself. That could only be because there was no reasonable explanation to excuse what he had done. Angrily, Mabel threw the blouse onto her dressing table and buried her face in her pillow. Life seemed full of insuperable mysteries and challenges and her whole body ached with the pain of loss.

However much she was hurting, though, she had to do her job. In some ways, she was glad to be kept busy by Lord and Lady Cardburn's schedule as they embarked on a flurry of entertaining. It prevented her from dwelling on what had happened. Below stairs, in the privacy of the servants' hall, there was plenty of moaning about the extra work involved in the fashion of serving dinners à la russe, where every course was brought in separately and dished up to each guest by the staff, rather than the old way of à la française where everything was put onto the table at the same time and diners helped themselves. But Mabel didn't care how hard she had to toil. Usually, it was because she loved the glamour and the buzz, seeing the guests dressed up to the nines, smelling of divine perfumes and sporting the latest hairstyles. Now, though, she couldn't care less about what anyone was saying or wearing but threw herself into her work as a way to stop herself ruminating on Archie's absence.

On the evening before one of the dinners, Mabel was doing her ladyship's hair when the bedroom door opened. She paused, shocked. No one entered a lady's boudoir without invitation

– not even her husband. In the mirror's reflection, Mabel saw Alexandra's friend Anna Lawless march over the threshold. Miss Lawless, it was said in the servants' hall, was an example of that radical breed of women, a suffragette. Mabel was utterly in awe of her; she was so suave and confident and outspoken – totally different from most of Lady Cardburn's other friends, and from Lady Cardburn herself, who never overstepped the mark but was the model Edwardian lady. Mabel's mother Mary would have called Anna 'modern' because she rarely observed the formalities – or perhaps something even less complimentary, if she heard the way she sometimes swore.

'Oh, I am so fed up,' cried Anna, flumping down onto the chaise longue with an almighty sigh.

Mabel continued her hairdressing, pretending she was invisible, as a good lady's maid should.

Lady Cardburn, her back turned to Anna, regarded her through the mirror.

'Poor thing,' she said, benignly. She was used to indulging Anna's mercurial moods. 'What is the problem?'

'It's Dennis,' said Anna, flatly. She took a cigarette from her purse, put it into an elaborate ivory holder and lit it, taking a long drag and exhaling the smoke in a hazy cloud that floated around her like mist in the early morning.

'And what has he done to fall out of favour with you now?'

Mabel wasn't entirely sure what the relationship between Miss Lawless and Dennis Whitfield was. They weren't married, but Anna talked of him so often that they must be officially courting.

'He's only gone to Ceylon, hasn't he,' Anna responded, grumpily. 'And left me all alone just when there's a ball or a party every night of the week and two on a Saturday!'

'Outrageous!' Lady Cardburn was smiling, holding back a laugh.

'Oh you, you're not sympathetic at all. Just because boring old Henry Cardburn never goes anywhere further than his club on the Mall. You have no idea what it's like, constantly being deserted.'

'Hardly deserted, darling,' interjected Alexandra. 'And I'm sure he gave you something lovely to remember him by.'

Anna turned up her nose and gave a disparaging sniff. 'Diamond earrings. But time is more valuable than money, is it not?'

Lady Cardburn avoided Mabel's eyes in the mirror. 'I think that depends on who you are,' she said, carefully. 'But anyway – you haven't told me why he's shipped out to Ceylon. Business, I suppose?'

'Some exhibition about rubber,' Anna replied, yawning. 'About as boring as it sounds, I should say. It's being held in the Royal Botanic Gardens somewhere unpronounceable – Peradeniya? Pterodactyl? I don't know.'

They both laughed.

Mabel, who had been daydreaming and not taking much notice, pricked up her ears at the mention of rubber. She wondered what it had to do with Ceylon, when Katharine had told her that rubber came primarily from the Amazon or, to a lesser extent, the Congo.

'Perhaps if you showed a little more interest in his business affairs, he'd include you more? Take you with him?' suggested Lady Cardburn with a mischievous grin.

'Oh no!' Anna threw her cigarette stub into an ebony ashtray on a side table. She stood up and stretched, her body long and languid, sinuous like a cat. Mabel found her movements fascinating, so controlled and contained.

'Why would I want that? What interest do I have in a mouldy old display of plantation rubber? They say it's going to wipe out the Amazon, but really, who cares?'

Mabel gulped a sharp intake of breath. Wipe out the Amazon? That meant Katharine. And, she supposed, Mac. But Anna couldn't be serious. It was impossible to think that anything could destroy the all-powerful Mac. Losing her concentration momentarily, she dropped a lock of Alexandra's hair across her face.

'Careful, Mabel.' The reprimand was sharp. Lady Cardburn hated it when anyone's focus was less than total.

'Sorry, my lady,' mumbled Mabel. She wanted to hear more about the rubber, this threat to her sister's livelihood, was hoping Anna would oblige.

'No, I'm not going on a long boat journey with my terrible sea legs for any money. Of course, for Dennis it's really a chance to hobnob with his chums from the City in more exotic climes. Goodness knows what else he gets up to.'

Anna gave a snort of derision, sat back down on the chaise longue and lit another cigarette.

Mabel waited, breath held, for further information. She was sure that the two women would be able to sense how intensely she was following their conversation.

'You are terrible,' laughed Alexandra. 'I'm sure he's the model of sobriety and rectitude wherever he is. And no Eastern beauty could rival you, in any case.'

Anna inclined her head gracefully in acceptance of the compliment. She leant back and blew smoke rings into the air. Mabel watched in admiration, wishing she had half the sophistication and poise of this alarmingly exciting woman.

'Let's just hope Dennis makes enough money in this new venture that he can come back and marry me and keep me in the manner to which I am accustomed!'

Lady Cardburn gave a snort of derision. 'Unlike Henry, who's never made a penny in his life. Thank God father is as rich as he is and happy to share it. Or we'd be on the poverty line.'

Mabel just managed to stop the pin she was working with stabbing into Alexandra's scalp. The idea that anyone in Hanover Terrace had any notion of what the poverty line looked like was preposterous. She wanted them to stop waffling on about money and go back to talking about rubber.

Alexandra obliged, briefly. 'You're right, though. My father also says the future of rubber is in the East. I think he's investing.'

Mabel coughed to hide her gasp of astonishment. She waited desperately for more. But that conversation was over.

Anna went to the window to look out. 'By the way,' she pondered out loud, 'I was sorry not to see your handsome second footman at the door. He was such a gentle giant, always so unbearably polite and deferential. What happened to him?'

Mabel's heart turned over. It was becoming hard to maintain an innocuous expression in the midst of so many revelations.

Lady Cardburn shrugged. 'There was a little problem, so he had to be let go. That's all.'

Mabel wondered why Alexandra didn't want to go into details but was secretly grateful. She couldn't bear to hear it all being picked over, wanted to forget all about it.

'Shame,' Anna responded, eventually. 'There was something rather attractive about him, wasn't there? The strong and silent type. Don't you ever lust after a touch of rough?'

Frozen in disbelief, Mabel bit down hard on her cheek to stop herself from saying something. How could Anna make fun of Archie like that? And so crude! She felt Alexandra's displeasure in the sudden rigidity of her shoulders.

'Anna! Please behave yourself,' Alexandra reprimanded her friend, her voice sharp and uncompromising. 'You go too far sometimes.'

Anna laughed. But she didn't mention Archie again.

'Anyway,' she continued, changing the subject seamlessly, 'I can't go gallivanting to Ceylon because I'm far too busy with the WSPU. I know you say you can't join, what with being titled and all of that old-fashioned stuff, but I so wish you could. We'd have such fun! I honestly think we should dump all this Lord and Lady, Duke and Duchess nonsense, become a republic like France or America.'

Mabel's disappointment at the dropping of the rubber conversation, and her pain at the discussion of Archie, was immediately replaced by fascination at Anna's dismissal of the class system that underpinned the whole of British society. She had never heard anyone express such revolutionary views so openly. Lady Cardburn stiffened again.

'Really, Anna.' Alexandra's voice was cold. 'You need to know when to stop with your rebellious notions. Mess around with votes for women if you must – but please leave the rest of us alone. You have no idea what such careless talk could unleash.'

Here she paused and Mabel could tell she was trying to give silent 'not in front of the servants' messages to Anna. Normally she'd have spoken in French if she didn't want to be understood. But Mabel knew more French than she did, after all these years of diligent study at the Working Women's College. Mabel suppressed the urge to giggle. It was nice to have at least one thing over these two rich women, even though she liked Alexandra, who had been good to her. And Anna's crazy notions were intriguing but so unlikely ever to come to pass as to be hardly worth bothering about.

The only thing that really mattered was the talk about rubber. Could it really be true that the Amazon was over? She must write urgently to Katharine and warn her.

Chapter Forty-Three

Manaus, 1907

The baby was due at the beginning of July. Katharine hoped and prayed that it would come early so that she could have the best of both worlds – give birth in Manaus and then jump on the Booth Line steamer to Liverpool. No matter the rigours of the journey, the rough seas, the sickness – she would be able to spend August in England with her new baby and her son, and of course all the rest of the family. The post had been even more abysmal than usual of late, and she had had no news from home in months. She was desperate to get to London and catch up with all of those she had not seen in so many years.

In the throes of delight about the forthcoming arrival and the journey, she set off to the city with her head held high, Thomas equally stalwart and proud by her side. She had nothing to be ashamed of. Love was free and she had made her choice. Other people could judge as they pleased.

And judge they did, of course – starting with Mayhew. Katharine had not even considered staying anywhere else but at the establishment that Mayhew had set up from where he could run Norwood Enterprises' Manaus operation. Apart from anything else, news of their arrival would be out within twenty-four hours. There was no way they could avoid Mayhew so they might as well meet him straight on.

'So, you're having a Black man's spawn,' he said disdainfully, taking exactly the standpoint that Katharine had anticipated. 'I suppose we see the results of miscegenation all around us in this god-forsaken place. But my own sister. Giving birth to a half-caste.'

'If you wish to think of it like that,' retorted Katharine. She knew that Mayhew was taunting her, wanting a reaction. 'I prefer to call it a baby. A baby I will love beyond measure.' She was determined not to rise to Mayhew's bait.

'No, I've got a better word for it, actually,' continued Mayhew, ignoring her. 'A disgrace. An embarrassment.'

'I'm sorry you feel that way. Thomas and I do not.'

Mayhew took a slug from the glass of whisky he was holding. It was only five o'clock. Katharine had noticed how his nose had become red and bulbous, and his cheeks flecked with purple veins, both signs of long years of excessive drinking. He seemed coarser than ever, the last vestiges of the good looks and charm that had always been there to serve him – when he had felt like it – eradicated.

'Does the boy know?'

Katharine assumed he was referring to Antonio.

'No.'

'You think he'll be happy to share his inheritance with a—?'

Katharine clicked her tongue against her teeth in irritation. 'Why do you assume the worst? Let him decide how he feels about his sibling.'

'It's a black and white case, dear sister, plain and simple.'

A slow count to ten inside her head prevented Katharine from exploding.

'Just my little joke,' mumbled Mayhew, as if sensing her unspoken outrage. He poured himself more whisky. 'I'd forgotten your lack of a sense of humour,' he added, unable to resist another jibe.

Though Katharine knew he was talking nonsense, Mayhew's words still touched a nerve. She had spoken with a confidence she didn't feel – earlier in the pregnancy she had convinced herself that Antonio would be happy to have a sibling. But she'd had no reply to her letter telling him about forthcoming arrival and she felt that she no longer knew how Antonio would react to anything. She hardly knew her teenage son. The sadness this brought to her was constant and profound.

To take her mind off it, and despite the suffocating heat made worse by being heavily pregnant, she and Thomas went out to see what had changed. The Manaus that Katharine remembered from her solitary walks all those years ago was almost unrecognisable. Then, it had been big, but now it was a megalopolis of paved roads, gigantic banks and office blocks, hospitals, schools and universities.

In the day time, the blue and gold roof tiles of the now completed opera house gleamed under the equatorial sun, and by night the city blazed with the brightness and brilliance of full electrification, installed here long before it had reached the greatest cities of North America and Europe. Parisian stores lined the streets – Au Bon Marché, La Ville de Paris, Parc Royal. Motor cars cruised up and down the avenues and boulevards, their Goodyear tyres made of Amazonian rubber. Rubber barons, always competitive, rivalled each other for the most ostentatious purchases – yachts, tame lions, swimming pools. Horse races were now held at the Derby Club in the Prado Amazonense and theatres had sprung up everywhere.

But, amidst the glamour and the luxury, the talk, in hushed murmurs and secretive asides, was of the Peruvian Amazon Company run by Julio César Arana in the no-man's land between Brazil, Peru and Colombia. Gossip abounded of terrible deeds in Arana's empire on the river Putumayo; *La Sanción* newspaper in Iquitos had openly accused him of using any means possible to extort more work from the Indian tappers: torture, rape, murder.

'Do you think it's true?' Katharine asked Thomas, after being part of a whispered conversation at a soirée held by one of Mayhew's rubber baron friends. 'And supposing it is – can we justify being part of such a deplorable industry?'

'You've put everything into this. It's your life,' replied Thomas. 'You've never hurt anyone and your employees depend on you. If you left – where would they go? What would they do? They might end up working for a boss as bad as Arana, or even Arana himself – and then how would you feel?'

'Yes.' Katharine tried to sound – and feel – convinced. 'Perhaps you are right.'

'I think your focus should be on the baby just now,' Thomas suggested gently. 'You can put the world to rights once you're back from England.'

'All right,' she agreed reluctantly, squeezing Thomas' arm in thanks. He didn't want her to go, Katharine knew. But he was far too good and true a man to deprive her of seeing her beloved son.

They went to the opera house to see Lucília Peres, the building's Renaissance magnificence as out of the place in the jungle as an Indian hut would be in the centre of Rome. On the way out, they promenaded with the hordes in the Praça do Comércio, both feeling underdressed. All around them, men wore suits and ties and bowler hats, their wives boasting elaborately feathered headpieces and gloves.

'I've forgotten how to dress for society,' Katharine said to Thomas. 'In a way it's wonderful to live somewhere where fashions and frippery count for nothing. But then again...' Her words tapered off as her gaze followed a particularly striking woman in an eye-catching blue striped dress. 'Sometimes it would be nice to wear beautiful clothes and to – well, to feel beautiful, I suppose.'

Thomas rolled his eyes. 'For a start, how many times do I have to tell you that you are beautiful to me in every way?'

Katharine pulled a face of exaggerated gratefulness. 'I wasn't fishing for compliments,' she protested.

'Of course not,' agreed Thomas, indulgently. 'But if you feel so strongly about it – why don't you buy yourself something special? You can wear it to impress the potoos and the puffbirds when we get back to Norwood.'

Katharine thumped him in mock protest. 'All right. You win. I'm being ridiculous.'

299

Over the next few weeks, thoughts of the baby put everything else out of Katharine's mind. She tried every old wife's
tale she'd ever heard to bring on labour – exercise, sexual inter-
course, gin – desperate for it to come in time for her to get to
England as planned. But nothing worked. The month turned
and there was no indication that the baby was about to put in
an appearance. Early July had become mid-July by the time
her labour started, at which stage she was not only fed up but
enormous.

In the hospital room, as the contractions built up – slowly
at first – Katharine chatted and laughed with the nurses, whose
many nationalities reflected the city outside the white walls.
But hours into the labour, amid the fug of pain, she began to
notice the looks on her attendants' faces turn anxious. They
gave her chloroform and it helped a bit, but like the herbal tea
the Indian women had plied her with when having Antonio, it
also caused her to drift in and out of consciousness, and to have
hideous dreams in which she gave birth to a monster.

'This is what happens when you lie with a Black man,' she
was sure she heard someone say, the words thumping into her
dream as if they had been kicked there. 'White women are not
designed to give birth to baby savages.'

Eventually, after how many hours Katharine had no idea,
a doctor came. Immediately assessing the seriousness of the
situation, he whisked her away on her wheeled bed into the
operating theatre.

When she regained consciousness, Katharine felt like she was
returning from a very long journey, but without having any idea
where she had been or why. Looking around at the bare white
room with bars on the windows, her first thought was that she
was in a mental hospital or a prison. Did they think she was
mad because her husband was not white? Had they incarcerated
her because it was against the law to have a relationship with a
Black man?

But then she felt her breasts tingling, and glanced down to
see them full and heavy with milk, and remembered that she had

been pregnant, that she had come to a hospital for her confinement, that presumably she was still there. Panic subsumed her.

'Where's my baby?' she called. There was no one to hear. She tried to sit up and fell back down onto the bed, broadsided with pain. Sweat broke out, prickling on her skin, soaking her back.

She shouted, but nobody came. Sobbing, she clawed at her hair and flailed around in the bed, but every movement was torture. She didn't know how long she waited, just that she was frantic with distress by the time the door finally opened. She held her breath.

It was Thomas.

'My baby,' she cried. 'Where is it? Where, Thomas?'

He bent towards her and only then did she notice that he was carrying something, a white bundle from which a wisp of black hair protruded. It was not moving.

'What's happened, what's going on?' Her panic was uncontrolled, desperate.

Thomas smiled and sat down on the wooden chair beside her bed. 'Be quiet, my love. You must lie still.'

He lifted the bundle and pulled back the shawl so that she could see the baby inside, its little, shrivelled face and scrunched up eyes, tightly closed.

'Is it – is it...' she blinked and tried again, unable to make her words any more than a whisper, 'alive?'

She could not look at the baby, in fear of the answer. Instead, she stared at Thomas, trying to read his face.

A huge smile broke out across it. 'She is most certainly alive. And she is beautiful.'

At that moment, the baby's mouth opened and she let out a huge, tremulous scream, that soon turned into rhythmic, insistent crying.

'I think she's hungry,' said Thomas. 'And a little cross.'

Katharine smiled and laughed, tears of joy and gratitude flooding her face and falling onto the white bed sheets. A nurse came and propped her up as much as the pain allowed. Katharine took her baby in her arms and fed her, instantly experiencing a rush of pure, wonderful love.

'I shall call her Lily,' she murmured, letting the infant's tiny hand wrap around her finger. 'Because the lily flower is a symbol of innocence, purity and beauty, and she will be all those things.'

Thomas nodded. 'As you wish, my love.'

Over the next few hours, he told Katharine about the terrible birth and the emergency caesarean section that the doctor had performed. They were lucky that he'd had the training and the expertise. Without the operation, she and the baby would almost certainly have died. But it was a major procedure and it meant that Katharine would have to stay in hospital for at least three or four weeks and then recuperate for another few months before she could think of travelling anywhere.

'Senhor Garcia was right to send us to Manaus,' Thomas concluded, 'even though he did it for the wrong reasons. She most certainly is not too small – on the contrary she weighed nearly 9lbs!'

They both laughed, slightly hysterical with relief. When the night nurse took the baby away so that Katharine could sleep, she cried again. But this time it was partly in happiness for Lily's life – and her own – and partly in searing sadness.

There was no possibility of making the journey to England to see Antonio now.

Chapter Forty-Four

England and Scotland, 1907

Watching Anthony exit the historic gates of Winchester school always gave Mayhew a profound sense of satisfaction. Though it had to be said that his nephew was not exactly wowing the world with his academic prowess, the fact remained that he was moving in the highest echelons of British society and making connections that would last for the rest of his life. It wasn't as if any other members of the Bird family were going to raise the family's status; this task was clearly down to Mayhew and Anthony alone. What did grades and exam results matter, compared to that?

Always happy to take control where Anthony was concerned, Mayhew had gallantly offered to step into the breach when Katharine had found herself unable to travel to England for the summer. He hadn't even made too much of a fuss about it. He didn't mind the sea voyage, and much as he liked Manaus and had everything arranged there to his satisfaction, a change of scene was welcome every now and again. It was good to go back to England with money in his pocket and status on his side.

It was, after all, exactly what he had left for all those years ago.

'Good afternoon, Uncle,' said Anthony, politely shaking Mayhew's hand. He was always a little stiff on first release, Mayhew found, always needed a little time to unwind. A plan formulated in his mind at that very moment.

During dinner at his club in Piccadilly, he ordered a bottle of very good claret. Plying Anthony with alcohol usually worked to loosen him up a bit. At first the chat was desultory, bits and pieces about events at school, rubber news.

But then Anthony asked about the baby.

Mayhew shrugged. 'A little girl,' he replied. 'You have a sister.'

Anthony nodded.

They both concentrated on the food for a few minutes. Anthony pushed a roast potato to the side of his plate, and half of his chop.

'I've hardly written to Mother lately,' he said. He was at the age now that letter writing in school was no longer compulsory. 'Not since she told me about the baby.'

'That's understandable.' Mayhew was eyeing up the potato, wondering if Anthony was going to eat it or whether perhaps he could have it. They were so incomparably better here than in Brazil, light and fluffy inside, with properly crispy outsides.

'This summer,' continued Anthony, 'when she came here, I thought we could have it all out.'

'I see.' Mayhew lost all hope of the potato as Anthony started mashing it into the remaining gravy with the tines of his fork.

'And now she's not coming anyway,' concluded Anthony, as if he hadn't heard what Mayhew had said.

'She had better things to do,' Mayhew agreed.

The man and the boy sat in silence for a while, watching the waiter clear their plates and bring them the cheese selection. If Anthony felt betrayed by his mother deserting him for her manager, transferring her affections from her son to her new lover, how was he, Mayhew, supposed to feel? His sister had betrayed *him*, getting together with the man he'd brought to be a lowly employee.

Mayhew had heard on the grapevine that Mac's wife was in very poor health, not only an invalid but by all accounts also a lunatic. She was surely not long for this world. Mac and Katharine got on so well. *They* could have married and then – well, then just think how rich they'd all be. Mayhew had spent some time mulling on this; the prospect of such a beneficial union, although entirely a figment of his imagination, had excited him enormously and the decimation of it incensed him to the same degree.

He asked the waiter to call a cab for when they'd finished their dessert. It was time for the next step in his nephew's education.

At the brothel, Mayhew almost had to push Anthony through the door. His face was sheet white, his fists clenched, knuckles like pale pebbles in his olive skin. Mayhew had the fleeting thought that he hoped, if Kitty had had a boy, that he was more of a man in such matters than his nephew appeared to be. Was it a shame that he would never know? He mentally slapped himself in the face. Of course not. Kitty had betrayed him by allowing a pregnancy to happen; the consequences were hers, and hers alone, to deal with.

'Go on, boy,' he commanded Anthony, unequivocally. 'You're old enough now.'

Afterwards, Anthony sat in stony silence in the carriage back to their rooms at Mayhew's club.

'So how was it?' Mayhew questioned, irritated by Anthony's withdrawn state.

Anthony shrugged. 'How the other boys told me it would be.'

Mayhew waited, expectantly, but Anthony said nothing further. With a sigh, he dismissed the whole episode, remembering the shock of his first time. The crucial thing was to keep at it, in his experience. Get back on the horse and have another go, so to speak. But maybe, in Anthony's case, not for a while.

'Let's go to Scotland,' he said, jovially, as he bid Anthony good night. 'Mac's invited us to his grouse shoot.'

Before catching the train, Mayhew took Anthony to the London rubber market in Mincing Lane. The clamour inside the dark, cramped building was deafening, the atmosphere fervid and tense. Rubber samples from all around the world – Brazil, Borneo, Madagascar, the Congo – were laid out on long, rickety trestle tables for inspection by potential buyers. As traders competed to get hold of the material upon which whole industries depended, the hysteria became palpable. The prize amongst prizes was dry, fine Pará and that, Mayhew congratulated himself, was what Norwood Enterprises produced in abundance.

'Look at this!' He indicated with an expansive sweep of his arm the frenetic scene, shouting to make himself heard above the din. 'This is what rubber induces – paranoia, fever. Could you ever imagine it, stuck in that benighted bit of forest of your mother's, far from the rest of the world?'

Anthony shrugged. He'd been morose all day. Mayhew shook his head and clicked his tongue in irritation.

'Let's get to the station,' he ordered. Perhaps the fresh air would bring the boy to his senses.

–

On the moors, the heather was purple, the hills a distant lilac ribbon. The wide-open expanses could not be more different from the enveloping vegetation of the rainforest. It was August, and not cold, but nevertheless there was that nip in the air that never seems to leave the Highlands, whatever the season.

Mayhew could feel his chest expanding, and it wasn't just the full English breakfasts he was consuming every day.

'Makes you feel you can breathe, doesn't it?' he said, exhaling loudly.

Mac, inspecting his gun, nodded. 'The chance to see a distance, a horizon – what you never get amidst all those damn trees.'

They both laughed.

'It's almost as good as back home in Ireland.'

Mayhew smiled wryly. As far as he knew, Patrick McNamara hadn't set foot in County Kerry for over thirty years. But he had been somewhere lately; not in the Amazon, nor in London but in some undisclosed location. Mayhew wondered briefly what his business rival was up to, but then put the thought aside. Why should he care?

'Don't know how those *seringueiros* do it though,' said Mayhew, shaking his head. 'Festering deep in the jungle for months and years on end.'

Mac made a moue of reflection. 'They have their reasons, I suppose. Everybody's searching for something,' he concluded.

A shot rang out, making both men pause in their conversation. Beside them Anthony, grim-faced, tracked another bird and brought it down.

'Oh, good shot,' called one of the other guests, as a setter ran out to retrieve the bird.

'You really have become an English gentleman, haven't you?' congratulated Mac. 'You've got your old uncle to thank for that.' He raised his gun, attempted a shot, missed. 'Sending you off to school was the making of you.'

The keeper signalled for the guns to move to the next butt.

'Pity your mother couldn't make it out here, after all,' Mac continued, waiting for an opportunity to take aim.

Anthony narrowed his eyes, scanning the cloud-laden sky. 'She wants me to go and see Aunt Mabel,' he said. His voice sounded rusty as if from lack of use. He'd barely spoken since the brothel. 'Take her to a photographer, get some pictures done to send back with Uncle Mayhew. To show the baby, when it's older.'

Mac glanced at him sharply, a frown creasing his forehead.

'Oh no, old chap, you don't want to do that. Wouldn't do at all, a public-school boy like you hobnobbing with a lady's maid. Stay away from Mabel!' He laughed, long and loud, the artificial sound echoing off the hills and moorland.

Anthony raised his gun again, aimed and fired. Another hit. Mac nodded admiringly.

307

'What did you say about Aunt Mabel?'

Mac hooked his thumbs into the pocket of his britches. 'Say? I didn't say anything, did I?'

Anthony clicked his tongue against his teeth impatiently. 'You said she was a lady's maid.'

'Ah yes.' Mac lifted his gun, followed a bird in the sky, realised he would miss and brought the gun down again. 'That's because she is a lady's maid. For my daughter, actually. Lady Alexandra Cardburn.'

'Oh.'

'You didn't know?'

'Of course I did.' It was such an obvious lie that Anthony realised as soon as he said it that it would make him sound stupid. But if that was what Mac thought, he didn't say anything. In fact, he just walked away, strolling towards where the rest of the guns were gathering for a shot from their hip flasks.

Anthony went to stand by his uncle's side.

'Mac says that Mabel is a lady's maid for his daughter. Nobody told me.'

Mayhew shifted awkwardly from one foot to the other, cleared his throat, coughed. 'No, well. I suppose it just never occurred to anyone to do so.'

Another blatant lie.

'Does my mother know?'

'Tsk.' Mayhew was annoyed. Mabel was of little consequence but Anthony being aware of her circumstances – which Mayhew himself had only found out about by chance when Mac had drunkenly let it slip a few weeks ago during a dinner engagement – was not ideal. Anthony needed not only to act like a gentleman but to believe he really was one; this was Mayhew's grand plan for him. That was a whole lot harder to do if the boy knew he had a family member in service.

'It's her choice,' he stated, bluntly. 'Wants to be independent, earn her own money. Doesn't want your mother to know so don't you be the one to tell her.'

Mayhew lit a cigarette to calm his nerves. He offered one to Anthony but he merely shook his head and stomped off in the direction the rest of the party were headed.

Later, over whisky, Mac and Mayhew sat by the outdoor fire. Anthony was nowhere to be seen. The midges were out in force, undeterred by wood or cigar smoke.

'Just like the bloody Amazon,' joked Mayhew, batting them away with his large, flat hands.

'Not for much longer.' Mac was staring into his whisky glass, looking at something far away.

'What do you mean?' Mayhew was finding Mac's cryptic utterances more and more exasperating.

'Nothing. Nothing at all, old sport.'

Mayhew felt a momentary flash of irritation. Why was Mac talking in this maddening way, using all these over-familiar forms of address? He never did that in Brazil. He wasn't even English, he was Irish, so why try to sound like a member of the English landed gentry?

Mac got up, announced he was going to bed and left the room. Mayhew wondered if he was feeling his age. He must be pushing fifty or fifty-five these days. It was natural to slow down. He drained his glass and called to the waiting servant for another. If there was a hint that Mac wanted to sell up in the Amazon, he should tell Katharine. Finally, the money was rolling in hand over fist from the Norwood *estradas* and Mayhew envisaged this continuing for years into the future. What could possibly stop it? There were no sizeable stocks of rubber anywhere else in the world, not even the Congo came close and there were so many problems there anyway. King Leopold had really messed up, the horrors of his reign now out in the open. Buying more land in Brazil would be a very sound investment.

Mayhew thought of his savings, the money he was squirrelling away. The deal he'd done with Katharine paid him handsomely and it was only a little clerical error if the price he got the exporters to invoice him for was a little less than he actually received. Everyone understood this way of doing business out there – it was the Brazilian method, the *jeitinho*, the little way, oiling the wheels of commerce so that everything ran smoothly. Katharine was far from a fool and her mathematical ability was second to none – but even she could only add up figures that were in front of her. And when the price of raw rubber changed daily, it was impossible to keep track of it from so far upriver.

Most important of all, she trusted him – her brother – to do right by her. And so he had, by and large, and taken care of her son. She was lucky to have such a shrewd and canny business partner and supporter, not to mention surrogate father to Anthony.

Next morning, Mayhew came down the shooting lodge stairs to find Mac's servant manhandling a large trunk into a waiting carriage.

'I'm leaving early,' Mac said, tersely. 'Got to get back to London for my daughter and son-in-law's annual ball.'

'That's a shame.' Mayhew wasn't really that bothered, but he knew what was polite.

Mac nodded.

'Shall I pass on your best wishes to your sister?'

Mayhew frowned. 'My sister? But she's in the Am… Oh, I see, you mean Mabel. That sister.'

Mayhew was still not entirely used to the idea that Mabel was employed by Mac's daughter, and therefore by Mac, as everyone knew Mac had been keeping the Cardburns financially afloat for decades. Henry Cardburn was a typical aristocrat – all the credentials of lineage and ancestry and not the first idea how to actually do anything useful like run a business or make money. He was also known to be monumentally stupid. Not like Mayhew and Mac, who were both shrewd-minded master negotiators. Nothing like them at all.

His eyes narrowed as he pictured Mabel in his mind. 'The beautiful one!' he cried, chortling. 'Oh, yes, do give her my regards.'

Mayhew watched as the footman finished loading Mac's belongings. He and Anthony were staying a few days longer, and then he'd take the boy back to Winchester before departing for the Amazon.

He'd see Mac again soon enough, he reflected, as the carriage pulled away. Bad pennies always turn up. He chuckled to himself at his joke, then waved goodbye.

Anthony was standing by the corner of the house, waiting for the rest of the shooting party to gather. Mac called out to him as he trundled past.

'Come and see me when you've finished school. I've got opportunities for a boy like you. Out East. I think you'll like it there.'

Chapter Forty-Five

London, 1907

Ideas of both revolution and of rubber receded into the background as work took all the hours of Mabel's days. Whatever was happening on the Amazon or in the suffragette meetings, the routines and rituals of the aristocracy continued unchanged. Mabel had shoved all thoughts of Archie out of her mind. His dishonesty was still incomprehensible but given the indisputable truth, there was nothing to be done but forget him. And in any case, they were back in the frenzy of social activity again, and it was time for the Cardburns' annual ball.

Invitations had been sent out far and wide and the house was bursting at the seams with guests staying for a few nights or several weeks. Mabel was rushed off her feet in the run up, coping with Lady Cardburn's exacting demands for every aspect of her wardrobe, including new dresses, jackets and underwear. Her ball gown would be made at a specialist supplier, but Mabel's stitching was so exquisite and her work so accurate, that she had somehow acquired the job of making most of her ladyship's other requirements. Sewing the silk chemises and bloomers and a racy garment called French knickers that were the last word in Gallic sophistication and style, she sometimes fell asleep over her needle, she was so tired. But she'd been promised a couple of days off when it was all over and she held that in her mind as her goal.

On the day of the ball itself, tensions were high across the household, and not just amongst the servants. Lady Cardburn was short-tempered, anxious that everything should be just so. His lordship upset Mr Robson by suggesting that the silver was not highly polished enough and Mrs Bustle looked as if she were going to be stricken by apoplexy at any moment.

Mabel kept her head down and got on with her chores, while trying to ignore everyone else. Despite the hard work, she adored such occasions, seeing all the ladies in their finery and the men in their suits, moustaches oiled and shining. She had to keep up with Lady Cardburn's love of late nights, because she had to help her get undressed and ready for bed however late the hour. The advent of electricity and hot and cold running water hadn't changed the length of Mabel's days one iota.

The ball went on forever. There was a formal dinner before-hand, and then a supper brought out at midnight. At one o'clock the dancing was still going on. Mabel saw lots of people she recognised, including Anna Lawless, who had no shortage of dance partners, despite the absence of Dennis Whitfield, apparently in the Far East again. Mabel wondered if he'd be jealous if he knew how many times she partnered with the Earl of Blackshire.

Mac was there, of course, relishing his position as the father of the hostess, his pale skin wind-burnt and healthy-looking after his time on the grouse moors, gaily dancing Irish reels and conversing with the other men, laughing heartily and drinking whisky. She wondered where Mrs McNamara was; she'd never seen her in Hanover Terrace. The other servants said she was in poor health these days and had become a recluse, rarely if ever emerging from the Highgate mansion. Some even whispered that she'd gone mad. Mabel felt sorry for her, for being unwell and having to miss so much jollity.

At one point, as she was searching the room for Lady Card-burn to ensure she wasn't needed for anything, Mac caught her eye and winked. Mabel, flustered, looked hastily away. It was a peculiar gesture but everyone was in high spirits and little bit drunk. Eventually, Alexandra gestured to her that she was ready to retire for the night. Mabel scurried off upstairs to get everything ready. Her ladyship was tired and soon dismissed Mabel. In the dressing room, Mabel carefully hung the discarded garments and tidied Alexandra's shoes away. Work finally done, she made her weary way across the corridor to her own room, longing to take the weight off her feet.

She was at her bedroom door and almost through it when she became aware of someone behind her. A flashback to the master passed through her mind and she jumped, involuntarily emitting a gasp of surprise.

A soft voice said, 'Don't worry, it's only me.'

Mac.

Mabel blinked in surprise. 'Mr McNamara!' In her aston-ishment, she forgot to call him by his nickname. 'Wh-what are you doing here?'

He ignored her, just quietly gestured her through the door and followed her in. Once inside, he slipped the latch and locked it.

'I thought I'd come and see those gloves of yours that I gave you,' he said. His words were slightly slurred, his eyes hazy. Mabel could smell the whisky on his breath, and the stench of cigarettes emanating from his clothing. 'I still haven't seen you wearing them.'

It was true. Mabel had been too nervous to take them out of her room, especially since Archie's disgrace. Apart from not wanting Lady Cardburn to question her about them, or think she was trying to rival her, if the other servants saw her with them, they might think she had stolen them, that Archie had infected her with his dishonesty – and something deep inside told her she could not let on where they had really come from. She wore them in her room, on her own, just so that she could feel and enjoy the softness of the leather, the luscious smell of them.

'You haven't lost them, have you?' Mac was asking. His voice was concerned and understanding, not censorious.

'Oh no,' she stuttered, 'they're here, I just – I don't want to spoil them, is all.' She still wasn't sure why he was there, in her room. The gloves didn't seem to be enough of a reason.

Mac smiled, his blue eyes twinkling. 'Wear them and spoil them all you like. And when they are ruined – I shall buy you a new pair.'

Mabel gulped. 'You're very kind,' she murmured. 'Too kind.'

'Not at all.' Mac gestured to the bed. 'Sit down.' Mabel sat, perched nervously on the edge of the mattress. Mac took the chair, turning it around from the dressing table and sitting astride it.

'Did you – did you want something?' Mabel asked, help-lessly, utterly unsure of how to deal with this unprecedented situation.

Mac frowned. 'I suppose so,' he replied, enigmatically.

He reached into his jacket pocket and pulled out a silver flask. 'I've brought something for both of us.' Mac removed the stopper and the smell hit her, pungent and heady. He took a swig and handed the flask to Mabel. She didn't really want any but it seemed rude to refuse. She sipped daintily from it. It tasted disgusting, like earth and mud and rainwater in puddles, and it scoured her throat as she swallowed, burning all the way to her stomach.

'Gosh,' she hiccupped, 'that's strong.'

'God, this is good.' Mac looked around him as if he hadn't heard what she'd said. 'Away from the fuss and hullabaloo, all those bores and shrieking banshees.' He stared at the floor and carried on, as if he'd forgotten Mabel was there and was talking to himself. 'That's what I like about the Amazon. When I want to get away from it all, I go to Lagona and nobody bothers me there.'

Mabel nodded, though Mac wasn't looking. She had a hazy vision of Lagona from Katharine's letters and imagined a grand house surrounded by a garden of banana, mango and pineapple trees and the river roaring by.

Suddenly, he sat up straight and handed Mabel the flask again. 'Have some more,' he said, 'have lots. Plenty more where that came from.'

This was certainly true. Mabel had seen the cellar beneath the house; she'd been amazed by the sheer number of bottles, too many to count, too many to take in: wine, whisky, brandy, gin – the quantities were endless.

'I've invested a fair bit in wine,' Mac mused, 'Claret, mainly. And good port. But there comes a time when there's nothing left to spend one's money on. And then—' He snapped his fingers in his air as if to signify the futility of it all.

Mabel felt sorry for him. He was rich beyond measure but she now saw what she'd probably been semi-conscious of all along – his wife was crazy, his children grown up and he was lonely. It was a shame. He was so handsome, so generous and kind.

She drank some more of the liquid, enjoying the burn this time. When she put the flask down, it hit the table with a bump as she misjudged the distance. She felt lightheaded and fuzzy, but enjoyably so, and as if everything was funnier that it had been before. Mac started to tell a joke about three men in a pub, an Englishman, a Scottish man and an Irish man. Mabel lost the thread long before the punch line but laughed heartily anyway.

'It's always the Irish man,' Mac was saying, 'always the Irish man who's the butt of the joke. But look at me. Rich as Croesus, I am. They can't laugh at me now, so they can't.'

Mabel shook her head. 'No, nobody should laugh at you. Never.' She drank some more and handed the flask to Mac and suddenly they were both chuckling gaily away and Mabel realised that she was lonely too, had been since Archie left. It was good to have company.

She lost all track of time. It could have been a few seconds or many minutes, but all at once Mac moved from the chair and was sitting beside her, very close to her, and then he had his arm around her and his mouth, smelling of cigarettes and alcohol, was close to hers. And then it was upon hers, kissing her, wrenching her lips apart, shoving his tongue between her teeth.

'No,' she yelped, instantly terrified, 'no, stop.'

'Don't be silly.' Mac's lips were on her ear, his words, though whispered, booming into it. 'You don't want me to stop. You've led me on for weeks, years, with those beseeching eyes, those enticing smiles. Now you're going to get what you've been asking for. And you're going to love it, trust me.'

And then he was kissing her again and pushing her onto the bed, holding her arms down, and no matter how she struggled she couldn't get him off because he wasn't a big man but even so he was far stronger than her.

'Relax,' whispered Mac. His breath was hot on her neck. He leant into her, bent his head and started nibbling at her skin, her throat. Releasing one of her arms, his hand reached down to her skirt and began to pull it up.

Seizing her chance, Mabel stretched out her arm to the dressing table. She had a looking glass there; perhaps if she could get hold of it, she could hit him with it, get him to stop. Her fumbling fingers made contact with the glass' silver handle and she picked it up. Fleetingly, she glimpsed her reflection, saw her own stricken look of fear like a cornered animal.

And then the glass was gone. Mac had snatched for it, whipped it out of her hand and thrown it onto the floor where it shattered, the sound of tinkling glass momentarily filling the air.

Seven years bad luck, thought Mabel, and uttered a hysterical burst of laughter at the horror and absurdity of it all.

'Don't do that, you little silly thing,' Mac hissed, his hands tight around her ears now, holding her head still. 'You know you want it. All this struggling – just false modesty, a pretence.' He sounded really drunk now, his voice thick with alcohol, his words slurring badly. 'You're more than old enough to enjoy it, too old really. Much older than my Indian girls. Usually I prefer the young ones, ten, twelve – but with someone as beautiful as you, age is immaterial.'

Mabel thought her heart had stopped. She looked into Mac's cornflower blue eyes. They were devoid of all emotion, as if the charming twinkle had never existed. She had completely misjudged him, just as she had misjudged Archie. In the bedroom across the hall was Lady Cardburn, Mac's daughter. If Mabel screamed, she would hear her.

'Don't even think about it,' muttered Mac silkily, reading her mind. He ran his fingers delicately over her mouth and then clamped his hand upon it. 'This is our little secret, our little treat. I'm not going to do anything to you that you won't like. Girls like you – they love it once they know how. Once they've had expert tuition. But if you tell anyone – if you tell my daughter – you'll live to regret it. Remember that no one would believe you, anyway. It would be your word against mine – and I would win.'

His weight was on top of her, the weight of rocks or mountains, the weight of the whole world. Mabel's head spun and her body drifted away in a haze of alcohol and nausea, and with it all her dreams of the future, of being a French teacher, of working in a school.

The alcohol coursed through her veins and she floated in and out of consciousness. She was only dimly aware of what Mac was doing, where he was touching her, how much it hurt. Once the worst of the sick feeling from the alcohol had passed, she began to appreciate the numbness, the distance it gave her from what was going on. What Mac was doing. It was nice to be in another world, another state of being. Better to be drunk.

The alternative was to be sober, and to know.

318

Chapter Forty-Six

The Amazon, 1908

In the end, Thomas and Katharine lingered in Manaus until the end of the year and then into the next. Katharine hated to say it, but much as the city disgusted her on the one hand, there was something to be said for the luxury of urban life. A bathtub, for one. Fresh running water for another. And now it was so built up, the insects and mosquitoes were far fewer than in 1890, during her first prolonged stay in the city.

If you ignored the brothels and bordellos that openly occupied a quarter of the buildings in town, you could enjoy the culture – the theatre, the art galleries, the concerts, the bookshops. And despite her initial worries, Lily's mixed heritage went largely unnoticed. Katharine remembered the evening she and Anselmo had arrived nearly two decades before, how bemused she had been by the huge variety of people on the crowded dockside, the mixing of races that had all generated their own specific term. Now she was part of that human melting pot, and it didn't seem as bad, or as frightening, as all that after all.

'I wonder what will happen when we take her to London,' she mused to Thomas one night. 'She'll never fit in there.'

Thomas shrugged. 'Neither will I.'

'I know,' responded Katharine. 'But I love her and I love you and that's all that matters.'

'Exactly,' agreed Thomas. 'What else do we need?'

In July of that year, just before Lily's first birthday and after the huge swell of the Rio Negro that occurred every rainy

319

season had subsided, they finally headed home. There were regular sailings all the way to Lagona now, no need to strike special deals with the captain as Anselmo had had to do. And there were water closets on board, plus fully enclosed cabins for first class passengers. Incredibly, there was also a steamer to Norwood. An enterprising young Welshman had bought a small vessel, sailed her to the isthmus, taken her apart piece by piece and carried her over the narrow strip of land that separated the Largo and the Poderoso. There he had painstakingly reassembled her and now the *Good Prospects* made regular trips as far past Norwood as the river was navigable and back again. It was the first steamer on that part of the river since Anselmo's had sunk.

'I'm getting too used to luxury,' sighed Katharine, as she settled Lily into her bassinet in their spacious presidential suite. It was a far cry from a hammock, and the bucket with a basin of water that had been their bathroom on her first journey upriver. The new Lagona steamer was also bigger and had more powerful engines than previous models and they arrived at Mac's compound in only four weeks. There they had to wait awhile before the *Good Prospects* arrived. The settlement's opulence had not diminished over the years, even though Mac was spending less and less time there. And on closer inspection, Katharine saw that the beetles had got into some of his Chippendale furniture and woodworm had taken up residence in the flooring.

Lily, caring nothing for mahogany or oak, was delighted daily by a family of capuchin monkeys that played in the compound garden. Katharine watched how the mother cared for her baby, so tenderly picking the fleas from its fur, grooming and feeding it with utmost dedication. They really are so like us, she thought, and hugged Lily tight and covered her with kisses because all mothers love their babies.

Approaching Norwood some weeks later Katharine felt, as she always did, a frisson of trepidation, a lurch of the stomach, in memory of that terrible return that had revealed the devastation of her home and the destruction of her rubber. But this time, all was well, a gentle breeze stirring amidst the tree branches, the sounds of a thriving and prosperous compound drifting over the wide river and just audible above the rumble of the steamer's engines.

Life settled back to normal quickly, except that everything about normal was different. With Thomas, Jonathan and Santiago all capable of running the business, Katharine no longer had to work night and day with her baby strapped to her back, as she had when Antonio had been born. She could spend precious time with her daughter, singing to her, playing pat-a-cake with her pudgy starfish hands, or round-and-round-the-garden on her pink palms. It was a revelation and she loved every moment of it – apart from the times when she was filled with regret that she had not been able to do these things with Antonio.

Her preoccupation with her daughter caused her to put out of her mind the rumblings of problems on the Amazon that were doing the rounds during their sojourn in Manaus, rumours rippling up and down the river of iniquities committed for the love of rubber, not just by Arana but by many others. She didn't want to think about everything that was wrong, preferred to focus on what was right, which was her new family of three and the extended family of her compound and all of those who lived on it. And the fact that she had now not only repaid her father in full but also given much more, enough to ensure that her parents enjoyed a financially secure future into old age.

The weeks and months passed, and though Katharine's happiness continued, there was just one thing that troubled her. She was finding Mabel's letters stranger and stranger, ever more distant and often disjointed somehow as if she was not quite with it when she wrote. And there were few of them, many fewer than in past times.

More and more, Katharine began to worry that something might be wrong. But so many, many miles away, what could she do about it?

322

Chapter Forty-Seven

London, 1908

Mac's visits started weekly, soon became daily. Mabel was paralysed, unable to react in any way. She could tell no one and had no one to tell. And even if she had, Mac had repeatedly warned her: 'Say anything, you're out on your ear.' He'd told her also not to even think of writing to her sister about it. 'I'll know if you do,' he'd said. 'I have you followed – everywhere you go, any visit you might make the Post Office, I'll know about, so I will.' The addition of the Irish phrasing seemed to make his words more sinister and threatening. But in his tone there was also a hint of reproach. 'You should be enjoying it by now,' he'd slurred into her ear one night. 'They always do, in the end.'

At first Mabel cried. Then she became enraged, imagining thrusting a knife into his heart – did he even have a heart? – and watching the red blood run forth. Finally she succumbed, knowing resistance was futile. Mac plied her with alcohol, abused her and raped her, and then left. In the mornings, head throbbing, she would rise from her bed and attempt to do her job. She couldn't believe that Lady Cardburn didn't notice that something was wrong; she suspected that she probably did – but chose not to do anything about it.

One day, her suspicions were confirmed. She was in the dressing room, mending stockings and underwear, when she heard a knock on the bedroom door. Hastily, she stabbed the needle into the pincushion, threw the garment to one side, and leapt up. But before she'd reached the door, the visitor had entered the boudoir and the opportunity to escape had disappeared. Moments later, the lilting cadence of Mac's voice filtered through to her.

'I've put that money you asked for into your account,' he was saying.

Mabel could picture her ladyship, reclining on her chaise longue, resting. All she did was rest and shop, she thought vitriolically. She'd never had critical feelings about Alexandra before, but now she suddenly hated her and her pampered lifestyle. And she was sure she was unfaithful to her husband, that she was having an affair with the Duke of Huntingshire. She wondered whether, even if Lord Cardburn knew, he would care. He and his wife didn't seem particularly close. Like so much else to do with the upper classes, much of what they were was a sham, maintained only for appearance's sake.

Now father and daughter were alone together, Mabel wanted to shout out loud about Mac, wanted to scream to Lady Cardburn about what her father was doing to her. But she knew she never would, would simply never dare. She had asked for it, as Mac repeatedly told her, and now she was getting it. It was her fault. And telling on him would only result in the worst outcome for her, being thrown out on her ear, utterly disgraced.

'Thank you,' she heard Lady Cardburn reply, laconically.

That was how easy money was for them all. In recent years, it had become the same for Mabel's family – not to the same extent as Mac's obviously. But Katharine had bought all sorts of luxuries for their parents, including moving them to a newly built property in Highgate, complete with an indoor bathroom and electricity. Mabel had not visited. She could not bring herself to set foot in the same suburb that Mac resided in. And Katharine had written and offered Mabel money, but Mabel had not responded.

Once upon a time, she would have taken a small amount to give her and Archie a start, as long as he hadn't minded her having more to put into their marriage than he had. Now, all thoughts of a happy union had long been driven out. Her shame and self-disgust had eradicated everything she had ever been, cared about or wanted. The only thing she could do in retaliation, her only small rebellion, was to write it all down in her diary. She recorded everything, all Mac's revelations about his Indian girls, his new business ventures, all of it, immortalised in her precise, looping hand. Papers he left lying around her room she gathered up and stored within the diary's pages. She knew it was dangerous; if found, it would be her downfall. But she did it anyway.

Sitting back down, Mabel wondered if she should make some noise, remind Lady Cardburn that she was there. But she didn't. So what if she were accused of prying. She didn't care about any of it any more.

'Father,' said Lady Cardburn, her tone suddenly serious, harsh even. 'I'm worried about my—'

Mabel held her breath, straining her ears to hear. But she didn't catch Alexandra's last words.

Her next were clarion clear.

'I think you might be going a bit far this time.'

There was a pause. The silence was heavy, expectant.

'Look, it's all very well for you to mess around with those dirty, skinny little Indian girls you can't seem to resist. God forbid that Mother finds out about it – it would certainly kill her. But—'

Mabel nearly screamed in frustration as Lady Cardburn's words became inaudible once more. But she registered that what Mac had confessed to her, about his liaisons with his servants, was not the secret she had imagined it to be.

'We've already lost two housemaids because of you and servants are harder and harder to find, in case you hadn't noticed. So please, I'm begging you, leave her alone.' Alexandra's voice didn't sound in the least bit begging. It sounded weary and irritated, as if reprimanding her father was something she often had to do and had grown tired of. Was she talking about Mabel? If she was, that meant she knew. Mabel could hardly bear it. And then there was the fact that there had been others.

It was a long time since Mabel had felt special. But perhaps she had still retained the tiniest sliver of hope that was the case, that what Mac whispered in her ear about being the only one for him was true. Now she knew she was no different to any of those who had come before her. Something to use and dispose of, just like the housemaids and the Indian girls. Mabel felt sorry for them and wondered what had become of them. For herself, she could no longer think anything.

In the stillness, she heard the floorboards creak. She assumed Mac was pacing the room in that way he had. The footsteps stopped and were replaced by the gentle drumming of his fingers on the mantelpiece.

'I pay her wages. I pay your bills. I'll do what I like.'

Lady Cardburn sighed, heavily enough for Mabel to hear.

'When you come out East to see the plantations there, you'll understand. It's a lot of work I'm doing, a great deal of organisation and responsibility. I need a rest every once in a while, some light relief.' Mac was beginning to sound angry. 'If you don't want any more of my cash, you've only to say.'

Weighty footfalls and a slamming of the door.

Mabel hardly dared breathe. She waited, hoping Alexandra would leave, would follow her father out to continue remonstrating with him. But she didn't.

Eventually, Mabel had nothing else she could reasonably pretend to be occupied with in the dressing room. She was desperate to get out, to be anywhere other than this. She stood up and went into the boudoir. With a curtsy, she addressed Alexandra.

'I've done the mending, your ladyship,' she murmured. 'If there's nothing you need now, I'll go and fetch your evening shoes from the boot boy.'

Lady Cardburn regarded Mabel with a smile that was part sardonic, part pitying.

'Yes, Mabel,' she said. 'Thank you.'

Lady Cardburn, who Mabel had thought cared for her and respected her, as much as an employer ever respected a servant, had let her down. She'd had a lazy, half-hearted conversation with her father and then given up. His money was more important to her than Mabel. Of course it was. Mabel was a servant. How ironic to think that she had believed the position of lady's maid would protect her from abuse. Now she had discovered that nothing could be further from the truth.

On the way to the boot room, Mabel passed through the dining room. The table was laid for dinner, glass and silverware gleaming and shining in the dazzling light from the electric chandelier. In the Venetian decanters, the wine was acclimatising. Breathing, Mr Robson called it. Well, Mabel needed to breathe, needed to do so more than any of these stuck-up, entitled, posh rich people who'd be stuffing their fat, ugly faces around this table tonight.

She picked up one of the decanters and took a long, deep slug from it, followed by another one. Then she filled it up to the top from the jug of water that stood on the sideboard. Reeling slightly, she made her way to the door, misjudging the position of the handle and missing it, rapping her knuckles against the wood. As she tripped over the threshold, Arthur and Algernon, the two footmen, approached.

'Good evening,' she giggled, half falling against the panelled corridor. 'Enjoy yourselves!'

She was aware of their eyes following her as she stumbled back to the staircase. And she was drunk enough to care not one little bit.

Chapter Forty-Eight

Norwood, 1909

The rainy season of 1908–9 was one of prodigious precipitation. The heavens opened and it rained, day after day, week after week, with a ferocity of intent that startled even those Europeans who, like Katharine, had been in the Amazon for years. The Indians took it in their stride; for people whose history stretched back millennia, excessive rainfall was nothing new.

When the rain finally eased off, the forest, ready and poised, exploded into new life. Blossom burst forth on the orange trees and hummingbirds surrounded them, greedily drinking the nectar, orchid flowers erupted from bud to bloom in the blink of an eye and so many chicks in so many eggs broke their way out of their shells simultaneously that Katharine swore she could hear their tapping.

Katharine and Lily were playing at the water's edge, enjoying the river's song and the sunshine after so many cloudy days, when a canoe drew up, its Indian oarsman leaping out the minute the bottom hit the sand and running towards them as if his life depended on it.

'Urgent message, Mother,' he shouted, 'Mr Mayhew, he said very important!'

He thrust a slim letter towards her and immediately turned back around.

'Thank you,' responded Katharine and then, calling after him as he rapidly ran off, 'can't you wait for a reply?'

But the Indian was gone already, leaping into his canoe and paddling furiously away.

Katharine took Lily up to the house and gave her into Rosabel's care before opening the letter. Inside the envelope were two pieces of paper – one from Mayhew and one in Mabel's handwriting.

Mabel's was short. She was coming to the Amazon.

Mayhew's was equally brief, and blunt as always. He was in Manaus with Mabel and would be travelling down to Lagona with her. He would stay with her until the *Good Prospects* arrived and then send her on to Norwood alone.

The letters gave no idea about what had happened, or why Mabel had made this totally unexpected journey.

Katharine worried and worried at it, asking Thomas time and again what the matter could be, whether she should go to Lagona to meet her sister, how Mabel would cope with the heat and humidity of the jungle. Katharine remembered her as such a delicate, precious thing. The onslaught of the Amazon would knock her for six.

When the steamer finally docked, Katharine was waiting. As the gangplank was lowered, her heart skipped a beat. She was desperate to see Mabel, who had been only five years old when she had left London, but also a little nervous. She had received only a handful of family photographs in the intervening period, and these had soon deteriorated in the humidity, falling prey to fungi and mildew, so Katharine wasn't sure that she'd even recognise her beloved sister.

But in the event, it was easy. Only one person got off. A woman, stunningly beautiful, her white dress of Swiss dot with hat and matching veil somehow managing to look pristine and fresh despite the temperature. But nevertheless, a woman who was most definitely not the sweet, innocent child that Katharine had left behind all those years ago in London.

This woman was truly a grown up – and she was also with child.

Open-mouthed in astonishment, Katharine went towards her, moving slowly as if walking through water.

'Mabel,' she stuttered, 'Mabel, I can't believe it's really you.'
Disregarding Mabel's state for the time being, she flung her arms around her sister and kissed her over and over again.

'Oh Katharine,' sighed Mabel, and her eyes behind her veil brimmed over with tears. 'I'm sorry. I'm so sorry.'

Thomas arrived on the dock and opened his mouth to speak. Katharine shot him a silencing glance – now was not the time for questions – and led Mabel up to the house, to the shade of the veranda, calling to one of the servants to bring lemonade and wine.

Divested of her hat and veil, Katharine was able to properly take in the ethereal, other-worldly beauty of her sister. Mabel was every bit as lovely as she had promised to be as a child, and now even more so, the glow of pregnancy enhancing her gorgeousness. *If her face is her fortune*, their mother Mary had always said, *then Mabel is sitting on a goldmine*. But there was sadness behind her smile, and a haunted look in her melting brown eyes.

Katharine poured the drinks. She took lemonade for herself but Mabel asked for wine. She drained the cup almost instantly and then requested a refill. Katharine was shocked. It was hard to see her sister, who'd she'd last seen age five, downing alcohol like it was going out of fashion.

'What happened?' asked Katharine, gently.

That Mabel was pregnant and had presumably fled as far as possible to escape the opprobrium an unmarried mother would face in London was obvious. Coming to the Amazon must have seemed the only option, and the best one – to take her shame to the jungle where it could be swallowed up with all the other depravity. Katharine was inwardly seething, incandescent with rage, but the worst thing would be for Mabel to see this. In her condition, she needed unconditional love and succour.

'You can tell me, Mabel,' Katharine urged, taking her sister's hand in hers. 'I'm your sister. But you don't have to talk yet, if it's too soon.'

330

Mabel began to cry, silently and copiously. 'I couldn't write,' she sobbed, when she could speak again, 'I–I was too ashamed.'

Katharine bowed her head in sadness. She had been blissfully unaware of Mabel's undoing, enjoying her time with her own infant with no notion of what Mabel was going through.

Mabel took a handkerchief out of her bag and wiped her eyes and blew her nose. Beneath the beauty, Katharine saw that she was exhausted, her face washed out, white and drained like the Amazonian sky after a storm.

'I think you should get some rest now,' suggested Katharine, stroking Mabel's hair away from her face. It was wet with sweat and tears. 'Travelling is exhausting and you've come a long way. Sleep first, explanations later.'

Mabel nodded. 'Thank you, Katharine,' she whispered. 'Thank you so much. I–I didn't know if you would understand. But I knew you would be kind.'

That night, feeding Lily in the darkness, Katharine thought that, though she would always be kind and would try to be *understanding*, she didn't *understand* at all. Not yet. Not until she'd heard from Mabel exactly what had gone on, who was responsible for this.

It was a long, angry wait. Mabel slept for twelve hours. Not even the discomfort of her large belly was enough to stop her slumbering. Unlike Mabel, Katharine barely closed her eyes that night, running through in her mind the possible culprits – a rapist in the streets, a young man from a bad family who felt entitled to take whoever or whatever he wanted.

And it was always the women who took the blame, whose lives changed irrevocably after an incident such as this, while the men carried on regardless. Katharine burnt with indignation and fury. This was one of the reasons why the fight for women's votes was so important, she thought in the cacophonous reaches of the Amazonian night. Unless women had a say in laws and government, how would anything ever change? Men got away with taking advantage of women all the time and women could do nothing about it.

331

Next morning, she was playing with Lily beneath the arching fronds of a palm tree when Mabel approached. Katharine ordered coffee and bread and scrambled eggs; Mabel needed protein and sustenance for her baby. She was thin, Katharine saw now, beneath the bump.

'Mabel, I know this is all going to be difficult, and you can tell me the details when you feel ready,' Katharine said, 'but first of all, we need to make arrangements for your confinement. How far gone are you?'

Mabel bit her lip. 'I think about eight months now,' she replied. 'Mayhew took me to a doctor in Manaus and he said the same. Eight months, more or less.'

Katharine nodded. She wished they were in Manaus, where she had first-hand proof that the hospitals were excellent. She weighed it up in her mind. There wouldn't be another steamer for two to three weeks, and then it would take several more, with the current on their side, to get from Lagona to Manaus. They couldn't risk it, would never make it to the city in time. It would be better for Mabel to be here with the local women to help than end up giving birth on the boat.

'So, the baby will be born here at Norwood. Your baby. It will be fine.' Her voice was as calm and reassuring as she could make it. Mabel was young and healthy, and Katharine herself had had Antonio in the jungle to no ill-effect. She needed Mabel to feel confident, not afraid.

Katharine looked at her sister to gauge her reaction. But her eyes were glazed over, her skin white and translucent as porcelain.

Chicken soup, thought Katharine, slightly desperately. Rosabel's chicken soup would restore Mabel to health in the weeks before the baby's arrival. And she would call for Senhor Garcia, ask him to come and check Mabel over.

Mabel, seeming to rouse from her waking reverie, picked up her coffee and sipped at it, her nose wrinkling as if it were poison.

'Don't drink the coffee if you don't like it,' urged Katharine, anxiously. 'It's very bitter here, and we've given up on even tinned milk. There've been so many times when we haven't had any that we've all grown used to going without.'

She smiled, hoping to see Mabel reciprocate. But Mabel just stared at the cup, blank-eyed.

'Do you have any wine?' she suddenly blurted out. 'Or whisky, or brandy. Anything?'

Katharine gulped in astonishment. It was ten thirty in the morning. She wondered if alcohol was good for the baby. Or good for her sister, for that matter.

'We've probably got... I mean, yes, we have brandy, and wine. It's in the office; the Indians go crazy for it; they'd drink it all in a day if they got the chance. So, it's kept under lock and key.' She paused, reaching out her hand and taking Mabel's. It was limp, cold and clammy. Katharine curled her fingers around Mabel's palm. 'But it's a bit early for drinking quite yet, isn't it? Perhaps stick to lemonade for now. We can have a glass of wine with our dinner later.'

Mabel visibly quivered and Katharine saw something in her eyes that horrified her. Behind the empty gaze lay something worse, animal, visceral.

Fear.

A gasp rose in Katharine's throat. Her sister was terrified and she needed to know why.

'Mabel,' she implored, gently. 'Please tell me what happened. You know you can trust me. Who did this to you? Who are you afraid of?'

Mabel looked up, her brown eyes meeting Katharine's grey ones. Her bottom lip trembled just as it had done when she was a little girl, back in Hawthorn Road, and she'd hurt herself or one of the boys had been mean to her.

Mabel whispered something that Katharine couldn't make out.

'I can't hear you,' she murmured, leaning in close to her sister. 'Please tell me again.'

333

Mabel's eyes were swimming with tears.

'Mac,' she muttered, faintly.

Katharine's breath caught in her throat. Mac? What could he possibly have to do with this?

'I was working for Alexandra – his daughter, your friend,' continued Mabel, still mumbling but her words more distinct now. 'I was her lady's maid. You don't know, Katharine, we didn't tell you. Dad had a bad fall, he couldn't work any more so I had to. I haven't been at school. I won't ever be a teacher. Mac gave me a job.'

She paused. Katharine was silent, dumbstruck, her head reeling. How could all this have been going on and she knew nothing?

'It was there. It happened there. In her house. His daughter's house, that Mac bought for her.'

Katharine's heart broke for her baby sister and she gripped her hand tighter. Though nausea was churning inside her and bile rising in her throat she had a desperate urge to know everything.

'Tell me,' she whispered. 'It's better to talk about it than to keep it all inside.'

But Mabel just burst into sobs and was soon crying so hard that speech was impossible.

Over the next few days, Katharine remained furious about being kept in the dark regarding Bill's accident but stopped asking Mabel questions. She told herself that Mabel would tell her when the time was right and, in the meanwhile, she would concentrate on feeding her sister up and – as much as she could – weaning her off her desire for alcohol.

In her head, she devised all sorts of punishments and penalties for whoever had impregnated an innocent girl like Mabel and then abandoned her, without the decency of offering to marry her. Though the more Katharine thought about it, the more she realised that she didn't want her sister marrying anyone just for the sake of convenience, however society might judge

334

her for the lack of a ring on her finger. Here in the Amazon, Katharine consoled herself, Mabel and her baby could live without anyone wagging fingers. The Indians couldn't care less whether she was Mrs or Miss; they just loved all babies without question.

One morning, sitting at a table on the veranda on which Rosabel had laid lemonade and biscuits, Katharine reached out and took Mabel's hand.

'Can you tell me now?' Katharine queried, tentatively. 'I'd like to hear. About everything.'

'I don't know how to say it,' muttered Mabel, staring down at the table, its wooden surface smoothed by years of use. It had been one of the first things that Jonathan had made when Katharine had first arrived at Norwood and had been used day in, day out since then.

'I think I loved Archie – Terence,' she said, falteringly. 'I did love him. But he got dismissed. And then it started. It's… I know it was my fault. He told me it was my fault, that I wanted him, wanted…'

Her voice grew so faint that Katharine had to strain to hear.

'It was… He gave me alcohol. I thought he was being kind. But it was really to make me – to make me do… things.'

Her face was twisted into a grotesque grimace as she remembered.

'At first I was flattered, I felt special, the chosen one.' She gulped, breaking a biscuit into tiny pieces and dropping them to the ground. The ants descended in seconds, a black mound seething and writhing. 'But then he threatened me. He said he'd get me sacked, thrown out onto the streets, that I'd be disgraced, I'd never be able to set foot in my family home, or any home, again.'

'None of that is true,' Katharine murmured, putting her hand on Mabel's knee to steady her, to comfort her. She still had no real idea exactly was Mabel was talking about. 'No one has that power.'

335

'He told me that if I just relaxed, I'd enjoy it,' Mabel blurted out. 'Oh please, Katharine, can I have some wine now? Please.'

Katharine clenched the fist of her free hand, the one that was not caressing Mabel's. Who was this 'he' Mabel was so terrified of? She thought of the most omnipotent person she knew, the most inviolable.

'Not even Mac,' she enunciated slowly, 'the greatest rubber baron of them all, has that sort of power.'

Mabel stiffened, and froze. The little colour in her cheeks drained away, leaving her eyes stark and staring, searching frantically amongst the trees as if her tormentor were there, stalking her, waiting for her. Fear, anger and shock jolted through Katharine's spine as the dreadful truth dawned on her.

Mac.

When Mabel had mentioned his name just a few days before, Katharine had thought his connection to Mabel's downfall was that the dreadful event had happened in the house he owned. But now it slowly dawned on her what the real situation was.

'No,' she stuttered, 'n-no... I don't believe it. It can't be...' She fell silent, her gaze meeting Mabel's. 'It is, isn't it? Isn't it?' Her voice rose in a tone of disgusted resignation. 'It's Mac. Mac did this!' The last words hissed out like steam under pressure.

Mabel nodded, slowly and with the utmost sadness.

'No!' Katharine screamed; no restraint possible now. 'No, no, no. How could he?'

The noise woke Lily, who'd been sleeping in her pram. She began to cry, loud and insistent. Katharine did not go to her, instead pacing up and down, fists clenched, knuckles white with anger.

'It is, Katharine, it's Mac!' Mabel was suddenly shrieking too, her eyes wide with fear, her nose streaming with snot. She still looked beautiful, even like that, and Katharine's heart broke for her at the same time as her head raged, the name Mac exploding over and over again between her ears and behind her eyes. She hadn't even been aware that her sister knew Mac. And now this appalling revelation, that she not only knew him but that he had fathered her child.

'He... he... many times, so many times, he... I couldn't stop him, Katharine! He brought me a gift; I was grateful. But then it all changed. He came to my room; he forced me... I didn't know how to make it stop...'

Mabel faltered, then broke down into uncontrollable, heaving sobs, unable to continue.

Katharine took a deep breath and swallowed down her bile. She could not believe that Mac, her friend and mentor, her ally, could be guilty of such a heinous crime as rape. But that was clearly the truth of the matter. She focused on her breathing, in and out, one two three, one two three.

Thomas appeared on the veranda and stared, bewildered, at the wailing baby in her pram, the weeping Mabel in a chair, and his wife striding backwards and forwards with a look fit to kill.

'What's wrong?' he asked, quietly.

Katharine swung around and faced him, raising her arms at the elbows as if Thomas were Mac and she were about to challenge him to a brawl.

'Mac,' she hissed. Just that one word, *Mac*. And Thomas knew.

'No,' he breathed. 'How?' And then, 'Oh God. Oh, my good God.'

Katharine, come to her senses with Thomas' arrival, rushed to Mabel, who had suddenly slumped forward onto the table. She flung her arms around her sister.

'It's all right,' she crooned, 'it's all right. He can't hurt you any more. You're safe here with us. I promise that you're safe.'

Eventually, she and Thomas helped Mabel to bed. She'd asked for brandy and Katharine had fetched her some. For the shock, Mabel had said, and Katharine didn't know how to refuse her.

'I can't believe it,' she repeated, over and over, 'I just can't believe it. He's my friend, he *was* my friend, he knew full

337

well who Mabel was when he employed her on his daughter's behalf…'

'Calm, calm,' soothed Thomas. 'No good can come of getting all worked up. We need to be strong, and solid, for Mabel. Everything else can wait until another time.'

But Katharine could not be pacified. Her anger was like an erupting volcano, unstoppable, red hot, all-consuming.

'He'll pay for this,' she raged, 'If it's the last thing I do I swear I'll make him pay. However long it takes.'

Chapter Forty-Nine

Mabel was changed after that first revelation. It was as if, once the biggest truth was out, the floodgates opened. Katharine discovered that her sister found it easier to talk when she was walking, or out on the river, Katharine paddling the canoe and Mabel sitting behind her, trailing her fingers in the silky water.

It was in this way that Katharine discovered the stories behind a myriad more mysteries.

'He said there were others,' Mabel blurted out, as the prow cut a swathe through the glassy surface, 'Indian girls, young ones. He said he liked them young, that I was too old really but so beautiful it didn't matter. He told me that one of them died after she'd had a baby.'

Katharine paddled on, staring straight ahead. A kingfisher darted for a fish. They're such a disappointment, after British ones, Katharine thought as she always did, their colours nowhere near as bright and vibrant.

It was hard to listen to what Mabel was saying. To hear that Mac was guilty, not only of impregnating Mabel, but others too. And not just women, but children.

'He said he didn't know why the girl died. Quite a few of them had his children and they just went back to live in the forest or in Iquitos. But this one got sick, he said she got a fever and the women couldn't cure it and eventually she got so weak that she died. He doesn't know what happened to the baby.'

A catfish came to the surface and took a fly. Katharine wanted to hit it with the paddle, to batter it as she would like to batter Mac. But it was just a fish. It had done nothing wrong.

'The girl's name was Esperanza.'

Katharine's hands around the paddle tightened. Her finger-nails cut into her palms and she liked the pain. It was a small echo of that which was in her heart due to the injustice done to Mabel, to Esperanza and all the others whose lives Mac had ruined or blighted or ended. Little Esperanza. She had wondered where she had gone, just as she had wondered at the age of the other pregnant girl at that Christmas visit when she had met Alexandra. She had not had the faintest inkling that those girls had fallen victim to Mac.

Abruptly, she turned her head to face Mabel.

'He's disgusting. He's foul, nothing better than vermin. But you're never going to see him again. When he finds out you're here, he'll never dare set foot in the Amazon again. I'll make sure of that, don't you worry.'

As she spoke, she had no idea how she could actually keep that promise. But for the moment, it was what Mabel needed to hear. 'We'll take care of you, Mabel. That's all you have to worry about now.'

And inside, silently, *We have plenty of time to take revenge. Years, if need be. But take it we will.*

Back on shore, Katharine retrieved Lily from Thomas' care. She took the child, now twenty months old, and carried her to where Mabel was sitting, quietly weeping. She placed Lily in her sister's arms and watched as Mabel smiled down at her, her sadness lifting and her luminous beauty shining through once more. Mabel kissed the infant's cheeks and fingers and each of her ten little toes.

'She's so perfect, Katharine,' she breathed, unable to tear her eyes away from her niece. 'So lovely.'

Katharine leant towards her. 'And your baby will be, too,' she assured her. 'We will look after it and love it, no matter what. That's all you have to think about just now.'

Mabel nodded. 'I'll try.'

Katharine thought that Mabel would have nothing else to tell. But the disclosures continued. Over the time she spent at

Norwood, Mabel came to trust Thomas as much as she did her sister. And one evening, as the three of them strolled through the orchard, Mabel began to talk once more.

'You wrote to the family about Anselmo dying,' she began, tentatively. 'Even though I was still so young, I remember when Mother got that letter, how she cried, how she wrung her hands for you. And for him.'

'I'm sorry you had to hear that, Mabel,' replied Katharine. 'It must have been shocking and frightening for you.'

'I never forgot it,' Mabel continued. 'When Mac started to speak about it, I thought he wanted to get it off his chest, to talk about how distressing it was, how terrible.'

Katharine nodded.

'But it wasn't that at all.' Mabel paused, before her next words came splurting out. 'He wanted to confess what he did – that he sank the boat deliberately, an act of sabotage. He punched a hole in the hull so that it would ship water and sink. He scuttled it on purpose.'

For a moment, no one spoke. The silence was filled by the thrum of the rainforest, the unceasing noise, the constant throb of life, the singing of the river as it bowled towards the sea. Life and death, slipping from one to the other in a heartbeat.

But Mac had caused the death of Anselmo and the others on that steamer, had done it deliberately. Katharine felt faint, hot and cold and lightheaded. Thomas caught her as she was about to fall, held her until her head stopped spinning.

'I don't believe it,' she murmured. 'And yet I knew it. I knew there was something strange. Something he said – I remember the exact words – *when a boat starts shipping water, there's no chance.* As if he had known in advance what was going to happen, that the steamer wasn't going to make the journey. Those words always stayed with me; I sensed that there was something wrong about them but I couldn't work out what it was. I suppose it was impossible to think that anyone would intentionally do such a thing.'

She clutched Thomas' hands. 'But it's true. It wasn't an accident.'

Thomas' eyes darkened, and Katharine could see disbelief in them, combined with anger. Mabel was slumped against a tree trunk, motionless.

'But why, Katharine? Why would he do that?' she asked, her voice plaintive, pleading.

Her bewilderment broke Katharine's heart.

Katharine took a deep breath. 'Mac wanted Anselmo dead, out of the way. He didn't want the competition. He thought that without my husband, I'd give up, sell to him for a pittance.' She paused, running her hands over her face and through her hair. 'I trusted him. I believed him when he said he was on my side, that he'd help me any way he could, lending me money, sending me gifts. How could I have been so stupid?'

Thomas grimaced and turned his steely gaze towards the forest, the endless, limitless forest. It knew no bounds, just as Mac's evil knew no bounds.

'He fooled everyone, Katharine. Absolutely everyone. Beguiled us all, pulled the wool over our eyes. You can't blame yourself for being taken in.'

Mabel stirred, stood up straight and pointed to the river. 'Let's go down to the water.'

They sat in a row in the sand, Mabel in the middle. 'I wanted to write to you, Katharine. But Mac said he'd know if I did, that he had me followed, that he'd intercept any letters I tried to send. I believed him and I was scared.' She leant her head on Katharine's shoulder. 'I'm sorry.'

They stared out at the river that, as usual, took no notice. It was just the river, intent on running to the sea, no other aim in mind. It paid no regard to human folly.

'Katharine.' Mabel spoke, then immediately faltered.

'Yes?'

'That's not all.'

Katharine almost laughed. Not more. Not something else.

'Sinking the ship isn't the only thing Mac did,' Mabel muttered, hesitantly, and then, the decision to reveal all made the words came rushing out in a torrent. 'He – he organised the incursion by the tribe, the destruction of your compound, burning the huts, pushing all the rubber into the river. He paid them handsomely for it, apparently, with a lifetime's supply of weapons, *cachaça* and everything else they could possibly want.'

The words fell, like coconuts from a tall palm tree, thudding to the ground with the weight of bombs. Mabel paused, aware of both Katharine and Thomas staring at her, astounded.

'He asked them to make especially sure they killed your pet bird. He'd forgotten its name. But it was Po-Po, wasn't it?'

Katharine let out a loud, long, ironic laugh.

'For Christ's sake,' she intoned hollowly, blaspheming in a way she never normally did. She buried her head in her hands, grinding her teeth as she remembered that horrendous time, arriving home to find home annihilated.

'Again, why didn't I see? But Jonathan and Santiago – they knew, I know they did. When they said that not all snakes in the jungle come in serpent form, they meant Mac.' She looked around her wonderingly, at the peaceful compound and the waving leaves of banana trees, everything in order, just as it should be. It looked suddenly different. Alien. Things had gone on here that she had fundamentally misunderstood and that knowledge changed everything. 'They must have been so afraid of Mac and his evil that, in all these years, they never said a word.'

'Oh, Katharine,' cried Thomas, his face contorted with concern for his wife. 'I'm sorry you had to go through all this alone. You are so brave, you know that, don't you?'

Katharine shook her head. All Mac's friendliness, his offers of assistance, his protestations that he admired her – all had been fake, just a means to an end. 'I don't think so. I just didn't have a choice. I had to keep going, for Antonio and to pay my father back. But Mac – he's a wolf in sheep's clothing. Worse than that. When I think back now, I remember him asking me how much rubber I had, one night at Lagona. And – oh God – I answered truthfully! I was proud to share that information with him so that he'd see that I was competent, successful. When all he wanted was to know whether it was worth invading my compound yet.'

A wind blew up, ruffling the river's surface. 'I see now that his price rises were imposed whenever I achieved a success, whenever I threatened his pre-eminence in the upper Amazon. If he couldn't break me with guns and fires, or by buying me out, he'd break me financially. He'd sap my spirit and my will. He'd stop at nothing.'

She looked at Mabel and Thomas. 'Even murder.'

Katharine stood up, took a stone from the beach and skimmed it into the water. It failed miserably, plopping through the surface and sinking without a single jump.

'And to think I saved his pitiful bloody life when he fell into the river! He drowned my husband and I prevented him from drowning. I wish I'd left him to die.'

'I'm sorry,' whispered Mabel, 'I know it's awful. But I had to tell you. I was right to tell you, wasn't I?'

'Oh yes,' Katharine knelt beside her and took her hands. 'You were absolutely right.'

'I think he wasn't feeling well,' continued Mabel. 'He seemed to need to spill it all out. Sometimes I didn't want to hear any more, but I couldn't get him to stop.'

Katharine gave a disdainful snort. 'Expiation, of a sort. Admission, acknowledgement, atonement, I don't know. As if he could make it all better by telling a poor innocent girl he was busy destroying.'

Lily came toddling towards them, accompanied by Rosabel, a welcome distraction. Mabel seized the little girl in her arms and held her tight.

'I just want to forget him,' she muttered into Lily's curly hair, 'just never have to think of him again.'

'I think we all feel like that,' replied Katharine. *But,* she thought, *it's simply not possible.*

... ...ble

Chapter Fifty

They say that holding an infant brings on labour, so when Katharine woke in the night to the sound of a woman's screams, she knew that Mabel's time had come. Leaping up, she looked around for Thomas. His bed was empty. Rushing to the door and flinging it open, she followed the direction of the noise to Mabel's room. Halfway along the corridor Thomas appeared, looking uncharacteristically flushed and agitated.

'The baby,' he said, 'it's on its way.' His voice was low and Katharine could sense an element of 'oh no, not again' in his tone. So soon after Lily's hazardous delivery, she was not surprised he was apprehensive. Neither of them wanted to go through that horror a second time. She cursed that none of the help she'd organised had arrived – not Senhor Garcia nor the midwife from Iquitos – but in such a short amount of time, with such distances to travel, it would have been impossible.

Telling Thomas to go to the compound and rouse the servants, she rushed into Mabel's bedroom. She recognised immediately the flush of pain upon her face, the sweat streaked across her brow.

'How long has it been going on?' she asked, insistently. 'Why didn't you come and get me?'

'I thought it was stomach ache,' moaned Mabel. 'The food, you know, my tummy has been unsettled for days and…' She was silenced as a contraction came on, at its height starting once more to yelp in agony.

Two Indian women arrived, with clean cloths and hot water and the comforting manner of those who have seen many babies born in the past and expect to see many more in the future. But their air of confidence gradually diminished as the labour continued and Mabel's pain became relentless and unbearable.

'This isn't right,' Katharine kept thinking, 'it's not right.'

Having Antonio, when she had been a similar age to Mabel now, had been tough, no denying that – but not like this. The birth of Clara's baby had been a walk in the park compared to this.

'The baby is upside down,' said one of the Indian women, after extensive feeling of Mabel's distended belly. 'That is why so difficult.'

A breech baby. Anyone knew that this was dangerous. That often the babies didn't survive.

The labour went on and on. Mabel burnt with fever but as her temperature rose, her screams diminished. Katharine could sense her weakening, losing the will to carry on the fight. By the evening of the next day, Mabel was exhausted. This was beyond the limits of human endurance. Katharine steeled herself to what she felt was inevitable; the baby was unlikely to make it.

Eventually, when Katharine herself was hallucinating with tiredness, Mabel's baby was born. It was a little girl. She was blue and still and no cries disturbed the evening darkness, just the habitual sounds of monkeys, birds, frogs and insects.

The Indian woman who'd pulled the baby out handed her to Katharine, shaking her head sorrowfully. Though she knew it was hopeless, Katharine rubbed her little back and frail limbs, and blew in her mouth, but there was no response. A few tears fell upon the baby's blanket. But then a shriek and cries for help made her put the child down on the floor behind her and leap to Mabel's side.

The Indian women were bent over her sister, both pairs of eyes wide with terrified alarm. Mabel's own eyes had rolled back into their sockets and her head lay at an awkward angle, as if she had no control over it. Her lips were barely moving but Katharine could hear her moaning something and bent forward to listen.

347

'My baby, my baby,' she was muttering, over and over. Katharine recalled her own fear on waking up and not knowing where Lily was, what had happened to her. She didn't know what to say. Mabel's little girl was born on the Sabbath and as the traditional rhyme would have it, would be bonny and blithe and good and gay.

Except that she was stillborn, already gone to a better place.

Katharine held her sister's hand and kissed her cheeks and had absolutely no idea how to break this terrible news to her. As she stroked Mabel's hair and soothed her fevered brow, Katharine felt her hand go limp, her fingers lose their grasp. Mabel's face blanched from pale pink to blue-tinged white. Looking around in alarm, Katharine saw blood soaking the blankets Mabel was lying on, more and more blood, blood that kept on flowing.

As she watched, the stain spread, as fast as a flood in the rainy season, wide and dark and drenching.

The Indian women saw it, too, and snatched up towels and sheets to try to staunch the flow. They mopped and mopped but the blood continued to pour out in a torrent, an endless snake of blood that became a river and then a tidal wave.

'What's happening? What's happening to her?' Katharine shrieked, no longer able to keep calm for Mabel's sake.

The Indian women just shook their heads and the blood kept coming, inexorably. Katharine could not believe that one body could hold so much blood.

Mabel stirred, her eyes fluttering open and closed. Her lips moved. Katharine bent in low, straining to hear her sister's feeble voice.

'There's... more.' Mabel's breath was laboured, catching in her throat. But suddenly her voice was crystal clear. 'I need to tell you... about – about Archie... and the money. He didn't steal it, Katharine, he didn't... and about...'

But then the words trailed away and became inaudible. Mabel fell silent, her porcelain skin covered with a sheen of sweat. Her lips trembled once more and were still.

'What, Mabel, what?' cried Katharine, frantic, panicking. 'Who is Archie, and who said he stole money? What else is there to tell?'

But Mabel's eyelids had closed like the final slamming of a prison door. Katharine took her wrist and felt for a pulse, laid her ear close to her mouth.

There was nothing.

Her beautiful sister. Her brave, mistreated sister was dead.

Part III

1910

Chapter Fifty-One

Norwood, March 1910

On the banks of the river, two small girls played in the sand, one dark-skinned with black curly hair, one fair and blonde, with searing blue eyes. The older girl led the game, the younger following. Both seemed delighted with their play and with each other. They barely registered the arrival of a large launch; boats came often, now that Norwood was truly on the map as one of the Amazon's biggest rubber suppliers.

The boatman called out to them, and smiled and laughed at their slow reaction, their unwillingness to leave what was obviously an important part of their game. He knew their names, and shouted them out, 'Lily! Elspeth! Come to take the mail.'

The bigger girl dusted down her hands on her dress and the littler one copied, and then they both ran to him, giggling. First, he gave each a small banana, the variety that tastes of apples, and then the post. They took their treat and the letters, racing up the beach on plump, unsteady legs to the house where their mother was sitting at a table in the shade, finishing writing her own missives. Swapping the two bundles of paper, they immediately gambolled back down to the dock, handing the letters over for delivery to Manaus and onwards, down the river all the way to the sea and then across the wide ocean to Europe and to London.

Their mother had told them about London, about the dank weather and the smog, the grey days and winter snows, though

352

she knew they were too little to understand and anyway had no concept of what it was to be cold.

She had also told them about Elspeth's miraculous recovery, knowing her words meant nothing to such mites, how she had been placed on the floor straight after her birth because they had all believed her to be dead but how, ten or fifteen minutes later, she had begun to cry, a mewling little wail that stopped the women keening over her mother and drew all the attention to her.

Against all the odds, she had survived, and was now nearly one year old.

Katharine watched as the mail boat pulled away again and the girls resumed their playing. She had named her Elspeth after a favourite doll of Mabel's, and she had made sure that the child knew she had another mother who had died and gone to join the angels. She wanted her to grow up knowing about Mabel so that it would not come as a shock to her to find out that Katharine and Thomas were not her real mother and father. What she would tell Elspeth about Mac, Katharine had not worked out yet. In the meantime, it was a joy to see how Elspeth and Lily got along. The two girls, less than two years apart in age, were as close as twins, not just sisters.

Katharine leafed through the bundle of letters that had just arrived, stopping at one with large, scrawling handwriting. She considered it for a moment before opening it.

Once read, she let it fall onto the table. A few minutes later, Thomas found her there, staring into space with unseeing eyes.

'What's the matter?' he asked, his gaze immediately roving the compound, searching for the girls. Once he'd located them, safe and sound, he turned back to his wife. 'You seem preoccupied with something.'

'Antonio is coming.'

Thomas nodded, clicking his tongue between his teeth.

'I see.'

353

Katharine rose from her chair and went to his side. Together they surveyed the view, the river, wide and green today, with little choppy waves caused by a lively breeze.

'It's been so long,' Katharine said. 'I feel so – so guilty.'

The arrival of first Lily and then Elspeth in such rapid succession had precluded any further talk of Katharine travelling to England to visit her son for the foreseeable future. The rejoicing in Elspeth's survival had been short-lived; she was a sickly baby and it had taken all of Katharine's unremitting love and care to put her on the road to health. She could not have stood the journey and Katharine would not leave her behind. If anything good had come out of Mabel's death, it was Elspeth's life. It could not be risked for anything.

And anyway, immediately on finishing at Winchester, instead of pursuing a career in London, Antonio had chosen to go to Ceylon to take up a job there. At the time it had seemed like a great opportunity. Now, Katharine found it horrifying. It was Mac who had provided the contacts and the opening.

But the real reason Antonio's impending arrival filled Katharine with trepidation was that she was scared. She was scared of seeing her own son, was the honest truth. He had shown her no love over all the years they had been apart and she knew it was her fault. She had sent him away. She had done it with all good intentions, she reminded herself constantly, because he needed an education, because she had wanted the best for him, had wanted him away from the diseases and scourges of the Amazon. But these seemed scant reasons now.

In her heart of hearts, she knew she had failed him.

'We had better tell him about Elspeth,' Thomas suggested, gently. 'He should know.'

Mabel had made sure to keep her pregnancy a secret from everyone, even their mother and father. She wouldn't have started to show until she was on the boat to the Amazon. Katharine, for her part, hadn't told anyone about her sister's baby. She didn't know why. Life was running away with her;

she doubted her own decision making. The two little girls had changed everything; she and Thomas were blessed to have them. But was the forest the place for their future? Katharine wasn't sure she knew any more. She was sure, though, that she'd never send them away as she had Antonio. That was a deed that would dog her for the rest of her life.

Thomas shrugged and added, 'I'm sure Mayhew will spill the beans when Antonio reaches Manaus. If he hasn't already.'

He called to Lily and Elspeth and they set off on a fishing expedition, looking for piranha. The girls loved to see the fish gnashing their teeth or snapping at sticks, how their jaws chattered even after they were dead. And they all thought piranha soup delicious.

Katharine went to her study.

The rubber boom had made her a millionaire. She'd repaid her father's money in triplicate, and, just this year, given all her siblings cash to spend as they pleased. Mabel had always refused Katharine's money, wanted to be independent like Katharine was. She had been determined to make her own way in the world. Look how her ambitions had ended, Katharine chastised herself now. In misery and death.

It wasn't just Katharine who had made it in this toughest of environments. Many others were millionaires too, or multimillionaires – like Mac, that so-called friend she now knew to be a tyrant of the most despicable kind. But more and more the reality was being made public, of the enslavement and subjugation of the Indians, the terrible cruelty, the beatings and the torture. Once, it had just been hearsay – and Katharine's isolation at Norwood, so far from anywhere, had meant that whispers from far-flung stretches of the river only rarely trickled through to her. Now, everyone had heard the rumours – and knew them to be true.

It was always going to be only a matter of time before the world heard of the atrocities. And then all of them, even those who were fair and true employers, would be tainted. They would all have to share the blame, and the responsibility, for what had been done in the name of greed. Katharine had stuck to her earliest convictions and never knowingly exploited anyone. She had kept her *supply bases* well stocked with food for her tappers, and as places where they could gather together to combat the isolation of the forest. The building of a school and health centre at Norwood, begun six months ago, was nearly completed, and Katharine had employed a physician as well as a pharmacist, and teachers with the best of qualifications. But was it enough? Could it ever be enough? The Amazon had lost countless numbers of its children. And she had lost her son.

Unable to concentrate on work, Katharine wandered up to her bedroom. In the corner of the wardrobe lay a trunk. She knelt down, pulled it out and sat looking at it for a long time before her hands reached out to open it. She ran her fingers across the metal and down the leather straps which were green with mould, rotting away, the jungle devouring them as it wished to swallow everything. If they walked away from Norwood, within a matter of months the forest would have reclaimed it, their existence forgotten. Human beings were insignificant nothings in the face of the rampant nature all around them.

Carefully, Katharine undid the straps. One of the buckles fell onto the floor with a dull clang. She lifted the creaking lid and sifted through the sparse contents. Most of Mabel's things were gone, crumbled away, destroyed by the damp, eaten by beetles and ants. What was left was mouldy, emitting a fetid smell as Katharine delved amongst it.

I should get rid of it, she thought. *There's nothing here worth keeping. Nothing for Elspeth to remember her mother by.*

Except for the diary.

It was in a tin box with asbestos to absorb the moisture. Katharine knew it was there, had often thought about reading it. But until now, she hadn't. She wasn't sure if it was because it felt disrespectful, or because she was a coward. Maybe she didn't

356

want to revisit all the hideous details of what Mac had done to her sister. After all, it was her letters extolling the virtues of her friend Mac and his daughter that had made Mabel believe, unbeknownst to Katharine, they would be a good family to work for.

But despite her reluctance, Katharine knew she had to do it. She pulled out the tin, opening it to reveal a leather-bound book. Its pages were yellowing and heavy with moisture. Even asbestos could hardly cope with the Amazonian climate. She didn't know what secrets the journal contained, but she had to find out.

The leather covers cracked as she started to read. At first, she was only half paying attention, her mind still on Antonio's visit, her failings as a mother, the life she wasn't sure she had lived as well as she should have. But as she read, she became gradually more and more intent. The clock ticked on the landing, a grandfather she had brought from Manaus on a whim and regretted ever since because it was far too loud, its constant reminder of time passing too melancholy. The quarter hour sounded, then the half, then the next quarter and the hour itself. She read on.

Eventually, after two hours in which she hardly moved, she reached the last word. She shut the book and sat back on her heels. Her legs had gone to sleep and she was lightheaded with hunger.

She went in search of Thomas. He and the girls were playing catch with homemade rubber balls. Beside them, the captured piranhas in their bucket were still snapping at each other. They never gave up fighting.

Lily was prattling away, partly in English and partly in the Indian language of the compound, Elspeth babbling in reply. What they were saying was anyone's guess; they were so tiny, still learning to communicate with words.

'We need to talk,' Katharine said to Thomas.

He left the girls helping Rosabel to make the piranha soup and followed her to the office.

357

'We have to go to Manaus,' she told him, her voice calm but still managing to convey her urgency. 'We must leave immediately, get there before Antonio has arrived from Europe. We can meet him there – it will be a surprise. And after that, we'll travel on to London. I want the girls to meet their grandparents.'

Thomas nodded. He opened his mouth to say something, thought better of it, shut it again. Finally, he made his statement.

'You know when we get to England that they'll never be equal.'

Katharine made a moue of disinterestedness. 'One's a bastard orphan and one's a half-caste. Sounds pretty even to me.'

Thomas raised his eyebrows in patient resignation. There was no point arguing with his wife when she was in this mood.

'As soon as we get to Manaus,' continued Katharine, in the same quietly urgent voice, 'I need to visit the bank.'

Now Thomas looked at her sharply. He knew her inside out, could read her like a book. He was not fooled.

'Something's happened, hasn't it?' he said. 'And you're not going to tell me what it is, are you?'

Katharine broke into a sad, reluctant smile. She was, as always, grateful for his discretion, his quiet acceptance. 'You'll have to trust me,' she said.

'I do,' he replied. 'I always will.'

Katharine barely slept, all the things she had read whirling around her mind like a swarm of mosquitoes around a hurricane lamp. Most of it was what Mabel had divulged in those precious, fraught days between her arrival in Norwood and her death. Reading it in black and white brought all the revelations, of Mac's depravity, his callousness and his crimes, into the light once more. But it wasn't just Mac. Katharine had been horrified to discover that the abuse had started not with Mac, but before that, at Mabel's first job, when the master had crept up on her and forced himself upon her with an attitude of total entitlement. It made Katharine's blood boil and her skin crawl to think of her sister – any woman, for that matter – being mauled at like an object.

And on top of this, there was yet one more disclosure in the diary that Mabel had not made to Katharine during their chats, had presumably forgotten in her muddled, confused, alcohol-drenched state. Mabel had died before being able to take revenge, but in her writing she had given Katharine the information she needed. Katharine had the power to act – and act she would – to avenge her sister's death. Nothing, she thought to herself grimly, would give her greater pleasure.

Chapter Fifty-Two

The Amazon, April 1910

At first light they left, Lily and Elspeth bundled up on a pile of blankets under the boat's awning. Katharine remembered travelling with Antonio like this, together with a precious *bolacha* of rubber to show Mac, the proof that she could make it, that she could survive as a woman in a man's world. The rainforest had fascinated her then and it still did so now. It seemed to prove, without equivocation, all of Charles Darwin's radical theories of evolution. But at the same time, it could also provide evidence that there must be a God. Every animal, bird and insect had a perfect purpose. For so many diseases, the rainforest provided a cure. For mankind's needs, it offered up the raw materials necessary. It was a miracle that pointed to a benign divinity of some kind.

But alongside that was the terror that some humans meted out to those in their power, from innocent Indians to her own sister. When Katharine remembered that, she could not believe that God, if he did. indeed exist, could know and see and yet turn a blind eye.

At first, the girls were sleepy, dozing in their nest, and Katharine amused herself watching the gambolling families of capybaras upon the banks. But once the children awoke properly she pointed out to them all the wonders of the jungle that passed them by – the monkeys and the palms, the towering trees, the hyacinth macaws and the nests of the oropendola birds that had so entranced her on her first journey on the river sea. The girls humoured her and pretended to look until Katharine laughed at herself and gave up. They were no more interested than she would have been if someone had drawn her attention to every smoke-blackened brick house in London. The majestic, miraculous forest was not new and stupendous to these children.

It was their home; all they had ever known.

'Thomas,' blurted Katharine, suddenly.

'Yes?'

'What will we do if Mac lays claim to Elspeth? We can't let him take her. I'd *never* let him take her.'

The current had picked up and they were bowling down-river. 'We won't let that happen,' Thomas said, determinedly. '*I* won't let that happen.'

The two of them sat silently for a while, each involved in their own private thoughts.

'When I look at her blue eyes,' said Katharine, 'I make myself think of the Amazonian sky at midday, or of hyacinths in my mother's garden. I have to work really hard not to see Mac. There was something in his eyes which I always read as loneliness – but now I see was his depravity.'

Thomas took her hands and squeezed them. 'Don't let hatred eat you up, my love,' he cautioned. 'You are so brave. You were so young when you came to the Amazon and you had to go through so much. Everything Mac threw at you, every time he tried to destroy you, you fought back. Most people would have given up at the first hurdle, but you never did. You should be so proud.' He smiled and lifted her hands to his mouth and kissed her fingers. 'But you'll never be as proud of yourself as I am of you.'

The girls had fallen silent, their innocent faces creased in concentration as they listened to the adults' avid conversation and watched their every move.

'Mama, Mama, water,' said Lily, and Elspeth mimicked her. Scooping the girls up, Katharine handed them the water gourd and hugged them tight as they took it in turns to drink. Freshwater dolphins came alongside the boat to play, just as they had on Katharine's first canoe journey. The girls climbed down off her lap and leant over the side to watch them, laughing and screaming in delight.

A canoe filled with Peruvian traders and Panama hats passed them. They had travelled all the way from the high Andes and were headed for the coast to sell their wares. Thomas bought a hat from them and put it on, pulling funny faces for the girls, whose expressions turned from mystified to gleeful as they chuckled and giggled. He put the hat on each of them in turn and they mimicked their father's expressions and laughed until they were breathless. Katharine smiled at their delight, their ability to find fun in any silly thing. She envied their simple lives, their easy happiness.

She wasn't sure she would ever feel like that again.

–

In Manaus, Mayhew's house was more lavish than ever. He had had it decorated like a Rococo palace and fitted it out entirely with furniture imported from France.

'Wonderful isn't it?' he asked, proudly surveying his absurd extravagance, taking it for granted that Katharine and Thomas would agree. He was sweating profusely; he had gained more weight since Katharine had last been in the city and was clearly suffering for it in the drenching heat. 'Now you see what you're missing, holed up in that jungle hideout.'

All he has ever cared about is money, reflected Katharine, scrutinising her surroundings. It was impossible to imagine that he had once, a long, long time ago, had a charming side; all he exuded now was boorish conceit.

'This is your money he's wasting on such ridiculous profligacy,' fumed Thomas, when Mayhew had left the room.

Katharine gave a dismissive flick of her head. 'He struck a deal with me right from the beginning on the percentage of the profits he was entitled to as Norwood Enterprises' Manaus representative. He's worked hard, though it pains me to say it. He's entitled to what he has and I don't have any say over how he spends what he has rightfully earned – even if I do heartily disapprove.'

None of it mattered any more. Or it wouldn't, shortly, anyway. She headed out to the bank.

'Shall I come with you?' asked Thomas.

'No,' she replied, 'I have to do this alone.'

In the town centre, the *Diario do Amazonas* newspaper proclaimed the dizzying new heights of the rubber price in dollars, pounds sterling and milreis.

On another day, she would have found it impossible to walk past the University Bookshop without going in and spending a small fortune on books and periodicals that, once back at Norwood, she would read over and over again until the damp and insects got to them and they fell apart. But today, she passed on by, barely registering the notice in the window informing customers that the latest adventures of Buffalo Bill and Nick Carter were now in stock.

The bank was busy as always, full of people withdrawing and depositing funds, taking out loans, repaying debts – though less, as always, of the latter than the former. She had to go to several different counters on several different floors. At each one, her request was met with raised eyebrows but no comment. At her next port of call, it took rather longer to do what she had to do.

When Katharine got back to the house it was well past midday, but even so Antonio did not surface until several hours later. He and Mayhew had been out late the night before, carousing, Mayhew showing off his latest mistress to Antonio. The Polish woman, once the most highly prized and sought after concubine for the rubber elite, had been surplanted by an East Asian beauty: tiny, petite and perfect. Mayhew always had to have whatever was the height of fashion.

'Antonio,' cried Katharine, involuntarily stepping forward to take her son in her arms.

'Anthony,' he replied, neatly side-stepping her embrace.

After being introduced, Thomas excused himself, saying he would take the girls for a walk. Mayhew, showing uncharacteristic tact, also took his leave, citing numerous important matters to attend to.

Alone, Katharine and Antonio sat across the salon from each other, both avoiding the other's eyes.

'I've missed you,' said Katharine simply. 'I'm sorry it's been so long. I'm sorry you couldn't face the voyage and I wasn't able to come to visit you. I want you to know that you were always in my thoughts, that I always loved you. That I always will.'

Antonio shrugged off-handedly in the way that had always infuriated Katharine. Now it just made her profoundly sad.

She held out her hands towards her son. 'How could you think otherwise? I beg you to believe me. I loved you from the bottom of my heart; I cherished you, I nurtured you. I still do, now and always. But I couldn't educate you properly at Norwood, I couldn't keep you safe. I had no choice but to send you away.'

'That's the point, though, isn't it?' Antonio challenged. 'When Mayhew told me I had to go, I was so confused about why you were banishing me. But Mayhew explained – he told me on the boat – that it wasn't just about schooling, or safety. You wanted to leave the coast clear for you and Thomas to—to—' He faltered, bit his lip, then began again. 'I couldn't make any sense of it except to believe that you loved Thomas more than me. That Mayhew was right. That I wasn't the most important thing in the world to you any more. And that was hard, Mother, do you understand?' His eyes, that were so like his father Anselmo's eyes, were full of tears, darkened with anguised memories. 'It was so hard.'

Katharine fought back her own tears. Antonio had put two and two together and, at such a young age and with the help of Mayhew's poison, made fifty.

'I'm sorry, Ant… Anthony,' she whispered, misery impeding her ability to speak. 'Mayhew shouldn't have told you that. It's totally wrong. He was the one who finally persuaded me to take the decision to send you to school, who insisted that it was essential to do so. It wasn't because of Thomas. That wasn't the reason.'

Antonio had the sulky, sullen look on his face that Katharine knew so well. She was suddenly transported to when he was a little boy, fretting about some perceived injustice or slight. He had always believed the world to be against him and on their long journey together Mayhew had clearly stoked that fire until it was a raging furnace. The small boy had been unable to make sense of his feelings, the older boy unable to share them. And so, the embers of hurt, confusion, bewilderment and misunderstanding had smouldered on.

'The thing is, Mother,' Antonio was saying, 'I like Thomas. I really do. But that makes it even worse. I didn't know until Mayhew told me exactly how wrong it is for a white woman to go with a Black man. Of course, I didn't know! I lived here, in the Amazon, where mixing of races is normal. But Mayhew told me it was disgusting and at school – well, can you even imagine how much I was bullied when the other boys discovered my mother had married a – a slave? It's just not the done thing at all,' he added, his voice imitating the accent of the upper classes and loaded with sarcasm, wobbling with incipient tears, 'not at all.'

Now the tears began to slide down Katharine's cheeks. This was too much. She had had no idea that Antonio was persecuted because of her choice to live with and to marry a Black man. It simply hadn't occurred to her that this would be the inevitable outcome of her union with Thomas. How had she been so stupid, so blind and ignorant? She would never forgive herself. The least she should have done was explain it all to Antonio before he left, and warn him, perhaps, of the prejudice he might expect to face. Instead she had covered it up, thinking that was for the best.

'We can make it up,' she said, quietly. She had to believe this was possible. What else was left to her? To them? 'We can put it right. Please let me try.'

Antonio stood up and began pacing the room, shaking his head vehemently as he strode.

'Maybe. I don't know. Probably not.' He paused and went to a leather case that lay on a side table. 'I want to. I'd like to. But it might be too late.'

Katharine shook her head. How could it be too late? It would never be too late.

'The th-thing is,' Antonio stuttered. 'I have something to show you. I haven't been idle.'

Katharine wiped her eyes with her handkerchief and sat up straighter.

'You know I've been in Ceylon since school finished?'

'I heard as much.'

'Well, I took over a rubber plantation there. Idiot bastard who set it up drank himself stupid, had to sell at a loss. Mac put me onto the opportunity, lent me the money – it was a bargain in any case. Henry Wickham took rubber seeds from the Amazon years ago and they came good. The trees are ready to tap now – in fact, we're already doing so. We've had our first harvest. Best quality rubber at a fraction of the production and shipping costs of that from the Amazon. The trees in nice neat rows, accessible, a dedicated and disciplined colonial workforce desperate for employment, none of these peasants and savages you to have to deal with here. It's all so easy.'

He looked at Katharine as if expecting a reaction – horror, surprise, anger... He got nothing.

'Mac's heavily invested there himself too, did you know? He saw the future a while ago and started to pull his money out of Brazil and put it into plantations. He's been planning for the future for ages – you know how astute he is.' Antonio's tone was neutral, even.

Katharine stared impassively at her son. She'd learnt something of the Indian ability to give nothing away through their faces in all these years.

'In Ceylon, we're undercutting you and your competitors by 50 per cent. Dry, fine Pará has had its day. Once the news of how plantation rubber is trading in the markets in London and New York reaches this backwater dump, the banks will pretty soon stop accepting rubber land as collateral for loans. And that will be the beginning of the end. The boom is going to turn to bust in the blink of an eye.'

Abruptly, Antonio stopped his pacing and came to stand by his mother, his tall form looming above her like the Brazil nut trees tower over others in the rainforest. Then he noisily pulled up a chair and sat down next to her. He looked suddenly like a little boy again, longing for forgiveness.

'I didn't really mean to do it, Mother.' His voice was high-pitched, distraught. Agonised. 'Or at least I did, and I didn't. Sometimes I wanted to hurt you as you'd hurt me. Other times, I was desperate to throw it all in and come back to Norwood. But I'd borrowed the money and Mac's terms were strict.'

Katharine laughed inwardly, though it was a hollow laugh. Oh yes, being indebted to Mac was a sorry state to be in, and his terms were never anything but stringent. She, of all people, knew that.

'I didn't think it through!' Antonio's face was screwed up with distress. 'But the reality is that you will be ruined.' His face suddenly became blank, looking as Katharine imagined it might have when the school bullies were assailing him. It was a look of self-preservation, utterly closed-up.

She gazed sadly at her only son. 'It doesn't matter, Antonio. I'm your mother and I will love you from the bottom of my heart whatever you do. I wish you every success with your rubber plantation.'

She paused, thinking about what she'd read in Mabel's journal, of the conversation Mabel had overheard between her employer and a friend about rubber from the Far East wiping out the Amazon. Apparently, she'd written to Katharine to warn her but the letter, as was so often the case, had never arrived. Mabel had been trying to tell Katharine something with her last few breaths – Katharine was sure it was this – but death had come before the words were out. It was only Katharine's reading of her journal that had brought the truth to light.

She pushed the vision of Mabel's last moments firmly from her mind and turned to her son, hands folded matter-of-factly on the table.

'I would advise you to watch out for disease; if too many trees of the same type grow too close together, they are liable to infection.' Katharine's tone was brisk now, business-like. 'Hopefully yours will stay strong and healthy.'

Antonio nodded miserably. He seemed to have shrunk in size, overtaken by grief and remorse and love and huge amounts of emotion he had no idea how to express.

'Yes, yes. But that's a small concern. The real issue is that the Amazon is over. Your *estradas* are worthless. Mac has done the clever thing in getting out – but you – you've lost everything.'

'Oh, Antonio. Mac may have taken some astute decisions by investing elsewhere. But unfortunately he has made a lot of mistakes, too. Today he has been arrested and he is now languishing behind bars in Manaus prison, charged with embezzlement, tax evasion and fraud.'

As she spoke, Antonio's expression froze into one of utter disbelief and then, as he realised it must be the truth, morphed into a terrible acceptance.

'How... how did they find out? How did he get caught?'

'Mabel,' answered Katharine, simply. 'I found papers in her trunk that she'd gathered up after he'd carelessly left them lying around in...' she hesitated, unable to say the words *in her bedroom* because of the awful reality they brought to the surface, 'in London. I gave them, together with her diary in which she'd documented everything he told her, to the police and they acted immediately. No government or law enforcement agency anywhere in the world likes to be defrauded to the extent Mac has done. He will be incarcerated for many years to pay for his crimes.'

Now it was Katharine's turn to pace restlessly around the room. She could hardly bear to think of her little sister and what she had suffered – but through it all Mabel had managed to keep enough of her wits about her to save the papers and write down all of Mac's confessions.

Speechless, Antonio sat in silent bemusement. It was only when a clock on the wall began to chime that he jolted back to life.

'I don't understand. I don't understand at all.'

'Mac fathered Mabel's child,' explained Katharine, plainly and matter-of-factly. It seemed that Mayhew had not already spilled the beans. 'Under pressure and coercion and by making her drunk, not just once but time and time again. That is the calibre of the man we all trusted. He also committed other despicable, reprehensible crimes against his servants, several of them young girls. The man is a monster. I'm sorry. I know it will be hard for you to hear. But it's the truth, and not only must the truth come out but we all understand that, on occasion, the truth hurts. I reported all of this in addition to the financial matters, though I doubt that anything will come of it. The evidence is all gone, melted into the forest or buried beneath it. But at least Mac is under lock and key now, and cannot hurt anyone else.'

Antonio appeared unable to process what his mother was telling him. 'So – so he was busy destroying Mabel – and others, you say – and making himself rich by any means possible. But now – even if he's got his own comeuppance, you are left poor, your rubber trees worthless.'

Katharine settled back down at the table, calmer again now. This was no time for being over-emotional. She needed to keep a cool head.

'I can see how you might think this to be the case,' she said, slowly. 'But you are wrong.'

Katharine reached for her purse and took out a piece of paper which she slid over the table towards Anthony, keeping her fingers lightly resting on the edge. She allowed him time to read it and then withdrew it, folding it up and putting it back in her purse.

Antonio stared at her: eyes wide in amazement.

'As you see,' she said, slowly and calmly, 'I have sold up. Everything is gone. I got the best price possible. Everyone else is buying, not selling, the rubber price is so high. I would be rich beyond my wildest dreams – I probably still am. But as well as seeing that Jonathan, Santiago and all the compound Indians and rubber tappers are well provided for until the end of their lives, I have put nearly all the remaining money into a trust. Jonathan and Santiago will administer it, and they will use it to build schools, homes and healthcare facilities for all the Indians on the Rio Poderoso, in addition to the ones I have already established at Norwood. I hope that the money I have made will do some good in the world, to make up for the bad that Mac and his ilk have sowed and propagated here.'

She stood up and walked to the door, her head held high, though a voice of anguish and agony screamed in her head.

'It is unbearable for a mother to know she has failed her child so badly,' she said, upon reaching the threshold. 'But it's all right, Antonio. Anthony. You have nothing to feel guilty about and I will always be here for you when you need me or want me. Whenever that may be. We'll be in London for the foreseeable future, in case you are interested.'

She had tried so hard not to collapse, not to cave in beneath the weight of the terrible emotions she was feeling. At this moment, though, it all became too much. She bowed her head, felt her knees go weak, and leant against the doorjamb as stars darted behind her tightly closed eyes. She remained like this until a sudden screech of chair legs against the hard wooden floor caused her to look up. Antonio was approaching, cautiously, as if towards an injured animal, his demeanour broken and bereft.

'Mother, stop,' he cried, a suppressed sob clutching at his throat. 'Please stop.'

He halted a foot or so from her, as if some invisible force field prevented him from coming closer. 'We can't part like this. I'm sorry too, sorry for everything. I listened to Mayhew; I believed every word he said when I know I shouldn't have. I just didn't understand. But,' he paused, his eyes flitting from Katharine to the ceiling to the windows to the floor, 'I want to love you. I do love you. Remember when I saved you from the snake? And you rescued Mac and I from drowning. We have both saved each other. We will again. *I* will. I want to come with you to England.'

Katharine listened in stunned disbelief. Which suddenly transmuted to delight. 'Th-thank you. Thank you, Antonio.'

Each took a step forward and then they were hugging, the first close contact they had had with each other for so many years. Katharine felt that finally all was well, that she no longer had to live with regret and self-reproach. That perhaps her relationship with Antonio could be salvaged – which, if it were the case, was the only thing that really mattered.

When the embrace ceased, Katharine suggested they take a walk in the garden. They stopped by the dancing fountain, held their hands under its cooling water.

'You've saved me again, Antonio,' Katharine said. 'Just by coming here. Your imminent arrival prompted me to read Mabel's diary which I'd been ignoring all this time. As I said before, I wish you nothing but well with your venture in Ceylon. I, on the other hand, am done with rubber, with this magical substance that has done so much good, and so much harm. Everything has changed. I came to the Amazon a naïve girl, following my husband, no idea what I was doing, barely a sensible idea in my head. I leave an independent woman. I have learnt so much. Most of all, that it is an industry that is rotten through and through, run by men riddled with maggots like the *bolachas* themselves. I have repaid my debts, given away my money and now I want no further part in it.'

The fountain gurgled and splashed and the equatorial sun blazed in the shimmering sky. Together, mother and son turned and walked back to the house. They gathered up the two girls, Thomas, their goods and chattels and took them to the floating quay, where they boarded the steamer bound for Liverpool. Standing on deck, the whole family was silent as they set sail. Katharine gripped tight to the rails as she squeezed back the moisture in her eyes. She knew that none of them would ever see the Amazon again. This was the final farewell to the place where she had loved and lost, hoped and despaired, and shed so many tears of triumph and disaster. The fact that all five of them were alive was all Katharine cared about now.

She turned to Antonio. 'The truth is this, my beloved son. Whether it is what you once wanted, or what you feared, you have no need to worry. You haven't ruined me.'

She paused as the steamer let off its horn.

'On the contrary,' she continued, as the booming sound subsided. 'You've set me free.'

Epilogue

The crash began in May 1910. Plantation rubber flooded the market and the price, which had risen to an eye-watering $3 a pound, fell catastrophically. South America was forgotten and suddenly everyone wanted a part of the new industry, triggering crowds that verged on riots to descend on London banks, demanding shares in businesses in the Far East.

By 1913, the Amazonian rubber boom was over. The entire system had been built on credit and debt and once it started to fall, the collapse was dramatic and spectacular. Anyone who wanted their money out was disappointed. There was no money there in the first place.

It took only a further three years until British plantations were producing enough rubber to fulfil 95 per cent of world demand. The industry in the Amazon never recovered. By the end of the First World War, large-scale production in the region had all but ceased.

For many, the end of the rubber boom marked the end of slavery, exploitation and degradation. Some say that every ton of rubber cost two lives, others that the figure was seven. At the time, around 600 million pounds of British money was invested in the Amazon, a fact that became a national shame when Roger Casement's report into atrocities on the river Putumayo was published. The report makes grim reading: torture, rape and murder, burnings alive and live burials. It's said that the uncontacted tribes that still exist deep in the rainforest today were driven there in part by the horrors of the rubber boom.

They did not have to see much of the white man's world to know they did not wish to be part of it.

And what of Henry Wickham, the man arguably responsible for it all? It's impossible to say what would have happened if he hadn't stolen the seeds and imported them to England and to Kew. Most likely, if not him, it would have been someone else, just as had already happened with the cinchona tree that produces quinine. When he shipped out of Santarem on the *Amazonas*, he left behind most of his family, who had come to join him in Brazil – those who hadn't already died. He spent his life on hare-brained schemes in far flung lands, was knighted in 1920, and lived to the ripe old age of eighty-two.

He died alone and is barely remembered today, though his actions changed the world.

Acknowledgements

A massive thankyou to everyone who has helped me with the writing of this book. It goes without saying that my family is the first and foremost of these.

Thanks are also due to Megan Carroll, my agent at Watson Little, who has been instrumental in getting my work published, and to Emily Bedford at Canelo, who saw the potential in this book and added her invaluable enhancements.

I also want to thank my great friend Claire Wells, without whom I would probably never have gone to South America at all. Our first endeavour was a three-month backpacking trip through Venezuela, Colombia, Ecuador and Peru. We thought this was a perfectly sane and reasonable thing to do in our university summer holiday at the age of twenty-one and with £300 each in our pockets. I think our mothers begged to differ but nobody stopped us going and the experiences we had will stay with me forever. Back then, Colombia was said to be the most dangerous country on earth; we had the time of our lives there. We also visited the Amazon and it was then that my fascination began. After graduating, we went to Brazil to teach English and my Latin American love affair continued.

I hope this book embodies at least a small part of the wonder of the Amazon rainforest, one of Planet Earth's most valuable, and threatened, places.